"By the Dragon of the Depths!"

The furious drake lord tried another arrangement, evidently hoping that some combination of forces would overcome the unknown obstacle in the oracle. Both visions dwindled away, this time to be replaced by a thick, grayish cloud that sparkled as it turned slowly within itself, almost as if a legion of fireflies had gotten themselves trapped in the maelstrom. The Green Dragon stepped away, clearly taken aback by this latest result. After a moment of contemplation, though, he reached once more for the markings on the pedestal.

There was a flash. A sparkling field of light engulfed the unsuspecting drake.

As the flash died, a head filled the air above the artifact; it was the startled countenance of none other than the Crystal Dragon. There was no mistaking the other Dragon King. Only one drake had skin that gleamed like diamond.

His body quivering violently, the Green Dragon shrieked . . .

ALSO BY RICHARD A. KNAAK

Firedrake
Ice Dragon
Wolfhelm
Shadow Steed
The Shrouded Realm
Children of the Drake
Dragon Tome

THE DRAGONREALM
THE CRYSTAL DRAGON

RICHARD A. KNAAK

WARNER BOOKS

A Time Warner Company

WARNER BOOKS EDITION

Questar® is a registered trademark of Warner Books, Inc.

Cover design by Don Puckey
Cover illustration by Larry Elmore
Hand lettering by David Gatti

Warner Books, Inc.
1271 Avenue of the Americas
New York, NY 10020

Ⓦ A Time Warner Company

Printed in the United States of America

First Printing: May, 1993

10 9 8 7 6 5 4 3 2

I

He woke to find his world invaded. A shadowy plague in human form swarmed over the glittering, rocky landscape, tainting it by merely existing. He concentrated, allowing the crystalline chamber to show him more. A myriad collection of images related to his request filled the walls. He saw the three great ships, black as pitch, anchored off the shore and wondered how they could have come so far without him noting them. It was a troubling sign, an indication that he had slept deeper than he had desired.

Rather than contemplate it further, he studied the other reflections. One facet revealed a detailed image of some of the invaders and this he brought to the forefront. He hissed. They were familiar to him although the name by which they went did not come to him at first. In contrast to the sun-drenched region they now occupied, the figures wore armor the color of night, armor unadorned save for the helm. Atop each, a crest fashioned into the snarling visage of a wolf's head leered down, a reflection in many ways of the men themselves. In the distance he could see the banners fluttering in the wind. The profile of the same wolf, surrounded by a field of deep crimson, watched over the army, for that was what it was.

The name came to him at last. As a people, they referred to themselves as the Aramites. Yet to those they had preyed upon for generation after generation, there was another, more apt title.

The wolf raiders.

Now they were here, in his domain. He released the image he had chosen and sought among the others. At first glance they seemed all the same, reflection upon reflection of dark-armored men infesting his kingdom. He hissed again, growing ever more frustrated. None of this aided him.

The desire to return to his slumber, to ignore the situation, grew stronger. He knew, though, that falling prey to such a tempting choice was to invite the downfall of all that was his. Despite the danger to his mind . . . to his very being . . . he had

1

to stay awake. The wolf raiders were familiar enough to him that he knew they could not be left unattended.

"Aaaah . . ." There they were. The officers. The overall commander the Aramites termed Pack Leader was not there, but the rest of the jackals, his subordinates, were.

With the exception of the black and crimson cloaks they wore, there was little to mark them as anything other than common soldiers. In addition to the cloak, the Pack Leader would have a more elaborate helm and a single badge with the mark of the wolf upon it, but that was all. The Aramites cared little for insignias of rank otherwise. An officer was an officer, whatever his level, and that was all that mattered. Officers were meant to be obeyed in all things. Blind obedience was part of the wolf raider creed.

His first glance at them revealed nothing of significance and he was almost tempted to seek another reflection when the scene as a whole suddenly registered. The wolf raiders had a *prisoner*. He could not see who or what it was at first, for the ebony-garbed soldiers surrounded the hapless soul, as if fascinated by what they had captured. They poked at the unfortunate with short swords and talked among themselves.

There was one among them who did not laugh, but rather stood to the side, his round, young face a mask of boredom. He might have seemed entirely indifferent to the world around him if not for the hunger visible in his eyes. They darted back and forth, drinking in everything yet never resting on any object for more than a few moments. Interested despite himself, the watcher sought a reflection giving him a closer view of this one raider.

He was smaller of stature and unassuming at first glance, but there was that about him that made one wary. When the eyes of the young Aramite suddenly turned in his direction, the intensity with which they stared was so unsettling that the watcher almost thought he had been discovered. Then, the wolf raider returned his own attention to the captive, breaking the spell.

Chagrined, the master of the crystalline chamber followed the Aramite's gaze and, for the first time, beheld the wolf raiders' captive.

It was a Quel. Even bound and on his knees, he was nearly as tall as the humans. Gray netting enshrouded him from the top of his armored head to the ground, but enough was visible. The watcher marveled that any rope could hold the creature, especially a male as huge as this one. The Quel's long, tapering snout had also been bound, either to put an end to his hooting or to prevent him from snapping off the fingers of any raider foolish enough to reach too close. The raiders had also been clever enough to pull their prisoner's thick arms back so that the Quel could not make proper use of his lengthy claws. Designed to dig through the harsh soil of this land, the claws of the underground dweller would easily pass through the armor and flesh of an Aramite soldier without pause. Likely, the wolf raiders had already learned that fact the hard way, for it was doubtful that the capture had been an easy task. Even *he* respected the incredible strength behind those rending hooks.

Why a Quel? He pondered that. Had the Quel attacked the camp? Had they somehow simply caught this one unaware as he had surfaced? The latter seemed unlikely, considering how well the subterranean creatures knew this region, for they had been here longer than even he. It *was* possible that the raiders merely thought their prisoner a beast of some sort and not of a race older than their own. Humans could be presumptuous when it came to their place in the scheme of things.

He had no care himself for the fate of the Quel. The race stayed clear of his domain, despite the fact that it had meant abandoning what had once been a part of their mighty, subterranean city. To a Quel, nothing short of death would make one of them invade his realm. They feared not only him, but the power he controlled.

The power he controlled . . . For a moment the watcher forgot his own task and laughed silently at himself. If he controlled the power, then it controlled him just as much. Likely more. He could never be free of it, for to be free would be to lose himself forever.

His mind began to drift and the chamber, responding to his every thought, conscious or otherwise, allowed the multitude of images to fade, almost immediately to be replaced by one and one alone copied over and over in the facets of the crystalline walls. It was a single, rough-hewed face partly obscured by a helm and a beard, a face in many ways too akin to the visages of the wolf raiders. A warrior, a soldier obsessively obedient in character no matter what the cause.

It was too much. Roaring, he rose from his resting place and waved a huge, taloned hand at the array of faces. The images vanished as swiftly as they had materialized. In their place returned the encampment of the invaders. Slowly, the fear and anger dwindled, albeit not completely. Once more, the Quel and his captors took the stage. They were almost welcome now, for anything was better than lingering too much on a past so long dead it no longer seemed anything more than another dream.

When he gazed at the walls this time, however, he saw that all was *not* yet well. Something, in fact, was terribly wrong. The reflections wavered, twisted, making it seem as if the world beyond the chamber had become fluid. At first, he thought it was his own raging mind, but that was not the case. He had lived with the chamber for so long that he knew its ways, knew both its limitations and idiosyncrasies as well as he knew himself. Possibly better.

Whatever the cause, it came from without and he could not doubt that somehow its roots led back to those who had dared to think they could make his dominion into theirs.

Reaching out with his thoughts, he used the power of the chamber to seek out the source. The pictures wavered further and many of them altered as he narrowed his focus. The cause was near where the Quel was being held, but try as he might, it was impossible to focus exactly on the location he wanted. That, too, was peculiar; nothing ever long escaped the chamber's intrusive ability.

Briefly, the milky vision of a tent surfaced in several of the facets of the glittering walls. Peering closer, the watcher struggled to strengthen the images. He was rewarded with new visions, just as murky as the first, of an armored man seated in the tent. There was a glimpse of a beast of some sort wrapped around his shoulders and another picture that indicated a second figure standing behind the first. Of the second all that could be said was that he was as tall as the young raider guarding the Quel had been short and his skin appeared to be, of all things, a vivid blue.

More! I must know more! Few times had the chamber, his

sanctum, failed him so. That it did now only made the need to discover the truth even more essential to him. If the wolf raiders were the cause of this, then they were truly a threat to the fragile balance he had maintained for so long.

His talons scraped at the floor, gouging the already ravaged surface. His breathing grew rapid. It was a strain to have to concentrate so, especially without sufficient rest. Now more than ever, there was danger that he might lose himself, become as the others before him had become . . .

Almost he had the image, a thing held in one hand of the seated Aramite, likely the Pack Leader he had sought earlier. In his eagerness to see it, however, he allowed his control to slip ever so slightly. The vision wavered again . . . then became a meaningless blur.

"Cursssssse you, you malevolent mirror!" He roared, forgetting himself and the danger such rages represented to him.

Flame licked the multiple images of the wolf raider camp as his frustration became action. His tail lashed out and struck the opposing wall, where more than a dozen identical Quel gazed up into the dark eyes of more than a dozen identical young officers, each of whom had removed a foot-long rod from his belt. A second burst of flame momentarily scorched the reflections of a score of soldiers searching among the crystal-encrusted rock, their purpose in doing so a mystery that, for the time, held no interest to the maddened watcher.

As his eyes reddened in fury and he prepared to lash out again, the wolf raiders once more faded away. For a single breath, the chamber of crystal turned opaque. Then, the dull gray walls gave way to a new reflection. The flame within him died an abrupt death. He stared, paralyzed, at the legion of maddened, reptilian visages. They, in turn, stared back, a gleaming array of monstrous heads all bearing the same expression of disbelief and horror that he did. The toothy maws were open wide and from each a forked tongue flickered in and out. Eyes narrow and inhuman burned into his head. Gemlike skin rippled with each harsh, halting breath. Leathery wings unfurled and furled.

He recoiled from the condemning images, but there was no escaping the fact that each and every reflection was of him.

Yessss . . . I am the masssster of the Legar Peninssssula, am

I not? I am the monster men call the Crysssstal Dragon . . . He faced the reflections again, this time in defiance. *But I am also myself and I shall always be!*

Despite his defiant stance, however, he knew he had come much too close to succumbing, closer than he had in centuries. The past few years were much to blame. Nearly two decades before, he had been forced to spend himself rescuing the Dragonrealm from his fatalistic counterpart to the north, the unlamented Ice Dragon. Reversing the spell of chilling death that the mad drake had unleashed had taken too much. The rage had almost overtaken him then. He had not come as close as now to being lost, but he had come close.

The wolf raiders would not leave of their own will. Like the parasites they were, they would remain until they had either been eradicated or had wrung from the land all that they could. If they did not know of the Quel's legacy yet, the Crystal Dragon had no doubt that they would before long . . . and that legacy would also lead them to him. The monarch of the Legar Peninsula understood all too well that even his presence would not deter men such as these. Their tenacity was almost reminiscent of another time, another people.

And so, in the end, I must fight . . . even should it mean a victory in which all I desire to save is lost! He tried to erase the repellent notion from his mind, but it had already embedded itself firmly within. There would be no escaping it. It would haunt him awake and asleep. Finally surrendering to that inevitable fact, the Dragon King settled down. Sleep, which he needed, was no longer really even an option for him. He could rest, but he could not afford the luxury of deep, enshrouding oblivion. The blight upon his realm had to be removed before it spread beyond his ability to control.

The Crystal Dragon shuddered at the thought of what he would be forced to do if that happened. There would be only *one* choice left to him then . . . and it might leave behind a legacy compared to which the devastation attempted by the Ice Dragon would seem a *blessing.*

Still, to *him* it would be worth the cost.

II

The Manor had no other name, none that had stuck, anyway. Many called it the Green Manor, but that was more a description than a true title. To Cabe Bedlam, it was simply called the Manor. How long ago it had been built and by whom was a matter of conjecture. The style was like nothing the dark-haired warlock had ever seen before or since. Though much of the building had been cut from stone, the right side was actually formed by a massive tree as old as time. Depending where one stood in front of it, the Manor was either two or three stories tall. Marble columns jutted upward on each side of the doorway. Near the roof, the metallic effigy of one of the Seekers seemed ready to swoop down on any intruder.

Some assumed it had been built by the avian race, in part because much of the statuary and artwork seemed to revolve around the lives of the bird folk. That a tree formed part of the Manor strengthened that theory. Yet, it always seemed strange that creatures who normally lived in the heavens and made their rookeries in high mountain caves would build so earthbound a home. It seemed more likely to Cabe that the statues and such had actually been added later on, long after the departure of the original builders.

Actually, the history of the Manor meant far less to him than the fact that he was now its master. Here in the midst of the Dagora Forest, he and his wife, the enchantress Gwendolyn, ruled as lord and lady. Here, they raised the children . . . both human and drake.

From his position on the second-floor balcony of their private quarters, Cabe could survey much of the vast garden of the Manor. He watched as servants of both races went about their duties or spent their free time enjoying the day. *The first time I saw this place, I was running for my life.*

The Dragon Kings had discovered him, the unknown and unassuming grandson of Nathan Bedlam, a sorcerer who had nearly brought down the ruling drakes. The silver streak in his

7

hair, the mark of sorcery, would have been enough to condemn him already, for the drakes despised human mages, but the discovery of his ancestry had sealed his fate. Some of the Dragon Kings had panicked and sought to kill him immediately, but instead one of their own had perished, in the process stirring the long-dormant magical powers of Cabe to life. He had fled here and found Gwen, the Lady of the Amber, frozen for more than a hundred years by the novice warlock's own father, Azran. Together, Cabe and the enchantress had survived Dragon Kings, armies, and mad sorcerers. After Azran's death and the scattering of Duke Toma's army, they had come back to the Manor and made it their own . . . if it was possible for anyone to actually lay claim to the ancient structure.

A giggle made him look down. Cabe stiffened as he saw his daughter, Valea, come charging into sight, a greenish yellow drake as large as a full-grown man behind her. Just coming into womanhood, she was the image of her mother down to the fiery red tresses. Clad in a riding outfit of emerald green, much more practical than the dresses Gwen tried to make her wear, she should have been able to outrun the beast.

She did nothing of the sort. Instead, Valea whirled about and reached for the running drake with open arms. Cabe raised a hand to defend her, then held back as the beast suddenly began to shimmer. Reptilian legs straightened and softened. Leathery wings shriveled to nothing, as did the tail. As the shifting creature stood on what had once been its hind legs, the draconian visage pulled inward, becoming more and more human with each passing breath. Hair of the same greenish yellow sprouted from the top of the head.

Where once had stood a monster, there now stood a beautiful maiden only a few years older than Valea. She was clad in an outfit identical to that of her companion save that it was of a pale rose, not emerald green.

Valea came up and hugged her tight. From where he stood, Cabe could hear both of them.

"That's the fastest you shifted yet, Ursa! I wish I could do that!"

"You think I'm doing better?" the older girl asked hopefully. Her narrow eyes contrasted sharply with Valea's almond-shaped ones. Like all female drakes when in their human forms, she was breathtaking and exotic. Her shape already vied with human women twice her age and her face was that of a siren, full-lipped and inviting. Only her childlike manner prevented her from already being a seductress. "Kyl keeps saying I'm so slow I should be with the *minors*!" She sniffed. "I don't, do I?"

Cabe grimaced. Minor drakes were beasts, pure and simple, and what he had mistaken the drake girl for a moment before. They were little more than giant lizards with wings and were generally used by their brethren as riding animals. In what was possibly the most peculiar aspect of the drake race, both minor drakes and the intelligent ones could be born in the same hatching. Even the drakes could not say why. To call Ursa a minor drake was the worst of all insults among her kind. He would have to speak to Kyl, something that was never easy.

The two girls were laughing now, Valea having evidently said something that Cabe had missed. The duo ran off. Cabe marveled at how easy it was for his daughter to accept a playmate who shifted from human to monster form, especially as the latter was the girl's birth form. He still felt uneasy around most of the drakes and was not reconciled by the fact that they, in turn, had a very healthy respect for his sorcerous abilities.

Darkhorse would laugh if he knew . . . He wondered where the elemental was. Still chasing the ghost of the warlock Shade? He hoped not. Shade was dead; the shadowy steed had seen it himself. Yet, Darkhorse had searched the Dragonrealm time and time again, never trusting what his own eyes had shown him. There was, admittedly, some justification. It had been Shade's curse to be reborn after each death, ever shifting from darkness to light to darkness again depending on which side his previous incarnation had followed. The last death had *sounded* final . . .

Cabe dropped the thought before he, too, began to see ghosts. There were other matters of importance. The news that King Melicard of Talak had passed on to them was disturbing, more so because one did not know what to believe and what not to believe. Oddly enough, it was not the more substantial rumors of a possible confederation made up of the survivors of decimated drake clans or the rise of a new generation of human warlocks that remained lodged in his mind, but rather the least likely one.

Someone had claimed to have sighted three great black ships on the northwestern seas of the Dragonrealm. Ships that had been sailing south.

It seemed unlikely, though, since the source of the rumor was said to be hill dwarfs, well known for creating tall tales. The Aramites hardly had the time and resources to start a new venture of the magnitude that the rumors indicated. Three such vessels meant hundreds of sorely needed soldiers taken from the defense of the wolf raiders' crumbling empire.

Yet . . . no news of the great revolt overseas had reached the Dragonrealm in about a year. At last word, one of the mightiest seaports left to the raiders had been ripe for falling. The forces of the Gryphon had been only days away.

He hoped the tide had not turned somehow.

"What are you thinking too much about now?"

The warlock turned to his wife, who had just entered the room. Gwendolyn Bedlam was a tall woman with fiery red hair that cascaded downward, falling nearly to her waist. A single wide stripe of silver ran back across her hair, marking her, as it did Queen Erini of Talak and Cabe, as a magic user. She had emerald eyes that sparkled when she was pleased and full lips that were presently curled into a smile. The forest green robe she wore was more free-flowing than his dark blue one, yet somehow it clung to her form, perfectly outlining her voluptuous body. He met her halfway across the room and took her in his arms. Their kiss was as long and as lingering as the first time they had ever kissed. Cabe, with his slightly crooked nose and roundish face, had often wondered how someone of such ordinary features and mild build as himself had ever been so fortunate as to win her hand.

When he was at last able to separate himself from her, Cabe replied, "I was thinking of many things, but mostly about what we learned in Talak."

"The black ships?"

He nodded. "Maybe I'm just worried about the Gryphon. He did so much for me when I was confused and afraid all those years ago. He gave us refuge. Now, not a word in so much time . . . and then this sudden rumor."

"The trip across takes a long time, Cabe." Gwen took his arm and started to lead him out of the room. "Perhaps the last ship was delayed."

He nodded, but the nagging feeling would not disappear. "Maybe, but I can't help feeling that something has happened."

"Troia and Demion would not let anything happen to him. Demion sounds very protective of his father." Although they had never met the Gryphon's mate or his son, they knew them almost as well as if they had visited them every day.

"I suppose . . ."

His father was a bear of a man, taller than he was and with so commanding a presence that he always felt compelled to kneel before him. Both of them were clad in the same green dragon-scale armor, but whereas he merely felt hot and uncomfortable, his father truly was the warrior incarnate, a true standard by which the rest of the clan measured itself.

The bearded figure looked down at him. "I expect complete loyalty from all of my sons! You won't fail me like your brothers, will you?"

And it seemed that more than one voice answered, for it seemed there were others beside him, all kneeling before the man they called father. . . .

"Cabe?"

"Father?" He blinked. "Gwen?"

She turned him so that they faced each other. There was deep concern in her eyes, concern bordering on fear for him. She stroked his cheek. "Are you all right? You froze there for a moment and your eyes turned upward. I thought you were about to pass out!"

"I . . ." What *had* happened? "I had . . . a flash of something."

The enchantress pushed aside several locks of crimson hair that had fallen over her face in the excitement. Her expression clouded. "You muttered 'father.' Was it . . . was it Azran?"

The name still sent chills running through him. "Azran's dead and I'd never call him father, anyway. He was only responsible for my birth. Hadeen, the half-elf my grandfather got to raise me . . . he was my father if anyone was. Besides, this was someone else's father . . . though I felt as if he and I were the same for that moment."

"What did you see?"

He described the scene to her, discovering then how murky

everything had been. It was as if the vision were very old. Cabe mentioned as much to Gwen.

"A ghost of the far past . . ." she suggested, glancing around at their surroundings. "The Manor is very, very old. It could be you walked into one of its memories." In the time since they had made the Manor their home, they had discovered that it was haunted. Not by true ghosts and undead, but rather by living memories of the many who had either lived here or stayed for a time. Most of the visions were quick, foggy things. A glimpse of a tall, severe-looking woman in a gown of gold. A creature like a wolf, but more upright, possibly of a race now dead.

A few images were more distinct. Short-lived events like the one that Gwen had seen in the first days. It had been a wedding, but the image had lasted only long enough for her to hear the two participants give their agreement. There were other visions, darker ones, but they were rare and only those very gifted in sorcery even noticed the most ordinary memories. The Bedlams had learned to live with them, for there was nothing in those memories that could hurt anyone.

"This was stronger than usual," Cabe muttered. "But it did follow the pattern of the others. I'd just never seen this one before."

"There's probably a lot we haven't seen. When I was here the first time, in Nathan's time, I experienced a few that I have yet to see again." Her grip on him tightened. "Are you still suffering from it?"

He shook his head. Even the last vestiges of it were no more than memories of a memory in his head. "I'm fine."

She nodded, but he could see that she was still not satisfied. Cabe knew that she was thinking of another possibility.

"No, it wasn't a Seeker. I know how their mindspeak feels and this wasn't like that. This truly felt *ancient*. I could sense that. What I saw was something that had happened long ago, maybe even before the Dragon Kings, the Seekers, and the Quel had ever been, although I didn't think humans went back that far in the history of the Dragonrealm."

His reply seemed to relieve her. She kissed him lightly, then cupped his chin in one hand. "Very well, but if it happens again, I want to know."

"Agreed."

They walked slowly down the hallway, their conversation turning to the more mundane concerns of managing what was turning into a small village. Both Toos the Regent, ruler of Penacles, and the Green Dragon, who controlled the vast forest region surrounding their home, insisted on adding to their already vast number of servants. With some effort, the Bedlams had increased the area covered by the protective spell of the Manor. The humans and drakes in their service already needed to build new homes, for the smaller buildings that made up the Manor estate could no longer hold everyone. Once Cabe had joked about slowly becoming master of a tiny but growing kingdom. Now, he was beginning to think that the joke was becoming fact.

Their conversation came to an abrupt stop as something small dashed across the hall.

"What was that?" Gwen's brow furrowed in thought. "It almost looked like a . . . like a . . ."

A twin of the first creature raced past in the same direction. This time, the two had a better look.

"Were you going to say 'a stick man'?" Cabe asked in innocent tones.

Yet a third darted into the hall. This one paused and stared at the two huge figures despite having no eyes to speak of. Like the others, its head was merely an extension of the stick that made up its torso. Its arms and legs were twigs that someone had tied to the larger stick with string.

Its curiosity apparently assuaged, the ludicrous figure scurried off after its brethren.

"We have enough folk living here without adding these now," the enchantress decided. "It might be a good idea to see where they're going."

"Or where they came from," added Cabe. "Do you want to follow them or should I?"

"I'll follow them. You find out who's responsible, although I think we both know."

He did not reply. She was likely right. When tiny men made of twigs wandered the hallways of the Manor or bronze statues turned into large and lethal flying missiles, there could only be one person responsible.

The stick men had come from the stairway leading to the ground floor. Cabe descended as swiftly as was safe; there was no telling if he might trip over yet another tiny figure. He reached the bottom of the stairway easily enough, but perhaps a bit too much at ease because of that, the warlock almost did not notice the living wall coming from his right.

"Do pardon me, my Lord Bedlam. I must admit my eyes and my mind were elsewhere or I would have certainly made note of you."

Benjin Traske stood before Cabe, an imposing sight if ever there was one. Traske was more than six feet in height and had the girth to match. His face was full and round and on any other person would have seemed the jovial kind. On the scholar, however, it was more reminiscent of a judge about to pass sentence. He wore a cowled scholar's cloak, a gray, enveloping thing with gold trim at the collar, and the ebony robes of his profession. Traske also wore a blade, not part of the usual fare for a man of his occupation, but the warlock had learned the day of the tutor's arrival that he was a survivor of Mito Pica, a city razed to the ground by the armies of the Dragon Emperor in their search for one young Cabe Bedlam. Benjin Traske had seen his wife and child die because he had only had his bare hands with which to protect them. He himself had barely survived a wound to his stomach. The blade had remained with him since then, a symbol of his willingness to defend those under his care at the cost of his own life.

There had been some question as to whether he would be able to live among drakes, much less teach their young, but the Dragon King Green, who had discovered him, had assured the Bedlams that Benjin Traske saw cooperation between the two races as the only possible future.

Even when he was not tutoring, Traske sounded as if he were lecturing. Cabe found he could never listen to the man without feeling like one of his charges. "No apologies, Master Traske! I was hardly paying attention myself."

The tutor ran a hand through thin gray hair peppered slightly with silver. An expression of exasperation crossed his face. "You have seen your prodigy's latest effort, then. I feared as much. They have journeyed upstairs, I take it?"

Cabe nodded. "All three of them. The Lady Gwen is hunting them down now."

"Only three of them? There should be five."

Such knowledge in no way encouraged Cabe in the efforts of his son. "We saw only three."

Traske sighed. "Then, if you will excuse me, Lord Bedlam, I will hunt out the other two while your good bride deals with the three above. I feel at some fault, for when he lost control, my mind was elsewhere."

"You were teaching him magic?" While there was a hint of sorcery about the tutor, he had never struck Cabe as an adept.

His remark seemed to amuse the man. "Teach him magic? Only if young Master Aurim desires to know how to lift a feather for the space of three seconds. No, my lord, my skills will never be much more than wishful thought. If I were an adept, the fall of Mito Pica might have taken a different turn. I was merely his audience. I believe your son was trying to impress the teacher, so to speak. No, the magic of mathematics and history is the only magic I can teach."

"Well, I think I'd better teach him a little about concentration and patience . . . again. Where is he?"

"In the center of the garden." Benjin Traske performed a bow, a momentous achievement for one of his build. "If you will excuse me, my lord, I do not want my quarry getting too far afield and if the other two are not upstairs, then that means they must be headed in the direction of the kitchen."

"Mistress Belima will have a fit if she sees one." Belima was the peasant woman who ran the kitchens as her own kingdom. Considering the results she achieved, Cabe was more than willing to grant her that territory.

"Indeed." The hefty scholar departed, moving with a swiftness and grace that the warlock could only marvel at.

It took only minutes for Cabe to reach the location where Traske had said his son would be. Aurim was seated by himself on one of the many stone benches located here and there around the garden. His head was bowed and his face was buried in his hands. The silver streak across the middle of his head contrasted sharply to his shoulder-length, golden hair. He wore a robe similar to his father's, save that it was of dark red.

"You'll never find them like that."

Aurim looked up, his expression changing from one of frustration to embarrassment. Overall, he resembled his father, but fortunately, as far as Cabe was concerned, he had inherited from his mother's side a more noble chin and a straighter nose. Although only a few years older than Valea, he was generally able to pass for someone several years into adulthood . . . except when failure reared its ugly head.

"You know."

"I *saw* them. So did your mother."

The boy rose. He could already meet Cabe at eye level even if he could not meet Cabe's eyes themselves. "It was a *simple* thing! You and Scholar Traske are always telling me my problem is patience or concentration! I made the stick men to practice. There's ten different routines I can make them do, all to prove I'm being more careful and concentrating better!"

"And so?" He tried to be encouraging. Unlike Aurim, Cabe had come into his powers almost full-flung. The experience and patience that his grandfather, Nathan, had *literally* passed on to him had given him an advantage no other spellcaster had ever had. Even then, his own inexperience and uncertainty had made for a constant battle of wits with himself playing both sides. He still had much to learn. His son had no such advantage; everything he learned he learned from the beginning. Sorcery, while it looked simple to understand and utilize, was anything but.

"And so I lost control again! Halfway through the second set. They just ran off." A sullen look crossed the lad's countenance. "And now you can lecture me again."

"Aurim . . ."

His son clenched fists. "If that stupid vision hadn't—"

"*What* vision?" All thought of Aurim's recklessness vanished.

"Like the other ones. The memories of the Manor, you and Mother say. Only this one was sharper. Men in scale armor. One big one talking to others. I think . . . I think they were all his sons."

"And you were one of them. He spoke to you about loyalty. How he demanded it from you."

The boy looked at him, wide-eyed. "You know it?"

"I had the *same* vision . . . probably the same time as you, in fact." Cabe grew uneasy. Nothing like that had ever occurred before. The visions generally only appeared to one person, usually Gwen or him. Only lately had Aurim started to sense them and he, knowing of them from his parents, had had little trouble accepting them. If the things were changing, becoming more intrusive into the world of the present, would it mean that some day they would have to abandon the Manor?

Aurim, who knew his father well, put aside his own troubles for the moment and asked seriously, "Does this mean something?"

"It might." He no longer had the memories of Nathan Bedlam to guide him, but Gwen knew far more about the whims of sorcery than anyone now alive save the Dragon Kings and possibly the Gryphon. She might be able to shed some light on this sudden turn.

Gwen! She was still hunting down the stick men! "We need to discuss this further, but first we have to take care of a little problem still running loose."

The tall boy's cheeks turned crimson. "I've been trying to think about what to do. Couldn't we just summon them with a spell?"

"Have you tried a summoning?"

"Yes." The defeat in Aurim's tone increased tenfold.

"I was afraid of that." In the heat of the moment, the idea had not even occurred to Cabe, but he knew that at some point Gwen would have thought of it. The warlock was doubtful it would have worked, anyway. Aurim's creations were never easy to deal with. It was a sign of his great potential. "Did you maintain your concentration?"

"I did! This time I *swear* it!"

"Then they probably won't listen to anyone . . . and we have to go hunting. You go after Master Traske; he'll need the help. I'll find your mother."

"Yes, Father." Aurim paused. "I still can't get the vision out of my mind. Are there others so vivid?"

"Only a few. We'll have to talk about how to shield yourself from them if they bother you so much."

"Oh, I don't mind them; any other time, they're interesting. Who do you suppose they were?"

Cabe knew that his son was stalling now, mostly because Aurim had little desire to face his tutor after such an abysmal display. Still, for once it was a question that the warlock wished he could answer. "I don't know. They remind me of something I've read, but nothing specific comes to mind now."

"What's the Legar Peninsula like?"

There were questions and there were questions and Cabe, who tried to be an understanding father even though he considered nearly two decades not near enough time to learn how to be one, had had enough. "I think Master Traske would *truly* appreciate your help soon, Aurim. Then, when you're done, *he* can give you a lecture on the geography of Legar or anywhere else."

Frustrated, Aurim grumbled, "I only wondered if it really glitters as much as it did in the vision . . ."

"What was that?" Stepping face-to-face to his son, Cabe repeated his question and added, "You saw Legar in the vision?"

Aurim swallowed, not knowing what he had done wrong now. He nodded slowly and gasped, "In the background. It was there sometimes. I . . . I thought it was. You've always talked about how much it sparkles and Master Traske said once it was covered with diamonds."

"Not diamonds. Not exactly," Cabe halfheartedly corrected him. "Crystals, yes." He looked away. "And it does glitter; enough to blind a person during midday if you look the wrong direction." *And I didn't see it. Why?*

The visions of the Manor had never extended to regions so far away. They had always dealt with the ancient structure itself or the lands it occupied. If Aurim had seen Legar, and Cabe did not doubt him, then this was more than a simple time-lost memory.

He could not say why or how he knew, but somehow, standing there, Cabe Bedlam was certain that the answer to this mysterious vision had to do with three black ships.

The beast was dead. It was not often that Orril D'Marr overestimated his prey, but the blasted creature had seemed so impervious to pain that he had pushed too hard. It was a pity. Lord D'Farany would be displeased, which was always a danger, but D'Marr was certain that what little he had gained out of the creature just before the end would more than make up for his error.

The young Aramite officer scratched his chin while he watched the soldiers drag the Quel's body away. That it had been more than a simple animal had surprised him at first, but he should have known that when the blue man said something was true it was most definitely true. D'Rance was a fountain of knowledge

and had, fortunately for the expedition, studied the history of
this abysmal land in great detail. It was a shame he had not been
born a true Aramite rather than one of the untrustworthy, blue-
skinned folk of the northern reaches of the empire. Everyone
knew it was only a matter of time before one of his kind turned
on you. D'Marr hoped he would be the one given the order to
kill the northerner. It would be interesting to see how the blue
man died.

The sun was going down rapidly. That was fine with D'Marr.
The weather here was beastly, fit only for creatures like the
overgrown armadillo he had just killed. The sun burned all day,
making the black armor seem like a fire-hot kettle. What made
it worse was that no one else seemed to notice it.

D'Marr turned and started for a ridge to the west of the camp.
It was a long walk, but he knew that was where he would find
the Pack Leader and possibly D'Rance, too, although the blue
man was supposed to be leading the hunt for the cavern entrance
now. One never knew about the northerner, though. What he did
often went against what a wolf raider was supposed to do. No
doubt only the fact that he achieved results kept Lord D'Farany
from putting a rather permanent end to the blue man's antics.

Yes, it would be interesting to see him die.

He reached the ridge some ten minutes later. The sentries
positioned near the bottom saluted him and immediately stepped
out of his way. Most soldiers were quick-witted enough to know
that one did not stand in Orril D'Marr's way for very long. As
he walked between them, the young officer smiled lazily at the
taller of the two. The man's eyes widened, then looked away.
Once past, D'Marr dropped the smile and forgot them completely. They were nothing to him. Only one man among all
those who had become part of this desperate venture had earned
his respect and obedience . . . not to mention his fear.

As he neared the top, a snarling sound made him look up. A
savage creature the size of a small dog but built more along the
lines of a giant rat peered down at him. Its ugly face was flat,
almost as if at birth someone had pushed it in, and when the jaws
opened, there were jagged teeth everywhere. When D'Marr came
almost within reach, it snapped at him. The mask of boredom
slipped from his visage as the Aramite silently cursed the animal
and swatted at it with one mailed hand. Still snarling, his furry

adversary trotted back several steps. D'Marr hated verloks and would have gladly done away with this one save that it was his master's pet. Only Lord D'Farany would ever consider such a vicious creature for a plaything.

No longer with an advantage, the verlok trotted back to its master. D'Marr took a moment to both catch his breath and organize his thoughts. He stared at the backside of the Pack Leader, who stood at the opposite edge of the cliff gazing out at the sea. The evening wind whipped Lord D'Farany's cloak like some mad dervish, but otherwise the master raider was as still as stone.

The Aramite commander was alone, but as D'Marr strode toward him, he heard D'Farany's voice.

"Can you feel it? So very near yet so far. The land fairly glows with power . . ."

D'Marr came within arm's reach of his commander and knelt beside him. The verlok moved away, glaring. "My lord."

"You killed him, D'Marr."

He glanced around to see if somehow he had missed someone else, someone who could have informed Lord D'Farany about his mistake. There was no one. The anxious raider looked down at the ground. Time and time again he reminded himself that his master was no longer a *keeper*, no longer one of the Aramite sorcerers whose souls had been tied to the wolf raiders' savage and very real god, the *Ravager*. When their god had abandoned them just prior to the revolt, he had taken his gifts with him. That had meant madness and death to most of the keepers, for the power of the Ravager had used as much as it had been used. It had enslaved them to the will of the wolf god. Without it, the survivors had become as helpless as newborn pups . . . all of them save Ivon D'Farany.

D'Marr realized he had not yet responded. "Yes, my lord."

"You were overzealous."

"I was, my lord."

"Rise, Orril, and join me." The Aramite commander had still not shifted his gaze from the sea. D'Marr stood up and waited, knowing that his master would speak when he chose to.

More than a minute had passed before Lord D'Farany finally commented, "From here, they still resemble hunters, don't they, Orril?"

It took D'Marr the space of a breath or two to understand what his master meant. Then his eyes fixed upon the three massive ships that had carried the wolf raiders this far. It was true; they still did resemble the hunters they had once been. Tall, black, and, despite their great size, as swift as any other vessel sailing the seas.

And swift enough to carry us away from the revolt while our tails still hung between our legs . . . "They've served us well, my lord."

"And suffered because of us."

"Yes, sir." Suffered, indeed. From a distance they might still resemble the terrors of the sea they had once been, but up close the ravages of the empire-wide revolt became all too evident. The sails had been patched so many times that there were now more patches than original sail. Scorch marks and cracked timber on the hull spoke of the accuracy of the enemy's weapons. On board, it was even worse. Most of the rails were either broken or completely missing. There were still gaping holes in the decks because there was no longer enough material with which to repair them. Aboard one vessel, the crew had barely managed to secure the main mast after one strike had nearly torn it free. It was a wonder the raiders had made it so far with only a few losses at sea.

The three ebony ships were hunters no longer. They were merely shadows now.

"Scuttle them. Tonight."

"My lord?"

The raider commander turned then. D'Marr swallowed. Lord D'Farany had not escaped the madness that had taken his fellow keepers and the vestiges of that madness remained forever a part of his countenance. His skin was pale, almost white, and there were scars, insufficiently hidden by a short, well-groomed beard, where he had tried to claw his own skin off during that period. Three days of screaming had left his lipless mouth forever curled upward at the ends, making it seem as if the former keeper found the world around him ever amusing. Worst of all, though, were the eyes, for they never seemed to focus, yet somehow they snared one's attention, forced one to look at them. To D'Marr, to whom the world was an enemy ever needing to be watched, being bound to stare into those eyes and those eyes alone was sheer horror.

"Scuttle them. Tonight. They deserve to rest." The eyes drifted to the direction of the sea but did not quite reach it.

"Y-yes, my lord." D'Marr found himself shaking as he broke contact. Then his fear faded as he contemplated what the Pack Leader's command truly implied. They would be trapped here, then. They would be forced to not only survive, but to strengthen themselves as swiftly as possible. They would have to make this realm theirs or perish.

It did not occur to D'Marr to protest, to refuse the order. One did not question the Pack Leader. It was not the Aramite way. "I will do it myself, my lord. There's something I wish to test and this will give me the chance."

"You should have been more careful, Orril," Lord D'Farany said, switching back to the previous subject as was often his habit. He snapped his fingers. The verlok came trotting over to him. Reaching down, the Pack Leader took the monstrosity in his arms. It growled quietly as he began to stroke it, the closest it could come to a purr. "This . . . this . . . *Quel* . . . was valuable."

Here was his chance to redeem himself. "Yes, my lord, he was. More so than we could've ever realized."

The hand stroking the backside of the verlok paused. Pale, gray eyes shifted to a spot just to the side of the officer's head. Not a word was said, but D'Marr still knew that he had just been commanded to speak.

"I know now where the surface entrance to the caverns lies, my lord," he began. "The entrance to the city of the underdwellers. To their power. All the searching in the world would not have uncovered it, Lord D'Farany. It's extremely well hidden."

"But you can find it."

"Yes, my lord. Easily."

Nodding his approval, the Pack Leader turned away. D'Marr, however, did not take that as a signal that he had been dismissed. He knew his master too well to assume such a thing.

"Tomorrow, then. You will lead the search."

"As you desire." Despite his hatred of the heat and the blinding sunlight he would be forced to suffer, the young raider was pleased. The glory would be his, not the blue man's.

"There is something else, is there not?"

Something else? D'Marr could not recall anything of significance other than what he had reported. The location of the monster's home had been his only trump card, the only one he had thought necessary.

"What of the dragon, Orril?"

The dragon! How could he have forgotten? The dragon who ruled here had been the only worrisome question, the only threat to the advancement of their plans.

"The Dragon King will be of little concern to us, my lord. This one hides in his citadel and never comes out. This I learned through the Quel. So long as we do not seek to enter, he and the handful that make up his clan will not bother with us. We may do as we please. All he seems to do is watch. Watch and do nothing." The last statement was pure conjecture on the Aramite's part, but it made sense to him. The Crystal Dragon apparently cared not who trespassed in the region that was supposedly his so long as he was left alone. "So we may proceed and the dragon may be left for later when we are more secure in our power."

Lord D'Farany did not immediately respond. Instead, he turned slowly back to his subordinate and, for the first time since D'Marr had joined him, fixed his eyes on the young officer. The verlok grew oddly still, as if as frightened as D'Marr. "You had best be correct in your assumption, Orril. The dragon cannot be taken lightly. He could not have lived so long surrounded by so much power and not been affected by it." The Pack Leader began stroking his pet again, but this time the animal was in no way soothed. "Should it come to a confrontation between the dragon and me, rest assured that I will bait a proper trap for the reptile . . . and you will be the *bait*." The eyes unfocused again and the Pack Leader began to turn away. "You are dismissed."

It took all of Orril D'Marr's willpower *not* to run as he departed the ridge. Someone in the camp would suffer tonight; someone would have to suffer to assuage his fears. It was the only way he could purge himself, the only way he could face the tasks tomorrow with the mask of indifference in place.

Better the dragon any day, he thought, than the wrath of his master.

* * *

Cleaving its way through the turbulent waters of the Eastern Sea, the lone vessel neared the Dragonrealm. Where the ships that Cabe Bedlam pondered about had been deadly leviathans, giants designed for terror, this one was low and sleek, a tiny juggernaut built to carry a mere handful of passengers swiftly to their destination. There was, in fact, only one trait it shared with the three massive raider ships.

It was utterly black.

III

"We are very close now. I can hear its call. It was good of the Quel not to lie to us," Lord D'Farany commented as he watched his men advance across the gleaming land toward the place where the dying Quel had claimed the entrance to his city was hidden. Lord Ivon D'Farany did little to stem the madness in his voice. He knew the others could not sense what he sensed, for none of them had ever been trained as a keeper. They were to be both pitied and envied, he decided. Pitied because they had never known the seductive power of the Aramites' great god, the Ravager, and envied because they had not had to suffer the soul-wrenching horror of withdrawal when that power had been abruptly torn away just prior to the war. He was considered one of the fortunate ones, but then no one else could ever understand the emptiness that was now ever with him. His hand twitched as old reflex actions still sought the talisman he had once owned, the link to his god.

"But that will change . . ." he whispered. "So much will change, then." The ends of D'Farany's thin mouth rose ever so slightly, the closest he generally came to a smile. It was never a good idea to smile, for it upset the men so.

When the power of his god had been torn from his soul, he, like the rest, had fallen into madness. He had screamed and then laughed, a laugh that had chilled his watchers. In his mind, he had died, completely and utterly. When sanity at last returned, a different man occupied the body. The desperate commanders had sought the power of a keeper to aid them in the sudden and overwhelming revolt that had arisen, but they had found something else instead. Something that would not be manipulated but rather would manipulate in turn.

Recalling where he was, Lord D'Farany glanced about him. Despite the sun and heat, his men were still moving at a brisk pace. The common ranks did not know what they truly sought, only that their leaders had ordered them to watch for a cavern and be prepared for battle.

It might be that he was wrong, that this was not the place that he had dreamed of for the past few weeks. He had not, of course, told anyone else of the dreams. He never did. The ship captains had obeyed his command to steer toward this land rather than one of the more lush regions to the north, but it was clear that they considered the gleaming peninsula an interesting but hardly useful bit of dirt. Vegetation was sparse and older reports had warned that the interior was inhospitable, consisting mainly of endless hills of rock and crystal. There was nothing here of value to the average wolf raider; the crystals were fascinating, but they were, for the most part, common.

He knew otherwise. He had first felt the power emanating from the near-barren domain *days* before they had landed. Now, ashore, he more than felt it; he *lived* it. Here was a force that could fill the emptiness inside, make him complete at last.

All his men had to do was take it from the beasts below.

"This is a mistake, yes?" came a knowing voice to his left. While phrased as a question, as much of what his companion said was, the comment was actually a statement.

"Give Orril his opportunity, Kanaan. It is both his reward and his punishment."

"There is another way, my lord. A better way, I think."

D'Farany knew what his aide meant. He nodded slowly. "When it is needed. Patience, Kanaan."

The tall figure beside him grew silent, but the Aramite leader knew that Kanaan D'Rance was by no means mollified. Like most of his kind, he was impatient and ambitious, a combination of traits that would have had him executed on the first day by most commanders but suited Ivon D'Farany just right. The Pack

Leader had a fondness for things mercurial and the blue man was certainly that. He was also a fount of information. D'Rance had made the Dragonrealm his obsession.

The gaunt northerner had been a rare find. His talents perfectly complemented Orril D'Marr's own considerable skills, yet the two were of such different minds that their constant competition also served D'Farany. The latter also assured that the two would never combine forces and cause him threat. He would have hated to see that happen. It would have meant the need to eliminate two valuable weapons. He did not dare do that until he was complete again.

Complete . . . the Pack Leader frowned. Even this would not make him truly complete. Nothing save his glorious god's return could do that. *Still, I will be close.*

It was then he felt the power around him shift and shape and though he *knew* what it meant, Ivon D'Farany merely stood there and drank in the sensation.

The world exploded in light . . . and the belated screams of men.

"I *warned*, did I not? I warned that this would happen, yes!"

D'Farany forced his eyes to focus. He did not see as normal men did, not anymore, but there were times when it became necessary to try. When the raider leader did at last see what the underdwellers had done, he could not help but smile, despite the horrific sight he knew he created. "Magnificent!"

Before him, his soldiers scattered in an attempt to make themselves less of an inviting target. The Pack Leader barely noticed their frantic efforts. His eyes only saw the wonderful result of so much power, power that was to be *his.*

There had been a small rise where the beasts had struck with their sorcery, a small rise populated by a few scraggly plants and, at the moment of the attack, likely a dozen or so soldiers. Now, the rise was a flat, iron-hot pool of *glass* and the plants and the men unfortunate enough to be there at the time . . . were nothing.

Yet still the raider force moved on, for they had been given a command and that was all they needed.

"Magnificent . . ." the Aramite commander whispered again. His hand twitched as he once more sought the talisman that would have let him manipulate such power.

The same sensation swept over him. A second flash burned away the world in a sea of light. D'Rance and the others were forced to fall back and shield their eyes, but Lord D'Farany barely noticed. He breathed in the holocaust air and felt a strength he had not felt in years.

With an almost wistful expression on his ravaged countenance, he slowly turned toward the blue man and quietly commanded, "Bring me the box now, Kanaan."

Still blinking, the bearded northerner reached into the depths of his cloak and pulled out a tiny, rectangular container. The Pack Leader nodded pleasantly, having known all the time that the blue man would have it on him despite orders to the contrary. He forgave D'Rance such things, because it pleased him to do so. There would come a time when he overstepped himself and when that happened D'Farany would either punish him properly or turn him over to D'Marr, who had never made it a secret that he wanted the blue man's skin.

The Aramite commander liked to think of himself as a fair man. He was also perfectly willing to give the younger officer to the northerner if circumstances warranted it.

He removed his gloves and, with great respect, took the tiny black box from D'Rance. The former keeper ran one finger over the lid, outlining the wolf's head engraved there. It had taken him much effort and time to gather the forces stored within and he treated them with the care they deserved.

A third burst of light raised anew the shouts and screams, but the sounds were merely insignificant irritations to him as he opened the top and admired his prize.

In the days of the keepers, it would have been called the *Ravager's Tooth*. A curved artifact shaped to resemble a hound's fang, it was small enough to fit in his palm. He had once had one like it, before the day of emptiness. With great eagerness, Lord D'Farany removed the talisman from the box and cupped it in his left hand. The terrible smile stretched tighter as he allowed himself to briefly become ensorcelled by the tooth.

My master, why have you forsaken us? In the talisman was the residue of the Ravager's unholy will. Long ago, a younger D'Farany had discovered that although their god had vanished and taken his power with him, there were traces in the talismans of the keepers . . . even traces in the keepers themselves. It had meant dark work, locating the artifacts and the bodies and drawing the lingering power from them, but he had prevailed. Yet the power this piece contained was limited; each use drained the talisman. It would soon be as empty as he was.

"But not for long . . ." The Pack Leader cradled the piece in his hand and returned the box to the blue man. He then turned back to where his men fought to survive and held out the talisman toward the gleaming landscape where he supposed the cavern entrance was.

Yet again the earth was shaken by a burst of deadly light. The Quel might no longer be masters of the realm, but they still wielded power. Their strikes were also systematic; each time the raiders shifted away from the previous blow, they were attacked anew from the opposite direction.

A silence seemed to surround the former keeper as he held the talisman up to the sky. The only one still daring to stand near him was D'Rance, who eyed his commander with both anticipation and envy.

D'Farany whispered, "Behold the legacy of my Lord Ravager. Behold his glory."

The carved tooth glowed bright.

Its effect was not something that was seen, not, at least, by the wolf raiders who were there. At most, a few who were sensitive, such as Orril D'Marr, felt a rippling in the fabric of the world itself. The rippling washed across the area like a tide coming into shore. It passed through rank after rank, moving swiftly toward the front and then beyond.

"Mustn't destroy," muttered the Pack Leader to himself. "Mustn't take the chance. Merely take the fight from them."

The silence around D'Farany spread as well. Even the screams and shouts seemed to fade away as the power unleashed by the talisman blanketed the land. Those who did not have the touch of sorcery within them still could feel that something was different.

At last, the tooth ceased to glow. Lord D'Farany looked at it with great sadness. The spell had drained it of everything he had collected. Now, it was no more than a useless trinket. Nonetheless, the Pack Leader did not throw it away, but rather returned it to an overawed D'Rance, who gingerly placed it back in the box.

"They may advance again."

The command proved to be unnecessary. Already, soldiers were reorganizing and moving forward. D'Marr had understood what had happened. The Aramite leader nodded to himself. It was an example of why the young officer was one of his favorites.

Now the raiders moved unimpeded. Even Lord D'Farany did not know what he had unleashed, but he knew that the Quel would be helpless now. Their power had been negated for a time and that time would be enough to ensure total Aramite victory.

"Come, Kanaan. It's time to join them."

The blue man bowed. "Yes, my lord."

As they trailed slowly after the advancing troops, D'Farany contemplated what he would do with that power now that it was his. Building new ships was a possibility, but what sense was there in returning to rescue the fools who still fought back home? How much better to claim a portion of this realm and begin expanding here. How much more satisfying to take from the Gryphon's friends the same thing the birdman had taken from the Aramites.

D'Marr peered into the darkness of the cavern entrance. The walls gleamed faintly from the torch he had directed one of his men to throw inside. There was nothing to be seen, but that did not mean that there was no danger. D'Marr was not that naive.

He turned to the man nearest him. "Inside. Double file. Do watch the ground and the walls . . . and the ceiling, for that matter. They could come from anywhere."

The raider blinked, then hurried to obey as D'Marr's free hand slowly shifted toward the rod hanging from his belt. The Aramite officer nodded and watched as two ranks quickly formed. He allowed the first three pairs to enter, then tightened his grip on his sword and entered with the next.

Where are you, my little beasts? Even with the intervention of Lord D'Farany, it could not be this easy. There had to be resistance. There had to be battle.

Farther and deeper they marched and yet still they did not encounter the creatures whose lair this was. A sense of unease spread throughout the lines, even infecting D'Marr. No enemy gave up so easy. Lord D'Farany's magical counterattack, while potent, should not have been able to eliminate *all* opposition.

He was almost pleased when the first man finally died.

He had commanded them to be wary of all directions, but no one save those who had been involved with the capture of the first Quel could have understood the speed at which they could burst through the earth and strike at their foes. Suddenly there was a huge, taloned hand erupting from the tunnel floor. It took hold of the ankle of the nearest soldier and withdrew as swiftly as it had come. That the hole that had been created was far too small for the human form did not matter. The helpless raider was pulled as far as the gap in the floor allowed and then pulled farther.

It was not a pleasant sight, but it gave D'Marr new respect for the strength of the overgrown armadillos.

"Leave it," he warned the two who started to reach for the remains in some vain hope that there was still a chance. "I want spears and torches ready." He had had some of the men bring light spears, weapons about a foot longer than a short sword and quite useful in tight areas. As light as they were, the spears were very, very sharp and highly resilient. "Right flank watch right wall and ceiling. Left flank watch left wall and floor. The man who misses the next one will not have to fear death at the beasts' claws. I shall be more than happy to oblige him myself."

Yet, even as he spoke, another arm burst through the wall across from him, seizing the nearest man by the throat and bringing his head hard against the rock face. The crack and snap echoed throughout the cavern, then was drowned out by the noises of belated action as the raiders closest tried to cut the hand of the creature off. One man managed to slice the back of the huge paw, but the digger quickly retreated into the earth.

How do they move through it so quickly? It might as well be water the way they come and go! There was only a small, collapsed hole to mark where the second attack had originated from.

He did not have time to consider the matter further, for the third attack was directed at *him*. D'Marr was turning when the talons came shooting from the wall next to him. With a swiftness he did not know he had, the officer ducked back. Even still, his reaction was nearly too slow. Huge claws slashed at his jaw, leaving a bloody trail. His sword was up in almost the same instant. The raider had the great satisfaction of watching the blade cut up through the arm just past the wrist of his attacker. A shower of blood drenched his breastplate.

The Quel's arm shook, its actions nearly twisting the sword free of D'Marr's grip. He took hold of it with both hands and held on for dear life. One of the soldiers raised his own weapon and brought it down on the still exposed limb. The armored hide of the Quel was thick, but not thick enough. The edge of the sword embedded itself in the arm, causing a new shower of blood.

The attacker tried to withdraw, but the swords prevented that. A soldier with a spear moved forward and thrust into the hole. D'Marr again wondered at the vast stamina and strength of the armored beast. Even as badly wounded as the Quel had to be, there was no sign of weakness.

The wall before him shattered, pelting men with bits of rock. The Quel, unable to retreat into the earth, had chosen to come to them instead.

The subterranean dweller filled the passage. D'Marr could not tell whether it was male, like the first, or female and did not really care. As an *it*, the Quel was terrible enough. With its good arm, it took the man with the spear and threw him into the soldiers behind him. The raider with the sword had wisely re-treated already. D'Marr released his hold on his own weapon, having realized that he would be next if he insisted on main-taining his grip any longer. The young officer had no delusions that he could take on one of the beasts single-handed.

Still . . . he reached for the rod by his side even as the Quel pawed at the blade buried in its wrist. Both arm wounds still bled profusely but the monster moved as if nothing were wrong.

"Don't just gawk! Bring the spears in!"

There was a scream and then much commotion farther down the line. The Quel were no longer attacking one at a time. He had no time to concern himself with the others, however, for the one who had tried to kill him evidently was intent on completing its task. D'Marr suspected that the creatures had known all along that he was the leader of the invading force. The initial attacks might even have been made so that they could better locate him among the rest. He suspected that the Quel relied greatly on their sense of hearing or some similar trait when they moved through the ground.

With a loud, long hoot, the monster swung at him with one huge paw. D'Marr ducked away and pulled his staff free of his belt. He held the long rod before him. Several men with spears had now closed on the Quel. Two feinted from the left of the huge digger. When the Quel turned toward them, those on the right jabbed with their own spears. One caught the massive creature in the arm that had been wounded. This time, D'Marr's adversary unleashed a shrill, unmistakable cry of agony. While it was thus occupied, the other lancers also attacked. Three spears penetrated the armored hide of the Quel.

So you do have a soft shell in places, the Aramite officer noted with some satisfaction. Like the creature it resembled, the Quel had less protection near the stomach region. That was not to say it was not protected well there, for two of the spears had snapped in that initial thrust, but of necessity the subterranean monster could not have as thick and hard a shell as it wore on its back. D'Marr had suspected as much from his time with the prisoner, but knew better than to trust that all the creatures were built the same way.

The Quel was staggering now, even its great stamina unable to compensate for the many dripping wounds. It took one last swipe at him and then began to back into the wall from which it had emerged.

"You'll not be leaving us so soon," hissed D'Marr. He thrust at the retreating Quel with his rod.

The wounded creature's howl shook the tunnel and echoed on and on long after the huge figure had collapsed to its knees.

Orril D'Marr touched the tip of the rod to the armored head. He smiled with grim satisfaction as the Quel shivered, hooted mournfully, and finally slumped.

"Yesss . . . I thought all it needed was a little adjustment." He looked from his conquered foe to his favorite toy. With the prisoner, he had overcompensated with the rod, killing the Quel. The short staff was a magical tool that he had inherited from his late predecessor, who had, in turn, paid dearly to have a sorcerer not of the keeper caste create it. It had thirty-two levels of pain, many of which could kill. The captive Quel had died from level twenty-one. He had given this one level twenty. D'Marr was quite pleased. Lord D'Farany would want hostages to question. It would make up for his earlier overzealousness.

The raider leader turned to aid in the other attacks, only to find that there were no longer any. He summoned one of the lesser officers.

The wolf raider, a bearded veteran named D'Roch who, like most of the men, had to look down at D'Marr, saluted him and nervously explained, "They simply withdrew, my lord. Right after that beast you took down howled."

It seemed odd that they would abandon the attack simply because one of their number had fallen. Such cowardice went against the Aramite way. "How many were there?"

"Counting yours, sir, four."

"Four?" D'Marr frowned slightly. They had only dared expend *four* of their kind in defense of the tunnel against a force the size of his? There was a piece of the puzzle missing. "This place is too lightly defended."

It was clear that the other officer did not think so, but he was wise enough not to say anything.

A soldier returned D'Marr's sword, carefully cleansed of all blood, to him. The young raider inspected the weapon, then sheathed it. The rod would serve him better, it seemed. With the blade, he would be dead long before he finished hacking up one of the beasts. They now feared the rod and D'Marr enjoyed nothing more than wielding fear.

He glanced down at the Quel. It still lived, if only barely. "Bind that thing tight and put it somewhere safe. Lord D'Farany may desire to see it."

D'Roch saluted. "Yes, sir."

"Re-form ranks. I see no reason why we shouldn't continue on, do you?"

"No, sir. At once, sir."

He had them under way in little more than a minute. They continued on down the passage, ever wandering deeper and deeper into the bowels of the earth. Once more, the trek became quiet, uneventful. The wolf raiders remained wary, however, for they had fallen prey to that trap once already.

D'Marr tapped the side of the rod against his leg. *Where are you, you cowardly monsters? Come out and play with me!*

The men began to mutter among themselves. There were whispers of plots involving the collapse of the entire length of the tunnel. The notion had entered D'Marr's mind earlier, but he had felt no need to mention it. Lord D'Farany had given a command and it was their duty to obey. Now, destroying the passageway did not even seem a likely trick, for if they had wanted to do it, he was certain that the Quel would have been better off if they had collapsed the passage earlier. They had not done so, preferring to risk themselves in more personal assaults that, to him, indicated again that something was amiss.

It was at the end of the passage that he found the first clue to the truth. The cavern that suddenly materialized before them took everyone by surprise, so accustomed had the raiders become to the narrow tunnel by that point. D'Marr pushed his way past the foremost rank and stared, his eyes drinking in everything. The mask of indifference barely remained in place, for although he had had time to contemplate the world of the Quel, the Aramite had failed to fully imagine its scope.

In a cavern that was nearly a world of its own, the vast city of the subterranean race silently greeted its invaders.

Enough of it resembled a human city that they understood instantly what it was. There were buildings that rose several stories and paths that could only be roads of a sort. Everything had been carved from the very rock. The path on which D'Marr found himself standing circled around the edges of the expansive cave. At various points, new tunnels branched off into the earth.

There was one peculiarity that would forever forbid anyone from thinking that humans had built this place, for while with great effort it would have been possible for men to carve out part of the city in the cavern walls, no human would have been able to live in places turned at such haphazard angles as these. Hundreds of gaps and outcroppings had been turned into tunnels and quite obvious living quarters, but to utilize them, the inhabitants would have had to virtually hang by their feet and hands at all times at heights that would have meant instant death to even the hardiest. Only creatures with long claws that could dig into rock would be able to make use of so peculiar a design. Only something like a Quel could call this home.

That the invaders could see all of this was the result of yet another marvel. Even despite the fact that they were likely hundreds of feet below the surface, the vast cave glowed as if the sun itself shone above the city. Instead of a burning orb, however, a fantastic array of crystals somehow gave off enough light to fill the chamber with day. Gazing up at them, Orril D'Marr knew that they were somehow linked to the outside, that, in a sense, the sun *did* shine on this subterranean spectacle.

"It appears to be a little larger than we expected," D'Marr muttered to no one in particular. He was beginning to appreciate the Quel and what they had accomplished. He was also beginning to appreciate what he had been sent to face by Lord D'Farany.

Granting him command of the assault forces had not been so much a reward for the information he had recovered from the captive, but rather a punishment for killing the beast before all his knowledge could have been squeezed from him.

Somewhere, he was certain, the blue man was laughing.

As the wonder of the place faded, the reality of what he saw finally sank into D'Marr's mind. *Where are they? Where are the cursed little beasts?*

"D'Roch."

"Yes, sir?"

"Tell me what you see."

The other raider frowned, not certain whether he was the focus of some game his superior was playing. He studied the city for a moment, hesitated, and then replied, "I see a vast underground city, the home of those abominations. It seems to be empty, but that shouldn't be surprising since we've broken through their defenses."

All in all, it was not a bad summation; the only one that could be given. Yet, it did not wholly describe what D'Marr saw and felt when he stared at the city of the Quel. "Nothing more?"

"Nothing."

"And how long ago would you say that it had been abandoned? Minutes? An hour?"

D'Roch squinted as he studied the sight before him again. With great trepidation, the older raider answered, "It seems . . . it seems longer, sir. It seems . . . *much* longer."

Slowly Orril D'Marr walked along the edge of the path. He tapped the head of the scepter lightly against the rock wall. After he had surveyed all he had desired to, the Aramite commander turned his bland visage back to his men. His voice was nearly a whisper. "Much longer, indeed. Look carefully at the dust, at the wear and tear that even a place buried so deep in the earth cannot escape. Think in terms of years. Try, perhaps, even *centuries*.''

There was confusion among the ranks. Word began to filter back. D'Roch and the other officers looked at one another, then at D'Marr.

He laughed then. It was not a pleasant sound, even to his ears, but he could not resist. When D'Marr realized that the others did not understand, he pointed at the city. "You unmitigated oafs! Look at our enemy! There he is! A city of the dead where maybe a handful of survivors still play with the power of their race! We are an army fighting the skeleton of a race!"

They still did not understand, he saw. D'Marr shook his head. He suspected now that there were probably no more than a dozen or so of the Quel, maybe even less. It would explain why only four had attacked them in the cramped quarters of the tunnel when a dozen, a hundred, could possibly have even eradicated them. He thought he understood why they had not collapsed the tunnel; they did not have the strength.

It was possible his suppositions were off the mark, but he was certain he was close. There was only one way to find out. The wolf raider glanced at each of the branch tunnels breaking off from the path circling the city. Most of them were exceedingly ordinary, but one to the right was wider and higher and D'Marr almost thought he saw some light source within.

"Re-form line. Single file," he called back. Then, without waiting to see if they had obeyed his command, D'Marr started toward the other branch. "Follow me."

There *was* a light source at the other end of the tunnel. The passage itself was not a long one, not after the first one, and it was wide enough to let four men pass side by side without being cramped. He had the officers redivide the ranks to accommodate, then pressed on. The glow teased him, taunted him. He was near to the truth, of that he was certain.

As if to add credence to his belief, the Quel renewed their attack.

The ceiling collapsed in the center of the tunnel, crushing several men and battering a number of others. From the hole dropped three of the armored leviathans, long, wicked battle-axes in their paws. Even as their feet touched ground, the Quel were swinging their weapons, taking full advantage of the wider and higher dimensions of this passage.

D'Marr cursed as the nearest ranks were decimated by the horrendous onslaught of the trio. With their tremendous reach and long weapons, the Quel had an advantage that not even the spears could overcome.

There are only three, he scolded himself. *Only three.*

Three they might be, but they were worth three times their number even without the advantages of their weapons. Two of the creatures were pushing back the men advancing into the tunnel while the third dealt with those, like D'Marr, who had been in front of the attempted çave-in.

Still, Orril D'Marr had planned for even worse than this. It was annoying that the creatures had already wreaked such havoc, but it had not been entirely unexpected. Having hunted one Quel, he had devised ways of dealing with them . . . if his men were still capable of following commands.

"D'Roch!" He searched for the other officer and found his battered corpse half buried under the rock from the collapse. D'Roch had probably not even seen his end coming. The loss was more of an annoyance than anything else; it meant that he would have to do the work himself.

Scepter in hand, he moved closer to the battle and shouted, "Keep the lines steady! Get the nets up front!"

A quick glance at the lancers showed that they had already spread out as best they could along the length of the tunnel. His own side was in a much worse position. He had only a few lancers and one of those died, his breastplate and chest sliced open like a piece of fruit, even as D'Marr looked on. His side also had none of the nets, for the men carrying those had perished with D'Roch in the tunnel collapse. There were, however, men with torches. Most of them were using the flames much the way D'Marr planned to, but with far less results than he hoped to have. The frustrated officer grabbed one of the men in the back and pulled him close.

"You'll die wasting your time and mine like that, you lack-head! There's a better way! Give me that!" He hooked the rod back onto his belt and stripped the blazing torch from the soldier's hand. With his other hand, he reached into one of the small pouches that most raiders wore on their belts. From it, D'Marr removed a tiny leather bag with a single, thin string attached to the top. It was something he had been toying with just prior to Lord D'Farany's decision to take the three ships and flee to the western edge of the Dragonrealm. He had experimented with three just like it only recently . . . and they had performed with perfection, enabling him to scuttle the vast raider ships virtually on his own.

As he adjusted the string, he calmly told the soldier, "Tell them to retreat three steps. Quickly if you please."

D'Marr gave the man the count of five to warn his fellows, then lit the string. It sizzled and began burning down, the flame edging closer and closer to the bag and its contents. When he was satisfied that the string had burned low enough, the Aramite let the small pouch fly.

His aim, of course, was flawless. The bag struck the Quel in the chest, then fell to the ground. D'Marr was pleased to note that the beast's reaction was what he would have expected from a human. The armored creature paused to glance down at the insignificant object, likely both puzzled and amused by the harmless assault.

The bag promptly *exploded*.

It was a much smaller amount than he had used on each of the ships, but it was still enough to tear the Quel to pieces. D'Marr brought his cloak up to avoid the majority of bits that he and his men were showered with. He smiled as he saw that he had been correct; the blast had not been strong enough to further weaken the ceiling. It would have been a bit embarrassing.

To his surprise, however, there was a second benefit to his attack of genius. The remaining Quel were on their knees, their weapons forgotten and their heads almost buried in the tunnel floor. They were hooting madly and rocking back and forth, clawing at the ground.

D'Marr was not one too slow to act when good fortune came his way. "Get the nets in fast while they're stunned. Do hurry."

The agonized creatures were still trouble despite their present state and for a short time he was tempted to take the scepter to each one in order to hurry things. Finally, when it became apparent that the injured Quel would indeed soon be nicely bound and out of the way, the wolf raider turned his attention to the haunting glow mere yards from him. Without hesitation, D'Marr started toward it, his sub-officers quickly following after, albeit with much more trepidation.

We've stepped into the heart of a diamond, was his first thought as he froze at the entrance to the chamber. Nothing else he had seen in the glittering realm of Legar, or anywhere else, for that matter, could have prepared him for this. *Is there no end to your surprises, Dragonrealm? First, a glittering land, then a city beneath the surface, and now . . . this.*

The walls were covered almost entirely in crystal, save where three other tunnels led off to other parts of the Quel domain. It was obvious that nature had not created this marvel. There were too many patterns, too many intricate designs, for it to be pure chance. The gemstones also came in a variety of colors that could never have formed together. Staring at it, D'Marr was reminded of the empty city and its light source. The crystals there had been arranged so that the subterranean dwellers could bring the sun to their world. Who was to say that this was not similar?

All this passed through the Aramite's mind in the space of a breath. It was during the second that he noticed the Quel.

The hulking creature leaned across a platform of sorts upon which had been placed a large gem that was in turn surrounded by an array of smaller crystals. The Quel, a male, D'Marr judged, was waving his clawed hands above the arrangement in what was most definitely a desperate manner. Inhuman eyes glared back at the intruders, specifically the young officer. The creature was saying something, his hooting rising and falling with a rhythm that made it impossible not to listen. D'Marr was struck by the nagging thought that the Quel was working to keep their attention.

"I'm afraid that won't work," he quietly informed the armored underdweller. He knew that the Quel understood him by the narrowing of his black orbs. "Your power has been smothered by my Lord D'Farany's might." The raider commander inclined his head toward the officers to his left side. "Take him. Kill him if need be."

As the wolf raiders rushed toward him, the Quel made one last pass over the crystal.

It glimmered. Only for a second, but it glimmered. The spell cast by Lord D'Farany still held, but D'Marr knew it must be weakening badly for something to happen this soon. It was fortunate, he thought, that they had not met any more resistance than they had. The power the beasts controlled was even greater than he had assumed.

The Quel hooted in satisfaction, then stepped away as he was surrounded. Unlike his fellows, he made no move to resist. At another time, Orril D'Marr would have been amused by the absurd sight of the creature calmly holding out his huge arms to be bound, but the Quel's note of triumph disturbed his sensibilities. He studied the chamber carefully, seeking what clue he could not say.

Then it came to him that there were only two other tunnel entrances besides his own. When he had scanned the chamber earlier, D'Marr had been certain that there had been *three*. He turned to the nearest man and asked, "How many ways out of here were there when you came in?"

Looking puzzled and nervous, the soldier glanced around and answered, "I see two, my lord. Besides the one we entered by."

"That's not what I asked." It was futile to explain, the young raider decided. Instead, he stalked over to the area where he recalled the missing entrance being and placed a hand against the wall. It was very solid. D'Marr ran his hand along the crystal, searching for anything that seemed not quite right. As far as he could discover, however, it was very, very real.

Taking the rod, he tapped lightly on the wall. A quiet but solid thud argued against there being a thin, false partition before him. This was a barrier of rock and crystal and a very thick one at that.

He was tempted to test its strength against one of his exploding bags, but knew that the Pack Leader would never forgive him if the chamber was damaged.

"You have my congratulations, Orril."

His round visage carefully banal, D'Marr turned and saluted his master. He nearly grimaced when he saw that the blue man was with the Pack Leader. "I thank you, Lord D'Farany."

The Aramite leader walked slowly into the room, his unnerving features fairly aglow with delight. "Yesss, this is it! This is what I felt!" He put a hand on the platform that the Quel had vacated. "A bit of study . . . and then we shall put it to use."

D'Marr glanced at the Quel as Lord D'Farany finished speaking. If it was possible for one of the monsters to look almost smug, then this creature was exactly that. *You have a secret, my little beast, and it's yours for now. Enjoy that time. When the opportunity arises, I'll take that secret of yours and everything else your mind holds.*

He would be more careful than with the last one. This time, D'Marr would not let death rescue his prisoner. This time, he would squeeze every bit of knowledge from the beast no matter how long it took and how much pain it meant.

As his eyes returned to the glittering wall, he met his own gaze. The multifaceted crystals made the face behind the gaze a twisted, distorted thing, a creature almost as inhuman in appearance as the Quel . . . and far, far darker within.

------ **IV** ------

Two days passed while Cabe sought news that might confirm his fears. There was, in that period, no reoccurrence of the vision and as evening of the second day came and aged, he began to have small doubts. Not about what both he and Aurim had seen, but how he had interpreted it.

That very night, those doubts were erased as he slept.

He was among them again. One of them. Clad in the green dragon-scale armor, they mounted their flying drakes and took to the air. The wind was hot against his face. There was something horribly wrong with the heavens, for there was no blue, but rather a sickly green vying with a bloody red. Clouds swirled like whirlpools and wild, free magic was rampant.

The lead rider—his father—turned to him and, in a voice that demanded obedience, called, "Don't dawdle back there! We've far to go!"

Suddenly his father's face stretched beyond belief. His body hunched over and his arms and legs became twisted. Wings burst forth from his backside . . .

A dragon loomed over him. He tried to turn his drake, but now he lay sprawled on a rocky plain, the animal nowhere to be found. The dragon, huge and terrible, lowered his head and hissed, "You cannot essscape what isss inevitable . . . you cannot escape . . ."

Then he, Cabe, found himself in the Legar Peninsula. He had barely time to register it when a shadow covered the land. The warlock raised his head and saw a vast sailing ship, black as pitch, slowly sinking toward him from the very sky. He tried to move, but pain suddenly jolted him. His head was on fire. It felt as if he were being torn apart.

Cabe glanced down at his hands, which tingled, and saw with horror that they were stretching, becoming more beastlike than human. Frantic, the spellcaster tried to reverse the effect, but it was as if his magic were no more. He could not even perceive the lines of force from which he drew his power.

The looming shape of the black vessel grew larger and larger. The ground beneath his feet trembled. Cabe was certain that he saw movement around him, as if large creatures lurked just below the surface.

The ship was almost upon him now. Cabe raised his hands in hopeless defense, then could not help stare at them despite the oncoming leviathan.

His hands were reptilian, the clawed paws of a dragon, but that was not what held his gaze so. It was the skin, a dragon hide that fairly glittered even in the shadow of the ebony ship.

He had become the Crystal Dragon.

Cabe woke sitting bolt upright, raw magical energy dancing and crackling at his fingertips. He shivered uncontrollably, not so much because of fear, but because the vision had looked and *felt* so very real.

Slim arms took hold of him in the dark and a concerned, caring voice whispered, "It's all right, Cabe. Nothing was real. Nothing in the dream. You are in the Manor. You're home."

The quivering slowed, then finally ceased. He looked down at his upturned fingers and watched with vague satisfaction and relief as the glow about them dwindled to nothing.

"Cabe?"

"Gwen?" Blinking, the warlock turned toward the voice. His eyes adjusted to the dark, allowing him to make out the dim image of his wife. He conjured a small light instead of using his abilities to adjust his eyesight further. Changing any part of one's form, even temporarily, was a task that required precise concentration for all but a few human mages. It was one area where the drakes would always be superior in the arts of sorcery. He was surprised that he was even able to create the light, considering how turbulent his mind presently was.

She pulled him close and kissed him, more from relief than anything else. They held each other tight for several moments, then Cabe finally broke the embrace. He looked into her eyes. "I had another vision."

"I suspected as much. It's not a memory of the Manor, is it?"

"Hardly." Wiping his hand across his face, he related to her the various images and events he had suffered through. Describing them, however, brought them back to life for him and by tale's end he was shaking again, albeit not near as much as the first time.

Gwen took his hands and held them until long after the shaking had ended. "Something has to be done."

"We both know what, Gwen."

The enchantress squeezed hard. The strength in her hands was amazing. "Don't even think of it, my love."

"What other way is there? This is too demanding. I am either wanted by someone or something or I'm suffering some sort of premonition . . . and it all points to the Legar Peninsula in the end. That means the Crystal Dragon."

She did not want to believe that, he saw. In truth, he really did not want to believe it, either. Of all the Dragon Kings, the Crystal Dragon was the most enigmatic, the most ominous. Even the late Ice Dragon or Storm, the drake lord who ruled Wenslis, the marshy, rain-drenched land far to the northeast, were definable dangers. No one knew much about the Crystal Dragon, not even his fellow monarchs. He had stepped in during the last rage of his northern counterpart, Ice, and, with what seemed a simple gesture, had helped turn inevitable defeat into salvaged victory. In the years since then, he had been silent, ignoring the vast changes in the Dragonrealm that steered it closer and closer to being a human world.

"The lord of Legar tolerates intruders in his domain, Cabe, but not when their interest lies in him. His predecessors were all the same, it's said. Secretive and hermitic, yet more than willing to raise their power against those few who dared to disturb them.

The Crystal Dragon, whether this one or any of his ancestors, has always been a creature to avoid at all costs. Look what arrogance cost the Ice Dragon.''

"I've been to the peninsula before, Gwen, and not always by choice.''

"But you never sought *him* out! That's the difference, Cabe! This time, you may end up confronting him! I don't like the thought of that happening!''

The warlock sighed. "I don't like it, either, but what else can I do?''

Gwen paused, then suggested, "Why not go to the Dagora Forest? Perhaps he can help.''

"The Green Dragon?''

Her voice took on an urgent tone. "You know he will do for you what he can. At least hear his advice.''

He considered her words. Green's borders, now extending into the realm once called the Barren Lands, were close to those of the Crystal Dragon. The Barren Lands had once been ruled by their counterpart, Brown, but after his death, which a young Cabe had unwittingly caused, the Master of the Dagora Forest had claimed them for his own. The Crystal Dragon, in typical fashion, had remained silent on the matter.

If anyone might be aware of something amiss in the peninsula, it would be the Dragon King Green.

"All right, I'll go to him. It's possible that he might be able to explain what's happening to me." Cabe stiffened. "Or to *Aurim!*''

"Aurim!'' Gwen released his hands, recalling what her husband had told her about their son's sharing of the vision. The warlock was suddenly alone in bed. It took him a moment to realize what she had done. By that time, the enchantress had already returned.

"He's sleeping,'' she said, relief paramount in her voice. "Sleeping quietly. This time he must not have shared it with you.''

Cabe rubbed his chin. "Why earlier and not now? It doesn't make sense.'' He frowned. "No, it does. This is no premonition. Someone does want me . . . me alone. It *must* be the Crystal Dragon!''

Gwen took his hands again. "Even if it is, talk to Lord Green first. *Please.*"

"Don't worry; I will." He took her in his arms and the two of them lay down again. "I promise you that."

It was near dawn when Cabe was at last able to relax enough to sleep.

Although he had known the Green Dragon since his earliest days as a spellcaster, it made his audience with the monarch of the great forest land of Dagora no less imposing. He was, after all, facing one of the Dragon Kings, the legendary rulers of the continent. Until his own involvement with them, Cabe would have never believed that the drake lords were in the twilight of their reign. There were few things in the Dragonrealm he found as overwhelming as the draconian monarchs even after having watched their empire crumble to a few deeply divided kingdoms suspicious of each other and of the humans who were taking their place.

Green was different, though. He had accepted the decline of power as a natural course for his race, yet the drake had no intention of merely letting his people fade away. He wanted to see both races working together, for in that was his own future.

Cabe liked to consider the reptilian monarch his friend as well as his ally and he hoped that the Dragon King felt the same way.

"To what do I owe this visitation, Cabe Bedlam? It is not yet the time for a report on the progress of the emperor's hatchlings."

"They fare well enough, though," Cabe informed him. "The same problems still exist with Kyl."

"Of course. He is like his progenitor."

The lord of the Dagora Forest sat in an immense, human-style throne carved from rock and situated atop a marble dais in the back of the vast underground cavern complex that was the lair of his clans. Like so many of the drake race, he had a fondness for the humanoid shape, eschewing his original dragon form for it for months at a time. In Cabe's opinion, the dragon people were becoming more and more human with each generation.

There were those, however, who would argue that and would point out the Green Dragon as their example. Humanoid though he was, the Dragon King was most definitely not human. To the eye, the seated monarch resembled a tall, massive knight clad in dragon-scale armor of the finest detail. He would have been more than seven feet in height had he been standing. In truth, the drake lord resembled more what an elfin lord would have looked like were those folk inclined to such warriorlike garb and not the lighter woodland outfits they wore. The armor was a vibrant shade of green, a forest green that spoke of the strength and majesty of the vast wooded region. It covered the Dragon King from his feet to his neck, only giving way above, where the helm, with its intricate dragon's head crest, nearly covered all else.

It was impossible not to stare at the dragon head, for anyone who stood before one of the drake lords would certainly feel that the head was staring back. The crests of the wolf raiders were crude in comparison. With their long snouts, toothy maws curled back in what was almost a smile, and narrow, seeking eyes, the dragon heads looked almost alive . . . and very hungry. It was not so surprising. The crest was more than simple decoration; it was the true visage of the Dragon King. The face within the helm was a mere parody of humanity. The face *above* the helm was the reality. In fact, the entire image the drake presented was false. What seemed like armor was actually his very skin. The scale armor was dragonscale still attached to the original. His helm could not have been removed, for it *was* his head as much as what was within pretended to be. In attempting to make use of the human form, which they had found so practical for so many things, this had been as close as the male drakes could come. Their progress was slower than that of the female drakes, although no one could say why. Yet, if Kyl and Grath were any indication, the next generation of males had finally crossed the barrier . . . in terms of appearance. Like the Dragon King before him, they still had much to learn about humanity itself.

For that matter, so did many humans.

Cabe forced himself not to focus on the crest, which always tended to draw his eyes first. "I come on a matter of great urgency, my Lord Green, and I thank you for this swift audience. I realize I was very abrupt when I requested it."

The Dragon King lifted his head, and if there had been anyone in the chamber still thinking that the figure before Cabe could be human, now would have crushed any such foolish notion. From within the false helm, two bloodred eyes burned into those of the warlock. Although the helm obscured much, there were glimpses of a flat and scaly visage. There was no nose, only two slits. When the drake lord spoke, his lipless mouth revealed the sharp teeth of a predator. A parody it might be, but the humanoid visage that the Dragon King wore was in its own way almost as terrible because of that.

A narrow, forked tongue darted out on occasion when the Dragon King spoke, yet except for some slight sibilance every now and then, he spoke more clearly and precisely than many humans. "Sssso formal, friend warlock! It truly must be an urgent matter then, if you would speak to me so."

The chamber was empty of all save them, which had been as Cabe had requested. Torches lit the great chamber. Its rock walls were too smooth, which long ago had led Cabe to the conjecture that one of the Dragon King's ancestors had dug it all out. There were plants of all shapes and sizes in the cavern and skillfully woven tapestries, some incredibly ancient, decorated most of the walls. Some Dragon King long ago had worked hard to make his lair a thing of beauty and had succeeded, but the dark-haired mage was by no means calmed by the regal setting. It was never possible to forget that this was the nest of a dragon and had been so for countless generations.

Cabe had debated on a number of ways to begin, but none of them had seemed satisfactory. Being blunt still appeared to be the best route. "My lord, I seek information concerning events in the realm of your brother, the Crystal Dragon."

"Do you?" The Dragon King could not entirely mask his surprise. "And why do you desssire this?"

The warlock stepped closer, stopping only when he stood at the bottom of the dais. He kept his face devoid of all emotion. "I believe something is happening there. I believe it may involve the wolf raiders."

"Aaah?" Now he truly had the drake lord's attention. If there was a threat other than human magic that the Dragon Kings respected, it was the ever-hungry wolf packs of the Aramites. The black ships had been a scourge that even the most cunning of the Dragon Kings had been unable to put an end to. The revolt that had forced the Aramites to abandon their plundering had been a blessing. "Tell me more, friend Cabe."

Cabe told him of the visions, leaving out nothing. The Dragon King was silent throughout. The warlock knew that his host was already considering possible meanings to the visions and what those meanings might demand of him. By the time Cabe was finished, the drake lord had already formulated some thoughts of his own on the subject.

"I have heard rumors, but this . . . It should not surprissse me that the wolf raiders have come to the Dragonrealm. They are your kind at their most tenacious. If they have chosen the lands of my brother Crystal, then I cannot possibly predict what might occur. The lord of Legar is an enigma even to his brethren." The Dragon Kings all called one another brother, but the term referred to their supposedly equal status, not any blood relation. As far as the mage knew, none of the surviving kings were truly brothers.

"Have you no contact with him . . . in any way?"

"He is not one for conversation, human. Ever has his line kept to itself. He does not seek our company, and in truth, we have ever avoided his."

Cabe considered this. "You have *no* contact with him?"

The drake lord bared his teeth, but not because of any anger toward the mage. Rather, he appeared frustrated at himself. "I have no contact, friend warlock. No spies. Through no method have I ever succeeded in divining his purposes . . . if he has any. Do not think that I have not tried. Do not think that my brothers have not tried, too."

"What about the rest of Legar?"

A reptilian smile briefly crossed the shadowed countenance. The Green Dragon straightened, then rose from his throne. Cabe did not step back, as many would have done, but merely crooked his neck and looked up. He knew the Green Dragon well enough to know that the monarch respected more those who stood up to him. "Of the rest of Legar, there is generally nothing of interest, friend Cabe. The land glitters, but it is devoid of a soul. One might as well observe the snow-smothered Northern Wastes, for there is just as likely something happening there as there is in the hot, dry domain my brother rules." The smile died. The Dragon King stepped down from the dais so that he was more or less at eye level with his guest. "Yet, I trust your word and your judgment when you say that now that may have changed.

You make me curious for the first time." He paused, then hissed. "If you will join me on a short walk, perhaps there is a way to answer your questions . . . and your fears."

"Where are we going?"

"I have been awaiting the opportunity to test a creation of mine. I see no reason why this should not be the perfect time. Come. It would be better to show it to you before I explain."

The drake lord led him into one of the branching tunnels and through the mazelike passages that were common among the lairs of his kind. Some of the passages were huge, perfect for a full-grown dragon, but others, newer, were designed strictly for creatures the size of a man or a drake in human form. Cabe knew that many Dragon Kings, especially the line that had ruled Dagora, often had human servants, but they did not generally dig their tunnels to accommodate those servants. The smaller pathways had come into existence about the time that the drakes had begun to favor the humanoid forms.

They came at last to a pair of plain bronze doors, something rare in the depths of a dragon lair. The bronze doors indicated how valuable the contents of the chamber behind them were to the woodland monarch. Four guards, all *human*, interestingly enough, were another good sign that any who trespassed here forfeited everything.

At a gesture from the drake lord, the guards stepped aside and the doors swung open. The reptilian ruler waved a taloned hand at the warlock, indicating he should enter first.

Cabe never knew what to expect when he was brought to the Green Dragon's inner sanctum. Each time, something was different. The lords of Dagora had always been scholars, their prime interests tending to run either to the vast history of the continent or the workings of magic as various races used it. There was no one save perhaps the Crystal Dragon who knew as much.

To a mage, the chamber was a collection worthy of envy. Seeker medallions hung next to tapestries by a race whose face and form not even the Dragon King knew. The tapestries were older than anything else and the images always revolved around landscapes that did not exist, at least now, anywhere in the realm. There were bottles filled with specimens of both animal and vegetable origin and row upon row of great tomes, many of which the drake lord had long ago admitted he had yet to decipher.

The Dragon King turned to the guards. "You may close the doors. No one is to enter, no matter what you might hear. That includes everyone."

"Yes, my lord," the men chorused. Two of them took hold of the handles and pulled the bronze doors shut. The Green Dragon's human servants were ever swift and thorough in their obedience, but unlike those who served many of the other drake lords, these obeyed out of pure loyalty. The Masters of the Dagora Forest had almost always cared for their humans as much as they did their own kind.

When they were alone, the reptilian knight turned back to his guest. "Have no concern, Massster Cabe. The warning was more for the sake of our privacy than to hint of any danger to our beings."

"I hoped as much." Despite the words of his host, however, Cabe was not completely at ease. Any venture that involved delving into the realm of the Crystal Dragon had to have at least a tiny element of danger inherent in it.

The Green Dragon stalked toward a small alcove in which a pedestal no higher than the warlock's waist stood. Carved into the flat top of the marble artifact was an array of symbols that looked vaguely familiar to him. The memory was so distant and hazy, however, that he wondered if perhaps it was not one of his own but rather something left over from when he had shared the memories of Nathan.

"This is what I wished to show you. It isss far superior to anything that my brothers have . . . save perhaps the one we seek to learn more of. I have only recently completed its creation; one would almost think that your request had been foreseen by the Dragonrealm itself."

The warlock did not like to think about that. Too often, it seemed that the Dragonrealm somehow controlled his life and the lives of those he cared for. "What does it do? How does it work?"

"An explanation now would pale against the actuality. It is best if you simply observe."

Cabe watched as the Dragon King first passed his hand over the symbols and then touched three of them. Again, a memory of the far past teased Cabe, but he forced it down. All that he knew was that the patterns carved into the pedestal were of a language of sorts, but not the common tongue spoken by humans and drakes. However, there had been many races that had preceded the Dragon Kings and at least some of them had spoken and written in other tongues. In the Dragonrealm, there were even those kingdoms where the written form of Common was undecipherable by any save those who had grown up learning it. When time permitted, he would ask the Dragon King about the markings, but now there were more important tasks at hand.

As he completed a second arrangement of symbols, the drake lord explained some of what he was doing. "The patterns are directly tied to specific forces in the Dragonrealm, almost the way a sorcerer's mind is when he reaches out to use power, but more precisely. There isss less chance for random failure due to a lack of concentration and a greater ability to focus on specific regions or even individualsss." The drake's sibilance grew as he became excited about the subject. "It alssso drains the mage usssing it less than mosssst mechanisms becaussse it does not require the great amount of willpower that cryssstals often do."

The Green Dragon performed one more pass over the pedestal, then stepped back.

"What happens now?"

"Wait . . . and watch."

At first, it was only a small black spot. It hovered over the center of the artifact, slowly growing. When it was the size of his hand, its form shifted, making it look more like a dark cloud about to unleash a tempest. He almost expected to see lightning and torrential rains. Slowly, though, the cloud thinned until it was almost transparent. As it thinned it continued to grow. Only when the dark mass was the size of Cabe's chest did it stop. By this point, he could see the wall beyond through it, but other than that, there was nothing, not even the most vague of images. After several anxious breaths, he finally could wait no longer. "Is there something wrong?"

"No," was all the drake replied.

Even as the Dragon King spoke, the thin cloud convulsed. Cabe almost took a step back, but when he saw that the Dragon King was nodding his head, he realized that this was part of the spell. The cloud continued to convulse, but now the changes in its form became specific things. Leaning forward, Cabe held his breath as he realized what he was seeing. The things became true shapes and the shapes became distinct features. Tiny hills sprouted and ravines deepened. The upper half of the vision turned blue as the heavens divided from the earth. The now nearly formed landscape suddenly glistened as light from an unseen source blanketed it.

A miniature world had blossomed into being. No, not a world, Cabe corrected himself, but simply a portion of one. A very familiar one.

It was the rocky, glittering hills of Legar. They floated before the two, not as some flat image, but as a very real place. It was as if someone had stolen a part of the land, shrunken it down, and brought it before them. The warlock wanted to reach forward and see if he could touch it, but he knew that the sight before him was illusion, nothing more.

"What do you think, Master Bedlam?"

"It's . . . nothing's good enough, my lord. The detail is unbelievable!"

"We can focus on even smaller areas. Like so."

The image changed. This time, it had magnified so much that Cabe could now make out individual leaves on one of the few hardy bushes that dotted the viewed region. A small creature no bigger than his hand scuttled from under a rock to the bush.

"That wasss the easy part," his host commented. The Green Dragon's entire body spoke of sudden uncertainty. "What we see is on the very borders of the peninsula. Now, we mussst delve deeper into Legar . . . and that will most certainly invite the interest of my brother!"

"You don't intend to try to contact him?"

"It may be that we can learn what we need to know without resorting to that."

The dark-haired spellcaster glanced surreptitiously at his companion. *He's afraid of the Crystal Dragon!* Immediately after thinking that, Cabe felt ashamed. Not afraid. More wary than afraid. The Green Dragon knew and respected the power of his counterpart to the west. Cabe, having witnessed that power in the past, understood some of what the Master of Dagora must be thinking. No one, not even the most vicious of the Dragon Kings, wanted to invite the wrath of the Crystal Dragon down upon them.

Yet, if the lord of Legar was so great a power in the realm, what did Cabe's visions mean? What was there that might threaten the enigmatic drake lord and the rest of the Dragonrealm as well?

How were the wolf raiders involved? By themselves could they possibly be so great a danger? He wished that he knew more about the Crystal Dragon.

He wished that *someone* did.

The Green Dragon touched the markings again. The image wavered, then shifted as the Dragon King sought to journey deeper into the domain of his counterpart. They saw nothing unusual at first, simply the same crystal-encrusted hills and the occasional bit of plant life. Now and then, a bird flew overhead, likely on its way to more hospitable climes. The image of the first such avian amused Cabe, who almost expected it to go flying beyond the edge of the scene and on into the chamber where he stood.

After several minutes of this, however, the warlock grew impatient. He began to wonder whether the Green Dragon might be just a little hesitant about moving toward the western shores of the peninsula. Cabe very much respected the monarch of Legar, probably at least as much as the drake lord beside him, but Green had not suffered through the visions. Cabe wanted an answer and he wanted it soon. At the present rate of progression, it would be some time before they even reached the central lands, the region where the clan caverns of the Crystal Dragon were supposed to start.

"My lord." His determination slipped a bit as the drake turned his blazing eyes to him, but Cabe persevered. "My lord, can't we leap from where we are now and view the western tip of Legar? If, as I believe, the answer lies out there, then we may discover it and be done with this within a matter of minutes."

The Dragon King vacillated, then, with great reluctance, nodded agreement. "Asss you say, it might indeed speed the matter to an end. Very well, give me but a moment, warlock, and I will sssee what I can do."

Cabe wished he could help, if only to encourage the drake to greater swiftness, but the Dragon King did not ask for his assistance and there was no way that he could offer it without the reptilian monarch taking the offer as a slight to his courage. He satisfied himself with trying to ready his own courage in the face of whatever the magical window revealed to them, especially if what it revealed was the enraged visage of the Crystal Dragon.

"Odd. Very odd."

The warlock glanced up. "What?"

"There is . . . something . . . blocking our view. See for yourself, Cabe."

He looked. Over the pedestal, the image that had earlier been conjured wavered and twisted, becoming more of a distorted shadow of its former self. Superimposed on that vision, however, was another. In that one, a much less distinct image than even the first had become, Cabe could make out the movement of several figures. Whether they were human or not was impossible to say, but Cabe stiffened when he realized that all of them were dark, possibly black.

"Sssomething is *fighting* it!" snarled the Dragon King. His unease had vanished, replaced now by annoyance that something had dared wreak havoc with his creation. He passed his taloned hands over a different arrangement of symbols. The images only became more tangled. Now it looked as if the ghostly figures were trying to walk through the hills.

"By the Dragon of the Depths!" The furious drake lord tried another arrangement, evidently hoping that some combination of forces would overcome the unknown obstacle. Both visions dwindled away, this time to be replaced by a thick, grayish cloud that sparkled as it turned slowly within itself, almost as if a legion of fireflies had gotten themselves trapped in the maelstrom. The Green Dragon stepped away, clearly taken aback by this latest result. After a moment of contemplation, though, he reached once more for the markings on the pedestal.

There was a flash. A sparkling field of light engulfed the unsuspecting drake.

As the flash died, a head filled the air above the artifact; it was the startled countenance of none other than the Crystal Dragon. There was no mistaking the other Dragon King. Only one drake had skin that gleamed like diamond.

His body quivering violently, the Green Dragon shrieked and then fell backward; the face vanished.

Cabe leapt to the side of his companion, the magical window all but forgotten in his concern. He knelt beside the drake, who still quivered, and checked his breathing. It was ragged, but strong enough that the warlock was fairly certain he would live. Taking the Dragon King's hands, Cabe saw that the drake had been burned bad in each palm. He used a spell to ease the damage and was relieved to note that it was successful. Injuries caused by high magic were sometimes impossible to repair.

As he lowered the Dragon King's hands, he became aware of the heavy silence that had befallen the chamber. It was the sort of silence, Cabe somehow felt, that preceded utter catastrophe.

From where he knelt, the warlock turned.

An ebony hand vast enough to engulf both Cabe and the Dragon King stretched forth from the pedestal.

Cabe knew that unleashing sheer power at the thing might result in devastation encompassing more than just the chamber, for the Seeker medallions on the shelves alone likely held enough potent force in them to do that. If his wild spell destroyed the talismans, that power would also be released. With all that the Master of the Dagora Forest's collection held, it went without saying that the medallions would surely not be the only magical artifacts to unleash their long-imprisoned forces.

With no time to consider a counterattack, Cabe chose instead to simply defend. Moving one hand in a swift arc, he surrounded the two of them with a transparent shield. It was basic but potent, one of the earliest spells that he had learned to use by instinct alone.

The fingers of the darksome hand struck the surface of the invisible shield and stopped. Cabe could almost sense the frustration. The guiding force behind the hand was not deterred, however. Readjusting so that its fingers completely gripped the outer limits of the barrier, the malevolent extremity *squeezed*.

Cabe Bedlam knew that the scene above him was merely the visible representation of two spells seeking to counter each other, but it was impossible not to believe that a real hand was slowly closing upon him. His own spell was buckling already, a sign that whoever or whatever fought him was not only adept at sorcery but was able to draw together forces that would have overwhelmed even Cabe, whose own ability was not slight.

Yet, in the end, the shield accomplished its task. Given a precious moment, he now struck back. There was no need to waste further seconds seeking some elaborate solution. Cabe summoned up a spell that was as much a part of him as it had once been a part of Nathan, his grandfather. A golden bow formed before him, a golden bow that had, in the past, killed a Dragon King. It was a legacy from Nathan. The few sorcerers who had been able to create and make use of it, for the binding of the necessary powers was a time-consuming and touchy matter, had been called such things as the Sunlancers, although Sun Archers would have been more appropriate. The spell took much out of those mages and they were often not able to re-create the bow for months after, but one shot was all that was ever needed. As much as it took out of the spellcaster, it took more out of the target.

A single, gleaming shaft, a streak of blinding brilliance, shot forth from the bow. The shaft flew unimpeded through the shield, since they shared both common origin and cause, and struck the menacing hand. Barely slowed, it continued through the palm and out the other end before Cabe could even blink.

As the sunlit arrow exited, the black hand released its grip and thrashed madly in the air above the warlock. Breathing heavily, Cabe strengthened his shield as best he could, but the act proved unneeded, for the hand was already fading, its magic disrupted and, hopefully, its caster painfully regretting his assault on the two. By the time Cabe drew another breath, the magical menace was no more. Had not the Green Dragon been lying unconscious and injured by his side, he almost would not have believed that the attack had ever happened, for nothing else in the room had been touched by it, not even the pedestal.

Secure, the warlock removed the defensive barrier and hurried to the bronze doors. He took hold of one and flung it open. The anxious but ready gazes of more than two dozen guards, both human and drake, met his own. Cabe pointed behind himself. "Get in here, quick! Your master may need aid! I can't promise that my spell of healing dealt with all the injuries he suffered!"

There was much visible apprehension. The Dragon King had never allowed more than a handful of his subjects, be they drake or men, into his sanctum. Fortunately, the health of their master outweighed their fear of disobedience. A half-dozen or so sentries darted around Cabe and seized the unconscious Dragon King by the arms and legs. With great care but also great speed, they carried their master out of the chamber. Cabe assured himself that all was now calm in the room, then followed.

He turned at the doorway and quickly commanded, "No one is to enter again without your lord's permission. There may yet be some danger in there. Is that understood?"

The remaining guards nodded. The spellcaster wasted no more time on them. He knew that the Green Dragon would receive the best of aid from his people and that there was no real need for him to attend, but guilt forced him on after the injured monarch and his attendants. It was his fault that the Dragon King had become involved in this, his fault that the drake had pushed further than had been safe.

Now more than ever, Cabe knew he had to journey to the inhospitable land of Legar. The images and the attack had only fueled his curiosity and resolve. It was not likely, based on what he had seen, that the Crystal Dragon had been at the heart of the attack. Moreover, that Dragon King had looked truly stunned by the intrusion into his kingdom. No, the attack had come from elsewhere, and although it was hardly evidence enough, the black hand that had nearly taken the two of them seemed to speak to Cabe of the wolf raiders. Worse, it spoke of wolf raiders with power, keepers such as the Gryphon had once spoken of. Cabe had thought that the Aramite sorcerer caste was no more; at least, the lionbird had hinted as much.

Whatever it was that threatened from the domain of the Crystal Dragon, he would have to face it, but he would have to face it alone. The Green Dragon was helpless. Gwen, the warlock knew, would desire to join him once she saw that he could not be turned from this, but they had long ago made a rule, one that even *she* would be forced to abide by, wherein one parent would remain with the children during such times. There had to be someone to watch over them. They could not risk both of them and possibly leave Aurim and Valea, not to mention the drakes under their care, without a ready protector. Aurim was too wild to leave in control yet and Kyl . . . Kyl was not ready, either.

There was no choice. Cabe would have to journey to the Legar Peninsula on his own.

Unless . . . he hesitated in the passageway, the servants and their burden momentarily pushed from his immediate concerns.

There *was* one other he could turn to for help, *if* he could only find him. The trouble there was that Cabe might search the entire Dragonrealm without success, for the one he sought was not bound by this world nor any other. The warlock could not waste the time on such a prolonged search; whatever events were unfurling in the domain of the Crystal Dragon might at any moment come to a head. At most, Cabe could spare a day, maybe two.

Still, it would be worth it if he could find Darkhorse.

"D'Rance! There you are. Rummaging through garbage again?"

The blue man, his cloak wrapped around his angular form almost like a shroud, turned to face his shorter counterpart. Unlike the others, his cloak also had a hood, which was presently pulled so far forward that it almost reached his eyes. His helm and gloves lay to the side on a makeshift table he was using for his work. One hand emerged from the obscuring cape and deposited a small, crystalline statuette onto the same table. The chamber that he had chosen for his work—and his privacy—had evidently once been the equivalent of a Quel library, but only a few loose fragments of scrollwork and crystal still remained. D'Rance was of the opinion that the rest had been spirited away by diggers that still remained at large, but he had so far not seen any reason to share his theory with his companions. "I have been here some time, Orril D'Marr, yes, and what I do is not rummaging. My lord has instructed me to inspect all questionable items of the diggers. There may be artifacts of power, talismans, yes, among what you so blindly label 'garbage.' "

The young officer responded with an indifferent shrug. The blue man silently cursed the Quel for being unable to rid his life of the insolent little martinet. He had a knack of stepping in at the wrong times, almost as if he had a sixth sense. Steeling himself, D'Rance grated, "I must assume, D'Marr, that you have some reason for disturbing me, yes? Or is it that you have come to love my company?"

"Something happened . . . some surge from the beastmen's thing, that magical device. *Our* Lord D'Farany requests your presence so that you might aid him in unraveling the mystery. He's been requesting your presence for several minutes now and he doesn't like being kept waiting. You and I both know that."

The blue man turned away from D'Marr and, using the same hand as before, picked up another of the artifacts the blindly obedient soldiers under his command had gathered for him. He pretended to study it, but in reality he had been forced to turn because at that moment it had come close to being impossible to hide the truth of what he was actually doing. The strain would have shown on his face. Unlike D'Marr, Kanaan D'Rance was a creature of emotions, more so than even many of his own kind. *But just this once and only in this matter, I would wish to wear a mask with the skills that you do, little man, yes!*

"I will be but a moment. You need not wait, yes."

"Lord D'Farany's waiting. I think he has something."

Forcing his hand not to shake, the blue man put down the second figurine. He looked over his shoulder. "As I said, I will be but a moment."

A thin smile played fleetingly across D'Marr's countenance. D'Rance knew that it was because one took a deadly chance when one did not leap to respond to a summons from the Pack Leader. It was something that D'Rance had never adjusted to and he knew that only his usefulness to his master had kept him from being punished for his continuous transgressions. D'Marr, he knew, was hoping that this latest might be the final straw. The blue man did not care. He needed a few more minutes before he could dare go before Lord D'Farany. Summons or not, he risked more by responding now rather than waiting until he was better able to compose himself. His secrets had to remain *his* secrets.

He noted how one of Orril D'Marr's hands touched the pommel of the Aramite's favorite toy, the magical rod he liked to use too often on others. The scepter would be the death of him if D'Rance did not kill him first.

"I'll inform our lord of your response."

"Do that, yes."

With obvious anticipation, a silent D'Marr departed. The blue man watched him disappear from sight, then exhaled sharply. He thought of how his counterpart would relate his response to the Pack Leader. There would be much embellishment. D'Rance would have to speak with a silver tongue, but he had always been good at that. It had gotten him across the vast sea to the land of his goals and it would keep him in the good graces of the Pack Leader until the blue man was ready to abandon the raiders to whatever fate was in store for them. *You have shown me much, yes, my Lord Ivon D'Farany, and I thank you, although you could not know just how much you truly taught me, no . . .*

Allowing the cloak to fall away, he stared at the hand he had hidden from D'Marr.

Visibly, there was no sign of a wound, not even the smallest mark. Yet the pain still coursed through him as if someone had thrust a knife into his palm. The hand was twisted into a shape more the parody of a bird's claw than a human extremity. Even the slightest movement caused the pain to increase a hundredfold, but he could wait no longer. He had to straighten it now.

Gritting his teeth, the blue man strained to bend his fingers back. Sweat poured down his forehead as he fought the pain. Slowly, the hand resumed a somewhat more normal appearance, although even achieving that resulted in yet more excruciating torture. In the end, D'Rance could not help moan under his breath. He would somehow find the one who had done this and make him regret it all.

It had been foolish, he knew, to test himself so soon, but the opportunity had presented itself like a gift and the blue man, unable to resist, had leapt in. His reward had been the agony.

But it goes better, he consoled himself. *I grow more skilled, yes . . .*

Forcing himself to use his injured hand, the better to begin living with the pain, D'Rance removed his hood. He began to pick up the helm, then thought better of it. Glancing around to make certain that he would not be interrupted, he pulled from one of the pouches on his belt a small looking glass. Raising it to eye level, the northerner held it so that he could see the left side of his head.

A tiny streak of silver in his hair, a streak that had only weeks ago not existed at all, greeted his gaze.

The blue man smiled. He was making definite progress, yes.

V

"If you think that I'll let you make this journey alone, Cabe, then you've not known the true me even after all these years!"

Had he been anyone else, the warlock would have been more than a little fearful at the sight his wife now presented. She was, for the moment, the woodland goddess, the Lady of the Amber, that many still thought her. Power radiated from her. Her brilliant scarlet tresses fluttered with a life of their own and she seemed to stand almost twice as tall as Cabe. Her emerald eyes sparkled bright, twin green flames that, at other times, had driven him to pleasant distraction. The expression on her face he had only seen once or twice in the past and both those times had been when her children had been threatened.

It hurt him to see her like this, for he knew that it was only her love and fear for him that had raised such a fury.

"You know what we agreed, Gwen. It's not for us; it's for the children. It isn't fair to risk both of us. Someone has to be there for them . . . just in case. You were the one who originally thought that up, remember."

"I know." She looked bitter. "But it would be easier if it was me who had to take the risk. Then I'd know that you were safe and watching the children. Whatever I faced, I would be able to face it better knowing that."

"And I wouldn't? Gwen, you know that you're my partner as well as my mate, but this time it has to be me and me alone. The visions came to me—"

"And Aurim."

He conceded her point. "But I think it might be because he and I are so much alike in many ways. The second time, only I saw the images. Besides, I can't take *him* with me. He's not ready . . . unless his control has greatly benefited from the other day."

Gwen managed a smile. "This morning I found one of the stick men wandering through the garden. Apparently, when Aurim tried to reverse his spell, he couldn't keep track of them

61

all and this one escaped. No, even if I was willing to risk our son—which I am *not*—I agree that he is not ready.''

''Good.''

''But I will not let you go alone, either. At least wait for the Green Dragon to recover.''

''It'll be too late. Physically, the attack did little, but magically, it's drained him. He'll be too weak for some time.'' The warlock strode the length of the bedroom to one of the windows overlooking the gardens. Below, the people whose lives he guided went about their daily activities, only vaguely aware that some important event now occupied the interests of their lord and lady. The two spellcasters had been at this since waking . . . actually, since the night before, when he had broached the subject. He had waited until he was certain of the Dragon King's condition, because he had hoped the same as her. The Master of the Dagora Forest had agreed that the situation was too great to ignore and had wanted to join him, but at the moment he was even less capable of aiding Cabe than the warlock's young daughter Valea was.

''Then I *have* to go with you.'' She joined him by the window, leaning against his back and putting her arms around him. ''We will have to ask Toos to watch the children.''

''I can just see that. I have another idea.''

''What?'' Her tone indicated that any idea would be welcome as long as it meant that he would be safe. Unfortunately, both of them knew that there could be no such idea as long as he planned to journey into the depths of Legar, especially if there were wolf raiders there.

''I'm going to try to find Darkhorse. I think I know where he might be and I think that he would be willing to help.''

There had been a time, long ago, when the mere mention of the demonic creature would have brought nothing but a stone silence from the enchantress. Darkhorse was a thing of the Void, an empty place beyond the plane of men. Though he had long worn the form of a giant, shadowy steed, he was more a living hole. His ways were not always the ways of other living creatures, if *living* was a term that could be applied to what he was.

In truth, it was not only what he was that had made him a thing somewhat repulsive to the enchantress, but also the company he had kept. Darkhorse had been a companion to Shade, the warlock whose quest for immortality and power had made him a force swinging from light to darkness with each new incarnation. Only Darkhorse—and perhaps Cabe and Queen Erini, who had come to know the faceless warlock best toward the end—mourned Shade.

Gwen had finally reconciled with Darkhorse, in great part because of his friendship with Cabe. "If you could find him, I would feel much better about this, but that raises the point. How do you hope to find him quickly? He could be anywhere and you yourself said that you really only had this one day, a day we've already used part of. He could be anywhere, even beyond the Dragonrealm, you know."

The dark-haired warlock exhaled. "Other than us, there's only one person he ever truly visits."

"Erini."

"Erini. I'll visit her and ask if she's seen him or has news of him. I only wish I'd thought of it when we were there last."

The enchantress released him and came to his side. She joined him in watching some of the drake and human workers carry a pair of long benches into the depths of the garden. The Bedlams had encouraged their people to make use of the sculpted land, providing they were careful about maintaining it. The population of their tiny domain had grown, however, and so it had become necessary to make some additions and changes to the gardens.

"Melicard may not be too pleased to see you back so soon. I've often wondered whether he still blames us in part for his father."

"Blames me, you mean. Kyrg and Toma were hunting for me when Kyrg brought his army to the gates of Talak." Cabe frowned, recalling the young prince he had first met. At the time, he had shared much in common with Melicard. Both of them had been unseasoned, naive, when they had been thrust into the center of things. It had cost Melicard his father, but at the same time it had cost Cabe more. He had lost not only the elf who had raised him and had been more of a father to him than Azran ever could have, but also, albeit only in spirit, his grandfather. "I suppose it doesn't really matter what the truth is in this case. Melicard is Melicard. We have to live with that and I've got to put up with that when I arrive there."

"Then you had best depart now."

Cabe realized that he had been hesitating, that he could have left minutes before but had talked on. He leaned forward and kissed his wife. It was a kiss that spoke too much of the fact that while they would likely see each other again before he departed for Legar itself, it would only be for a very, very short time.

"Good-bye," he whispered . . . and disappeared.

Under normal circumstances, Cabe would have materialized in one of the greeting areas where dignitaries from other kingdoms awaited an audience with Melicard. Times were not normal, however, and so the warlock chose to instead appear in the most likely chamber where he might find the queen. He hoped to locate her and find out what information he could, then leave before Melicard discovered his presence. It would be easier that way.

Erini took her lessons and tested her magical skills in what had once been an auxiliary training room for the palace guard. Much to his misfortune, though, she was not there this day. Cabe had hoped she had been practicing. It was the right time of day, but he knew that Erini occasionally altered her schedule. Scratching his chin, he contemplated his next move. There were perhaps two or three other places he might find the queen alone, no more. Other than those locations, he stood a good chance of confronting the king, too.

She was not in the riding range nor was she in the next location he visited, the private rooms of Princess Lynnette, only child of the king and queen. Standing among the elegant but fanciful pictures of woodland creatures that decorated the princess's chambers, Cabe quietly swore; he did not have time to go running about searching for Queen Erini. Time was short enough. There was still the monumental task of locating Darkhorse.

He recalled then another place. There was a possibility that the king might also be there, but it was less likely than his remaining choices. He teleported.

She was sitting in a chair, a tiny globe of light shining above her head, when Cabe manifested not more than an arm's length before her. Queen Erini dropped the book she had been reading and gasped, but she was quick-witted enough to recognize the warlock and thereby stifle the scream that would have surely followed.

"Cabe! By Rheena! You know that you are always welcome in my presence, but certainly *this* is rather extreme!"

Queen Erini of Talak did not much resemble the image of a sorceress or a witch as most in the Dragonrealm thought of the type. She seemed, in fact, more the perfect storybook princess. Slim and delicate in appearance, with long tresses the color of summer accenting her oval face, Erini looked hardly out of her teens even though she was long past that time. Her pale features were without flaw. Unlike the day of her last lesson, she was now clad in a more sensible and less formal silver and red dress, one that a person could actually walk around and sit down in. It still had its share of jewels sewn into it and the typical puffed sleeves of royal garments, but otherwise it was actually rather plain. He suspected it was probably her favorite dress for that very reason. When last he had seen her, she had been wearing an elaborate gown of gold, an affectation of her former homeland, Gordag-Ai. It had completed the image of a young queen who should have been more at home doing embroidery in the company of her ladies-in-waiting than attempting to perform a magical spell of moderate complexity. Yet while it was true that Erini was fond of embroidery, she was also a woman who had let it be known long ago that she would be more than a showpiece for her husband, King Melicard I. She was a person who followed her own mind in all things, although she did respect the opinions and thoughts of others, especially her husband.

The king, to the surprise of many in those first years, had argued little. He loved his wife for what she was, not what she represented.

Cabe Bedlam quickly knelt before her. It was likely not necessary, for Erini considered both spellcasters her social equals, but it made Cabe feel better for the shock he had given her. "Forgive me, Queen Erini! I searched for you in the most obvious places and then recalled your fondness for the royal library." The blue-robed warlock glanced around at the impressive array of tomes that had been collected in the oak-paneled room. Other than Penacles, the City of Knowledge, Talak boasted one of the finest collections of writing in the Dragonrealm. The books were, for the most part, copies, however. Melicard had sent scribes throughout the continent on quests to obtain access to whatever bits of writing they could find. At Erini's urging, he was now also having some of the *copies* copied so that others could share in what his people had discovered. "I've come on urgent business so my arrival was a bit more abrupt than I would've wished. I hope that you will overlook my transgression."

"Only if you take a chair and cease to be so formal, *Master* Bedlam." She indicated one of the half-dozen elegant and padded chairs situated in the carpeted room. A slight smile played at her lips. "And you need not fear my husband's presence. He is engaged in some proper time with his daughter, someone he sees too little of considering the great love he bears for her."

"My thanks, Que—Erini." Although Cabe's body was tense with anxiety, he forced himself to sit across from the queen.

The warlock waited until she had picked up her book and put it on the tiny table beside her. The ball of light, which had bobbled about during her initial fright, remained situated above her head. Cabe nodded at the magical lamp. "I see you've been practicing. It's very steady."

"I only wish I'd practiced years ago. To think of the time I've wasted!"

He shook his head. "I wish you'd quit thinking that. Erini, if there's one thing I know, you've not wasted time. You have a husband and a beautiful young daughter. You've made Melicard a king more accessible to the people's needs." Cabe waved a hand at the rows of neatly arranged books. "You've encouraged learning to read. The only access I ever had to reading was what Hadeen the elf owned. In fact, the only reason I ever learned to read was because of him. Now, you threaten to make Talak second only to Penacles in the education of its subjects." He folded his arms. "I could give more examples, but that should be sufficient."

"I threaten to make Talak second to none, actually," the slim monarch replied. The smile had not only returned, but it had spread. "You are correct, Cabe, but I still cannot help feeling angry at myself for all those years I left my power to languish."

"You'd seen too much death and destruction. It wasn't what you were raised for."

"Neither were you."

Cabe shook his head. "I am Nathan Bedlam's grandson and the birth child of Azran. If I wasn't raised to be in the midst of trouble, I don't know who is. Somehow, trouble generally finds me . . . which brings me back to why I'm here." The warlock leaned forward, his voice quiet. "I'd hoped to find Darkhorse here. I can detect traces of his presence, but nothing strong enough to tell me if he is near or where he might have gone. I need his aid, if he's willing to give it, on a journey into the midst of the Legar Peninsula."

"You are talking about the Crystal Dragon's domain!"

"I am. This is no ordinary trek, either. If it were, I might be willing to travel alone. Under normal circumstances, the Crystal Dragon would ignore me unless I tried to invade his caverns."

Erini's gaze was steady. "And now?"

"And now, there may be an army camped in the very midst of his kingdom. An army under the banner of the wolf."

"The Aramites? The rumors are true?" She paled slightly. "I think that perhaps Melicard *should* be here. Commander Iston, too." Iston, a native of Erini's homeland, had, for the past several years, been Talak's chief intelligence gatherer.

"Please!" Cabe almost jumped from his chair. "Not until I'm gone. Then you can tell him everything. The important thing is that I need to discover just exactly what *is* happening. That's why I was hoping to find Darkhorse."

"And if you don't find him?"

"Then I'll go there alone."

Her left hand tightened into a fist and her voice grew deathly quiet. "Gwendolyn would never accept that."

"She won't know until it's too late. I'll make certain of that if I have to, Erini. I won't have her coming after me."

It was clear that she did not agree with him, but she finally nodded. "As you wish, Cabe. This means that I must help you find Darkhorse no matter what. I would never be able to face Gwen if something happened to you because I failed to locate him for you."

"She'd never hold you responsible."

"No, but *I* would." The queen rose, smoothed her dress with her hands, and stared off into space, her perfect features twisting into an expression of intense concentration. "He's not been here of late and I've not been expecting him. Therein lies our greatest problem. There are two places that we generally meet, though. One lies within the palace and the other far beyond Talak's high walls."

"Outside?" The notion that Melicard would allow Erini to wander beyond the safety of the city rather surprised the warlock.

"If you think that your relationship with my husband has its tentative moments, you should ask Darkhorse about his own experiences. The only thing that truly holds them together is me, Cabe. Melicard is grateful for what the shadow steed did for me when Mal Quorin, my husband's traitorous counselor, sought to take Talak for his master, the Silver Dragon. Darkhorse knows that I love Melicard. Both of them, however, remember the circumstances under which they met, when my husband-to-be had poor Drayfitt snare and imprison the eternal and even torture him in his quest to make Darkhorse his servant."

Cabe shivered. He recalled that. Darkhorse was not a forgiving sort, either, not that anyone could blame him.

"Sometimes, especially when I am around, they are very cordial, almost friendly, but their mutual past always returns. That's why there are times when it is better to visit Darkhorse in a place far from the eyes of my husband. I love my husband but I will not abandon my friends . . . as you know."

"I do." Rising, the blue-robed spellcaster readied himself for what was to come. "Where's the first location? The one in the palace."

"My private rooms." She took his hand. "Please. Allow me."

Even as the queen finished speaking, the scene around them shifted. They now stood in the midst of a vast, elegant suite of the like that made Cabe stare in open awe. Huge columns stood in each corner of the chamber, the white marble decorated with golden flowers so lifelike he at first thought them real. The floor was also marble, but of different colors arranged in a beautiful abstract pattern. Long, thick fur rugs ran from the massive wooden bed to each of the four doorways. Where there were no doors, gay tapestries decorated the walls. A row of closets spoke of the volumes of clothing royalty wore, as did the wide mirror to the side of the closets.

The bed and the rest of the wooden furniture in the suite had all been carved from the now rare northern oak. The wood had not been so rare at the time of their creation, but the winter of the Ice Dragon had created enough damage that the oaks had still not yet recovered. Despite the magic that had been used to reverse the effects of the magical winter, the most northern places had still suffered much too much.

As impressive as his surroundings were, they paled in comparison to what the queen had just done. "You did that without flaw, Erini! I waited, thinking I'd probably have to help you along, but you brought us here as if you'd been practicing for years."

"No, for some reason I find that spell easier to perform. It only took me three or four attempts to master the proper concentration for it. Why is that, do you think?"

Cabe shrugged. "Gwen is the one who usually has the answers. With me, magic came almost full-blown. That saved my life in the beginning, but it means I never really had the incentive to learn *why* spells work the way they do. Gwen's taught me much since then, but that still doesn't mean I understand completely." He gave her a rueful smile. "Which is why for the fine points, my wife has been instructing you."

"You have both been excellent teachers."

"I muddle through." The warlock again glanced around at the sumptuous apartment. "A room definitely fit for a queen, Erini."

"It is exactly the way it was when I first arrived in Talak. Such a waste of a room," the queen commented dryly. "Since I do not sleep here, the only use it usually gets is when I must be dressed for yet another interminable ball for some ambassador and the necessary gown is not among those in my closets in our royal suite. Still, there are times when it's nice to be alone . . . and it gives Darkhorse and me a place to talk. The library is too cramped, too."

"Then why do you need the other location? This seems private enough."

"Darkhorse rarely talks below a roar, Cabe. You should know that." Erini strolled around the room, visibly recalling memories. Cabe knew that this was where she had first stayed after her arrival in Talak. This apartment had been her refuge in the days when she had first struggled to be accepted by the disfigured king, whose torn mind had been further turned to the dark by his malicious counselor. He did not doubt that she kept it as it was rather than alter it to some other use simply *because* of those precious memories.

As loath as he was to interrupt her reverie, he knew he had to. The day was advancing quickly. "Your Majesty . . . Erini . . ."

"Yes, he is not here, of course." Her memories put aside for now, the slim monarch pondered the matter at hand. "That only leaves the hills. I wish I could be more help to you. Can you not follow his trace?"

"Too old and too faint. It also crosses itself so many times, I couldn't tell which way he went last. If he teleported, that makes it even closer to impossible."

"And I thought magic made everything easy."

"Sometimes it makes things more convoluted and frustrating, not to mention life-threatening. There're times when I wish I was back in that tavern, still waiting on tables and getting threatened by half-drunk ogres. Dragon Kings, Seekers, Quel . . . I could do without all of them."

"But not without the Lady Gwendolyn, I imagine." The queen moved to the center of the room and reached out a hand to him.

"Makes everything else worthwhile." Cabe took her hand and steadied himself, more comfortable now that he knew that Erini was adept at this spell.

"I hope you tell her that on occasion," Erini responded even as their surroundings shifted from the planned elegance of civilization to the raw beauty of nature. She released his hand and stepped away from him in order to better survey the region. The hills were actually the beginning of the Tyber Mountains, but somewhere in the planning, they had been cheated of the great height of their brothers. While few folk ever cared to make the journey through the treacherous chain, the hills did garner some traffic of their own. There was good grazing land here, not to mention the only decent wood within a day's ride of the city. Talak, for all it had, was forced to go to its more outward lands to fill its wood needs.

There were dangers here, of course, but generally only the ordinary ones such as wolves and the rare wyvern or minor drake. Since the death of the Dragon Emperor, Melicard's vast forces had worked hard to clear every corner of the kingdom of the monsters and larger beasts that had once preyed on travelers. For the most part, they had been quite successful.

"I was afraid of this, Cabe. I doubted he would be here, but it was the only place left that I could bring you."

He nodded, his smile one of resignation rather than pleasure. "I didn't think it would be easy. I've got a few other ideas, but I was hoping that I'd find him with or near you."

Erini was downcast, but then her face brightened. "I can *help* you search for him! The teleportation spell is my best. I should have thought of that before. It will cut your searching by nearly half!"

"No."

"No?" Her tone became frost. "Do you think to command me, Cabe?"

"In this instance, yes, *Your Majesty*. You are too important to Melicard, Talak, and, because of both, the rest of the Dragonrealm. If anything happened to you, what would the king do? Think on that before you answer me."

She did. He watched as her face fell. Both of them were too familiar with Melicard's moods. It was Erini who had changed him for the better, but those changes might slip away if she was injured or even . . .

Her eyes suddenly widened. "There's . . . I think there might be one more place to search, Cabe. It's a thin possibility, but it just might be . . ."

"Where?"

"I'll have to take you there; it's . . . it's the only way to make certain we arrive at the proper location."

The warlock caught the hesitation in her voice. "Where *is* it, Erini?"

"In the *Northern Wastes*."

"I forbid you from coming! Tell me approximately where and I'll go there my—"

Erini stalked up to Cabe and gave him her most royal glare. He hesitated just long enough for her to interject, "You can forbid me nothing this time, Cabe Bedlam! As frustrating as it is to me personally, I concede to you that it would be better for us if I did not risk myself! I love Melicard, but I agree that if I were injured or even came close to harm he might, in his unreasoning anger, do something that we would all regret! I have a very good reason, however, for needing to lead you to this one last location. The Northern Wastes are nearly half the size of the rest of the continent and far more troublesome to search. You could pass within yards of the area and not see Darkhorse standing before you. I can lead you to the exact spot; like him, I will never forget it.''

Her skin was pale and her body trembled. Queen Erini stared at Cabe in such a manner that he knew she would have actually preferred *not* to make this final trek. Only the importance of his mission compelled her to do so.

''What is this place, Erini?'' he asked quietly. ''And why would it have such a hold on both you and Darkhorse?''

''Because it is where the warlock *Shade* died.''

He had never been able to convince himself that the blur-faced warlock was dead. At the same time, he had never been able to convince himself that Shade was still alive.

So Darkhorse had searched the world and beyond for nearly a decade, always wondering if the human who had been both his friend and enemy was merely one step ahead of him, watching and waiting for the proper time to emerge. One part of the shadow steed hoped and prayed that the weary sorcerer was at last at peace. The other missed the good incarnations of the man, for only Shade had ever come close to understanding Darkhorse's own emptiness.

Which was why, Erini told Cabe before they departed for the Wastes, he often stood for days at the site where the warlock had simply faded away after expending all his might in a last effort to make up for what he had become.

When they materialized in the midst of the freezing, wind-wracked tundra of the Northern Wastes, it was almost as if he had been waiting for them. The queen brought them to a point barely ten feet from where the huge ebony stallion was situated.

Darkhorse slowly turned his massive head toward them. His ice-blue eyes seemed to burn into the warlock's very soul. The eternal's voice was a thunderous rumble even despite the rather subdued tone. ''Erini. Cabe. It's good to see both of you. This is not a place for your kind, however.''

''We . . . we came in . . . in search of you, Darkhorse,'' the queen managed.

Studying her, Cabe Bedlam grew worried. Erini was a competent sorceress, but it was possible that she had overextended herself. He had provided himself with a heavy cloak to offset the cold, but she had not done the same even though the need should have been obvious. The warlock quickly remedied the situation.

Erini gave him a weak smile. "Thank you."

Darkhorse's hooves kicked away snow and ice as he moved closer. At his present height, he was half again the size of a normal steed. Size, however, was irrelevant to a creature who could manipulate his form in ways no other shapeshifter could. Had he chosen, the ebony eternal could have become as small as a rabbit, even smaller. He need not have resembled a horse, either. Somewhere in the far, forgotten past, Darkhorse had hit upon the form and found it to his liking. The black stallion rarely shifted anymore, although occasionally his body would resemble more the shadow of a horse than the real animal. Cabe had decided that this last was an almost unconscious action. There were things that were normal for a human to do; the same likely could be said even for as unique an entity as the black leviathan before them.

"You should not be out here in the cold, Queen Erini!" roared Darkhorse. It was almost necessary to roar; the wind had picked up. A storm was building. It was hard for the warlock to believe that anything could live in the Northern Wastes, but many creatures did. "We should return to Talak! It will be much more cozy there . . . at least for you two!" The demonic steed chuckled.

"I—" was as far as Erini got. Suddenly she was falling toward Cabe. He caught her at the last moment and stumbled back under her sudden weight. Darkhorse's eyes glittered. He trotted a few more steps toward them.

"What ails her?"

Cabe adjusted his grip. "She pushed herself too far! She insisted that she be the one to bring us here and like a fool I agreed!"

Darkhorse snorted. "I doubt you had much choice with her! Best take her back to her chambers quick!"

"The private ones where you two sometimes meet?"

"You know them? Good! Take her there! I shall follow! Perhaps, if we are fortunate, good Melicard will be out running down drakes or some such foolishness! Hurry now!"

Tightening his hold, the warlock teleported—

—and found himself face-to-face with *King Melicard*, who stood within the suite, one hand on the door handle. Another moment and it was likely they would have missed one another, for he was turned as if just planning to depart.

There were still those to whom the lord of Talak was an effrontery or even a thing of horror. Melicard no longer cared what those people thought. Erini and Princess Lynnette were the only two whose opinions mattered to him and they, of course, loved him dearly.

Despite the yoke of leadership he had worn for almost two decades, Melicard at first glance still looked very much like the handsome young prince that Cabe, with his own rather ordinary features, had always secretly envied. Tall and athletic with brownish hair just now turning a bit to gray, he had once been the desire of many a woman, both royal and common. If Erini was the storybook princess, then Melicard, with his strong, angular features and commanding presence, was the hero of the tale.

He was still handsome . . . but now more than half of his face was a magical reconstruction. The left side from above the eye down to the lower jaw was completely *silver* in color, for that was the natural shade of elfwood. Much of the nose was the same and there were even streaks of silver stretching across to the right side, almost like a pattern of roots seizing hold of what little good flesh remained of the king's visage.

Magic had stolen most of his face and because of that, the damage had proved impossible to repair. Only elfwood, carved into a reproduction of his very features, could give King Melicard the illusion of normalcy. The wondrous wood, blessed, so legend said, by the spirit of a dying forest elf, was capable of mimicking the movements of true flesh. The more the wearer believed in it, the better it pretended. It could never replace what had been lost, but for Melicard the choice had been the mask or the monster beneath. For the sake of his own sanity and the princess he was to marry, Melicard had chosen the former.

He was clad in a black riding outfit that covered him from neck to foot, including his hands. Melicard generally wore outfits with long sleeves and always used gloves, but not for reasons of fashion. The ravaging forces that had taken much of his face had also taken from him his left arm. Had he removed his gloves, Cabe knew that the king's hand would also be silver. The king could not so easily disguise his features, but he could at least hide his arm.

"Warlock! What are you—" His eyes, both real and not, focused on his beloved queen. "Erini!"

"She'll be all right, Your Majesty," Cabe quickly said. "Just help me carry her to the bed, if you please."

Melicard was already moving. The two of them helped Erini walk to the bed; the novice sorceress was not actually unconscious, but seemed lost to the world around her.

When they had her lying down comfortably, Melicard hastened to the door and flung it open. Cabe, glancing up, saw two very nervous guards come to attention.

"Get Magda!" the disfigured monarch roared. "Get Galea! Get someone for the queen! She's been hurt! Now!" He did not wait for them to respond, but rather turned immediately back to the bed, slamming the heavy door shut behind him as he did.

Cabe immediately stood up and faced him. He could not allow Melicard's anger any leverage. He had to meet the king man-to-man and make him listen.

It was at that time that Darkhorse made the unfortunate decision to materialize. Melicard fell back from the newcomer, but Darkhorse did not notice him at first. "Does she fare better? How—" The pupilless eyes froze when they fell upon the furious king, who stood against one side as if the shadow steed filled the entire room. "Melicard . . ."

"I should have known you would be involved, demon! You may be virtually indestructible, but my queen is not! My Erini—"

"Is to blame for her troubles, my love."

The three turned to the bed, where a still pale Erini was forcing herself up to a sitting position. She succeeded only as far as leaning on one elbow. Lines of strain marred her beauty.

"Erini!" Melicard, forgetting any pretense of dignity, ran to the side of the bed and hugged the queen.

"Gently, dear Melicard," she gasped. "I'm not yet fully recovered."

"Praise be!" Darkhorse bellowed. "You had us all fearful, dear Erini! You must take greater care in the future!"

"Greater care . . ." The king turned to face the warlock and the steed. "What did you make her do?"

"They . . . they did nothing, Melicard. I overextended myself. Cabe would have performed the spell, but I did not think he would find Darkhorse. I knew exactly where he would be if he was anywhere in . . . in that region.''

"Where *were* you?" He touched her skin. "You're cold, Erini; I should have noticed that sooner . . . you've been to the *Wastes*, haven't you?"

It was clear it was a strain for her to keep speaking, but the queen was not one to let others take the blame when she considered herself at fault. Cabe felt guilty that he allowed her to continue, but if anyone could make the ruler of Talak see reason, it was Erini.

"Listen to me, my love. I have to tell you everything the first time. I do not have the strength to repeat myself. Do you understand?"

Much of Melicard's anger dwindled away as he realized what effect his fury was having on her. Still holding her, he sat down on the bed. "Very well; I'm listening, my queen."

They were interrupted by a knock on the door. An older, plump woman, one of Erini's two longtime companions from her former homeland, peered inside anxiously. "Your Majesties . . ."

Erini steadied herself. "Please wait without until I call for you, Galea. It will be but a moment."

It was not to the woman's liking, but she nodded and withdrew. The queen's ladies were very protective of their charge, especially Galea and Magda.

"Now," began the queen. "Let me tell you what happened, my beloved."

She told him everything, glancing at the warlock for understanding. Cabe nodded; he agreed that there was no longer any reason to keep the purpose of his mission a secret. Melicard deserved the explanation even if, to the warlock, it might complicate something already too complicated. The king's face was a mask in more ways than one now. Neither the real nor the elfwood side betrayed any emotion. Melicard was simply absorbing the facts. Afterward, when he had had a chance to consider what she had relayed to him, he might again become the living fury he had been a moment ago. The warlock hoped not, but there was no predicting Melicard. He would have to wait and see.

Erini was forced to pause several times in order to regain her strength, but at last she finished. More drained than before, the exhausted queen fell back onto the bed. Melicard rose to call her ladies in, but she reached up, put her hand on his, and said, "Not just yet, my lord. Let us finish here first. I'm only tired; nothing more. I promise you."

"You're certain, Erini?"

"I am."

"I would never let anything happen to her, Your Majesty," Cabe added. "My power stands ready to aid her if necessary. She's overtaxed herself like she said. It can happen . . . I know that too well . . . when a fairly new mage succeeds too quickly with some spell. I apologize, however, for letting her go as far as she did. That was *my* mistake."

"Erini has a stubbornness worthy of me!" commented Darkhorse. He was more his old self now. Cabe was thankful for that; if his old friend agreed to join him, he would need Darkhorse at his best. Distracted, he could become more of a danger, for Cabe would then himself be distracted from his course. "When she chooses to do something, she does it! One might as well ask the Tybers to move aside for them rather than convince the queen to change her mind on certain subjects!"

"I am . . ." the king began, "very much aware of my wife's qualities. Foremost of those is a tendency to be open and straightforward with the truth. That and her beauty were what struck me that first day we met as adults." He turned to face the two. His expression was calm, but his tone was just slightly cold. "I take what she says now as the true and complete story . . . as she knows it. You have my apologies, Master Bedlam, for my accusing you of being responsible for her condition."

"There's no need to apologize, Your Majesty. Under the circumstances, you reacted as anyone might have."

"Indeed." King Melicard rose. "And now that you've found what you were searching for, Master Bedlam, I am sure that you must be on your way. This news of Legar and the wolf raiders I will pass on to Iston. I will respect your mission. We will do nothing for now except watch. When you've discovered what you can, I would appreciate being told."

They were being asked to leave and leave now. Melicard's

words teetered on the edge of bluntness, but at the same time he was sounding civil. It was all that could have been expected from him at a time like this. Cabe was more than ready to depart. As the king had almost said, he had found *who* he had been searching for. *Thank the stars Darkhorse didn't take him to task for that slight!*

"I was glad . . . glad to be what help I could, Cabe," whispered Erini from the bed. She managed to lean up a bit. "Good luck."

"And where do we go from here, Cabe?" asked Darkhorse. There seemed no question in his mind that he would follow the sorcerer to the inhospitable peninsula. Darkhorse was very loyal to those he considered his friends.

"Thank you, Erini, and you, too, Darkhorse. First to the Manor, I suppose, to let Gwen know I've found you. Then, I think on to Zuu."

"Zuu?"

Much to Cabe's surprise, it was Melicard who answered the demon steed for him. "Zuu would be appropriate. There is no human city closer to the domain of the Crystal Dragon. They may have some word there that has not reached us yet." He hesitated, then added, "Good luck, Master Bedlam."

The warlock bowed. "Thank you, Your Majesty. It may be that this will be simple and swift. The danger may be limited. There *is* something going on there, though, and for reasons I don't understand, I seem to have been included."

"Have no fear now, Cabe!" Darkhorse roared. "With me at your side, it is our foes who must worry!"

The demon steed's brash confidence, while not enough to change Cabe's own dour opinion on the matter, still succeeded in bringing a smile to his face. It was hard not to be at least a bit more hopeful when he was with Darkhorse.

"Give Gwen my love," Erini added from the bed.

"I will." He looked at his unearthly companion. "Are you ready?"

"I was ready long ago, Cabe! I look forward to this adventure with great anticipation!"

The warlock concentrated. "I'm glad someone is."

Darkhorse was still laughing when they vanished.

* * *

At the southeastern edge of the land of Irillian, a longboat from the lone black ship slowly made its way toward shore. The black ship had waited until just the right time to come close enough to deposit its cargo. There were those who would have gladly sunk the vessel without so much as a question or a warning. Its mere presence, even in the distance, would have sealed its fate no matter who had been aboard.

There were three aboard the longboat, all of whom wore heavy cloaks designed not only to protect them from the spray and rain, but also, if need be, to protect their identities. Only one rowed; the other two sat and watched, wary.

They did not beach the longboat. Instead, when they were near enough, the two passengers climbed out into waist-deep water and waded their way toward shore. The third figure slowly began to turn the boat around so that he could return to the other vessel.

Both passengers moved swiftly through the sea. Their reactions were those of folk who little loved the water and suffered it now only because it was necessary. When they were at last on the beach, the duo shook themselves off, the wild wind and their cloaks making them look like the specters of dead seamen rising from the depths. They then turned and briefly watched their companion row back to the dark hunter. Satisfied that the ship would depart undetected, the two quietly conferred and then started inland, the taller one leading the way.

The journey ahead would be long and tiring, but they were undeterred by that thought. All that concerned them was the reason that had brought them to this shore in the first place. They were hunters, both of them, and they had come to the Dragonrealm because that was where their prey was. Whether it took ten days or ten years, they would complete their quest, for with them it had also become an obsession. Either they succeeded or they died. Living with failure did not occur to them; it was not their way. Either their prey was vanquished or they were killed in the attempt. Those were the only choices.

At the top of a rise overlooking the cloud-enshrouded, rolling landscape of southern Irillian, the lead figure stopped. He motioned to the other, then pointed to the far southwest in a direction that would take them on a route north of the distant city of Penacles. His companion nodded, but said nothing. They had discussed the route in advance. They knew their destination and how long it would likely take to reach it. All that mattered now was getting there without being discovered, a difficult task, but not an impossible one for two with their skills.

Confident and determined, they began both the climb down the other side of the rise . . . and the final leg of their journey to the Dagora Forest.

—— VI ——

"I still do not see why we cannot just teleport to where you want to search in Legar and then leap back!" Darkhorse grumbled. In order to converse with Cabe, who rode on his back, he had twisted his head around in a manner that would have broken the neck of any true steed. Fortunately, it was dark now and they were some distance from the actual city, having materialized so far away for safety's sake. Mages were still a rare and gossip-stirring sight. The warlock wanted no interference with his mission.

Cabe sighed and adjusted the hood of the traveler's cloak he wore. The hood was the only way he could properly hide the great stretch of silver in his hair. Dyes merely washed away before they even had time to set. It was said that a god had created the mark as a symbol of his respect for the legendary Lord Drazeree, who had borne a similar streak, but if so, Cabe thought that the least the unthinking deity could have done was allow for times when a spellcaster *had* to hide his nature. Mages were always forced to resort to hats, cloaks, helms, and rather touchy illusion spells to obscure the silver. There were times when that made their lives tricky.

"You weren't there when the Green Dragon was struck down, Darkhorse. I don't want to go blindly into Legar. We need to move with stealth. I also want to see if I can find out any information beforehand. It's possible that not all news has made it back to Talak yet."

"You should have asked Melicard to give you the names of his spies! We could ask them and be done with it!"

"I'm sure that would've pleased the king. Now, for the last time, you'd better start behaving like a real horse. I'd like to avoid too much notice; it's possible that the wolf raiders, if they are in Legar, might also have spies in Zuu."

The shadow steed snorted and turned his head to a more savory position. Cabe relaxed a little. For a creature who had lived for thousands of years, the eternal could be very impatient at times. Tonight, he was even more restless than was normal. The warlock was certain that Darkhorse's anxiety focused around Shade. Darkhorse had done little in the past few years besides search for traces of the ageless sorcerer.

They would have to talk about this some time in the future. Whether Shade was truly dead or not, Darkhorse could not spend eternity thinking about it. He had to be made to see that there were other matters—and friends—waiting for him.

"There is the city," whispered Darkhorse. Unfortunately, his concept of whispering still resembled more of a shout.

"I see," Cabe responded quickly. "We'll have to be doubly careful. We may encounter other riders at any moment."

His ploy worked. The demon steed nodded and resumed his role of faithful horse.

To the eyes of another traveler, one who carried a good torch, that is, the two would resemble a weary rider and his large ebony stallion. Darkhorse had shrunk down to a more tolerable size, although he was still large for most breeds. Cabe, meanwhile, was clad in a simple gray outfit consisting of pants, cloth shirt, knee-high leather boots, and the aforementioned riding cloak. While his outfit was a bit old-fashioned, it was not an uncommon sight. The style was a throwback to his life near the now ruined city-state of Mito Pica, which had been destroyed by the Dragon Emperor's forces for having unknowingly secreted a young Cabe Bedlam. Many survivors had become wanderers since then, even almost two decades after the event. Hence, the warlock would look like one of the youngest ones finally grown up. Most people respected the privacy of such wanderers, especially the people of Zuu.

Cabe had never journeyed to the low, sprawling city of Zuu, possibly, he now admitted to himself, out of some small guilt. During the brief war that had been instigated by the Dragon Kings' search for him, the rather independent-minded folk of

Zuu had sent a contingent of their famous horse soldiers to the aid of Penacles. The young warlock vividly recalled the band of huge blond warriors clad in leather and how they had wanted to come to his aid when airdrakes had flown down and attacked Cabe and Gwen. He especially remembered their leader, a scarred man named Blane, the second or third son of the king at that time.

Blane had died defending Penacles, but not before he had killed Duke Kyrg, the drake commander and brother to Toma. It was no surprise that Talak and Zuu were on excellent political terms with each other, not that such prevented each from having their share of spies.

Blane's brother, someone named Lanith XII, was now king, but Cabe had no intention of introducing himself to the man. If things went according to plan, he wanted to be out of the city before morning. That meant little or no sleep, but to a spellcaster of his ability, one night missed meant nothing. For the past several years, he had enjoyed a full night's slumber all but a handful of days. In truth, Cabe did not miss the sleep so much as the peace and quiet.

He gently prodded Darkhorse's sides, the signal for speed. There would be no peace and quiet tonight nor likely the next.

Zuu lay in a valley that was vaguely bowl-shaped. Around it were miles and miles of grassland. The nomadic founders of the city had chosen this location for the latter feature. Horses had been and still were the most valuable possession of any citizen of Zuu. Merchants from all over the continent came to this region to purchase the best animals.

Because of their obsession with their horses, it was not so surprising to Cabe that even in the dark Zuu resembled one endless array of stables. With few exceptions, no building generally topped more than two floors. Most of the structures had a boxy appearance that was evident even from where the warlock was. Adding to the effect was the one drawback to having business in the city: Zuu also *smelled* like one vast stable.

Cabe had wanted to avoid spells, for they had a way of drawing the attention of other mages, but he could already see that the odor was going to become more pungent with each successive step nearer. With a single thought, he adjusted his sense of smell. He did not go so far as to make the odor pleasant, but he made it less noticeable. That required less manipulation. Cabe disliked using sorcery to alter his form. It was there that a mage could cause himself irreparable harm; his concentration might waver just enough that his spell would go awry. There were legends of spellcasters who had died like that. Too often, the ease with which some learned magic made them too careless.

It was not long before they approached the city gates. Up close, Zuu was a well-lit city, a sign of its prosperity in the horse trade. Behind the walls, Cabe could make out some of the nearer structures. Zuu did not have high walls to protect it; the people relied on their own skills. There were few forces, either drake or human, who willingly went against the horsemen of Zuu. Not only were they expert riders, but they could fire arrows or throw spears with amazing accuracy even when their horses were at full gallop. More important, it was not just the men an enemy had to be wary of. Under Zuu law, every adult, male or female, was a fighter. There were many women in this city who could have stood among the finest warriors in the land. Even the children could be dangerous should a battle somehow reach behind the walls. The citizens of Zuu were of the opinion that it was never too early to teach a child how to defend his own.

It was something to consider, especially since six of those horsemen were now waiting for him at the gate.

They were typical of what Cabe had known. Tall, blond, and looking as if they had been riding since birth. Most of them were wearing leather pants and jerkins, the latter not entirely succeeding in covering their bronzed chests. They wore short helms with nose protectors, but otherwise no armor. Not all the inhabitants of Zuu resembled the nomadic image, but the city guards most certainly did. Many of them were likely the latest in a long family line of city guards. People here tended to follow in their parents' footsteps . . . or maybe horsetracks.

The evident leader, a somewhat heavier man with a blond and gray beard, urged his horse toward Cabe. He was followed a few steps behind by another rider who carried a torch. The other guards had their bows ready. The warlock wondered if he could teleport away fast enough if he somehow offended them. The archers of Zuu were not only accurate; they were swift.

"Welcome, stranger! What do you have to declare, eh?"

There had been the temptation to simply materialize in the

midst of the city and forgo meeting the city guards, but despite its reputation for respecting the privacy of its visitors, Zuu paradoxically also liked to keep track of everyone. Had he given in to the temptation, Cabe soon might have found himself the object of several curious and suspicious soldiers. No, passing through the front gates like a normal traveler would much better aid him in the long run.

"Only myself and my steed. A few supplies for travel, but nothing else."

The guard leader was eyeing him up and down. "You've never been to Zuu, have you, man?"

Had he done something wrong? "No."

"Hilfa." At the summons, a sentry from the back of the group rode forward. A woman. She was perhaps a year or two younger than the warlock looked, tall, and just as capable-looking if not more so than some of her companions. Modesty, Cabe saw, was not a strong point of the folk here. Hilfa wore the same outfit as her companions, which made for some distraction above the waist. She seemed unconcerned about his slight embarrassment. How foreigners acted was only a concern if they broke the law.

When she was even with the guard captain, Hilfa waggled the bow in her hand, a salute of sorts to her superior.

"Give him a marker."

Reaching into a saddlebag, the woman quickly produced a small, U-shaped talisman on a chain. This she tossed to the waiting spellcaster without preamble. Cabe had to move with swiftness to catch the marker before it fell past him.

The leader pointed at the talisman. "That's your marker. Carry it with you at all times, either around your neck or in your pocket, but carry it, man. When you buy somethin' or talk to anyone from our city, produce it."

Cabe inspected it. There was a touch of magic to it, but so little it could not be meant to harm him. Unwilling to remove his hood, he thrust the marker into a belt pouch. Zuu evidently had one or more mages who worked for them. An interesting aspect he would remember for the future. How many more were there and what were *they* doing?

"Let him pass."

Hilfa backed her horse up, allowing the sorcerer access. As Cabe rode by, however, she reached out and put a hand on his.

He looked at her. Up close, she had strong features, but not unattractive ones. Like many of the inhabitants, Hilfa looked like she was related to her companions. "That's a remarkable animal you have there. I've not seen one like that anywhere. What breed is it?"

"It's unique. A mix." Cabe had considered this problem. Folk as interested in horse breeding as these would not let a steed like Darkhorse pass through their city without some questions. Mixes were not considered as valuable as purebreds, however, so he had hoped that by calling the eternal a mix, he would be able to dampen some of that interest.

That was not the case. In the end, a good horse was a good horse to some. "Would you consider selling it?"

"I don't think he'd let me. Sorry."

She removed her hand, somewhat puzzled by his response. The gates had opened while the two of them had talked, so Cabe quickly took advantage of her silence and urged Darkhorse forward.

This was the entrance through which most of the foreign visitors first passed and so Cabe found himself entering a bustling market still filled despite the night. Merchants from both Zuu and beyond had set up their tents along his path. Travelers from all the continent over, even far Irillian, wandered about admiring and often buying things they did not necessarily need. The two men from the seaport of Irillian, recognizable in their sailor-style shirts and wide, blue pants, were discussing the need for a pair of small daggers with silver handles. A merchant family wearing the bulky, elaborate garments of Gordag-Ai was sitting at a row of benches eating freshly purchased meat pies. Cabe wondered what sort of meat might be in it. He was discovering that he was now hungry enough to eat almost anything, even horse.

Soon he would eat. He had forced himself not to so that he might be able to order meals at more than one inn. From his early days, when he had been but a simple steward at the Wyvern's Head Tavern, the warlock knew that one of the best places to overhear the local rumors was a tavern or inn. Good company, food, and plenty of drink could loosen a man's tongue just as quickly as a mage's spell.

There were sure to be many such places and Cabe was prepared to visit most of them, but he wanted to find one frequented just as much by the citizenry as it was by strangers. It was more likely he would hear news from a home source than from a stranger, but he did not want to rule out the latter hope.

Finding a stable would be easier, he soon discovered. They were everywhere. Compared to even the royal stables of Penacles or Talak, these were also the cleanest. The dark-haired spellcaster finally chose one near an inn entitled Belfour's Champion. From the image painted on the sign, he gathered that the name had something to do with an actual horse once prominent with this quarter of the city.

At the stable he showed the marker to a groom, who led them to a private stall after an exchange of money. On the pretext that he desired to personally take care of his own mount, Cabe succeeded in being alone with Darkhorse.

"I like this place," the shadow steed rumbled. "They know how best to treat an animal. I should visit Zuu again in the near future!"

"They won't treat you so well if they find out it's you scaring all their other horses."

What Cabe had said was true. Around them, the other mounts were stirring, the voice of Darkhorse unnerving them. The shadowy stallion tried to speak quieter. "I wish I could enter with you, friend Cabe."

"That would certainly raise a few eyebrows and shut more than a few mouths. I don't think even the locals treat their horses *that* well anymore. You'd best stay here for the time being. It won't be a loss, either. This close, you should be able to pick up a number of the voices outside. You'll also have people coming and going here, too."

Darkhorse scraped the floor of his stall, gouging out a valley in the rock-hard dirt. He was not pleased with his end of the mission, but he understood that there was no way he could blend among people. Given time—more than they had now—the eternal might be able to copy the basic structure of a human, but he would *not* be able to copy their ways. A human-looking Darkhorse would still garner too much attention; despite the centuries among men, the demon steed had a rather unique thought pattern and personality. He did not and could not act like a mortal. Neither, for that matter, would he have been able to pass for an elf or any of the other races.

There was and there would always be only one Darkhorse.

The inn was surprisingly clean compared to many that Cabe had experienced. His sense of smell, despite having been dulled, was still able enough to pick up the delicious odors coming from the back. The warlock's stomach grumbled, hoping to remind him that while he had a mission here, so did it.

The interior of Belfour's Champion had much in common with many inns, of course, save that here there was no escaping the symbol of the place, the horse for which it had been named. There were small statuettes, trophies won by the selfsame steed, lining one wall. Tapestries revealing the various feats of a chestnut goliath covered most of the others. If even half of them were true, the animal had been a wonder.

Perhaps the most unusual bit of decor was the clean, polished skull that hung above the rock fireplace across from him. From the small wreath below it, he gathered that this had once belonged to the famous horse. It was, to the warlock, a peculiar way to honor even a most favored companion, but this *was* Zuu, after all, and it was Cabe who was the foreigner here.

Cabe found an empty bench off to one side of the eating area and sat down. Almost the second he was comfortable, a sun-haired serving girl was at his table. Unlike the guards, she was dressed in a more conventional outfit. Yet while the skirt and bodice were of a style that might have been found in any tavern across the Dragonrealm, the form barely hidden within was not. Cabe was of the opinion that there must be much to be said for the Zuu way of life; both the men and the women seemed remarkably fit.

"What can I get *you*?" she asked after he had revealed the marker. She had slightly elfin features, but with what could only be described as a saucy touch to them. The warlock was uncomfortably reminded of a serving girl named Deidra who had been all but able to wrap him around her finger when they had worked together in the Wyvern's Head.

"What's best? Food, I mean."

"That'd be the stew."

Cabe's stomach rumbled again. "That's fine. Stew and cider."

She vanished in a swirl of skirts, leaving Cabe to recover. He loved Gwen, but a man had to be blind not to notice some women, just as he was certain it worked the other way.

There were a number of other travelers in the place, not to mention three good-sized parties of native Zuuans or Zuuites or whatever they called themselves. A few scattered individuals here and there verified that Cabe would not stick out. He picked out the loudest conversation, that of a trio of horse merchants, and started to listen.

His meal and drink came a couple of minutes later, by which time he was more than ready to abandon his first attempt. The serving girl dropped a heaping bowl of delicious-smelling stew in front of him along with a chunk of brown bread. As she reached over and put down the mug of cider, she hesitated long enough for him to admire the view if he desired. Cabe, who was familiar with the ways of some taverns and inns, gave her a noncommittal thank you and enough coins to satisfy both the bill and her. Once she had disappeared back into the crowd, he started in on the stew while at the same time choosing his next target.

The stew was superb, which made concentrating a bit harder at first, but he soon picked up on one of the other conversations. This one, between a pair of the locals, at first sounded like yet another talk about horseflesh, but then switched.

The first man, a thin elder, was muttering, ". . . dwarfs keep insisting. Even said they saw the place glow once."

"Ain't nothing happens in that godforsaken place. I don't even think there's no Dragon King there. Never hear anythin'." His companion, about half his age and with as thick a beard as any the warlock had ever seen, picked up his mug and drank long from it.

"So? We ever hear anything from our drake? You see a few in the city near the king's place, but old Green never shows up or demands anything. Could be the same with this one."

The younger man put down the mug. "But still . . ."

Their conversation shifted again, talking about Dragon Kings and kings in general. Cabe held back a grimace. The glow and the dwarfs interested him, but he could hardly walk over to the men and ask them. He wished that he could be like Shade had been. The master warlock had not only been able to hide his presence in a full inn, but he would blatantly summon people, ask them questions, and send them away without them recalling or anyone else taking the slightest notice. Cabe could have done the same, but he felt wrong about doing so.

He focused on two other discussions, found nothing, then discovered that even with his concentration, he could not make out any of the others clearly enough. The stew lost some of its flavor as he realized that he would have to resort to sorcery and modify his hearing. Again, it was a simple spell, but he still did not care for any transformation, however minor.

It took him but a moment to do it. Now, he was not only able to hear conversations on the far side of the room, but he could pick them out of all the others and hear those speaking as if no one else were making a sound.

Much to his regret, however, it turned out that no one had anything concrete to add to what he knew. Cabe had expected it, but had hoped for more. He would have to search elsewhere. Rising, he left the nearly empty bowl and mostly untouched cider and departed before the serving girl returned.

There was no dearth of inns in this quarter. Not all of them were up to the standards of Belfour's Champion, but all of them were surprisingly neat. Compared to the worst, Wyvern's Head had been a stable.

No, not a stable, Cabe thought as he entered the next one. *You can literally eat off the floor in these stables*.

At the next two places, the warlock picked up a smattering of information. An intruder killed in the west, his identity unknown. He had been carrying a pouchful of foreign gold and a few valuable gemstones. Two guards had died in taking him . . . and the patrol had originally only wanted to ask him the same simple questions they asked every visitor. Another body found, this one stripped of all his possessions. Oddly, the two did not seem directly connected.

There was mention of the glow again, a brief brightness that had lit up part of the western sky the *very* night that Cabe had had the second vision. Only a few had actually seen it; most of those he listened to knew of it only secondhand. Evidently Zuu did actually keep a few hours aside for rest.

After the fifth inn, Cabe came to the conclusion that he had heard all he would hear this evening. While he had not garnered much more than he had begun with, he was not unsatisfied.

Slightly fatigued, the warlock started back to the stable where Darkhorse was no doubt impatiently waiting for him. The eternal would probably be disappointed in his findings, but that did not matter.

He was just passing Belfour's Champion when he sensed something amiss, although what it was he could not say.

"Well, it's our visitor who eats and runs without saying farewell to a girl."

It was the serving woman from the inn. In the flickering light of the torches, she almost reminded him of a drake woman, so magical did her beauty seem. She had a shawl over her shoulders that could not have served to keep her warm and certainly had not been chosen to protect her modesty.

"Is that a custom I missed?"

The woman, who appeared to have been walking quietly along the avenue, smiled and shook her head. "Only an opportunity." Slowly she pulled away the shawl. "But there are always other opportunities, other chances, for the right man."

He stood his ground even though a part of him urged swift retreat. Before Gwen, he had never been better than inept with women. Cabe was still not certain how he had been so fortunate as to marry her. "I'm flattered, but I'll have to decline."

She hesitated for a brief moment, almost as if she was confused by his response. Then she advanced toward him again, growing somehow even more desirable than she had before.

Again, Cabe sensed that something was amiss. He blinked, then stared carefully at the girl. She mistook his expression for a positive response to her advances and reached out to him. The warlock took her proffered hand . . . then reached out with his power and froze her where she was. He allowed her only to speak.

"Let me go! What are you doing?"

"There are certain things an enchantress should be careful about doing and one of those is picking the wrong victim to use your spells on." Cabe led her by the hand to the side of the stable, where they would not so readily be seen. The wouldbe seductress followed, walking in jerky movements. He now controlled her actions; she could do nothing but breathe, see, and hear. Even her ability to talk hinged on Cabe's desire. He disliked having to do this, but he could not take chances with so wild a sorceress. There was no telling what other tricks she might know.

When they were safely ensconced, he whispered, "You will speak softly. I won't hurt you if you don't try anything and if you answer me honestly. Understand?"

"Yes."

"Good." Even with her spell of seduction removed, it was difficult for him to stand so close to her. If he backed away, however, he knew she would notice. That would throw some of the advantage back to her, which was not what he wanted. "Who are you? Why did you seek me out?" He studied her hair. His eyes had not been augmented for the dark, but up close, he should still have been able to see it.

"You may call me Tori, warlock, and what I wanted—and still want—is simply you." Her smile was dazzling. Understanding his confusion, she added, "The streak is on the left, buried beneath another layer of hair. All it takes is some artful combing."

That would not serve her forever, the warlock knew. Soon, the mark would make itself so evident that nothing short of false hair or a hood like his would be sufficient. However, that was not so important now as what she was doing here. "Why? Why do you want me?"

"Are you serious? What sort of life have—"

He waved her to silence. "You know that's not what I meant. There were certainly better choices in there than me."

She cocked her head to one side. Cabe had not realized that he had allowed her more mobility. That was a bad sign; it meant that she was either stronger than he had supposed or her influence on him was. Either way, it spelled trouble. "True, there were men who were *prettier*, master warlock, but pretty is not all I want. I want someone who thinks as well, someone with ambition and ability . . ."

He understood now. "And someone with skill in the art of sorcery."

"Yes. Very much so. Not just for the sake of that power, though that certainly sweetens things, but because I want someone who understands what it's like to be so . . . superior and different. I want someone of the same world as I. When I saw you, I sensed somehow that you were like me, that you were the one I was searching for. All my patience and sweat have been for something after all. I was beginning to believe that I would be working in taverns for the rest of my life, searching for someone else like me. Someone like you.''

Although it seemed that each week brought rumors of new mages, they were still few and far apart. Cabe understood Tori. Here she was, with skills she had not been tutored in the proper use of, trapped in a place where there was no one else like her. Or was there?

"There must be at least one other spellcaster here, Tori. These markers are magical.''

"There are a few, master warlock, but they are hardly the company I would keep. Besides, they work solely for Zuu and I will have my own life. You would be wise to watch that marker. It lets them know if a mage is in the city. That's how the king recruits.''

"Recruits?'' All thought of Tori's attempted seduction faded.

"King Lanith wants magic users. He hasn't decided what he wants to do with them, but he wants them.'' She put a cool hand to his chin. "You know, there may have been some prettier ones, but I like the character and strength in your face more. You could teach me how to use sorcery properly and I could—''

"That'll be enough of that. There's a certain enchantress, the mother of my children, who might take offense. She and I are very protective of each other. If you want training, then something can be arranged.''

"With you?'' With the swiftness of a feline pouncing on her prey, she was against him. Cabe started to push her away, but then both of them stopped and turned their attention to a sound coming from beyond the street. Tori glanced up into his face. "You had best be leaving, my love. I carry a false marker, so I'm safe, but you must have been using much magic tonight. Those little toys aren't usually so efficient.''

"What is it? What's coming?''

"Lanith's hired mages and the city guard.'' Even under the circumstances, she took the time to run a finger slowly over his chest. "They are not much to look at and separately they're inept, but the three of them together with the guards could give you trouble . . . and I wouldn't want that. We *will* meet again some day, my warlock.''

She leaned up, gave him a swift but powerful kiss, and vanished before he could ask her his next question. Tori had the potential to be a very adept mage, it seemed, if her skills were honed so well already.

Disconcerted, Cabe stood there for several seconds. He had come to Zuu for information, not in order to be involved in some enchantress's wild notions or another king's murky ambitions. Legar was beginning to look more and more inviting with each passing moment.

There was a clatter in the street, a clatter with a very definite military sound to it. Cabe felt the presence of other mages. Unlike Tori, they made no attempt to mask themselves. He sensed them draw upon the natural forces of the world, but draw upon them in such haphazard manner that it was a wonder they did not accidentally unleash some wild spell on themselves.

"He's around, he is," came a gruff female voice.

"Well, it's your task to find him, mage. Do so."

"Do not proceed to tell us our duties." This voice, male, was more cultured than that of either of the previous two.

The warlock pressed himself against the wall, a frown on his lips. His best choice was to teleport to Darkhorse and for the two of them to leave instantly.

Thought was action. Cabe materialized a few stalls down from where he had left Darkhorse. The warlock purposely chose a spot near the stable wall, the better to avoid being seen by some boy or groom. Other than the horses, though, he saw no one. Cautiously he stepped away from the wall and started toward the shadowy steed.

"Dark—" The warlock bit off the rest of the name as he found himself staring at a tall figure clad in a long, flowing robe of white. The man stood like one of the storybook wizards Cabe had grown up hearing about, the ones that only existed in tales. He even had the long white beard.

The man stared at him. After a breath or two had passed, Cabe came to the realization that the man was not staring at him, but rather at the spot where he stood. He did not see the warlock at all. Becoming daring, the bemused warlock waved a hand in front of his counterpart's countenance. The bearded mage might have been a statue for all he noticed.

"He came barging in all important," mocked a voice from

behind the still figure. The gate to Darkhorse's stall opened of its own accord and the demon steed trotted out. "I think he must have been looking for you but sensed me instead. Then, just as he had decided to give up, you came along. His powers are not that great, not by far, but he *is* very sensitive to the presence of magic. I did the only thing I could do under the circumstances. Who was the hungry female?"

The question caught Cabe off-balance for a second, but he quickly replied, "Another spellcaster."

"They seem to be breeding like mice these days. There are two others nearby."

"I know; that's why I'm here. We have to leave."

"We would not think of letting you leave without first hearing the offer our most benevolent lord has commanded us to present to you."

It was the male spellcaster Cabe had heard moments earlier. In contrast to his companion, he was clad like a minister of state from one of the northern kingdoms, like Erini's own Gordag-Ai. In one hand, he carried a cane whose top was two silver-and-crystal horse heads. The mage himself was tall and narrow of face with a long mustache and thin, oiled hair. Beady eyes glanced at the petrified figure behind Cabe. The thin mouth curled up into a slight smile.

"I'm sorry, but I'm not interested." The warlock was feeling too popular of late. Unknown forces were summoning him to Legar, enchantresses were seeking him for . . . for many things . . . and now kings wanted his services. He only wanted to go home and spend the next couple of hundred years with his family and friends.

"You have not heard the offer yet." The other spellcaster tapped the end of his two-headed cane on the stable floor. "And you shall not leave until you do."

Cabe could feel a sudden change, as if a blanket had been thrown over the stable. There was a dull ache in his head. His counterpart was trying to cut him off from any use of power. While that likely worked against an untrained or novice sorcerer, Cabe Bedlam was neither. With a simple, forceful thought, he cut through the magical barrier and restored to full intensity his link to the Dragonrealm.

The other mage's cane promptly exploded.

"What? What?" The white-robed figure was mobile again. He glanced this way and that, trying desperately to figure out what was going on. Distracted by the surprising explosion, Darkhorse had lost control of the spell holding him in place.

Blinded briefly by the burst of sorcerous energy unleashed, Cabe could only now see what had happened to the elegant mage. The dull ache in his head had now become a raging headache, likely a backlash from the chaos of the cane's destruction. The blast had thrown the other spellcaster back into one of the stable doors, where he lay unconscious. He wondered what sort of idiotic matrix the man had incorporated into the staff that would make it backfire like that when the spell was disrupted. Having never faced someone of true power, the other must have been unaware of the dangers. The cane was an interesting device, but when one chose to tie an item to a particular spell in order to save one's concentration and strength for other things, one should make certain that the matrix, which stored or drew the power depending on the spell, was fortified in all dimensions. Obviously, there had been a weak link somewhere. Cabe was furious; it was not his intention to harm anyone. He did not wish to do anything that might strain relations between Zuu and himself. So far, no one knew who he was, but that might not be the case in the future. If King Lanith discovered it was Cabe Bedlam who had caused the chaos, there would likely be repercussions.

"What have you done? Hold there, young man!" The white-robed spellcaster reached for Cabe.

"Oh, do be still!" bellowed Darkhorse. Once more the figure froze. "Are we leaving now? This grows most tiresome!"

"Yes, we are! I—" His head still pounded. "I'd better ride you and let you teleport! That way we're guaranteed to be together! My head—"

"Feels much the way I do! My entire body feels twisted inside out! I should give that mage a sound kicking! Next time, I will! Where to? Legar?"

"No, not yet! Somewhere near what used to be the edge of the Barren Lands, where the Brown Dragon once ruled! I need time to clear my head!" Cabe scrambled aboard the darksome steed and clutched at the reins. Before now, they had been merely for show since Darkhorse obviously did not need to be led. Now, though, they were the warlock's lifeline. He swayed in the saddle as the pounding continued. His entire body felt sluggish. If this was what came of leaving new spellcasters to train themselves, then it was important that they start the new schools as soon as possible. Sorcerers left unchecked might someday gain the potential to ruin the world. It was a wonder it had never happened before.

He looked around. They were still in the stable and the sounds of soldiers outside warned that time was rapidly melting away. Cabe did not want to cause an incident. No one had recognized him so far, but he could not take the chance. "What's wrong? Why are we still here?"

"That infernal explosion has addled me! I cannot summon the concentration to depart! Me! Darkhorse! I *should* kick that prestidigitating popinjay all the way back to his master!"

The warlock put a hand to his head. It did not stop the pain, but it eased the pressure a little bit. "We'll have to ride through the city! Can you do that?"

"They shall have but a trail of dust to mark our time here!"

Mark? That made Cabe think of something else. He did not want anyone following them. Reaching for the U-shaped talisman, he took the item and threw it as far from him as possible. Did the Green Dragon know what was going on in his own kingdom? He was certain the draconian ruler would find all of this interesting. All Cabe had to do was find the time to tell him.

"I'm ready, then!" He heard pounding on the stable doors. Where the stableboy was, he did not know, but he thanked the stars that no one was there to immediately open the way for the guards. "We'll have to ride through the doors when they open!"

"Why wait?" Darkhorse laughed, reared, and went charging toward the thick wooden barriers.

The anxious warlock bent down low and prayed he had concentration enough to shield himself when the doors shattered.

As luck would have it or not, depending on the point of view, the guards managed to open the doors then. They were greeted by the sight of a huge stallion with gleaming blue eyes like the chill of winter coming at them at a speed that allowed no hesitation in choice. Most of the guards made the correct choice and dove to the side. A couple stood their ground, not experienced enough to understand why the veterans were scattering. After all, it was only a horse.

Darkhorse charged through the first one, then *leapt* over the head of the other.

The demon steed roared with laughter as he raced away from the stables. Cabe, still clutching tight, was thankful that none of the men could see that it was the mount and not the rider who was mocking them. Darkhorse was known well enough throughout the Dragonrealm, even if half of those who knew of him thought him legend. If word reached King Lanith that the shadow steed had been in Zuu and that a warlock of considerable skill had been seen with him, it would be reasonable for the monarch to assume that it was the warlock most known for his friendship with Darkhorse. What Lanith would or would not do was a question that Cabe did not want to have to consider.

Through the streets of Zuu the two raced. A few people here and there scattered as the great black beast fairly flew past them. One man actually stood his ground and raised a hand in encouragement as they went by. The last thing they heard from him was, "Aaryn's Spur! I'll give a hundred gold for the next colt he sires! What do you . . ."

They were just out of earshot when Darkhorse turned down a side avenue. Cabe looked up, noticing that they were now heading away from the gates of the city. "Where're you going? This is the quickest way out!"

"But not the best!" The eternal's voice was a subdued roar. It was still doubtful that in the dark anyone could tell that it was him talking. "Look before you!"

He did . . . and saw only the wall circling Zuu before them. There was no gate, only solid stone. "Are you—"

"Since I cannot teleport . . . yes!"

These streets were deserted, the only good thing to happen to them this night as far as the warlock was concerned. Cabe tried to concentrate again, but the headache only grew worse and his body tingled so much that he had to squirm despite his precarious balance. He would have to trust Darkhorse. Darkhorse had not and would not fail him. He would not.

The black stallion leapt into the air and over the wall. The harried mage took one look down at the shrinking world and decided that closing his eyes might be best after all.

They began to plummet earthward.

* * *

The pandemonium at the stable had drawn both natives and visitors and even several minutes after the escape by the unknown rider, many of the spectators were still milling around trying to piece together the story.

The mages, looking disgruntled, perplexed, and dismayed, quickly departed the scene, none of them uttering so much as a single word. Some of the guards, however, were more vocal, the common folk of Zuu liking to tell or hear a good story whenever possible. Soon, a very distorted version of what had happened spread among the populace. There had been a score of riders. A band of spellcasters had been using the stable for their rituals. The king's mages had been practicing, but something had gone wrong and they had summoned a demon out of the ether.

None of the stories was correct, but a careful listener who wandered about could piece together much from what was said, almost enough to re-create the true event.

To a spy clad in the stolen clothing of a murdered merchant, such a thing was child's play.

VII

They had lost two men in the tunnels during the night. Two men suspiciously close to the chamber where Lord D'Farany and the blue devil worked to decipher the monsters' secrets. Two men too many as far as Orril D'Marr was concerned. There was something special about the chamber, something other than the obvious, and he was the only one who suspected the truth. D'Marr was certain that the deaths had to do with a passage that was not there . . . at least not now.

It did not help that he was certain the beasts he held prisoner were laughing at him. Even when he questioned them, put them to the scepter, they seemed to be laughing. There was some great riddle that only they knew the answer to and they were not talking. He had come close to killing one, but for some reason the almost eager look in the beast's eyes had made him draw back.

Lord D'Farany would not hear his suspicions and the damned blue man merely gave him a smug smile each time. If there was a problem, Lord D'Farany had said, then it was up to D'Marr to deal with it. That was his function, after all.

I will deal with it, oh, yes . . . Each time his master descended into the tunnel, the Quel seemed to grow expectant. Each time he returned, they grew morose. The young officer had first thought that they were expecting an attack on the leader of their enemies, but then he saw that his assumption was wrong. The armored beasts *wanted* him to go to the chamber . . . but why?

To discover that reason, he had decided to drag one of the overgrown armadillos to the chamber and try a few tests.

Neither Lord D'Farany nor the northerner was in the chamber. That was as he had planned it. The only ones that D'Marr wanted here were the few men he needed to keep the Quel under control. This was *his* moment.

"Bring him forward so that he can see what I do."

The soldiers dragged the wary beast toward the center of the room. D'Marr removed the scepter from his belt and walked slowly over to his captive. Some of the wariness in those inhuman eyes faded. The Quel had almost become used to the magical rod. It was an enemy that the prisoners understood.

The young officer touched the tip of the scepter against the underside of the Quel's snout. As he had expected, the creature flinched. D'Marr smiled ever so briefly at the puzzlement he could read in the other's eyes. There had been no pain. D'Marr had not activated his toy.

"I know you can understand me, so listen well. There are two things you should note, my ugly beastie." He kept the tip of the scepter no more than a few inches from the Quel's eyes, now and then swinging it back and forth so as to keep the prisoner off-guard. "The first is that you should never think of me as predictable." He tapped the rod against the Quel's snout, this time giving him but the least of the pain levels.

He had the creature's attention now. D'Marr backed up and began to walk about the chamber. He continued to talk as he played at studying its interior. "The second item you should be aware of is that I have not bothered with the speech stone this time. Your answers would only be repetitive. Also, what I need to know from you now does not require words or images."

Out of the corner of his eye, he could see the look of cautious curiosity that had spread across that monstrous visage. D'Marr put a hand on the crystalline device. He sensed the Quel flinch almost as much as when he had put the scepter to the subterranean's head.

The Aramite officer brought the weapon dangerously close to the crystals aligned on the top of the alien creation. Then, as if unaware of both what he had nearly done and the Quel's reaction, D'Marr stepped away. He walked to the far end of the chamber and started pacing the outer edge, occasionally tapping the wall with his staff as he went. The Quel's eyes never left him.

"There are things you are hiding from us, beast." *Tap*. "I have been trying to be reasonable about this." *Tap*. "You must understand, my lord's becoming impatient." *Tap*. "And now your fellow monsters have taken two of our men." Orril D'Marr stopped and turned to face the captive. "Two men very near to this place. Two men, who might have seen . . . what?"

Still facing the Quel, he snapped his arm back and struck the wall beside him soundly with the top of the scepter.

The armored leviathan gave a muffled hoot and tried to leap forward despite being bound. His guards dragged him back, although it took some effort to do so. D'Marr allowed himself a rare full, satisfied smile as he watched the Quel's unsuccessful struggle. Noticing his tormentor's own reaction, a look that might have been equivalent to human consternation crossed the inhuman features.

"Thank you." The wolf raider glanced at the mace. Despite its somewhat fragile appearance, it was very sturdy. The head was not at all chipped. When his predecessor had had it created, he had wanted a weapon that could be used in combat as well. D'Marr was thankful for his forethought. It would take much to even scar the scepter.

He turned to inspect the area that he had struck. It was the same region where, on the first day, he had thought that he had seen another chamber or tunnel. That day, D'Marr had inspected the area and found only solid wall, but he had been nagged ever since by doubt. He was not one to imagine such things. Now, thanks to the Quel's violent and unthinking response, D'Marr was certain that there was indeed a chamber or passage hidden behind the glittering facade.

Even had the Quel not responded as he had expected, there would have been proof of a sort to back his suspicions. Each time he had brought the baton against the glittering wall, he had left a tiny trail of cracked crystal and rock behind him. Yet, despite utilizing the full strength of his arm, his last strike had not left so much as a single scratch in the surface of this section of the wall. It might be that he had happened to strike an area of exceptionally resilient crystal, but D'Marr doubted that. No, there was something special about this particular bit of wall.

The raider officer turned away from the others and ran his hand over the suspect area, as he had done the first day. There was no sign of a break. There was nothing that might betray the falseness of the wall. "Nonetheless," he whispered, "I shall have to tear you down. Stone by stone, if necessary."

"To do that, Orril, would be a most distressing thing to me."

He spun around. "My *lord*?"

As the officer fell to his knees, the Pack Leader slowly entered the chamber. He was accompanied by the blue man and his personal guard. Standing in the tunnel, just beyond the entrance, was what appeared to be a full squadron. Lord D'Farany looked about the chamber, his expression that of a man who is home at last. "You know nothing of the work of sorcery, Orril. Of the intricate matrices that must sometimes be arranged. Of the nuances of concentration, so simple in theory but perplexing in practice." D'Farany stroked the side edge of the Quel artifact. His eyes fixed on a location above D'Marr's head. "Of the *care* one must take. . . . If you understood such things, you would certainly realize what permanently damaging the integrity of this room might do to my prize."

The young officer had *not* considered that. He recalled the minute but very real damage he had already caused the wall. Would that be sufficient to upset the balance of the magical array? If so, then he had handed his own head to the blue man.

"Forgive me, my lord. I had our interests at heart. I'm certain that there's a hidden chamber behind the portion of the wall I was inspecting. The beasts know it; I've watched them. I tricked this one into betraying himself. There may be something, some threat to us, hidden there."

"And so trusting of the Quel, who would seek to trick, you would destroy all this, yes?" interjected D'Rance. The two men locked gazes. The northerner was enjoying this.

"There will be . . . none of that." The Pack Leader actually shuddered, as if the mere thought of any damage to this place physically pained him. He pointed in the direction of D'Marr. "The wall, Kanaan . . ."

"My lord." Bowing, the blue man stalked across the chamber. As he neared his rival, he smirked. D'Marr's grip on his scepter tightened. Given the least of excuses, he would have been willing to strike down the blue devil right there and then.

D'Rance ran both hands over the questionable section. His eyes were half-closed in concentration; he almost seemed in a trance. At last, he turned back to his master and said, "This wall feels like the others, my lord, yes, but I am only a simple soldier." After a moment's hesitation, he slyly added, "He does not seem to have damaged it yet, either."

"There will be no breaking down of walls." To Lord D'Farany, that was evidently the final word on the subject. He turned his attention to the Quel device. D'Marr exhaled quietly. He would find other ways to pursue the matter . . . and take the blue man to task while he was at it.

D'Rance was not finished with *him*, however. The northerner stepped past the Aramite and studied the floor. D'Marr grew still. After a brief inspection, the blue man looked up. "My lord, I fear that there may be damage to the chamber after all. There are several places where the crystal face has been chipped, perhaps by a blunt weapon, yes."

Perhaps I should chip your face with this blunt weapon . . . He readied himself for punishment. There would surely be no escaping it this time.

Lord D'Farany leaned over the crystalline device. He was silent for nearly a minute. Then, "We shall see what will happen, Kanaan. I do not like to execute a man for no reason."

Familiar with his master's ways, D'Marr was not at all comforted by the comment.

"Now come, Kanaan. I can wait no longer."

That there were not only more than a dozen soldiers present but also a Quel as well did not appear to disturb the Pack Leader in the slightest. He only had eyes for the crystalline magic of the chamber. His gauntlets put aside, he carefully inspected each and every major facet of the peculiar artifact.

The blue man, on the other hand, was not at all pleased with the crowd. As he joined the Aramite commander, he asked, "My lord, would it not be better if those unnecessary would depart, yes? They could cause distraction and perhaps also unknown harm. It would be best, yes, if they retreated back to the previous passage even."

"Do what you will," D'Farany responded rather distractedly, his response accompanied by a curt wave of his hand.

Kanaan D'Rance dismissed everyone, including even the guards that D'Marr had brought with him. The sentries urged the Quel to his feet, but as they were dragging him toward the tunnel leading to the surface, the Pack Leader turned his ambiguous gaze in their direction. "Leave it. Orril, the thing is your responsibility."

"Yes, my lord," responded the short raider. He rose quickly to his feet and took control of the prisoner. At his command, the Quel knelt again. Two guards remained long enough to bind the beastman's legs together, then, saluting, they hurried after their comrades.

"Would it not be wiser to—"

"It shall watch, Kanaan. I want it to watch."

There was no argument. One did not argue with the Pack Leader . . . at least not *often* if one wanted to keep one's head.

The raider leader touched several crystals. D'Marr felt a tingle, but it passed away. The Quel was leaning forward, his dark eyes narrowed. *You don't like what you see, do you, beastie? Did you underestimate my lord simply because his world is not always ours? What were you expecting? I wonder.* He observed with care the way the captive followed each and every gesture made by Lord D'Farany. There was growing apprehension in the monster's ugly countenance. This was more than what the Quel had expected, he thought. *He uses your toy like an adept, doesn't he? You expected less of him, didn't you?*

It was then that the chamber . . . *twinkled.* That was the only word that D'Marr thought appropriate. Even though they were well into the depths of the earth, stars now shone bright above them. A thousand points of light sparkled, almost a dizzying effect. Colors from one end of the spectrum to the other danced about like fairies wild and gay. There was a low, almost inaudible hum that seemed to course through the mind. The young Aramite gritted his teeth. The others were either unaware of it or affected in a different manner. D'Marr only knew that it set him on edge, made him want to flee the area. He could not, of course, do any such thing.

"Kanaan . . . I will take the box now." Perhaps it was some trick of his addled perceptions, but D'Marr thought it seemed as if it were a different Lord D'Farany who stood there. This one was almost sane in speech and manner. The eyes were nearly focused on what he was doing. His words did not come out in sometimes random phrases, but rather as complete and, for the most part, coherent statements.

Somehow, it only made him that much more frightening.

The blue man removed a small black box and turned it quickly over to the Pack Leader. Orril D'Marr squinted. He knew what was in the box, but could not fathom what purpose the Pack Leader had in mind for the contents. The thing within was dead, powerless. The Pack Leader had drained it during the initial assault against the Quel. It was nothing more than a memento of the past now . . . wasn't it?

Lord D'Farany opened the box and removed from it the Aramite talisman that he had used to silence the Quel's power.

A muffled hoot made D'Marr glance down at the captive. The Quel had evidently fathomed the raider leader's intentions. He squirmed anew, trying to free himself from bonds designed to hold creatures much stronger than he. D'Marr increased the intensity of his scepter and jolted the Quel back into submission. He would have liked to have asked the beastman what concerned him so, but he had neither the time nor the means to do so. *We will know soon enough . . .*

The former keeper inspected the curved artifact. "There can be no flaw," he explained to no one in particular. "All of my calculations of the past days demand that. Any flaw would mean disaster."

It was no comfort at all to the young raider that D'Rance was just as dismayed by the comment as he was. The blue man took an involuntary step backward and, if anything, was a much paler blue than he had been seconds before.

D'Farany looked up from his work. He gazed at the Quel as if seeing him for the first time. "This device is recent, isn't it? I thought as much. It lacks the care and design of so much else here, yet it holds so much more potential. Why did you build it?"

The Quel, of course, could not and would not answer. This was apparently unimportant to Lord D'Farany. He shrugged and returned his concern to the Aramite talisman and the peculiar creation of the armored underdwellers.

"It is incomplete. I shall complete it for y—for *me*."

With his free hand he rearranged the central pattern, plucking gemstones from their chosen locations and replacing them with others from the array. The Quel started to shake and twist, but still to no avail. D'Marr gave his captive another touch of the rod, but even then the massive figure continued to shift.

Satisfied with his alterations, the Pack Leader added the talisman to the arrangement.

The room crackled . . . and from each point of light a bolt of blue darted toward the Quel creation.

D'Marr covered his eyes and ducked down. The blue man pressed himself against the wall nearest to the entrance to the chamber and simply stared. Beside D'Marr, the underdweller rocked back and forth as if expecting the end of everything.

The wolf raider was almost inclined to agree with him.

Tenuous, frantic strands of light, the blue bolts struck the crystalline device, bathing it in brilliant color. D'Marr felt his hair stand of its own accord and saw that the others suffered the same effect. Only Lord D'Farany, standing within the bright cobalt glow, was untouched . . . at least on the surface.

He was smiling. Smiling as a lover might while in the tender embrace of his desire. It was perhaps a very apt description, the officer realized, for to the former keeper the power that bathed him *was* both his love and desire. The loss of it had killed most of his kind and sent him into madness.

Orril D'Marr was too young to really recall the keepers when they had been at the apex of their glory. He only knew the stories and the few survivors he had seen. He knew that without the will of the Ravager and the work of his most trusted servants, the keepers, the empire had begun to crumble. Part of him had always wondered at the speed of that decay. Why had the great armies so depended on a tiny minority in their ranks?

Seeing D'Farany, he thought he understood. A keeper at the peak of his power was an army unto himself.

The Pack Leader still smiled. His eyes stared upward at the spiderweb of energy pouring into the crystalline artifact. Blue sparks drifted from his fingers whenever he moved his hands. His *eyes* gleamed blue.

With each passing second, the glow surrounding both the Pack Leader and his newfound toy became less bearable. D'Marr turned away, but found himself facing the blinding glow in a thousand reflections. He turned farther, seeking some respite, something that did not reflect the light.

What the raider found instead was the very passage he had been searching for.

A gaping mouth, it was so blatant a sight he could not understand how it had taken him even this long to notice it. He took a step toward it, but then something caught him by the foot, nearly sending him crashing to the harsh floor. The Aramite regained his balance and glanced over his shoulder. He saw the desperate Quel, the inhuman eyes wide, struggling to roll over to him and somehow stop the raider's advance. D'Marr smiled briefly at the pathetic sight, but a sudden change in the Quel's eyes, a change from fear to burgeoning hope, shattered the smile and sent the raider's attention flying back to the secret entranceway.

It was already fading. The same crystal-encrusted wall was slowly re-forming, growing more solid with each passing breath. The Quel suddenly forgotten, D'Marr raced toward the vanishing passage. The wall was still transparent, but that was rapidly changing. Reaching out in desperation, he slammed a hand against it, but his efforts only rewarded him with pain. It was too late to cross through. The split-second delay caused by his gloating had lost him his opportunity.

Still, he had a moment, but only a short one, in which to glimpse what secret lay behind the cursed wall. It was a harried glimpse, made the worse by the lessening transparency of the stone and crystal. Nonetheless, he was able to make out shapes, hundreds of shapes, in a cavern that must have been nearly as immense as the one in which the city lay.

D'Marr saw no more than that. The wall became completely opaque, the stone and crystal completely innocent in appearance.

He slowly turned back to the others and was not at all surprised to find that Lord D'Farany had *just* completed his work. The tentacles of energy had withdrawn; if not for the blue glow about the top of the Quel device, the chamber would have looked exactly as it had before they had entered.

"Not the same . . ." the Pack Leader was muttering. Despite his words, however, a smile had crept across his scarred visage. "Not the same, but so *very* close . . . I will just have to accept that."

His eyes were *still* focused.

"My lord, I shall remove the tooth, yes?" D'Rance looked exceptionally eager. D'Marr momentarily put his discovery aside and started to mouth a protest. He knew, through careful observance, that the northerner had some trace of power. Was it possible that he had more? Did he have the will and ability to control the keeper talisman? That would take more skill than the Aramite had suspected him of having.

His words of protest never left his lips, for Lord D'Farany was quicker to respond. His eyes bore down on the blue man and D'Marr had the distinct pleasure of watching his rival cringe under the intensity of those suddenly alive orbs. "Your readiness to assist me in all is commendable, Kanaan, but you may leave it where it is. There is no more secure place for it now than where it presently stands."

D'Rance assumed a more servile position. "Yes, my lord. I meant nothing by it, my lord."

The Pack Leader had already dismissed him from his attention. Now those eyes focused on the peculiar scene of the Quel lying on his side far from where he had been earlier positioned and Orril D'Marr standing near the wall, *much* too far away from the prisoner that he had been charged with guarding. "And you, Orril?"

The raider wondered how he was to convince Lord D'Farany of what he had seen. An entire cavern lay hidden from the invasion force, yet only he believed—*knew*, rather—that it was there. The Pack Leader and the blue devil had been so engrossed in the spectacle above them that they had missed the unveiling of the Quel's secret.

"Forgive me also, Lord D'Farany. Sorcery is not my realm. I admit to having been somewhat . . . overwhelmed . . . by the results. I've seen things I'd never expected to see."

"*Wonderful* things . . . and there will be so much more . . ." The Pack Leader gazed down at the Quel creation, his eyes filled with great fondness. "We shall do so much together, the two of us . . ."

The eyes were losing focus.

With a last gentle touch, the Pack Leader separated himself from his prized possession and, to neither subordinate's surprise, departed without a word. Kanaan D'Rance remained behind only long enough to look from the device to his rival before he disappeared into the tunnel after the Aramite commander.

D'Marr stared thoughtfully at the wall that had, so far, beaten his efforts to unmask it for what it was. He would have to find another way in than this place, that was all. Perhaps there was another chamber that also shared a wall with the hidden cavern. It would be a simple matter of exploration, of hunting. He excelled in hunting, no matter what the prey. Then, with the aid of his explosive toys, he would create for himself a new and *permanent* way inside. There would be no magic to stop him then.

From the mouth of the tunnel, a wave of black armor flowed into the room. It was the guard contingent Lord D'Farany had brought with him. The ranks split as each man entered, one line moving to the left side of the chamber and the other to the right. D'Marr signaled two of the soldiers to take custody of the Quel. The captive departed without protest, but inhuman eyes watched the young officer until the depths of the tunnel swallowed the creature. The other guards shifted their ranks to make up for the slight loss to their number.

I will have to make measurements, D'Marr thought, returning with anticipation to the project ahead. Too much powder and the explosive would bring down not only the wall but the rest of the cavern as well. *Best to find the proper spot first. Then I can judge how much will be needed.*

There were already men mapping the complex system of caverns and tunnels that made up the Quel domain. While far from complete, he was certain that their charts already revealed enough for his present concerns. With so much importance placed on this particular section of the underground world, it had only been logical to map it first.

He had much work ahead of him, but Orril D'Marr was pleased. He was on the verge of shattering the last hope of the beastmen and discovering what great secret lay in that cavern behind the wall.

The guards came to even greater attention as he passed them on his way out of the chamber, but the raider officer paid their fear of him no mind this time. His only thought was on the coming success of his project and the look on the blue man's face when D'Marr revealed to Lord D'Farany the most closely guarded of the underdwellers' mysteries . . . whatever it was.

They did not know how close they had come.

The Crystal Dragon stirred himself from the self-imposed stupor. Trust the wolf raiders to be both predictable and unpredictable. He had been certain that they would somehow seize control of the Quel's domain. He had been fairly certain that they would have *some* success with the subterraneans' mechanisms. What he had not been prepared for was the *level* of that success. The invaders already had a grasp of the abilities of Quel might. Given just a little more time, they would grow adept. A little more . . . and they would dare to confront him.

He should strike before they grew too strong. He should risk himself, for delaying the inevitable only made the later consequences worse.

How? How do I sssstrike? It mussst be effective but taking the least effort and concentration possible! There cannot be too much risssk. That might lead to . . . If only there had been time to rest. That would have changed everything. They would have been insects to crush beneath his huge paws.

The glittering leviathan twisted his neck around and sought among the treasures he had accumulated over time. Some were there because of simple value, some because of purpose. Carefully he scoured the vast pile. There were times when he had thought of organizing it again, storing it anew in the lower cavern chambers, but that would mean leaving the protection of his sanctum and doing so might prove the final, fatal blow.

Sssomething . . .

Then, to one side of the pile, almost separate from it, the Dragon King sighted the answer to his plea. It was not what he had wanted, not in the least, but the longer he stared at it the more the dread monarch knew it was his only choice. Massive, daggerlike talons gently picked up a small crystalline sphere in which it seemed a tiny, reddish green cloud floated. There was something unhealthy about the cloud, for the colors did not speak of life, but long and lingering decay. The sphere was no larger than a human head, which made it tiny indeed for one such as he, but he had learned care in using this gargantuan form, for even shifting to the manlike image his counterparts preferred was dangerous now. Each transformation distracted him, made him more vulnerable to . . . to the danger of losing himself. Now especially he dared not transform. It might be just enough, combined with his lack of rest, to defeat his long efforts.

He was careful for another reason. What the cloud represented could not be accidentally released full-fledged upon the world, not even for as short as a single blink of an eye.

But what of a tiny fragment of its evil? Might that do?

With the tenderness of a parent holding a newborn babe, the Dragon King brought the sphere to near eye level. A distorted image of his monstrous face glared back at him, but he forced himself to ignore it as he always did.

"Yessss, you could aid me. You could act where I cannot. You could blind them; lead them assstray. Perhaps you could even remove this blight on my kingdom." The Dragon King laughed bitterly. "A blight to plague a blight. So very apt."

He continued to contemplate the sphere. The cloud swirled, briefly revealing a hellish landscape. The crystal artifact was not a thing designed to contain but was rather a door of sorts . . . a door to a nightmare that the drake lord had lived with since almost the beginning.

"Nooo . . ." whispered the crystalline-skinned dragon. "Not yet. I mussst consssider thisss firssst . . . yet . . ." He twisted his head to one side and looked at the deadly cloud from another angle. "If only the decision were not mine anymore."

Lowering his paw, the Dragon King summoned up the images of the raider camp. He stared long and hard at the army and its leaders, memories of another time and another invasion slowly seizing hold of him.

"Ssso very much alike they are," he hissed. "Asss if the world hasss gone full circle."

The malevolent cloud in his paw shifted violently, almost as if it were reacting to the words of the drake. The Crystal Dragon did not notice the change, caught up as he was in both the sights before him and the phantoms stirring anew in his mind. The scenes reflected in the multiple facets blended in with those phantoms, creating a myriad collection of twisted and misremembered pictures.

"Full circle," the Crystal Dragon muttered again. "Asss if a door to the passst had opened up . . ." The gleaming eyes narrowed to little more than slits as the drake lord became further enmeshed in the visions. "A door open . . ."

In the sphere, a storm began to rage.

VIII

It was not until well into the day that Cabe and Darkhorse were finally able to shake off the effects of the mishap with the magical staff. They had dared not enter Legar in such condition and so the two of them had been forced to simply wait. Cabe used the time to first compose a carefully worded message to be sent by magic back to Gwen and the children and then to rest; Darkhorse chose to make use of the wait by constantly grousing about time ever wasted. It was not that the wait was not necessary. Even the demon steed knew better; he could simply not stop himself from complaining over and over again. The warlock knew deep down that what drove his companion to such impatience and bickering was the ebony stallion's own knowledge that with nothing else to occupy his thoughts, the haunting memories of Shade would return. Darkhorse was seriously trying to free himself of his obsession, but it was a monumental task even for him.

Thinking of memories, Cabe could still not recall the night

before without shuddering a little. Darkhorse often forgot that as mighty as his friend was, the warlock was still guided by human instincts and preconceptions. Plummeting earthward from such a height had nearly been too catastrophic an event for the mage's heart. With his own skills in question, he had been forced to rely solely on the eternal. Even as good friends as they were, Cabe could not completely put himself into the care of a being who could never truly understand death as men did.

Fortunately, this time Darkhorse *had* known what he was doing. The shadow steed had landed hooves first on the ground, but the warlock had felt only the slightest of jolts. Such a landing would have shattered the legs of a real horse and killed both animal and rider instantly. Yet Darkhorse had ridden off into the nearby hills the moment he was certain that his passenger was secure and safe.

They now waited in the foothills of southern Esedi, the great western region that had once encompassed the domain of the Bronze Dragon. The kingdom of Gordag-Ai, Queen Erini's birthplace, was actually a part of the northernmost reaches of Esedi. That was not why Cabe had chosen it for sanctuary, though. Rather, he had chosen the location because from where they were they could look down into the northeastern borderlands of Legar.

"It is late, Cabe! How much longer need we wait?"

"How do you feel now?" the spellcaster asked. He presently sat on one of the many rocky outcroppings dominating this hill. This part of Esedi was actually related to the hills of Legar although it lacked the heavy growth of crystal unique to the peninsula.

The dark-haired sorcerer had cause to question his companion's condition. For him, it had been more than an hour since the last lingering effects had finally faded away. The eternal, however, had continued to suffer to some degree, enough to make Cabe hesitate to leave. Darkhorse, being, in essence, magical himself, had been affected much more severely.

In response, the dark stallion suddenly reared and struck out at one of the nearest formations with his hooves.

Fragments rained down upon them as the single blow pulverized the rock and sent it scattering.

"I am ready," concluded the massive steed.

"Then let's leave." He rose and swiftly mounted. In truth, Cabe, too, was anxious to begin the final leg of the journey. He had not wanted to mention anything to Darkhorse, but during his rest he had been visited by yet *another* vision. It had not been as strong as the others, perhaps coming only as a reminder. Still, it had been vivid enough to make him fear that his delays, both accidental and *intentional*, had cost them precious time.

Unlike the others, this vision had consisted of only one scene and a short one at that. Cabe had stood in the middle of the rocky landscape of Legar, but not with Darkhorse. Instead, he had found himself facing an armored figure, a bearded man clad in the same dragonscale of the previous visions. The man was an adversary, but he was also an ally, for even as the warlock had settled into the vision, a black shadow had spread across the land. Both of them had known at the same time that it was coming for them. His companion had pulled out a sword, but it was no ordinary weapon, for the blade was fire-drenched crystal. He had swung the blade again and again at the shadow, cutting it into fragments, but the pieces simply merged and sought them out anew.

The warlock had tried to help, but not even the least of spells had obeyed his will.

Before him, the armored figure had thrown down his sword and raised his hands in what was obviously the beginning of a spell of his own. There had been a look in his eyes, a fatalistic look, that Cabe had discovered he feared more than any threat from the black shadow. It reminded him too much of the eyes of the Ice Dragon. Somehow, he had been certain that the spell would destroy them as effectively as the shadow. It had also been clear that his companion had not cared the least.

He had run toward the man, shouting "No!"

Cabe had been too late.

It was at this point that he had stirred. The vision had lingered a second more, but all that the half-asleep spellcaster could recall was a shuddering sensation of nothingness worse than even what one felt in the empty dimension called the Void. Cabe Bedlam knew that what he had experienced had been a taste of utter *death*.

He had no intention of relating the experience to Darkhorse. The shadow steed might think to leave him behind, something that Cabe could not permit. As much as the latest vision unnerved him, it only made him more determined . . . and more curious.

Cabe had barely settled onto Darkhorse's back when he felt the massive figure stiffen. The eternal was staring out at the western horizon, ice-blue eyes focused on something that his human rider could evidently not see. The shadow steed sniffed the air around them. "What is it, Darkhorse? Something wrong?"

'It may be nothing, but . . . there is a fog or mist spreading across this region of Legar. Can you not see?"

Squinting, he tried to make out what Darkhorse claimed to have seen. The hills near the horizon had a vague, indistinct quality about them, but nothing that would normally make him worry. Then, as he continued to study it, the landscape just a bit closer also grew murky. A minute more and he could no longer even *see* the hills at the horizon. There *was* something there, he finally had to admit, and at the pace it was spreading eastward, there could be no doubt that it was nothing natural.

"It will have engulfed much of Legar already, Cabe."

"We'll have to travel by land, not teleportation. Will the fog cause you difficulty?"

Darkhorse snorted. "I will only know that when we are in the midst of it. What do you say?"

"I don't have a choice, but you—"

"That is all I need to know!" The ebony stallion started down the hillside at a pace and angle that made his rider cringe even though his abilities were now strong enough to protect him from any fall he might have.

Cabe's original intention had been to teleport to a region of Legar that he vaguely recalled from an undesired trek long ago. When he realized just how vague those memories were, however, he had then decided that a better plan would be to use short hops involving line-of-sight teleportation. After all, it was a rare day that did not find the sun-drenched peninsula a clear sight all the way to the horizon. A rare day like today, apparently.

They dared not materialize in the midst of so thick a fog, not when there might be raiders nearby. It was impossible to know exactly how great an infestation there was and it had been risky enough to consider teleporting when the two of them could *see* their surroundings. All of Legar might be under the watch of the Aramites. They were nothing if not efficient in that category.

Regrettably, they were only a short distance into the harsh land when the first tendrils of mist surrounded them. Before they could even react, the fog had already overwhelmed the sky above them. Legar no longer glittered; it was now merely a dull, rocky domain where life struggled. Darkhorse was almost immediately forced to slow to a crawl as the mist continued to thicken at an alarming rate. Cabe Bedlam shivered as they entered the enshrouded realm. The peculiar green and red coloring of the mist did not strike him as healthy for some reason.

"I'd almost swear that the fog surged directly toward us," whispered Cabe. He did not have to whisper, but something about the dank mist made him want to do so.

"That may be. It certainly shifted our direction with superb accuracy . . . and as far as I can ascertain, the wind does not blow hard enough to have done it."

"Do you sense anything out of the ordinary?"

The towering steed unleashed a short, mocking laugh. "I sense mostly that we will be journeying through this muck for some time to come. The fog seems to flow both around me and within. I cannot say that I expected less." He sniffed the air. "There is something obscenely familiar about this muck."

Cabe Bedlam did not understand the last, but he most certainly agreed with the rest of what the ebony stallion had said. With much effort, it was possible to sense his nearby surroundings, but trying to reach out and study the path far ahead was nearly impossible. At best, he had vague impressions of the landscape and the possible knowledge that there were a few life-forms, none of very significant size, lurking about in the strange fog.

Worse, he, too, felt it within, as if it sought to possess him, make him a part of it.

"I have come to the conclusion," mocked Darkhorse, "that the Dragonrealm likes nothing more than to see the creatures who inhabit it existing in constant frustration and despair! Yes, it makes perfect sense to me!" He pawed at the ground, strewing age-old rock behind him as easily as if it had been loose sand. "It will be slow going I am afraid. I might be more willing to risk myself and travel at a quicker pace, but your kind is not as durable. Should something happen, I would never forgive myself.''

The warlock tightened his grip and adjusted his seating. ''I want to get moving, too. Do what you can; I'm more durable than you think, Darkhorse.''

This brought a short but honest chuckle from his fearsome companion. ''You may be right! Very well, hold tight to the reins; you will need them *this* time!''

Darkhorse began to trot, but it was a trot no other horse could have matched. The massive stallion's pace quickly ate up ground. Even despite the swift pace, however, both were careful to keep themselves at their most wary. By this time, Cabe had become fairly certain that the wolf raider camp did exist. It was likely they were still too far away from it to be noticed, but there was still the danger of scouts. The raiders were not the only threat, either. What the Quel might be up to while all this was going on, he could not say, but the warlock was certain that they had to be involved somehow. It would have been impossible for the invaders not to have discovered some trace of them. Likewise, it was improbable that the Quel would share the Crystal Dragon's apparent unconcern about the overrunning of their domain. It was just not the Quel way. Cabe was too familiar with the underdwellers not to understand that.

The fog continued to thicken until it almost seemed they were traveling through a wall of rotting cotton rather than mist. Even after he had given in to the inevitable and had enhanced his vision, the frustrated spellcaster could still see no farther than two, maybe three yards in any one direction.

''It might as well be night!'' grumbled Darkhorse.

''At least we'd be able to see at night,'' returned Cabe. He wondered what things would be like when the sun did set. Could it be any worse than *this*? ''Are we at least heading the correct direction? I can't tell.''

''More or less yes is the best response I can give you, Cabe. This is a malevolent mist; it seeks to turn me in circles, I think.'' Again, he sniffed the air. ''There *is* a foulness here that I know from long ago. I cannot believe that it might be what I think it is, but what *else*? We would have been better off coming here half-dazed and stumbling in the darkness!''

''What can we do now?''

Darkhorse had no answer for that. A depressing silence lingered over the two for some time after. Cabe was certain that it was induced by the sinister haze. It was just too cloying a feeling. No matter how hard he sought to fling it off, it stuck to him.

They journeyed for what was at least three hours by Cabe's admittedly questionable reckoning, but forced to slow down because of the lack of visibility and their inability to sense much farther than they could see, the pair had hardly made any headway in that time. He hoped that anyone else they might encounter would at least be at the same disadvantage. His one fear was that this was a trick of the raiders, yet it would have been extremely complicated to create a spell that would blind one's adversaries but allow one's own army to see. Such a spell would require more than a simple thought. It would require such mental manipulation of the natural forces of the world that it would take days to even prepare for it.

The raiders also suffered from a lack of competent mages, if he recalled one of the Gryphon's earliest messages describing the beginning days of the war overseas. Admittedly, years had passed since that message and it was possible new sorcerers had risen since then, but nothing of that sort had ever been mentioned by the lionbird in any of his later dispatches. The Gryphon would not have excluded such news.

But we've heard nothing from him of late . . . Although that thought would continue to nag him, Cabe was still fairly certain that the fog was not the work of the Aramites. It was not their sort of weapon.

It was only minutes later that they heard the clattering of rock.

Darkhorse halted and swung his head toward the direction of the noise. He said nothing, but twisted enough so that he could meet his companion's eyes. Cabe nodded. One hand went to the short blade at his side. Magic was his foremost weapon, but he had learned to keep other options available.

They remained still. For a time, the only sound was the warlock's quiet breathing. Then they heard the shifting of more rock, closer and more to their right.

The black stallion abruptly raised his head. "I smell—"

A gray-brown form the size of a large dog leapt at Cabe.

The thing was almost upon him before he struck back with a crude but handy force spell. Cabe smelled breath so rancid his stomach nearly turned. The creature howled as it was thrust back from its prey. He had not used enough power to kill it, but the thing was stunned. There was no doubt of that.

Darkhorse did not wait to see what it was that had assaulted them. He reared and came down on the beast's head with both hooves. The skull might have been made from the most delicate crystal, so completely did it shatter under the tremendous strength of the shadow steed's legs.

The warlock turned away in disgust. The massive stallion peered down at the horrendous carnage he had caused, then finally muttered, "Only a minor drake! A *small* one at that!"

"It was large enough for me, thank you. Strange, I didn't even sense it with my sorcery."

"Nor I! It was my sense of smell that did it in and that only when it was near enough to spring!"

Cabe finally forced himself to look down at the mangled corpse of the creature. It was not large by the standards of its kind, but, as he had commented, definitely large enough. Its presence puzzled him, however. "It should've never attacked us."

"Yes, that was its undoing to be sure!"

"That's not what I meant." Cabe pointed at the still form. "A minor drake that small rarely attacks something our size. Maybe if it had been part of a pack, but it seems to be alone."

"That *is* true," Darkhorse conceded. "Perhaps it was confused by this infernal fog."

"Confused and frightened. Maybe more."

"Meaning?"

The human sighed. "Meaning that we had best be even more cautious. I think this fog's as much a danger to our minds and our bodies as it is to our eyes."

Darkhorse shook his mane and laughed. "We are far superior to this hapless beast! We know what this mist can do; therefore we are prepared!"

"I hope so."

They left the corpse and moved on. More time passed, but how much more, Cabe could no longer even estimate. When the twinkle of light caught his eye, the warlock was not certain whether it was a torch or perhaps a star. For all he knew, night had already come upon them. The longer one was trapped in the smothering mist, the duller the senses seemed to become. Still,

Cabe was fairly certain that what he had seen was real, not imagined. He pulled on the reins.

"A simple 'stop' will suffice, you know. I am *not* trained for the reins."

"Sorry." The warlock's voice was low, almost a whisper. "I saw something to"—if they were traveling west . . . *if*—"to the south. A light. It twinkled."

"Perhaps this blasted blanket is finally being thrown back, hmmm?" The eternal looked in the direction his rider had specified. "I see nothing nor do I sense anything out of the ordinary . . . not that there is much ordinary left."

"I was certain . . ." He saw the twinkle again. "There!"

Hesitation, then, "I see it. What would you have me do, Cabe? Shall we investigate it?"

"There doesn't seem to be any other choice. Have you noticed anything else that has had the ability to pierce this thick soup? I'd like to know what that is."

"Then it is settled. Good!"

Darkhorse picked his way carefully toward the glimmer. Cabe noticed for the first time that the shadow steed's hooves made no sound as he crossed the uneven, rock-strewn ground. They had probably not made a sound since the eternal had entered Legar. It was often hard for even Cabe to remember that his companion's external appearance in no way represented what Darkhorse truly was. The eternal simply admired the form. That did not mean that he obeyed every physical law demanded by such a shape. Darkhorse did what Darkhorse *chose* to do.

Below him, the shadow steed snorted in what was clearly anxiety. That bothered Cabe, for Darkhorse was not a being who often grew even the slightest bit nervous.

"I *know* this foulness . . ." he whispered. "I know this stench; I do!"

The light winked out again. The shadow steed halted. The two studied the area before them, but everywhere they looked, they only spotted the same murkiness.

"Where did it go? Do you see it, Cabe?"

"No . . . *there!*" His words were barely audible. Even sound seemed deadened by the murky fog.

Darkhorse followed his outstretched hand toward the light's new location. It was now to their right, which was west, the direction they had been originally headed. The ebony stallion snorted. "How did it come to be *there* now?"

"Magic."

The eternal slowed. "I will not go about this dismal land chasing phantom lights!"

"I don't blame—" The dark-haired spellcaster broke off as he noticed the twinkling light begin to move. "You won't have to! It's coming for *us*!"

Even Darkhorse could not have moved fast enough to avoid it. Cabe raised his arms over his face and summoned a shielding spell that he hoped would halt at least a substantial part of the oncoming juggernaut's power.

The light struck them . . . and scattered into a thousand tinier sparks that quickly faded away, leaving no trace of their fleeting existence.

"Someone wants to play *games* with us?" Darkhorse snorted and looked around for someone or something on which to vent his anger. "I will be more than happy to show them a new game!" He tore at the ground with one hoof, scattering rock.

"Quiet!" Cabe whirled around in the saddle.

"What is it?"

"I thought I heard . . ." Something clinked. It was the familiar and ominous sound of metal upon metal, a sound that from Cabe's vast experience spoke of men in armor. Men in armor who must be *very* near.

He heard it again, but this time it was in front of them. Below him, the shadow steed pricked up his ears, an equine habit learned during those long ago first days when the eternal had first experimented with the form.

A tall black figure coalesced before them.

Of the three of them, the wolf raider was the most surprised by the encounter, but that in no way meant that he was the slowest to react. His blade already out, he moved in on Cabe. There was no question, no demand for surrender, simply a strange, high cry and then an attack.

Darkhorse easily kept himself between the Aramite and the warlock. The raider slashed at him with the sword and Darkhorse, chuckling in an evil manner, allowed the edge to strike him in the neck. It was as if the attacker had tried to cut through solid stone. The blade snapped and the entire weapon fell from the startled raider's hand.

His confused hesitation was all the time the deadly stallion needed. Rising just a bit, Darkhorse kicked the Aramite in the chest. The force of the blow was enough to send the armored man flying back into the mist. Cabe winced as a heavy thud finally put an end note to the raider's haphazard flight.

Where there is one wolf raider, however, there must be others. The Gryphon had often written comments like that in his missives. The Aramites were, for the most part, pack creatures like the animal that was their namesake. Cabe, already cautious, sensed them before he heard them. They were coming from all sides in numbers enough to startle him.

"We've run into a patrol!" he whispered to his companion.

"Excellent! Rather would I fight something real than wander much longer in this thick morass!"

"That's not—" He had not time enough to finish, for the first shapes materialized then.

They moved in with fair but not exceptional precision. It was clear that the wolf raiders were put off by the rank fog, but they had been trained to suffer most any environment in the pursuit of their tasks and so they were adapting as best possible. Listening, Cabe now understood the purpose of the initial cry by the first raider. The Aramites were using it to keep in contact with one another, evidently deciding that stealth was not worth the cost of possibly losing every man to the mist.

"Well?" Darkhorse was suddenly shouting to the oncoming shadows. "Come, come! I have not all day! There are still other tasks I must deal with after I have finished with all of you!"

"Darkhorse . . ." This was not what the warlock had wanted. He had hoped to avoid danger as much as possible, which was one reason he had sought out the shadow steed. Darkhorse, while always willing to face an enemy, generally also respected the safety of his companions. Now, however, he was taking chances that Cabe felt were more than a little risky. The eternal was begging for a fight and it could only be because of Shade again. Wandering through the fog, seeing nothing, the shadow steed's thoughts must have returned to the subject that had become so much a part of his recent life.

It was too late to do anything about it now. The Aramites were coming at them from all directions and it would have been sheer folly to attempt to teleport away. Something within warned Cabe Bedlam that a teleport threatened his life more than this attack.

Two other swordsmen tried to cut Darkhorse's forelegs, but met with the same results as their predecessor. The demon steed kicked one of them back into the fog, but the other managed to avoid the blow. He pulled a curled dagger from his belt and threw it, but at Cabe, the rider, rather than Darkhorse. It still had not registered in the minds of the raiders that the horse was the greater of the threats to them. They assumed that with the rider under control or dead, the battle would be won.

The warlock saw the dagger coming and although he had shielded himself against ordinary weapons, he deflected it, deciding that it was not wise to risk himself because of overconfidence. Then he turned as both his magical senses and his ears warned him of several raiders coming from the rear. A lance came within a yard of him, but with a spell he lifted both the weapon and the man and used them to clear four other soldiers nearby. The spell suddenly went awry, however, and the lancer dropped to the ground like a rock. The raider scrambled to his feet and back into the fog.

"Careless," a voice said.

Cabe looked at Darkhorse, but the stallion was busy dealing with both the raider who had evaded his first assault and two others who had joined the survivor. One was trying to rope the eternal, a foolish maneuver if ever there was one. Darkhorse caught the rope in his teeth and, while the Aramite was still holding it, pulled with such might that he sent the soldier flying into his companion. Both collided with a harsh clang and crumpled to the ground. The soldier who had survived the earlier attack backed away, almost immediately disappearing into the fog. The shadow steed laughed.

Forgetting the voice, Cabe returned to his own dire situation. Where the eternal had no qualms about the destruction of his adversaries, Cabe still felt pain every time he was forced to kill, even though most often it was in self-defense. He held back as much as he could, trying instead to dissuade or knock senseless the attackers. With his abilities suddenly once again in doubt, the warlock felt justified in resorting to flying rocks and tiny windstorms to beat back his opponents.

This did not mean that he was not forced to kill. Some of the Aramites could not be stopped any other way. They brought their own deaths by charging wildly into the storm of rocks. One reached close enough to almost pull Cabe from the saddle. Try as he might, the sorcerer could not free himself and he discovered then that some Aramite weapons would hurt him regardless of his protective spells. The dagger that caught him slightly on the leg was bejeweled and also likely bewitched for just such a battle. Over their long history of war, it made sense that they would learn to deal with spellcasters. In the end, he had struck back out of sheer reflex . . . and had sent a jolt of energy so great in intensity that he had literally burned the man to death in less than a breath.

Still they kept coming. It was almost as if the entire raider force had found them.

"Unngh!" The blow against his head shook Cabe so hard he had to struggle to keep in the saddle. His first thought was that someone with a sling had caught him unaware, but his spell should have protected him regardless. When he heard *Darkhorse* grunt in pain, though, the warlock knew that it was no mundane weapon that had hurt him.

Where was it? None of the raiders he had sensed carried any such weapon. In truth, the greatest danger he and Darkhorse faced was likely not the Aramites, who only had sheer numbers on their side, but rather the malevolent fog, which continued to sap his will and play havoc with his magical abilities.

He kicked out at a swordsman who had somehow gotten past Darkhorse, then shocked the man before he could close the gap again. The Aramites were giving him little time to think. Even as the soldier fell twitching to the earth, Cabe himself was stung. Every bone in his body seemed to quiver. This time, the addled warlock slipped almost halfway off of his companion. It was only quick shifting on the demon steed's part that kept Cabe from falling.

"Cabe! You must hold tight! I cannot fight and maintain your balance!"

"I . . . can't." It was painful just to straighten. He was almost flung off again when Darkhorse spun about to defend his right flank.

"Very well . . ." The ebony stallion almost sounded disappointed with the turn of events. "Hold on as well as you can, Cabe! I will take us to safety!"

The warlock gripped the saddle tight and forced himself to look up. Darkhorse had abandoned the fight and was now clearing a path through the attackers. Several went down, but there always seemed to be more. Arrows struck both warlock and eternal, but Cabe's spell still held and Darkhorse was Darkhorse.

In the midst of the fog and chaos, the weakened spellcaster caught sight of a truly peculiar figure squatting atop a rock formation. The Aramites, who streamed past his very location, took no note of him. The mist partly obscured the figure, but Cabe made out long, spindly legs and arms and an obscenely round torso. The head was mostly covered by a long, wide-rimmed hat that fell down over the face . . . if indeed the odd parody had one.

A spider, was his first impression. *A human spider*.

The entire scene wavered then, but not because of Cabe's condition. Rather, a wave flowed over the area, shaking rider and mount and throwing the pursuing raiders into new turmoil.

Cabe recognized it although he had rarely experienced the sensation before and certainly not of the magnitude of this ripple. *Wild magic*. The term was not quite correct, but it was as close as any description could come to explaining what was happening.

One of the rock formations nearest to them melted. Flat ground began to rise. The warlock heard a scream and located the source just in time to see one of the raiders *fold* into himself and disappear. Several of the Aramites were struggling to free themselves from ground that had become liquefied. An empty suit of armor, half corroded, indicated that something else had happened, but Cabe was in a hurry to discover exactly what that was.

"What . . . what . . . what . . ." Darkhorse was shivering. The demon steed appeared caught in some sort of fit. He was changing, too, becoming stretched out like a true shadow. Cabe felt the saddle move. He looked down and saw that it was sinking into his companion.

The spellcaster threw himself off. The saddle disappeared within Darkhorse as if it had never existed. *Wild magic*. Once in existence, it could create earthquakes, fires, anything. The very fabric of reality would be turned about for the time it existed. Literally anything that magic was capable of doing might happen depending on the intensity of the wave. It could also concentrate in one area, become a well of sorts where anyone who entered became subject to its insanity.

Sometimes it was caused by an irregularity in the natural forces of the world. Most often, it was because some mage had been too careless. Reckless spellcasting could pull and bend those forces beyond safe limits. Sometimes the world repaired itself, but other times it tried to adjust to the new patterns of force and then would come the ripples or waves of pure energy. Pure, unfocused energy.

There was nothing that could be done. Cabe only hoped that the wave would play itself out and leave them alone.

"You! Keeper!"

He realized the voice was directed at him. The warlock twisted around. A gruff, bearded Aramite wearing the cloak of an officer was moving toward him, battle-ax in his huge hands. Cabe felt a buzzing in his head, then saw the small crystal hanging around the soldier's neck. A Quel talisman and one evidently designed to deflect sorcery.

"Stop what you're doing to my men, keeper, or I'll save the inquisitors the trouble of questioning you!"

The title by which the raider called him puzzled Cabe Bedlam until he recalled that to the Aramites the only mages were all of the keeper caste. "This isn't my doing!"

"You lie!" He swung the ax, coming within arm's length of the anxious warlock's chest. "Your last chance! Do it! Don't think you'll be able to take me, either! Your spells won't even touch me! I'm protected!"

"*Are* you now?" came a singsong voice. Cabe recognized it as the one he had heard only moments earlier. "Or *aren't* you?"

To Cabe, the voice cut through all else, demanding his complete attention. Not so for the Aramite, who still waited for the warlock to obey. Then, both of them looked at the crystal, which had, without warning, begun to glow with an internal fire.

The officer snarled. "What did you do?" He reached for the crystal with one hand. "You *can't* have—"

The Quel talisman melted through his breastplate before he

could even finish the statement. He dropped his ax and tried to take hold of the crystal, but it was already too deep for him to reach that way. The raider's eyes widened. He scrambled to tear the chain from his neck but his fumbling, gauntleted hands were too slow.

Cabe tried to help him even before the screaming began, but the man would not hold still and the warlock's spells would still not affect him. There was the smell of burning flesh.

It was over relatively swiftly. The crystal burned through his chest with rapid, unchecked success. When the end came, the Aramite literally had only time to stiffen and gasp before collapsing in a limp heap on the inhospitable ground.

"Not very strong it was. Strong it definitely wasn't."

"Who are you?" Cabe searched for the owner of the singsong voice, fairly certain that it was a strange creature with a round form and long, spidery appendages.

"Cabe . . ." At first he thought that the voice was mocking him, but it was not the same one. Turned about by the sudden series of events, it took him several seconds to recognize the demon steed.

Darkhorse still stood where he had been, but now he was able to move his head a bit. Cabe rushed over to him and would have taken hold of his companion, but Darkhorse vehemently shook his head. "No, do not touch me! I am not yet stable. You might be pulled in. I could never forgive myself for that!"

"Are you all right?"

"Not by far, Cabe! Now I recognize this madness! I thought it impossible. I thought the last traces had perished with Shade, but this is too real. This has the taste of Vraad about it . . . the taste of a cursed realm called *Nimth*."

They both knew of Nimth, the place from which, countless millennia ago, a race of sorcerers called the Vraad had fled into the Dragonrealm. Humans today were the descendants of the Vraad, although from what he had unearthed of them, Cabe would not have cared to call the dark race ancestor. They had flourished briefly in this new world, but had disappeared as a culture, if arrogance and indifference could be considered a culture, before the first generation finally died off.

Yet it was said their world still lived despite the damage they had done to it with their careless, godlike attitudes toward sorcery. Shade had hinted that and he, it had turned out, had been one of them. Darkhorse had even known them, although he refused to speak of that time and could not or would not remember much of it. Some Vraad, it appeared, had had a penchant for torture.

The ground rose under them again, but not much. There were fewer shouts now. Most of the wolf raiders had either vanished back into the mists or were dead. Only a few, either stubborn or trapped by the ever-shifting reality, still remained. At the moment none of them was very concerned with the horse and rider. They were either trying to help fallen comrades or simply trying to survive. "It can't be Nimth, Darkhorse! Nimth is lost, sealed off from everything!"

"Not so sealed. Shade always had a link with it. I tell you it is Nimth . . . or a taste of it at the very least."

"But how?"

"That, I cannot—"

A thing like a nightmare hodgepodge of plant, animal, and mineral formed from empty space. Without preamble, it charged the warlock before it was even fully solid. It had hundreds of vinelike tendrils for legs, reptilian forearms that ended in claws much like those of a crab, and an oval body that resembled a simple hunk of granite. Carved into the center of that was what at first glance appeared to be a crude image of a human face, but the jade eyes that stared with hunger at the warlock and the huge maw that opened and closed, constantly revealing row upon row of sharp teeth, looked real enough. It moved at an incredible speed, considering that each tendril had to push forward to give it momentum. It spattered a greenish slime about as it traveled. Cabe noticed with dismay that the trail it left behind it burned into the hard ground beneath as the monster passed. There was no doubt that it was a magical construct; no creature could have been born so.

"Stand away, Cabe!" Darkhorse demanded, putting himself between the monster and his friend. "I will deal with this abomination!"

The warlock stepped aside, but not to protect himself. There was no way that he could prevent Darkhorse from trying to defend him, but he was also not the kind of man who would let others do battle while he stood by watching.

The magical abomination slowed as it neared Darkhorse. It shifted to one side, as if trying to get around to the eternal's flank. Darkhorse kept the monster before him, which resulted in Cabe ending up behind the shadowy stallion. The warlock started toward the left, but then the abomination moved again and Cabe once more found himself standing to the rear of his companion.

The two leviathans continued to square off. Darkhorse, Cabe knew, was trying to evaluate the thing's abilities. Where anything associated with Nimth was concerned, the demon horse was unusually careful. He had a long and bitter memory of things spawned from that sorry realm.

The warlock once more tried to join Darkhorse and once more the madcap abomination shifted also, again leaving Cabe where he had started. Things were going from bad to worse, for in addition to the beast, the fog was thickening further. Already, both Darkhorse and his adversary were half-hidden from his view and that with the warlock only standing two or three yards from the ebony stallion's backside. If they had to battle this thing blind, there was no telling what the outcome would be. Darkhorse was *not* invulnerable and Cabe thought even less of his own chances.

Despite his wishes, the foul mist continued to thicken . . . no, at this point, *solidify* almost seemed a more fitting word. The magic-wrought beast was already little more than a shape. Not wanting to suddenly find himself alone against a threat that might be able to see when he could not, Cabe decided to risk the danger and come up on Darkhorse from behind. If he could not be at the shadow steed's side, he would at least remain close enough so as not to lose him.

As he took a step forward, however, the abomination backed away an equivalent distance. Darkhorse, needless to say, followed his monstrous adversary. Like Cabe, he had no intention of losing sight. Unfortunately, each step he took seemed to make him fade a little more.

"Darkhorse . . . Darkhorse! Don't follow it! Wait for me!"

Either Darkhorse chose to ignore him, which was not likely, or he could not hear the warlock, for the eternal not only did not reply, but also trotted even farther ahead. Now, not only could Cabe not even make out the vague shape of the magical monstrosity, he could barely even see the outline of the massive stallion.

Dignity aside, the anxious warlock shouted more frantically, "Darkhorse! It's a ploy! We're being separated! Come back!"

He tried running, but for every step he took, his companion took four. Little by little, Darkhorse became a thin shadow in the dank mist. Cabe's shouts went unheeded. Even when he tried to send a burst of sorcerous energy in the shadow steed's direction, the magical fireball only made it halfway before fading to nothing in midflight.

Something tangled in his legs and sent him falling. He rolled around for several seconds, trying to untangle himself from whatever had snared him. Whatever it was, though, it disappeared as quickly as it had appeared. Swearing to Lord Drazeree, the spellcaster rolled back onto his feet and turned his gaze quickly in the direction he had last seen Darkhorse.

Neither the demon steed nor his adversary was in sight. In fact, Cabe could see nothing at all, not even the ground just beyond his feet.

"Darkhorse!" He did not think that the other would hear him and so when there was no reply, it did not surprise him in the least. He was, for all practical purposes, entombed as good as if he had been buried miles beneath Legar's surface.

As dangerous as it might be to teleport in such a magical mire, Cabe knew he had to risk it. He would return to the hills of Esedi and hope that Darkhorse followed suit once he discovered that the human was missing. Then they could decide what to do about Legar.

He was careful and deliberate as he teleported in order to ensure that there was no mistake. A spell that normally would have taken him only a swift thought became an elaborate series of mental exercises, each designed to create success. Although all of that only took him the blink of an eye to complete, to the mage it was an eternity.

What made matters worse was finding himself still lost in the deadly reddish green mist when all was said and done.

"*Tsk*," came the singsong voice from behind him. "Not one of my better. One of my better it certainly was not."

He spun around, seeking the source. "Who are you? Where are you?"

"Good enough, though. Enough to be good."

Cabe squinted. Was the visibility just a bit better? He saw that it was, for now he could at least make out a few patches of ground beyond arm's reach. The fog continued to thin even as he watched. It was becoming too obvious that whoever had spoken must certainly be the reason behind his separation from Darkhorse. The warlock clenched both fists and carefully turned in a circle, seeking with his eyes, ears, and magical senses some evidence of where the culprit was located. This could not be the work of the Crystal Dragon, at least he thought not, and it did not seem the kind of weapon the wolf raiders appreciated.

That only left . . .

Then he saw the rock, a vague, miniature hill just off to his left. Atop the rock, spindly arms and legs bent, squatted the same outlandish form he had noticed earlier, the form he was certain had been responsible for the raider officer's gruesome death.

The fog parted slowly but certainly from the rock and its lone inhabitant. Cabe saw that the figure was more or less human, but as oddly shaped as anything he had ever seen. The bizarre figure was clad in a strangely patterned courtier's suit of purple and black that would have looked clownish on any other person but somehow was perfect for its present wearer and not just because of its shape. The hat's flap still covered most of the face. All he could see was a chin that ended in an almost extreme point.

The head lifted a little, allowing him then to see the curved line that was all there was to the mouth. "I am Plool the Great," the spidery figure abruptly said. Other than raising his head, he did not move, not even to remove his hat. "The Great Plool I am."

Cabe Bedlam shivered as he became aware of what it was he was facing here. Plool was at home in the foul mist. He manipulated it to his own desires in the manner of someone long accustomed to the practice. Yet Darkhorse had called the fog a thing of twisted, decaying Nimth, the hellish place from which the mage's own ancestors had fled.

He had never thought to wonder if perhaps some had *not* fled Nimth. He had never wondered what they or their descendants might have become, living as they did in a world where the natural laws had all been torn asunder and wild magic flowed forever unchecked.

Plool could only be a *Vraad* . . . and now he was loose on the Dragonrealm.

The missive from Cabe in no way calmed Gwen. She paced the floor of their bedroom, cursing the fact that she could not be with him. It *had* been her own idea to have one parent remain behind. Her own parents, long, oh, so long dead, had instilled in her the need for someone to be there for the children. Cabe was of the same mind, although the enchantress did not doubt for one moment that he would have also raised a protest if it had been her task and not his.

None of which made the waiting any easier. The magical message that she had received had given her a brief rundown of Cabe's time in Zuu, but knowledgeable as she was where her husband was concerned, the Lady Gwen knew there was more to the story than what he had written. His tale of King Lanith's rather heavy-handed recruiting of mages reminded her too much of the days when Melicard had sought out spellcasters, talismans, and even demons in his quest to eradicate the drake race. Lanith's ambitions would have to be looked into and not just by her. Toos and Melicard probably knew all about this already, which somewhat infuriated her since they had not seen fit to pass on that bit of knowledge. One was never certain just how much information was being held back at the "councils" she and Cabe attended with the two monarchs.

It was not the gathering of mages that bothered her, though. It was the thought that more had happened in Zuu. She could not help feeling that perhaps Cabe and Darkhorse had not simply entered Zuu, stayed there for a time, and departed. Because of that feeling, she wondered what else her husband might have left unsaid and what dangers he might still have to face.

Worry doesn't help him, she angrily reminded herself. It made her feel no better. Gwen sighed. There were other things that needed to be taken care of. Perhaps, she hoped, they would be enough to keep her from dwelling too much on what might be happening to the man she loved.

As she departed the bedroom, she almost walked into a figure just beyond the doorway. The other caught her in his arms and held her just a second too long for her tastes. She freed herself and backed a step away before realizing that doing so only added to the newcomer's amusement.

He was tall and lean, with arrogant but striking features that had many females, human and drake, eyeing him with speculation that he often encouraged. His eyes were narrow, burning orbs that could snare a person and almost make one kneel. He wore a tight-fitting, emerald and gold suit reminiscent of those of the royal court of Gordag-Ai. Gwen knew that he had chosen this particular one in part because it appealed to her tastes. Kyl and the younger drakes wore real human clothes, not magical constructs formed from their own skin, which was what the elder drakes often did. It was not quite the same color combination as his skin, which was a more elegant mixing of the green and gold, but it was still eye-catching. Still, Kyl could have probably created a perfect duplicate if he had wanted to do so. His skills were much more advanced than those of his older counterparts. Sometimes, the Lady of the Amber thought that they were *too* advanced.

"What are you doing up here, Kyl?"

He gave her a sly smile that long practice had made overwhelming against many a maiden, but Gwen simply had to look at the slightly edged teeth to remind herself that this was indeed a drake, not a man. "Your pardon, Lady Gwendolyn. I should not walk with ssssuch hasste. I hope that you were not disturbed in any way."

She held back the smile that she wanted so badly to display to him. Kyl, for all his perfection, still slipped back into drake sibilance more often than either his brother or his sister. He especially had difficulty when he was in her presence. "And what brings you here in such haste?"

"I come to tell you, gracious lady, that the Manor has visitorsss."

"A servant could have told me that." Try as she might, the enchantress could never warm to Kyl. He was always trying to be near her or, more to her dismay, near Valea. The young heir to the Dragon Emperor throne was always good with her daughter, but his constant "accidents," which always somehow involved touching Gwen, made her worry about the future. It would not be long before Valea was old enough to truly gain the attention of males. In that respect, she was already too pretty now. "You need not have troubled yourself so."

"These are special visitors, my lady. Ssspecial visitors demand special treatment."

"Who are they?" She could recall no one that she was expecting.

"They are clothed so as not to be recognized, but one hasss shown an insignia given to him by the Blue Dragon himself!"

The Lady Gwen ignored the way Kyl's eyes lit up whenever he mentioned another Dragon King. *Emissaries from Irillian? But why disguised, then?* "Lead me to them."

Kyl led her through the Manor and out the front. Any other time, the sorceress would have enjoyed a walk through the grounds. Kyl's close presence and the mystery of the two visitors, not to mention Cabe's situation, made that all but impossible.

The two visitors indeed resembled monks more than emissaries. Nothing but cloth was visible, but she thought that the taller of the two had to be the male that the drake had mentioned. The unknown duo stood just beyond the invisible barrier that protected the Manor grounds from unwanted guests and marauding beasts, which sometimes turned out to be the same thing.

"I am Lady Gwendolyn Bedlam. Before you say anything, let me see the ring that you revealed to the boy here." She heard Kyl hiss quietly. Perhaps he would stop trying to play her now that she had dropped him down a few levels. It was good to remind him on occasion that while he was the heir to a throne, he was also under *their* guardianship.

It looked as if the one she had directed her demand to was about to say something else, but then he shrugged and raised a hand toward her. The sleeve fell back. The enchantress glanced down to study the ring.

When she saw the hand that wore the ring, however, all interest in the Blue Dragon's gift vanished.

The hand was covered with *fur*, which by itself was unusual enough, but then Gwen noted a trace of *feathers* toward the wrist. Astounded, she looked up. With his free hand, the visitor was pulling back his hood. A dignified but weary avian face had been hidden under that hood. Toward the back and sides, the feathers gave way to fur. It was as if someone had crossed a lion, a bird of prey, and a man together.

"It's good to see you, my lady," the Gryphon politely whispered.

She could only gape. After so *long* . . .

"You have not changed, Lady Gwen," the Gryphon added when no comment was forthcoming from the enchantress. "Still as beautiful as ever."

"You . . . You're here!"

"That we are." There was something sad in the way the monarch of Penacles said that, but Gwen was still too shocked to really take note of it.

Her head jerked toward the other traveler. "Then, this must be—"

The smaller figure pulled back the hood. Again, the sorceress was taken aback. She had never met the Gryphon's bride, only corresponded with her. Seeing Troia now proved to Gwen that imagination had hardly readied herself for the truth. She was, as the Gryphon had first related, a cat woman.

More woman than cat, Gwen could not help noticing. Even the cloak could not completely hide the lithe body underneath. Every movement, no matter how small, was fluid. Her features were exotic. Her dark, arresting eyes, so truly catlike, were half-veiled. She had a tiny, well-formed nose that twitched now and then and long, full lips ever so inviting when she smiled. The hair on her head was cut short and went from pitch-black to dark brown. A closer glance revealed that the tawny, striped coloring was not her skin, but rather a short layer of fur that, if the enchantress recalled correctly, covered her entire body.

Seeing her for the first time, Gwen could not help but feel a little relieved that Troia had come here as the mate of the Gryphon and not a single female. Aurim was already too susceptible to the charms of women.

Only one thing marred Troia's appearance and that was the row of scars on the right side of her face. They did not succeed in detracting much from her beauty, but they made one curious. The Gryphon should have been able to remove them with ease. His sorcery was easily on a par with that of the Bedlams.

She realized she had never finished greeting the cat woman. "I have waited so long to actually see you, Troia!"

"And I you, Lady Gwen." Again there was the hint of sadness that the enchantress had first noticed in the Gryphon. What was wrong?

"May we enter?" asked the lionbird. "I was not certain if the barrier would still admit me and I knew that it would not admit Troia. Also, politeness dictated that we ask *permission* to enter." He glanced at his bride as if this had been a minor point of contention between them. From their letters, Gwen had been given to understand that there were times when Troia could make her look like a shrinking violet in comparison.

"Where are my manners? Of course, you can enter here!"

The duo stepped forward with caution. The barrier had various ways of dealing with outsiders, many of them seemingly of its own design. Having been given permission by the lady of the land, though, neither the Gryphon nor his mate was hindered in any way.

Gwen turned to Kyl. "Kyl, if you would be so kind as to alert someone that we have special guests, I would like some food and drink ready by the time we reach the garden terrace. Would you please do that for me?"

The drake lordling bowed gracefully to both his guardian and the two newcomers. "I should be happy to, my lady. If you will excussse me, Your Majessstiesss?"

The Gryphon tried to hold back a hint of amusement that had dared to rise against the sadness. "By all means."

With a surreptitious glance at both Gwen and Troia, the young heir departed. The three watched until he had disappeared from sight, then returned to their conversation.

The Gryphon shook his head, whether amused or annoyed by Kyl's ways, Gwen could not say. "I had not thought about how near to adulthood the hatchlings truly were. Aurim must be almost a man, too."

"Very much so, although there are lapses. One expects those, however, at his age." Something had been nagging at the red-headed sorceress's memory and now she knew what it was. "And where—"

Troia's eyes widened and the Gryphon raised his other hand in a request for silence. Gwen noticed with horror that two fingers, the lower two, were *missing*.

"*Gryphon!*"

He sighed. "I see there is no purpose in holding back."

"Tell her, Gryph," the cat woman hissed. "Tell her why we've braved pirates and raging sea storms to come to her."

The lionbird took hold of his wife, who shook as if every fiber of her being wanted to cry out at the world. Gwen's face went grim; she suspected that she already knew the answer to the question that the Gryphon had prevented her from finishing. *Rheena, please let it not be true! Let me be wrong!*

"You were going to ask about our son, Demion, were you not?"

"Yes, but—"

The Gryphon, his eyes chilling, would not let her continue. "Demion is in Sirvak Dragoth, Lady Bedlam, his home forever more now." His voice was toneless. "He died at the hands of the wolf raiders."

IX

For twenty minutes they had sat together in the privacy of the garden terrace and for twenty minutes Gwen had been unable to come any closer to the story behind the terrible words the Gryphon had spoken concerning his son. In truth, only she and Troia sat; the lionbird stood staring off into the main garden, his claws sheathing and unsheathing, his mane stiff. Neither he nor his bride had spoken more than a handful of words since their arrival.

Troia stared at her husband as if nothing else around her existed. *That may very well be the case to her,* the enchantress pondered. *With Demion . . . dead . . . they can only turn to each other.*

Still, there were limits to her respect for their turbulent emotions. It was clear that they had been dwelling on their loss since before their voyage, certainly a long time. Gwen did not believe that they should simply forget the loss of their sole offspring, but she was one who believed that life should go on, if only in the very name of the one who had been taken from them.

"Gryphon . . . Troia . . . I share your grief, you certainly must know that, but I need to know what happened; I need to know and I think you need to tell me.''

''You are correct, of course, my Lady of the Amber. I have been remiss.'' He turned back to the two women. A table stood between them, a table with food and wine. Neither had been touched even by the enchantress, but now the Gryphon took the decanter and poured some of the glistening plum wine into one of the gold and silver chalices. Quite suddenly, the avian features transformed into those of a handsome, silver-haired man with patrician features. That image, though, lasted only long enough for the lionbird to swallow the wine in one swift gulp.

The Gryphon returned the goblet to the table, then glanced at his wife. ''I will make this short . . . for all our sakes.''

She nodded, but said nothing more. A look had come into her eyes, but one directed toward neither her mate nor the enchantress. It was a look that could have only been directed toward the unknown wolf raiders who had stolen a precious life from her.

''How did it happen?'' Gwen encouraged. ''Is the war—''

He seemed to dismiss the war as something inconsequential to the topic. ''The war goes well. Morgis and the Master Guardians of hidden Sirvak Dragoth have helped lead many of the former slave states of the empire to freedom. We have also done our small part.''

Small part, indeed! thought the flame-tressed sorceress. She knew, through missives sent by the drake Morgis, of the many things that the Gryphon had accomplished. He, more than any other individual, had been the driving force behind the continent-wide revolt against the sons of the wolf. It was odd that she and Cabe had learned much of what they knew from one of the get of the Blue Dragon. It was odder still that a drake could become so loyal a friend and companion to the Gryphon. From respectful adversaries to comrades-in-arms.

''The war goes well,'' he repeated, ''but because of it, the Aramites grew—have grown—more desperate and treacherous in their actions. When we overthrew Luperion, they began to gather their forces in and around their original homeland, especially in Canisargos, the seat of their power.'' The Gryphon paused and gazed forlornly at his hostess. ''Lady Bedlam, Gwendolyn, you have to understand that we are not like your kind. I was created a hunter and Troia's people are born that way.''

"I made my first raider kill at the age of eight summers," whispered the cat woman. Her eyes were narrow slits. "Three of my brothers made theirs at seven. It's the way we are."

The lionbird nodded in agreement. "What I try to say is that Demion was not unfamiliar with the war. He had fought and made his first kill only months before . . . and that far, far later than he could have. We had barely been able to keep him in check for these past four years and believe me, we *tried*."

Gwen nodded, understanding. She understood quite well what it meant to grow up in wartime.

"Chaenylon, it was." The monarch of Penacles unsheathed both sets of claws again. "Chaenylon, which will forever mean despair to us."

They had only taken the Aramite port city some three months before, but in that short time it had quickly become a valuable part of their western campaign. Chaenylon gave them a new location to ship supplies to the forces ever inching closer to the heart of the empire, Canisargos. After all these years, the empire's great citadel was within striking distance. The Aramites had always been more willing to give up their slave states rather than leave Canisargos anything but much overdefended. Now, not even that would save them. The confederation of free kingdoms, with the help of the Gryphon and Duke Morgis, had put together a combination of armies that would soon launch an attack in the direction of the Aramite city. It was possible that the wolf raider empire would cease to exist within the next three years.

That did not mean that the raiders would be defeated. There would be pockets of resistance for years and more than a few ships had slipped away into the open sea.

Gwen flinched when she heard the last. She had still not told her guests of the wolf raider rumors, in part because she feared that they would leave the moment they knew, but also because she herself *needed* to know what had happened overseas.

"Either they knew about the impending attack or it was pure bad fortune, but whatever the case, one morning Chaenylon itself came under assault. *Six* warships simply sailed in. The harbor was madness. They utilized special catapults to bombard the city. There were gryph—gryphon riders everywhere. Worse, from every ship there came an armed force. We turned back the first wave, but there was no way of keeping the second from landing.'' The lionbird's eyes lost their focus. He was once again in the midst of battle. ''Western Chaenylon was in flames. The Aramites seized control of the docks, then spread through the city.''

Lady Bedlam recalled the siege of Penacles long ago. She and Cabe, fleeing the Dragon Kings who had sought the grandson of Nathan Bedlam, had been given refuge by the Gryphon. The drakes had not taken kindly to that. For days, they had tried to take Penacles. While the battle had never quite escalated to the sort of fighting that the defenders of Chaenylon must have gone through, it had been terrible enough. She could only imagine what her two guests had suffered through.

''We can never be certain of what happened.''

''We know *enough!*'' hissed Troia. ''We know that it was D'Farany again or at least one of his puppets!''

''Yesss, we know *that*. We know it was D'Farany's curs, Troia, or else why would we be here in the first place?'' Gwen would have spoken then, but the Gryphon, not noting her reaction to this latest revelation, continued with his horrific tale. ''It happened during the fighting. We thought he would be safe where we had placed him. Understand, Lady Bedlam, that we valued Demion above *all* else. He was our pride. Despite his desires, we kept him away as much as we could, but no one could count on wolf raider tenacity.''

They had moved Demion and several others to what was considered the safest quarter of the city. Well behind the haphazard line of fighting. Not only was there a line of defense to protect him, but there was also little in that quarter that should have interested the raiders. Chaenylon had been one of the empire's centers for cartographical study and thus great archives housing much of the sum of their seafaring knowledge had been built there. Maps dating back thousands of years were stored in the archives as were the most current. Whether drawn up by the Aramites themselves or stolen from some captured vessel, the maps were all carefully stored for future use. Much of the region where Demion had been placed was simply an outgrowth of those archives. There were only small stores of weapons and food there. Anything of true value to the invading force should have been near the fighting.

Yet, someone among the raiders had evidently found some need for those maps. Enough need to send a small but efficient force to hunt down the archives. They had somehow slipped past the lines, a trail of dead sentries marking their way. Their target they reached with minimal resistance, for everyone's attention was on the main struggle. Once inside the buildings, they had proceeded to ransack the archives.

There it was that they had also evidently come across Demion, who had left the safety of the building he had originally been housed in by his parents.

Here again the Gryphon straightened. His mane bristled and his voice was both proud and bitter as he added, "We know that he and a few soldiers evidently with him gave of themselves the best they could. Nine raiders met their end there, three of them definite kills by our son." He clenched his fists together. "But there were more than nine."

"And the coward that *cut* him down did so from behind!" roared the furious and frustrated cat woman. She was on her feet in an instant, her own claws flashing in and out as she no doubt pictured the scene in her mind.

Despite barely being able to keep her own composure, Gwen responded in soothing tones. "But he did not let them take him without paying for it, Troia, Gryphon! He did not let himself be taken without payment. He fought honorably to the end. I grieve for your loss, but it is the good memories of him you must keep in mind from here on. The memories of what he was to you and how he will *always* be with you no matter where you are." She was aware how different the thinking processes of the two were compared to that of either herself or Cabe. Both the Gryphon and his mate were civilized, but they were also predators, more than even humans were. She could only hope that her quick words carried some meaning to them. "Demion would want you to be looking forward, not dwelling in a maelstrom of hurt and anger."

"We look forward, Lady of the Amber. We look forward to the final hunt, the snaring, and the running down of the curs responsible for his death." The Gryphon's part-avian, part-human eyes glared at the empty sky. Both he and his bride calmed a bit, if only on the outside. "Curs who have run to the Dragonrealm, if what we discovered is true."

"The Dragonrealm?" It was a verification of everything she had feared, but Gwen did not reveal that fear to the duo.

Unwilling to sit down again, Troia began to pace gracefully back and forth. "In the end, we repulsed the damned dogs' attack. They lost two ships there, but Chaenylon was in ruins. It took us the better part of the day to discover . . . his body. Whether the raider who killed him returned to the ships with the other survivors or died in the city before he could flee, we'll probably never know, my lady. I wish we would . . . I'd follow him personally to the ends of the world . . . What we do know is that they seemed most interested in charts concerning the Dragonrealm."

"And we discovered then that three of the ships never returned to the empire," interjected the Gryphon. "Three ships, including the one carrying Lord D'Farany."

"You mentioned him twice now . . . who is he?"

"He is a keeper, Lady Bedlam. An Aramite sorcerer."

His words struck her with the force of a well-shot bolt. Having kept abreast of the distant war since its inception, the enchantress was aware of most of the major events. There was one in particular she recalled about the sinister keepers. "But they all died! Almost twenty years ago!"

"Died or gone *mad*, you mean? Lord Ivon D'Farany did not die; as to whether he went mad, that is another question."

"Even still, he should be powerless!" Was Cabe heading toward a confrontation with a sorcerer of the darkest arts? "You said they—"

"Had lost their link with their god, the unlamented Ravager, yes. You recall correctly. That loss, that withdrawal, was enough to kill most of them and leave the others mindless." He squawked. "Somehow, a young keeper named D'Farany survived and although it cannot be vouchsafed that he had no power of his own, he has time and time again brought forth sorcerous talismans and artifacts that were thought lost and used them to the raiders' advantage." The lionbird held up his maimed hand. "This is the work of Lord D'Farany; even my skill is insufficient to heal it proper. Troia, too, bears the mark of one of the keeper's discoveries." She turned so that Gwen could better see the scars across her face. For the first time, the enchantress noticed that they *glowed* ever so slightly. Glowed bloodred. "He, more than anything else, has slowed the course of the war by at least three, perhaps four years."

"And he does all this even though the dogs themselves mutter about his sanity!" Troia snorted, still pacing about.

Her quick, constant movements were disrupting Gwen's attempts to remain calm. "You think he's here."

"He *has* to be," the lionbird returned, almost pleading again. "There is no other place for him to hide so great a force. He cannot stay anywhere near the empire or the free lands. D'Farany, by abandoning the war, has in a sense made himself enemy of both. That is why he must be here."

"What about the war? What will happen with you gone?"

He looked closely at her. "The war now moves well even without us and especially without D'Farany to aid them. We have given more than a decade of our own lives in addition to the life of our one child. There was no one who did not think we were entitled to depart. I did not abandon them. In fact, Sirvak Dragoth would only be too happy to see an end made of the curs. D'Farany and his men, as long as they live to fight again, will forever be a fear covering the freed lands and the surrounding waters."

"We'll find him, my lady," hissed the cat woman. "He killed Demion as good as if he were the one who struck the blow. His death alone will pay for our son's."

The anxious sorceress could not help but blurt, "Do you truly think so?"

Neither of them could look at her then, but Troia slowly replied, "Nothing else will balance that scale, not even . . ." She held her tongue at the last moment, apparently unwilling to share some further revelation with her host. "Nothing."

"The voyage across did nothing but stir the embers to new life," the Gryphon added. It seemed whenever one faltered, the other was there to continue the tale. To Gwen, it revealed just how close the duo were to each other and in turn how close they had been to their son. "When we arrived on the shore of southeastern Irillian, I was barely able to control my desire to use sorcery to speed our journey to here along. Out of respect of the Blue Dragon, I held off until we reached the borders between his domain and that of the Storm Dragon. Then I found I could not wait any longer. Daring the lord of Wenslis's ire, I teleported us from his lands to the ruins of Mito Pica, just beyond your forest. We would have even materialized at the very border of your domain, but the Green Dragon has ever been a good neighbor to Penacles and I would not wish to cause my former home any ill will.''

''We've told you our story, Lady Bedlam.'' Troia stalked up to the enchantress, then nearly went down on one knee just before her. ''Gryph said that if anyone could help us, if anyone had some word, it would be the Bedlams.''

The Gryphon stood beside his mate, the maimed hand on her shoulder. ''Even if you have no word of the raiders, I ask that you might grant us the boon of letting us stay but one night so that we might be refreshed for the hunt ahead of us. You have my word that I will make amends for the trouble.''

She looked at them, at their eyes that both pleaded and hoped, and wanted to say that she had heard nothing. Like Darkhorse with Shade, they were obsessed. Gwen could not find it in herself to lie to them, though, possibly because she knew that under the circumstances she would have acted the same way.

''We think the wolf raiders are in Legar.''

They stood motionless before her, not at first comprehending her blunt statement.

''Cabe is there . . . and Darkhorse, too.''

The Gryphon did not question her reasons for not volunteering the information earlier. Perhaps he understood that she had wanted to hear his tale first. Instead, he asked, ''How long ago? Where exactly?''

Troia stood up and clutched his arm. Her claws dug into it, but the Gryphon did not seem to notice.

''We do not know. Cabe—and Aurim—had a vision. Then, Cabe had another. They were peculiar, but both pointed to Legar. Both pointed to the Crystal Dragon . . . and wolf raiders.''

''The Crystal Dragon.''

Familiar with the Dragonrealm only through the stories told by her husband, Troia did not note the significance. ''Can we speak with this Dragon King? Will he aid us?''

Again, the lionbird's mane bristled. ''The Crystal Dragon is not like Blue or Green, both of whom we might appeal to under certain circumstances. He is like none of his counterparts, Troia. He and his predecessors have ever been reclusive. He will toler-

ate those who, for one reason or another, find themselves travers-
ing the peninsula, but woe betide anyone who seeks to disturb
his peace. It was he who helped turn the tide against one of his
own, the Ice Dragon. Without his aid, the Dragonrealm might
now be a dead land under an eternal sheet of ice and snow.''
The Gryphon grew contemplative. ''Tell me about Cabe and his
journey. Tell me everything.''

Gwen did, describing the visions, the Bedlams' decisions, and
the attack on the person of the Dragon King Green. The Gryphon
tilted his head to one side during the telling of that incident and
also the mention of the black ship in the vision. Cabe's missive
from Zuu particularly attracted his attention. New life had come
into his eyes, but it was still a life dedicated to one cause, finding
the ones responsible for his son's death.

''Zuu. I remember Blane. His horsemen.''

''And Lanith?'' asked the enchantress.

''He is unknown to me and hardly a factor in this.''

She did not think so herself, but telling the Gryphon that was
not so easy. ''You're planning to go there.''

''Yes.''

''We should leave before the sun sets,'' urged Troia to her
mate.

He gave her an odd look, even for his avian visage. Then,
with some hesitation, he said, ''You are not going with me. Not
to Legar. Any other place, even the Northern Wastes, I would
take you, but not *Legar*.''

''What do you *mean*?'' The fine fur along the back of Troia's
head stood on end. ''I will not be left behind! Not now!''

''Legar is the one place where the risk is too great for the two
of you.''

Gwen glanced from one to the other. *The two of you?*

''Any other time, any other *place*, I would welcome you at
my side, Troia, but I will not lead you into Legar.''

''I'm far from helpless, Gryph! My stomach is not yet
rounded!''

She was pregnant. The enchantress cursed her own words. If
she had only known, she would have spoken to the Gryphon in
private. Like Queen Erini, Gwen was not the kind to sit demurely
to one side while others did the fighting, but one thing she found
very precious was the creation of new life. Chasing after wolf

raiders was terrible enough, but to do so now and in the domain of the unpredictable and possibly malevolent Crystal Dragon was sheer folly for an expectant mother, especially after having lost her only other child.

It was clear that they had discussed this issue several times in the past and it was clear that Troia had always won. That there should be someone capable of matching the Gryphon in stubborn determination would have been amusing under more pleasant circumstances. Now, however, it only threatened to muddle the situation further.

"Troia, you are with child?"

The cat woman spun on her, then recalled herself and settled down. She seemed more worn out than she had been before her burst of anger at her husband. "For these past eight weeks. I thought at first it was sickness from the trip; we're not fond of the sea, either of us. It stayed with me, though, and I soon recognized the symptoms from—from Demion's time."

"You have grown tired quicker these past few days, too," the lionbird reminded her. "In truth, I was beginning to worry even before we landed." His voice was more understanding, more concerned. Both he and his mate were mercurial creatures.

The years have changed you, Gryphon, or perhaps merely opened you up more. The sorceress studied Troia. Despite the litheness of her body, there were hints here and there of aging that had nothing to do with the years of war. How long did the cat people live? Troia had little or no sorcerous ability, which meant she, like King Melicard, would age faster than the one she loved. For that matter, it had never been clear just how long the Gryphon would live if permitted to die of old age. He was not like Cabe or Gwen; his life span might be as long as that of a Dragon King or maybe even *longer*. Likely he had thought about that, which meant his time with his wife was all the more precious to him. To know that her life span was limited in comparison to his . . . it only added to the importance of seeing that this new child was allowed to enter the world happy and whole.

And she has had only one child in all this time, the enchantress pondered, still studying the anxious cat woman. *This may very well be her last chance.* There was no doubt, either, that Troia very much wanted this child. From what little Gwen knew of her kind, they generally had many children. Troia, however, had only had the one and among her people children were precious and well cared for. She could not afford to lose this one.

"We made a pact that we would follow this through together, Gryph!"

The Gryphon flexed his claws again, but the action was not directed at his bride. "You will be with me, Troia, I promise you that. I also promise that I will return with D'Farany's head if need be to show you that Demion has been avenged, but I see now I must do it alone."

"You will not be alone, Gryphon," Gwen quickly pointed out. "My husband and Darkhorse are there ahead of you. Find them. Their quest is tied to yours." *And see to it that Cabe comes back to me!* she silently added.

"There is that." He took his wife in his arms. She was stiff at first, but then she took hold of him in a grip that vied with his own for pure intensity. "I know the Dragonrealm, Troia. Believe me when I say that this is one place I will not risk your health and that of our offspring. You know why Lady Bedlam remains behind; do you consider her any less than her husband because of that?"

The cat woman locked gazes with Gwen. "No. Never. I've known her too long in letters to believe foolishness like that. If only I could come, though! I left Demion in that place!"

"*We* left Demion in that place. There was no way either of us could have foreseen what happened." He squawked, the equivalent of a sigh. The Gryphon had a habit of switching between his human traits and his animalistic traits without thought. "We came to hunt and we will hunt, but this time I must make the kill alone. I will, too."

The tall sorceress shivered. Again, she was reminded that her guests were not to be completely judged by human standards, but that was not all there was to it. The war and Demion's death had indeed changed the Gryphon the way the Turning War never had. *It's become much too personal. Would that I could keep him from going, too.* Yet she welcomed his coming, for it meant more hope for Cabe.

"You will need food and rest, Gryphon. I will not allow you to leave until you have had a bit of both."

He nodded his thanks, then looked back down at his wife. "If the Lady Bedlam permits it, I would prefer you stay here. There is no better place for you than with her.''

''There's one place,'' Troia corrected him. ''That's with you.''

''After Legar.''

''She is welcome to stay as long as she needs, Gryphon. You know that.''

''Then tonight I will leave for Zuu, to see if I can pick up Cabe's trail.''

''You'll teleport?'' Troia sounded suddenly disturbed again.

The Gryphon did not appear to notice it. ''I am familiar with the region and it will save days of travel. From there, I will teleport as carefully as I can into the midst of Legar.''

''Is that not dangerous?'' Gwen asked. ''You might materialize before a patrol of wolf raiders.''

He gave her a look almost devoid of emotion. ''No one knows them as well as I do. Trust in me, my lady.''

''I still don't care for it. I should be with you, Gryph.''

''And you will be.'' The Gryphon put one hand on his heart. ''You will always be here.''

Gwen allowed them their peace while she thought of Cabe. She, like Troia, was still upset about being left behind even though both of them knew it was not because their husbands saw them as lessers. Even had the Gryphon offered to take her place and watch the children, she was aware that she would have turned the offer down. There had to be someone here for the children, especially with the Dragonrealm so volatile in other ways, and this *had* been Cabe's mission from the very beginning. He was the one who had been contacted. It was not the choice every parent would have made, but it was her choice and she would live by it.

She consoled herself with the fact that the Gryphon's presence would make Cabe's safety that much more possible. Between the lionbird, her husband, and the irrepressible Darkhorse, neither the wolf raiders nor the Crystal Dragon were tasks insurmountable. It was possible that the situation was not even as terrible as they had assumed. There was even the chance that Cabe might very well return before his old friend was able to depart.

That was assuming that nothing had happened to him already.

* * *

The blue man stumbled through the godforsaken fog, cursing its magic-spawned ability to creep even into the most obscure passages below the earth. It was hard enough to see even with the torches lit let alone with such a thick morass enshrouding everything around him.

Yet, there was something else, something inviting about the fog. He could taste power, raw, wild forces, coursing through the mist. D'Rance had seen the proof of that, too. He had watched floors twist and turn, a man sucked into the walls as if he had never been, and fantastical figures prancing about in the fog. Mere tips of the proverbial iceberg, the northerner knew. Above, those on the surface would be facing much more. The Quel city seemed to dampen the effects of the wild power. Whether that was intentional or simply chance, he did not know. That subject could wait until later, after he had reached the surface and explored farther. As much as he disliked the fog, it offered him possibilities that even Lord D'Farany could not match. He had to find out where it had originated from.

He was nearly to the mouth of the tunnel when a dog-sized form skittered over his feet, causing him to fall against one side of the passage. From near his left, he heard it growl.

Verlok. From his time in Canisargos he knew the sound well. There was only one verlok on this side of the world.

"Kanaan. How good of you to be where I wanted you."

"Lord D'Farany?" He could see nothing save the dim image of the verlok . . . and this with the light of day supposedly trying to cut through the murky fog.

"We were on our way down. It was not necessary to meet us."

"Yes, my lord." The blue man clenched both hands tight. "I must apologize, yes, for not noticing you sooner. This thrice-cursed mist wreaks havoc on the eyes, yes?"

A shape took form before him. The Pack Leader. "I suppose that could be troublesome, but it's hardly a concern compared to other things. Fascinating, wouldn't you say? As if entering another world."

A world gone mad, yes! Kanaan D'Rance wanted to study the magical forces involved, but he by no means cared for any other aspect of it. If he could find a way to manipulate it, that was all he desired. "It is unique, yes."

"But of course something must be done about it; it disturbs the men, you see. Disturbs my work."

And that is all it is doing? The blue man was often fascinated by the Pack Leader's peculiar pattern of thought.

"It's magical, as you've no doubt guessed. Not like anything else. Not at all like *his* power. A shame, truly." D'Farany reached down and picked up his vile pet. "It repels rather than attracts. I think I *must* remove it from this place and send it to wherever he unleashed it from."

"He?"

"The Crystal Dragon, of course." Lord D'Farany walked past him, the verlok taking the opportunity to snarl at the blue man. D'Rance quickly followed, knowing how easy it might be to lose someone in this mire.

The floor of the tunnel was shifting beneath their feet, but where the blue man struggled to keep his balance, the Pack Master simply stepped here and there, moving along as if nothing were the matter. A misshapen tentacle of rock darted out from beside them, but somehow missed D'Farany. The northerner, on the other hand, was forced to duck, not an easy act when the ground beneath his feet continued to move.

He acts as if this is the way of the normal world! Could this be what he sees, yes? If so, it explained much about Ivon D'Farany.

Although nothing major impeded their blind trek, it was still with relief that the blue man entered the chamber some minutes later. Relief and curiosity, for he immediately saw that the crystalline room was not touched as the others were. There was no fog even though the tunnel just beyond was dank and impossible to navigate by sight alone. For once, the sentries posted here must have felt themselves fortunate, he thought.

The Pack Leader, oblivious to all else, leaned over the Quel device and visibly sighed. Removing his gloves, he tenderly touched the various crystals in the arrangement, finishing with his own addition.

"Where is Orril?"

"I regret, my lord, that I do not know where he is." *He is hopefully lost forever.* D'Rance knew he could not be so fortunate. D'Marr would likely show his blank little face at the worst possible time.

"No matter." The former keeper began to activate the magical creation.

Interest was overcoming uncertainty. He had watched closely as Lord D'Farany had become quickly adept at the use of the diggers' tool. Watching the raider leader had been a learning experience, although soon he would not need to watch. Still, if Lord D'Farany had a plan to disperse the dank and decay-filled mist, then there were still things the blue man could learn from him. "If I may, my lord, you have a plan, yes? What will you do, please?"

He did not catch the fascinated smile on the Pack Leader's crystal-illuminated countenance but the tone and the words were enough. "I have no plan, Kanaan. I'm simply going to *play*."

D'Rance suddenly found himself envying the men on the surface. They only had the fog to fear.

X

In a place where darkness was unchallenged by light, a sleeper long undisturbed stirred briefly to sluggish life . . .

They were able to move mountains, create castles from nothing. A world had been theirs to play with and they had played ever so hard, tearing that world asunder and making it into a reflection of their own, uncaring souls.

Plool gazed down on Cabe in what appeared to be expectation. At least, Cabe thought so; the wide-brimmed hat still obscured the upper part of his incredibly narrow face. Everything about the odd figure was a parody of humanity, but the warlock found no humor in the other's physical appearance. Plool was a creature—an *inhabitant*—of dreaded Nimth. Worse, he had to be *Vraad*, one of the terrible race of sorcerers that had created the madness of Nimth in the first place.

"You are a curious creature," the macabre figure pronounced. "In a curious world. How curious."

He still spoke in the peculiar, singsong tone he had used earlier, but he changed his pattern of speech now and then, almost as if it were a game with him. Plool seemed of a whimsical nature in many ways, which did not necessarily mean that Cabe could relax. Whimsy had its dark side, especially where the Vraad were concerned. From his notes he had gathered that the race of sorcerers had had a dark sense of humor.

"Tell me, curious creature, your name?"

"Cabe. Cabe Bedlam."

"Bedlam. I like that. I am Plool."

The warlock nodded a cautious greeting, deciding that it would be better not to mention to Plool that he had already introduced himself. So far, the Vraad was acting quite civilized with him, but he was not about to forget that Plool had slowly and quite casually burned a hole through the Aramite officer's chest using a medallion that should have been resistant to most sorcery. The nightmarish mage was of a highly capricious nature and anything Cabe said might be enough to set him off. As long as the foul mist of Nimth surrounded him, it behooved the warlock to stay on the madcap figure's good side.

If that was possible.

"Where is Darkhorse?"

"The black beast? Following my imagination, the black beast is. Following my imagination the better so that we may speak. He, I understand. A thing of chaos, a thing that is not what he seems. You . . . you are different."

Different? "I'm simply who I am, Great Plool."

"And *that* is why you are so different! You are so much what you seem, so . . . constant. Constant you are, never changing. Yet, how long will you last, Bedlam?" Plool's head shifted under the vast hat. He appeared to be observing the shrouded landscape around him for the first time. "This is a new place; I've not seen its like formed before. Not ever, ever not. Will it stay long?"

Cabe had no idea what the other was referring to and so kept silent.

"All so . . . still. Quite a different little variation, with all

you ephemerals running around and the land so *unchanging*.
Like you . . . a novel thing.''

Unchanging? The wary spellcaster tried to recall what else he
had gleaned from his research on the Vraad and the ancestral
world of Nimth. There was very little, but one other thing that
had been hinted at was that in the violent, magic-tossed realm,
everything, *including* the creatures who lived there, faced dismal
and horrific existences in which they were twisted and reshaped
almost continuously. Nimth was supposed to be a world ever
decaying, ever collapsing. Yet, it still existed even now.

The ground beneath his feet suddenly burst upward.

Cabe barely had time to stumble and readjust his balance
before he found himself on a column of earth nearly the height
of Plool's rocky seat. The column then began to twist and turn,
drawing the warlock closer and closer to the madcap creature.
Girding himself, Cabe did nothing to prevent or even slow his
journey. If Plool had wanted to cause him harm, he would have
done so. It was more likely that he simply wanted to better study
the young warlock.

The column came to a halt just before the Vraad. Cabe noted
that Plool had worked it so that even at full height the warlock
would be a head shorter than the seated Nimthian.

"You *are* a most peculiar-looking piece of work," Plool commented. How he saw anything from under that hat was a miracle.
"Everything's so *orderly*. Would you like me to change that? It
must be awful for you. Awful it must be."

"Thank you, but I'm happy with the way I am." The words
flew from Cabe's lips. The dark-haired sorcerer tried to hide his
anxiety. He did not even want to imagine what the Vraad might
have in mind. A form like *his*? *Never!*

"Are you certain?" As he spoke, Plool at last lifted his head
enough for the warlock to view the rest of his narrow face.

Cabe almost gasped aloud. It was only with the best of efforts
that he prevented himself from stepping back in shock and possibly falling from his perch.

Only in Nimth could Plool have become possible. The lower
half of his countenance, while peculiar, was not overly unusual.
Even the nose, long, narrow, and pointed now, was within the
realm of reason.

But the *eyes* . . .

Both were set on the left side of his face.

They were positioned one right atop the other, like some madman's portrait. On the right side of the face, there was a blank area of skin where the one eye should have been. Had he been born that way or was it a later legacy of Nimth?

The eyes blinked. Once over the sight of the lids closing and opening in unison, Cabe discovered another peculiarity about them. Around the pupil, they looked almost crystalline, so crystalline, in fact, that they probably glittered in sunlight.

The disconcerting eyes were fixated on him. "You and yours are a strange sight; a strange sight you are. So much is strange this day. When I saw the hole, I could not be but curious, yes, curious I could not help but be. Where did it lead? Where had it come from? There are so many things of wonder in my world, but this . . . I think this is not Nimth."

Cabe remained silent.

The eyes blinked again. "The hole. It pulled me in and I found myself here. Then it was gone. Why is that, do you think?"

The warlock shook his head. He had ideas, all involving wolf raiders and Dragon Kings, but he was not about to relay any of them to Plool. The less the bizarre mage knew, the better.

Plool rose, at the same time extending the height of the earthen column so that Cabe was still a head shorter. The odd-looking figure stood atop the formation and once more gazed around at the mist-covered land. It was still impossible to see beyond a few yards, yet the Vraad studied his surroundings as if the fog did not even exist.

"And so where am I, Bedlam? Where has the great Plool, Plool the Great, found himself? What do you call this little place?"

"This is Legar." The answer was safe enough. It told Cabe's companion nothing, which was all he wanted Plool to ever know. Somehow, there had to be a way to return him to Nimth.

"Legarrrrr . . ." The spiderlike figure mulled over the word. His crystalline eyes closed for a time. When he opened them again, they were even brighter and livelier than before. "An amusing name."

"Great Plool, if I may ask you a question?"

He almost preened himself. "You may do so."

"Where was this hole you came through?"

Plool looked sly. "Trying to rid yourself of my presence?"

Cabe actually was, but he was not going to admit that to the Vraad. "I share your curiosity about things, about *your* world."

The answer satisfied Plool. He nodded, thankfully obscuring his unnerving eyes, and responded, "I like you, Bedlam. Would you like to see the hole?"

"If it is safe."

The Vraad shrugged, chuckling all the while. "What *is* safe, Bedlam?"

Cabe blinked. They now stood atop the peak of one of Legar's taller hills. The warlock looked down and saw nothing but the dire mist; he was on the edge of a precipice. Cabe quickly backed away, only to bump into Plool, who floated, legs crossed in a sitting position, just high enough to gaze down at the young mage.

"Sweet, sweet Nimth," the spiderlike Vraad nearly sang. "Your loveliness envelops all . . . and chokes it to death."

He doesn't sound very eager to return. I hope there's no trouble. Somehow I have to convince him to leave. "I don't see the hole, Great Plool. Where was it?"

"The hole is closed, but the door remains."

"And the door?"

"Below us."

Cabe turned his gaze downward once more and saw only murk. He could not even see the rest of the hill, merely a few feet of earth below them. Fog obscured the rest. "Down there?"

"Yes, here."

Every muscle in the warlock's body grew painfully taut as he once again found himself transported to another location. Plool had a habit of teleporting others from one spot to another without warning, something that Shade had often done and even Darkhorse still did without thinking. Cabe had never liked being pulled along in the past and he certainly did not like it now.

They were down in the murky soup he had just been observing from above. From where he stood now, Cabe could not see the top of the hill. How high did the fog go? All the way to the sun?

He reminded himself that it was not the fog that mattered. For now, he needed to concentrate on the magical doorway that had allowed all of this, including his erstwhile Vraad companion, to enter unchecked.

The object of his desire lay between them. A sphere. At first, Cabe studied it with some confusion. He had expected a portal or a tear in reality. Certainly not a glass ball. It looked more like a container than a doorway.

"Can I touch it?"

"If you like."

He did. A mild shock made him pluck his hand back. Plool chuckled. Cabe steeled himself and reached out again. The same mild shock coursed through him, but it was only momentary. Slowly he ran his hands over the artifact. It was not glass after all, but crystal. There was also still something inside. The mage could not be certain, but it appeared to be more fog.

"This is how you came to be here?"

There was a hint of annoyance in the Vraad's voice. "This is how I came to be here; I came to be here because of this. Do you want to ask again, Bedlam?"

"I'm sorry," he quickly responded, "it just amazes me."

Plool squatted. His legs seemed to be built for that. He now resembled the spider again or perhaps a spider and a frog combined. The round torso was so great in girth that it was a wonder the spindly legs could maintain such a balance, yet they did. "Came I through this little sphere, Bedlam, but the opening was much more vast. When I saw what had been the cause and it tried to fly away, I brought it down to this spot and with my might forced it to the ground. It stays there now until I deign to release it to its master."

To its master . . . There was only one being that Cabe could think of who might have been responsible. Certainly not the wolf raiders. Now he was certain that it could only have been the Crystal Dragon.

But why? This seemed a strange defense for a leviathan who had turned the might of the Ice Dragon back. It was, for all its strength, a rather halfhearted and in most ways foolish sort of attack. Cabe was certain that he, in the Dragon King's position, could have devised more than a score of countermeasures much more efficient and less haphazard than the unleashing of Nimthian decay. What happened if the deadly mist became permanent? Might it not also spread?

He sighed. Why was nothing ever simple? It was terrible enough that he had been forced to come here and seek out both the lord of Legar and the Aramites, but now he had the fog and a Vraad to deal with.

The Dragonrealm does like to play with us, doesn't it?

Thinking of that, he suddenly had a wary thought. Plool would not know the lay of the land, but he might know enough about this region in general to answer a few questions. "Great Plool, are we far from where we first met?"

"Nothing is far away . . . but Nimth now."

So perhaps the answers would not be forthcoming for now. Trust Plool to speak in riddles and poetry. Standing, Cabe studied what little he could see of the hill formation. The one thing he was certain of was that he was high in the sky. These hills were the closest Legar had to true mountains and only some arbitrary decision by ancient mapmakers had prevented them from falling into the other category. He could recall only one area in all the peninsula where such high hills were located. If his estimates were correct, and it was still quite possible they were not thanks to the concealing fog, then he was in a region very near the underground city of the Quel and the caverns where he suspected the Crystal Dragon's clans made their home. That would also put him near enough to the shoreline of the peninsula, which meant that the wolf raiders, too, might be his neighbors.

This is not what I had in mind when I began this journey. He looked at Plool. Could he convince him to leave Legar? The hills of Esedi would be the most likely place to reunite with Darkhorse, although what the demon steed and the Vraad would do when faced with each other worried him. Darkhorse he was certain he could calm, but the madcap figure beside him was more unpredictable. He had clearly been responsible for separating the two.

Cabe saw no other choice. His best chances for putting a finish to all these matters lay in combining his skills with those of Darkhorse and Plool, the latter because of his ability to work and exist in the Nimthian mist. Cabe also wanted Darkhorse with him in order to keep a better eye on the Vraad. True, the ebony stallion was weakened by the very fog that Plool thrived in, but between the two of them they should be able to keep him in check. The warlock hoped it would not come to that, however. Plool was not evil, not exactly; his was simply a different world. He might be willing to help if only because he found the situation entertaining.

"Great Plool, there is another place we should go, a place where there is someone I hope to meet. I think you'll find it a fascinating place, so alive with stability and so unchanging." *I begin to sound like him.*

"The black beast. You hope to meet him."

He had been careful not to mention Darkhorse, but Plool had made the connection regardless. "His name is Darkhorse. He means no harm to you." *I hope!* "He is my friend and companion on this journey."

Indignation. "I am Plool! I do not fear anything! I can create castles in the air! I can make monsters from mud!"

"I didn't mean—"

The indignation vanished, to be replaced by curiosity. "But so much . . . unchanging . . . not even Nimth has created such!" The eyes blinked. "I will enjoy this world . . . *yesss* . . . I will come with you and see this place, talk to the hole, too. The hole I will talk to, this Darkhorse!"

"Good," Cabe returned once he had pieced his way through the Vraad's quick and confusing words. The warlock had no idea what he would do if Darkhorse was not there. Return to Legar with Plool, he supposed. Not to this location, however. Better to choose one of those he was vaguely familiar with from long ago. Plool appeared willing to listen to him, although who knew why, and with the Vraad to aid him he should be able to find a better place to materialize than here.

First, however, he had to find a way to get Plool to teleport the two of them to Esedi. The Vraad had been quite agreeable so far to teleporting them from one place to another. Maybe he would do so again. Cabe did not want to risk his own sorcery if he could avoid it, not here in this malevolent mist. "Master Plool, if you could be so kind—"

The eerie figure executed a bow, an act that, considering his shape, bordered on the absurd. "I am ever benevolent to those in need; to those in need benevolent I ever am."

"My gratitude. First let me—"

Plool was already acting.

Cabe started toward him, hand out. "Wait!"

The familiar hilly and, thankfully, clear terrain of western Esedi manifested before him. Despite his not having described it to the Vraad, Plool had known where to go. He could have only done so by seizing the image from Cabe's *mind*.

His relief at escaping the fog made the invasion of his thoughts almost secondary, at least for the time being. Cabe exhaled in relief and started to look for the other mage.

He heard a gasp of pain from a voice that could only be Plool's, then the world around him began to spin. He struggled to maintain balance, but the force tugging at him was too strong.

Cabe was torn from the earth. Everything around him shimmered in an all too familiar way. There was a brief instant when he was surrounded by nothing. *Pure* nothing. The nothing was followed by a body-rending shock as the startled warlock was flattened against a rocky surface.

It was not enough to severely injure him, but it did leave him stunned and aching for several minutes. Eventually, he tried to see where he was, but his surroundings seemed but a blur no matter how many times he blinked.

No. Not a blur. As his head cleared, Cabe saw that it was not his vision that was at fault.

He was back in Legar. Back on the hill near where the sorcerer from Nimth had shown him the crystalline sphere.

What had happened to Plool? Cabe recalled the brief, agonized sound. He scanned the region, but his search was limited to a few yards at most in any one direction.

"Gngh!" A terrible force dragged him upward. His frantic thought was that the teleportation spell was still in effect, but then he ceased moving. Cabe simply hung where he was, his arms and legs mysteriously bereft of movement. There was an uncomfortable pressure around his chest that made it difficult to draw a breath.

"Bedlam, I do not like pain! Betray my faith, my goodwill! I have punished for less; much less have I punished for, *Bedlam!*"

"Ploo-ool?" Cabe managed to choke out.

The Vraad floated before him on a throne formed from the very mist. His round torso was tipped back so far that Plool had to practically peer over it. He was breathing hard and one hand shook. The maddening eyes were narrow in dark thought.

"Wh-what have I *done*?"

"The pain!" Plool roared. "The pain, the pain, and the pain! My very body twisted and boiled! Were I not Plool the Great, I would be dead, torn apart!" Somehow, Plool managed to lean forward. "As you shall be for my sport and vengeance!"

"I did nothing!"

"Lies and lies and lies and lies!"

It was growing nearly impossible to breathe, much less speak in his own defense. "You've freely invaded my mind, haven't you? Do it again, but this time seek out the truth about me! Try to prove that I betrayed you!"

He hoped his plan, born of the second, would succeed. Otherwise, Plool would use him as he desired. A Vraad's desire. The very notion turned his stomach. He knew the legends.

Plool's long, hodgepodge face leaned even closer. Was it Cabe's imagination or was the upper eye slightly more to the other side? That was preposterous, of course, the product of his predicament. It was a moot point, anyway. What mattered was what the furious Vraad drew from his mind.

One breath.

Two breaths.

Three and four, all harsh.

The pressure on his chest eased. Slowly, both he and Plool sank toward the ground. Plool ceased descending when he was roughly a man's length from the rocky surface of the hill. He still used the chair of mist to support his massive form. Cabe, on the other hand, was unceremoniously dumped. The gasping warlock managed to keep his balance.

From the Vraad there was no apology, but a careful study of Plool's insane countenance revealed to Cabe enough to satisfy him. Plool had read his mind and found what the desperate mage had wanted him to find.

Nothing more. Cabe was certain of it now. There were things his mind held, thoughts concerning the Dragonrealm and his fears of Plool, that the searching Vraad would have surely noticed and acted upon. That he had not noticed meant that like Darkhorse, Plool had limits as to how deep he could plunder another's mind. It was good to know. Cabe had feared that he would not have the power to direct his menacing companion's mental search toward specific thoughts only. His mind was his after all.

"I was in great and terrible pain, Bedlam," the floating spell-caster hissed. His tone bespoke his condition; Cabe grew more and more interested in what had happened to him. "Terrible and great pain."

"I feel your pain," Cabe returned, all politeness. "But I am not the one responsible, as you now know."

"Then *who? Who*, then, Bedlam, hmmm?"

The Crystal Dragon? It was unlikely. Not at all like the Dragon King, if the warlock's opinion was correct. The lord of Legar was generally satisfied with his enemies fleeing from his kingdom. He would have been more likely to take both of them and fling them farther from the peninsula, say all the way to the Dagora Forest. Still, nothing was predictable anymore. It might very well be the Crystal Dragon.

The Aramites certainly would not have left Cabe alone, so it could not be them. He also doubted it could have been some trick of Lanith's mages. They were not that organized.

Could it have simply been something about Esedi itself? Or Plool even?

Plool . . . yes, it was a possibility. He tried not to change his expression as he covertly studied the misshapen body of the Vraad. What had he thought earlier? Only in Nimth could some-one like Plool be possible?

Only in Nimth and not *beyond* the borders of its foul mists.

"I don't know," the warlock finally responded. He despised lying, but in this case he was not certain the truth was any better. Plool might choose to believe him or he might not. Besides, there might still come a time when Cabe would need that bit of knowledge to save himself; the Vraad had already proven his instability.

His reverie was interrupted by a look of sudden inspiration on the horrid visage. Plool's eyes widened, then narrowed. "But I think I know who it must be . . ."

Gods, no! If he blames Darkhorse, then the two of them could come to blows without any chance of explanation!

It was not Darkhorse. "They will boil in their suits of black armor. Their heads I shall use for a stairway in a citadel built from their bones; from their bones a citadel will be built. Even then, I shall not let them die, death being too good for them for having caused me such pain . . ."

Black armor. Plool had chosen the wolf raiders as his scape-goats.

The maddened Vraad was looking directly at him again. "And you, Bedlam, will aid me; aid me you will, Bedlam."

It had been Cabe's early hope that if the Aramites had truly landed on the shores of Legar, as he now knew they had, he would find some means, some allies, that would force the raiders from the Dragonrealm forever. What he had *not* been searching for was someone like *Plool*. Definitely not like Plool. To join the Vraad on his campaign of vengeance would be folly of the greatest kind.

The Vraad was quiet for a time, but his anger by no means diminished. He was thinking, contemplating. Cabe used the time to try to clear his own thoughts. How could he steer Plool from the direction the other sorcerer was heading to one in which the Vraad chose to return to Nimth?

The sphere! The doorway! In some ways, Plool was like a child. Cabe suspected that once turned toward the puzzle of how to open the doorway again, Plool would forget his insane vengeance on the wolf raiders. At the very least, it was worth the attempt. Plool was likely to cause more chaos than good by attacking the Aramite encampment.

Where *was* the sphere? The warlock looked around. It should have been in sight. Plool had embedded it in the rock, but from Cabe's angle it still should have been visible.

"What do you search for?"

"The sphere. Your doorway home. It's vanished."

Plool hardly seemed put out by that fact. "Then, I will be staying."

"You don't understand . . ." Neither, in fact, did Cabe. He did, however, have a very bad feeling that his assumptions had gone astray, that he had left out something.

He was even more certain when his feet began to sink into the hillside.

The spell that he cast in an attempt to free himself did nothing. Cabe was not even certain that it had completed, for there was no sign of any reaction, no twinge in the magical forces that held the Dragonrealm together. The warlock looked down; the earth had already swallowed him up to his shins and it was evident that the rate of sinking was increasing.

"Plool!" What was the Vraad doing? Watching him? Did he find this all entertaining?

When he looked up, Cabe saw that the truth was anything but. Plool was not standing over him, merrily watching his predicament. Plool might possibly not even be standing there, although it was hard to say, for in his place there was now a vast, opaque sphere, a glimmering monstrosity taller than a man. In some ways, it resembled the sphere that Cabe had investigated, but whereas that had been a doorway, a gate, this one was more likely a prison. A prison for a dangerous and unpredictable sorcerer like Plool.

The sphere, too, began to sink, but the struggling mage hardly cared now. He was more concerned with his own freedom, for without that he could hardly help the Vraad. His legs were now completely enveloped. At the rate he was being dragged under, he had only a minute, maybe two, to act.

Somewhere, Cabe found the strength. Tensing, he threw himself into the spell, stretched out a hand, and pointed at an outcropping. A single magical tendril shot forth and pierced the rock. The warlock attached it to himself, creating a lifeline.

His rate of sinking slowed, but that was not enough. Pleased with his success at casting a spell despite the malevolent mist, Cabe anchored himself in a similar manner to another outcropping. Now, his downward progress was nearly negligible. The strain on his body, however, was growing stronger by the moment. It felt as if a giant had taken him by the feet and head and was trying to tear him slowly apart like a piece of fruit. If he delayed too long, whoever sought to capture him might finally do so, but they would have to settle for half his body.

The third tendril was easier to create and cast than the previous two and while he wondered about that, there was no time to consider the reasons. This third he bonded to a formation before him, but not in the same manner as the ones on each side of it. This one Cabe kept bonded to his hands, so that it seemed as if he were holding on to a magical rope.

His concentration fixed upon the stream of power running from his hands to the rock, the warlock caused it to shorten ever so slightly. It did and to his joy he found that he rose a little. The strain was still incredible, but it was no worse than before. Still, he wished he could trust his abilities enough to do something else. He wished he had the *time* to think of something else. Yet Cabe was also aware that more complicated or stronger spells might not function as well here. More subtle spells, because they did not stir the forces as much as the greater ones, were less likely to go awry under present circumstances. His own attempt at teleportation was a fine example.

Becoming more daring, he shortened the strand by nearly half a foot. The warlock rose by a similar height. He allowed himself a quick smile, which promptly faded as his concentration slipped and he started to sink again. Another attempt brought him back up, but the effort was beginning to have a toll. His sides ached terribly and his breath was becoming a little ragged. Cabe dared not turn his attention to Plool's dilemma, assuming that Plool was indeed a prisoner of the sphere. He did not even know if the sphere was still visible or whether it had already sunk unchecked into the hill.

His next attempt faltered and instead of the foot that he hoped to rise, he barely gained more than an inch. Still, Cabe persevered. As long as he continued to rise, he would eventually triumph, he told himself.

On his next attempt, however, he felt a new force combating him. It was not magical, but physical.

Something had clamped on to his ankles and was pulling him under with renewed vigor.

One of the two lines linked to his body simply faded. Cabe sank to his waist almost instantly. He tried to strengthen the other one, but between his need to monitor the magical bond pulling him free and the strain on both his mind and body, the tiring spellcaster could add little. Cabe watched in frustration as whatever force had eliminated the first also caused the second to dissipate.

The ground was already creeping up to his chest. Cabe put his entire will into the one bond that remained to him. His sinking slowed, then stopped again. He even succeeded in winning back an inch or two of freedom.

Then, the ground behind him shook, something shot by the left side of his head . . . and Cabe Bedlam had a momentary glimpse of a massive, taloned paw just before it covered his face and, with the aid of others like it, finally pulled him underground.

─────── XI ───────

There is something different about this place.

Sometimes, it was hard to recall that more than twenty years had passed since his last visit to Zuu. It had been before the crisis centering around Cabe Bedlam and his emergence from hiding.

I live too long a life, the Gryphon thought not for the first time. Even the sorcerers he knew gradually aged and, if allowed, died peacefully. He, on the other hand, went on and on, fighting wars and trying to find his place in the world. Even when he had learned his own origins, learned that once his body had been that of one of the Faceless Ones of the other continent, he had not felt as if he knew who he was. There had only been two places where he had ever felt comfortable with himself. Safe. One was Penacles, which had embraced him as its leader despite his monstrous appearance.

The other place was wherever his family happened to be. With Troia and Demion, he had known *true* peace of mind, even during the worst years of the war.

Now Demion was dead and Troia, still chafing about being left behind, would someday also die.

When would he?

The Faceless Ones were virtually immortal; he was not so certain that he wanted to be. Yet neither was he the suicidal type.

Reshaped to pass for human, the Gryphon walked among the inhabitants of Zuu. Things *were* different. There was more order, more attention. Lanith, who he recalled vaguely as a young, obstinate child, must be more ambitious than his father. The Gryphon hoped that that ambition in no way mirrored that of King Melicard. The Dragonrealm looked to be in enough chaos without two human monarchs seeking to take on the mantle of conquest the Dragon Kings had given up.

He fingered the medallion given to him by the guards at the gate. More familiar with its like than Cabe was, the lionbird understood its true purpose. The talisman was crude, however, and so it had only taken a simple spell to adjust it so that anyone attuned to it would not notice the sudden presence of a master mage.

Two hours of wandering Zuu's market area had already told him most of what he wanted to know. Again, as with the talisman, he was more familiar with how the rumor and gossip system of cities worked. Cabe, for all his skills, had not lived in the lower reaches of civilization for as long as the Gryphon had. True, the human had grown up around the taverns, but there were other levels of information. He had not had to survive as the lionbird had had to do in the early days. Few, if anyone, had the sum total experience that the Gryphon had.

And how I envy you that, Cabe.

He saw no purpose in remaining any longer. The sun was already down and each minute he delayed added to the off-chance that one of the king's new spellcasters might, just might, detect him. The Gryphon, like Cabe, did not want to cause an incident. He already knew of the mysterious goings on in the city and suspected that the warlock and the demon steed had nearly been discovered. While it was possible the Gryphon would be able to call upon his role as monarch of Penacles to protect himself, it would be embarrassing to his former kingdom and good Toos to try to explain why he was skulking about in another's domain.

One item he had learned interested him most of all. There was some news about Legar. A dank fog had risen and those who had dared traverse the regions near the border had told of a mist so thick it was impossible to see anything. Curiously, this mist ended almost exactly at the inner edge of the peninsula, less than a few yards from where Esedi began. No one doubted it was magic, but having lived near the domain of the Crystal Dragon for so many generations, the people of Zuu were inclined to believe it was simply a step by the lord of Legar to further isolate himself from the world. After all, the fog *did* end before Esedi, not after. Not even the least tendril extended into those lands claimed by Lanith's kingdom.

It is amazing, the peace of mind some can have. The Gryphon was not so confident. To him the foul haze meant that the wolf raiders *must* be there, as the Bedlams had feared. That meant that Cabe might be in more danger than he was prepared for, even with the aid of Darkhorse. From experience, the lionbird knew of some of the Aramites' deadly tricks. He knew them better than anyone and knew also that D'Farany would be plotting others.

Abandoning his listening position at one of the danker establishments, which he still found of higher quality than many he had visited during his long life, the Gryphon sought out one of the more secluded alleys. It was time to begin following Cabe's trail and for that he needed to perform a little magic. It would be subtle enough to escape the attention of the third-rate sorcerers who had created the talismans, but still powerful enough to accomplish its mission.

In the darkness of the narrow street, he removed a single object from the folds of his weathered cloak. The object had been carefully wrapped in a piece of cloth so as to be affected as little as possible by his own presence. Both the cloth and what it enshrouded had come from the personal effects of Cabe Bedlam.

He quickly unfolded the cloth and removed his prize. It was a short blade of the type used for shaving. One of the warlock's foibles concerned shaving without the use of sorcery. Cabe's detestation of any sort of magical alteration to his physical being amused the Gryphon at times, but in this instance it had come in handy. Metal objects were always best for this sort of spell. They had a better affinity for their user, especially mages. There were reasons why this was so, but they were of no concern to the lionbird at the moment. Finding Cabe's trail was.

For one of his vast experience, the spell was nothing to perform. He felt the tingle as the blade became attuned. It would lead him along the path Cabe and Darkhorse had followed. The lionbird never considered following the magical trail left by the demon steed. As unique as that trail was, enough time had passed that following it would be more troublesome than what he was doing now. A physical object was always better, even in this case.

His hand and the blade once more buried in the voluminous folds of his cloak, he set out. The vague trail that most every spellcaster left led the Gryphon toward one of the countless stables he knew dotted the city. Likely Darkhorse had been stabled there. The trail grew confusing, however, which meant that not only had Cabe spent much time here, but he had moved around quite a bit in the nearby vicinity.

Some might have questioned the need to search at all, considering that the dark-haired spellcaster's last message had mentioned the hills of Esedi, but the Gryphon was concerned with more than just his human friend. The Lady Gwen had not been entirely forthcoming, but he was certain that she was very concerned too with what had happened in Zuu. Cabe's note was deceptively matter-of-fact. So much so, in fact, that the lionbird had agreed with the enchantress's assumption that Zuu had not been a simple pause in the warlock's journey.

Gwendolyn's concern was for the health and well-being of her mate. The Gryphon's concern included Cabe, but also the potential danger Zuu might now represent. Not merely Zuu, either. For all he knew there were already Aramite spies in the city. Again, the raiders were nothing if not efficient.

Much had happened at the stable, of that he was certain. That along with what he had heard verified much. He would have to relay his knowledge to Toos once this was over, assuming that the lanky former mercenary did not already know. This kingdom would bear watching.

It was impossible to avoid other folk, but this was hardly the first time the Gryphon had performed such covert activity. His every step was carefully planned despite how casual his actions might appear to an onlooker. At the stables he toyed with one of his boots, acting as if something had slipped inside and was now causing him annoyance. Dressed as an outsider and already having been in more than one tavern, it was hardly surprising that he also staggered to and fro a bit as he walked. Since he was clearly a visitor it was also no surprise that he would be glancing around at everything.

The trail left the stables simple enough, but near one of the local establishments, a strong pull made him turn. He stared at the well-lit entrance to a place called Belfour's Champion. There was another trail leading off into the far streets, but this one was stronger, almost as if it were so recent it had not had time to dissipate.

Now what do we have here? There was no reason for Cabe's return to Zuu. Knowing the human as he did, if Cabe had finished his mission, he would have returned home to the Manor the instant it was possible for him to do so. Yet, the blade tingled as if the warlock himself sat inside.

Only one way to discover the truth.

He entered the inn, all but ignoring the enticing smells. Belfour's Champion was a bustling place and it was everything he could do just to scan the crowd while not looking suspicious. The blade hidden in his hand gave him focus. He carefully stumbled in the direction, noting with satisfaction that there were a few empty spots on some of the benches ahead of him. Should it become necessary, he could take one and pretend to wait for a serving girl while he continued to search.

The Gryphon passed around the shapely backside of a particularly fetching girl, then immediately dodged by two very overstuffed patrons on their way out. He paused to get his bearings and could not help but frown. The direction had now changed. Not only had he passed the location, but it was *receding* from him even as he stood there.

The Gryphon eyed the path he had taken. He saw no one that resembled the warlock. It was possible that Cabe was disguised and that although the lionbird wore a human face nearly identical to the one Cabe had known him by long ago, he would not know to look for one of his old companions in this faraway city. Still, something was wrong. Could his spell have caused him to follow a coin that the warlock had spent? Unlikely. The trail was too strong. Even if the coin or coins had just left his hands, Bedlam would have had to handle them for quite some time. It also would have required more than a few coins to create such a pull. They passed through too many hands too quickly to generally have much attachment to any one person.

Pretending to have sighted someone who *might* be an old chum, the Gryphon started back. His eyes carefully inspected each person. He sidestepped several more patrons entering, the same serving girl, and—

And the trail altered again. Out of the corner of his eye, the Gryphon glanced at the woman he had twice now passed.

The more he studied her, which was something no one there would have found unusual anyway, the more he was of the opinion that she had some secret. What?

I am becoming senile! He knew what it was now. Only sorcerers of some ability would even recognize it, which still gave him no excuse for not having noted it before. Now that he knew, the woman's secret fairly screamed to him.

A sorceress! One of some mean skill, too, I would think!

What was her connection to Cabe? Why did his spell draw him to her?

She happened to turn in his direction then. Although his actions were still innocent enough, the look that passed briefly across her beautiful countenance told him that she knew he was not what he seemed. In fact, he was certain that she knew what *he* was, too.

It had to be the case. Suddenly the golden-haired woman found things to do that took her to the back of the inn. The Gryphon did not wonder whether she would return, only how many exits there might be back there. He doubted she would use her skills while still inside. A sorceress who worked in taverns and inns generally did so because she was hiding what she was. That meant he still had an opportunity to catch her.

The lionbird had not been idle while he had thought all this out. Already he was at the front doorway. If he could find her before she slipped away, it would simplify things for him. If the unknown enchantress *did* teleport away, he still had one trick up his sleeve. The same object that had first drawn him to her would allow him to find her again.

Despite the hour, or perhaps because of it, there were a number of folk wandering about. That encouraged him, for while it slowed his progress, she could hardly use her sorcery in front of people who might recognize her as working at the inn. The blade also informed him that she was still nearby, although it was possible that the sorceress had removed the item from her person. Since she could hardly know why he was after her, he did not think she would know to do that. If he was wrong . . .

The tug he had felt suddenly ceased.

Teleported! Cursing quietly, the Gryphon turned round. Nothing was ever too easy. Still, if she ran true to predictability, she was probably not too far away. Just far enough to consider herself safe.

Sure enough, he felt the same tug. Not for a moment did he think it was anything other than her. He had performed this spell too often, too.

Without hesitation, the Gryphon teleported after her.

She was facing his direction as he materialized, but caught off-guard, her reflexes were too slow. Moving with the inhuman swiftness that had allowed him to survive for so long, the lionbird reached forward and caught her with his good hand. Only after that was done did he become aware of where exactly they were. She was bolder than he had thought, for from their location, he could just make out the inn far to his left. The woman had been watching for him rather than simply escaping, an obvious sign that no matter how skilled she was, she was still a novice in many things.

"If you even think about escape, *don't*."

It was very clear that the serving woman understood. He could sense the tension coursing through her body. On the other hand, he could also sense the excitement she felt. The Gryphon was familiar with her type, having met more than his share. *Very fortunate that neither Gwen nor Troia came with me!* This was not the sort of woman either wife would care to see around their mates.

In the few seconds since his sudden arrival, she had already become bold enough to ask him questions. "Do we visit the king now?"

"Should we?" He decided to play along.

One thing she was, was quick. The toying smile that had started to spread across her exquisite face faltered. "You're not with the king's herd of pet mages."

The rumored spellcasters of King Lanith. Now he understood her earlier panic. She *was* hiding, hiding from her own monarch.

"I should have known." The smile had started spreading again. "You are much too talented for one of that bunch. Not to mention much more pleasant to look at."

He kept her from reaching up and stroking his cheek. Had Troia been here, the scene would have become very unpleasant by now. In her own way, the woman before him was just as much a predator as his bride.

"Thank you, but I am spoken for."

"From the way you followed me, I wouldn't have believed that." She leaned forward ever so slightly.

He leaned forward, too, but not because of the grand and glorious sight before him. "Do not play your games with me. I might surprise you."

His tone was menacing enough that she quickly withdrew. Even subdued for the moment, however, the young enchantress was still imposing. She would be much more trouble in the years to come.

"What do you want of me? If you're not from the king, then who are you?"

"My name is unimportant, but I believe you and I share an acquaintance. One from whom you have a token of remembrance."

Her smile twisted into a grimace and one hand flinched. The lionbird reached toward a small belt pouch hanging against her thigh. He tore the pouch off. Releasing her but still keeping his eyes focused in her direction, the Gryphon opened the pouch.

There were several small items in the pouch, but only one that could belong to Cabe. The Gryphon's high sensitivity to magical auras allowed him to pick it out. A small dagger that many people carried when traveling. It was more useful for mundane tasks than cutting thieves, but then Cabe Bedlam hardly had to worry about thieves . . . excepting this one, of course. "You planned to follow him at some point? Was not one rejection enough for you?"

"You're *his* friend?"

"We go back a long way. How did you come by this?"

One look at his eyes warned her about lying. Unleashing her dazzling smile, she replied, "He came into the inn. I could see that he was different, one of us."

"And so you tried to seduce him . . . for what?" He thought carefully. "Training and more, I imagine. The road to power for a mage."

He had come close to the truth. The Gryphon understood the present situation concerning spellcasters. Hunted for years by the Dragon Kings, they were only now reappearing in any number. Other than Cabe and Gwen, he had only known a handful of mages of any ability who had survived the constant purges. Toos, once his second-in-command during his mercenary days, was one.

"What is your name?"

"Tori. Tori Winddancer."

Winddancer, just the sort of name one found in this region. The appellation no doubt revolved around the swiftness of horses. She was a native of the kingdom of Zuu, then. There would be even less chance for her to find someone like her in this region.

Although the Green Dragon was an ally to humans now and his particular line had always treated people fairly well, the days after the Turning War had seen the beginning of the strongest of the mage purges. That cleansing had been under the control of the Dragon Emperor, and knowing his counterpart in the Dagora Forest, it was said that extra care had been taken to make the purge in and around Dagora very thorough.

"What happened to my friend while he was here?"

"You heard about what happened near the stables?" At his nod, she continued. "That was him. That was some horse he had, too. I heard some people claim it could fly, but they probably didn't know your friend was a warlock."

And you do not know about Darkhorse, evidently. So much the better. "Were the king's men after him?"

"The guards and the mages . . . or bumblers, after the way they handled him. He made fools out of them I hear."

"You hear?"

She smiled again. "I left the moment I knew they were coming. Your friend didn't understand about the medallion . . . but you do, I guess."

"I've been around longer." So now he had verification. Cabe and Darkhorse had run afoul of King Lanith's tame spellcasters. He could not blame the warlock for leaving the incident out of his message to the Lady Bedlam; she had more than enough to worry about without adding this. It was over and done.

"Are you through with me or would you like to talk of other things now?" From the way she looked at him, it was clear what she meant.

"There are those who will aid in your training without you having to resort to seduction."

"I'm looking for more than training as you know, silver hair." She tried to touch the hair, but he blocked her hand. "I'm looking for *much* more than that."

"My wife would claw you into little pieces if she knew you had even been this familiar with me. Literally claw you."

"What is she, a cat?"

"Yes."

She looked at him carefully, expecting some sign of amusement, then saw that he was deadly earnest. "Some people will marry into the strangest families. A human and a cat?"

"Did I say I was human?"

Tori had no response to that, but he noted that she leaned back a little, as if seeing him in a new and unnerving light. "I asked you a question. Are you finished with me?"

"Nearly. Are you familiar—" He paused as a drunken trader dressed in the clothes of Gordag-Ai stumbled in their direction. He heard other voices nearby. The Gryphon took Tori's arm. She did not resist but neither did she try her charms on him again. His comments concerning himself and his mate had her wondering. "Let us walk back to the inn. Be friendly."

The enchantress nodded. Ahead of them, the trader was trying to decide which side of the narrow street he wanted to give up to them. The Gryphon pointed to his left and the man steered that way. Turning his attention back to Tori, he started to ask his question again.

The footsteps of the drunken man stilled.

A normal man would have been too slow and that fact was perhaps all that saved the Gryphon, for it probably made his attacker just overconfident enough. He threw the woman to one side as the trader fell upon him, knife in one hand. The lionbird heard Tori gasp, but then his attention became completely focused on the battle situation. His adversary weighed far more than he should have, which made the Gryphon certain that beneath the outfit one would find armor.

Black armor.

He had grown careless, spending too much of his time on some things and forgetting his own thought that there might be spies here. He had also grown careless in another way, for the face he wore now was the one he often preferred. Cabe would not be the only one capable of recognizing it. After so many years of facing him, it was not surprising that many of the raiders, especially the spies, would recognize that striking countenance on sight. The Gryphon knew he had not only become careless, but also vain. Had he chosen faces of less distinction, he might have avoided this. His maimed hand might still have given him away, but not nearly as quickly as his vanity had.

They struggled on the ground, the wolf raider maintaining his advantage above through sheer weight and the Gryphon's inability to get a strong enough grip with his damaged hand. The raider's own features were nondescript, as was most common

with those in his profession, but the quiet determination he radiated told the Gryphon that his adversary was a veteran of many
a campaign. There would be no room for mistakes against this
man.

If physical strength was not enough to rid him of his assailant,
then the lionbird was more than willing to resort to his magical
skills. When the situation called for it, one took the advantages
one was given and sense of honor be damned, that was his belief.
Survival first and foremost.

The Aramite must have known what he was attempting, for
suddenly he abandoned the knife attack and, disregarding injury
to himself, swung his head down, catching the Gryphon square
in the forehead.

It was all the Gryphon could do to keep from blacking out.
Worse, the force was enough to make the back of his head
strike the ground. The world around him began to spin. His grip
weakened, allowing the wolf raider to press his advantage.

"My life for yours!" the dark figure hissed. "A small price
for the empire's triumph!"

So now it ends, he managed to think. *Cut down at night in a
street far from anything I might call home.*

He heard a small, startled grunt from the raider. The weight
on his body shifted to one side. Instinct took over. The Gryphon
followed the shifting of the weight and pushed his attacker off
in that direction. He heard a clatter and realized that the knife
had fallen from the Aramite's hand. Now, even with his head
still ringing, the advantage was becoming his.

The raider was by no means defeated, however. Once more
he tried to butt heads. The lionbird was ready for him, however,
and tipped his own head out of the way. Then he did the only
thing he could think of doing that would end the flight in swift
fashion.

He transformed. For most shapeshifters, such an act would
have left them helpless for a few precious seconds. For the
Gryphon, long practiced at shaping at a moment's notice, it was
not so. Two decades of war had kept that ability well honed.

The spy let out a yelp that the Gryphon's taloned hand all but
muffled. Taken back by the astonishing sight of his adversary
shifting form, the Aramite was too slow to block the attack

that came next. With grim satisfaction, the Gryphon twisted his adversary's head to one side, snapping his neck.

Verifying that the man was dead, he slowly rose and whispered, "Your life for that of my son . . . hardly a balance but certainly a beginning."

It was only then that he recalled Tori. He transformed back into a human even as he turned to where he had last left her. It was not surprising to find her gone. Still, something had caused the Aramite to grunt in pain and shift his weight. It could only have been an attack of some sort by the enchantress. A kick in the head, he suspected. Why bring attention to herself as a spellcaster when a simple physical assault worked as effectively?

The area had grown conspicuously devoid of people and the Gryphon knew that such emptiness usually preceded an appearance by the local guard. He regretted that he had allowed his anger to seize mastery; the spy might have given him some further information, including how many of his ilk had already spread through Zuu. The city guard would have to be satisfied with the corpse. Certainly any other spies in the city would go into hiding now that one of their number was dead and they had no way of knowing who was responsible. This one had acted on his own; if there had been more, they would have entered the struggle, for he was not flattering himself when he thought they considered him a target of prime importance.

The brief respite, however much it might have put him in danger of being sighted by the city guard, had served its purpose. His head still throbbed, but his concentration was sufficient for spellcasting. It was time to leave Zuu and follow Cabe's trail.

Trail. The Gryphon searched for the knife that the woman Tori had stolen from Cabe, but found nothing. It might have been thrown into the darkness during the struggle, but he suspected it was once more in the hands of the enchantress. She would gain small success with it now, however. In the short time he had held it, he had made a few magical alterations. If she sought out the warlock after this, she would simply reappear in the same location she had started from. Let her search for Cabe Bedlam if she chose, but she would have to do it on her own.

One of the first lessons in magic is to never assume it will always work the way you desire.

It was a lesson he tried to remind himself of each and every day. It was a lesson he was certain he would need to recall when he entered the desolate domain of the Crystal Dragon.

The city guard was near. With one last bitter glance at the raider's sprawled body, the Gryphon regripped the guiding blade and teleported away . . .

. . . to the hills of Esedi.

The trail was stronger here, as he had expected. The blade had probably brought him to within a few yards of where Cabe himself had materialized. He allowed himself a brief human smile, for teleportation was always a chancy thing when one was not familiar with the location, then let his human guise melt away since it was no longer needed.

Cabe and Darkhorse had done fairly well in their choice of locations. Under normal conditions, they would have enjoyed an excellent view of the eastern portion of the peninsula. Not all of it, of course, but enough to enable them to plan the journey's beginning. Legar was not as massive a region as Esedi or even the immense Dagora Forest, but it was filled with hills, crevices, and a system of underground caverns that rivaled those in the Tyber Mountains. Add to the treacherous, uneven landscape possible encounters with the Quel and now the wolf raiders, and you had very good reasons to move slowly and carefully through Legar.

And now this mist . . . He was familiar with the Grey Mists, the dank, mind-sapping haze that covered Lochivar. Lochivar, on the southeastern edge of the Dragonrealm, was the kingdom of the Black Dragon, who was the source of that magical fog. Knowing what the Grey Mists could do, the Gryphon was glad he had not simply decided to teleport into this murk. Even from here he could sense its evil. There was something wild about it, but it was the wildness of a thing in its death throes, for there was also a feeling of decay about it.

If this is how it seems under the dimness of the moons, then how is it in the daytime? Worse? How will it be when I actually enter it? He would find out soon enough. There was no real reason to remain here for even a fraction of the time he had spent in the city. Cabe and Darkhorse would have waited here only long enough to prepare themselves for Legar and the Gryphon was as prepared as he would ever be. He would learn nothing new from these silent hills, nothing that would aid his mission and his vengeance.

Nothing? He paused, noticing something for the first time. Why was it so deathly quiet here? Was the poison covering Legar so great that the wildlife could not stand to be even this close to it? That could not be. In the distance, the lionbird could barely make out a few of the normal sounds of night, nocturnal birds and animals. It was only this one region where the creatures had either grown silent or fled. Only the region in which he stood.

The Gryphon's sword was out and ready before his next breath.

"Well, I must admit I was not expecting *you!*"

From the darkness emerged a huge shape blacker than the night. Ice-blue eyes glittered without the aid of the moons' poor illumination.

"Darkhorse!"

The shadow steed dipped his head. "You are far from your war, Lord Gryphon, but then your war seems to have strayed as well!"

"You've seen them then. The raiders."

"Seen them and fought them!"

"Fought them . . . and where is Cabe, then, demon steed?" Was he too late for the warlock? Had D'Farany added to his list of victims already?

The leviathan's response did not encourage him. "I . . . lost him."

"He—"

"No!" Darkhorse grew vehement. "He is *not* dead! He cannot be! We were merely separated in the foul mist! He said nothing and I thought he must be behind me, keeping clear!"

The Gryphon cut him off with a curt gesture. His general uneasiness around the pitch-black creature had given way to his concern for Cabe Bedlam and the need to know what sort of things he might face in shrouded Legar. "Tell me from the beginning. Speak carefully, tell me all, but do so fairly quickly."

Darkhorse's easy acquiescence surprised him at first until he reminded himself that Cabe Bedlam was one of the eternal's few true friends. The telling of the tale was short and swift. When it was over, it was clear that Darkhorse was dismayed by what he considered his terrible carelessness. There was something more to what had happened than what the shadow steed had related to him, however. Whatever it was, its roots went deep. Some distraction in the eternal's mind that had caused Darkhorse not to notice that he and the warlock were being purposely separated.

Oddly, knowing that the creature from the Void could become so distraught lessened some of the Gryphon's wariness of him. He felt he understood the workings of Darkhorse's mind better than he ever had in the past.

"The monstrosity you fought was an illusion, you say?"

"Yes, and when I turned to comment so to Cabe, he was also gone! I never heard him call out!"

"He might have, but you still might not have heard him. In that place, I would not be surprised." The Gryphon stared at the mist, so unsettling, so hungry, even in the calm of night. "You couldn't find his trail, either."

"I detected nothing! I, Darkhorse, could not sense him!"

"Yes . . ." The lionbird contemplated the situation. The knowledge that the wolf raiders were active throughout Legar made his mane bristle and his claws unsheathe. He wanted to hunt down each and every one of the marauders like the animals they were and savor their deaths; yet the Gryphon knew that not only would it still not fill the hole inside, but he could not abandon a friend. In that he and the shadow steed were one. Cabe Bedlam was missing and if he had been captured by the Aramites, then there would be opportunity enough for the Gryphon to try to satiate his need for vengeance. If Cabe's fate was otherwise, then the raiders would have to wait. He had no doubt that they would still be there. Once the Aramites gained a foothold, the only way to remove them was to kill them.

He was willing to try, but not now.

"Do you think you can find the last place you left him?"

Darkhorse gazed out at the ominous mass blanketing Legar. "I might be able to take us that far, but what use will it be?"

"It may be of some use, believe me." The Gryphon revealed the small blade he had utilized to follow the warlock's trail this far. "You had nothing of his to aid you in your search."

"Even if I had, I do not think it would have worked. The mist has the taint of Nimth upon it, Lord Gryphon! You are one of the few with sufficient knowledge to understand what that means! You *also* knew Shade!" The shadow steed paused. "Nothing works as it should down there! The laws of magic—the laws of *nature*—cannot be trusted in Legar so long as that foulness remains!''

"We can only try." The lionbird gazed at the blade. "This may be Cabe's best, possibly only hope. Our combined skills might prove to be enough to overwhelm it."

"Overwhelm *Nimth*? You must surely jest! I knew the Vraad! I knew Shade!''

The black stallion's tone each time he spoke of the blur-faced warlock revealed volumes to the Gryphon. Shade was somehow tied to Darkhorse's troubles. What had the Bedlams' messages said? Darkhorse continued to search for Shade as if he might somehow have survived. Was he that afraid of the tortured warlock?

No, not afraid. If there was anyone who might understand Darkhorse and what he is, it would have been Shade.

He had no time to ponder further. Darkhorse's inner struggles would have to wait until there was peace, assuming that ever happened. Now it was time for Legar.

"This is not Nimth and neither the Crystal Dragon nor the wolf raiders are Vraad. What exists down there can only be a *reflection* of Nimth's chaos. I think that if we try the spell from as near as possible to the place where you two became separated, then we stand a chance. If it fails . . . we still have to enter. You know that Cabe would have returned here by now if he could have. He would know to do that."

Darkhorse kicked at the ground. "I know that, Lord Gryphon! Ha! I have been thinking about it since I materialized back here! I thought he might have accidentally teleported elsewhere, but there is no place here that I have not searched and if he in some way eluded my search he would, indeed, still have returned to this location by now!"

"Then we should not hesitate any longer."

"Very well." Darkhorse trotted closer. "You shall have to ride me as he did, Your Majesty! We did not trust that we would arrive at the same destination, this being the Crystal Dragon's realm. The foul fog makes the danger of that worse."

"I agree." As he mounted, the lionbird thought of what his companion had just said. "And do you also find it odd that the Dragon King has been so quiet even though he has in the past always dealt swiftly with those who would disturb his existence?"

A snort. "I still think that this was his doing! I, for one, would not call this doing nothing!"

"Nothing it certainly isn't, demon steed, but it's an unfocused, dangerous method by which to rid himself of the Aramites. If this was the Crystal Dragon's doing, I would like to know why he chose such madness as a tool. It is as much a risk, perhaps more, as the wolf raiders are."

"Be that as it may, we *still* have to journey through it!" The leviathan swung his head around so that he faced dark Legar. "Give me but a moment and I will be ready." Darkhorse's head tilted to one side. "Curious!"

The Gryphon leaned forward and tried to see what interested his mount so. "What is it? I don't see anything."

Darkhorse shook his head, sending his mane flying. "I suspect wishful thinking is all it is! When I stare at the fog, it looks not quite so dense as it was earlier! Truly, it must be the moonlight!"

Squinting, the Gryphon could see nothing. If there had been a change in the density of the fog, he could not tell. From the shadow horse's words, it would have happened before he had even teleported to here. Whether or not it *had* happened, the lionbird could still not make out even the slightest detail beneath the upper surface of the shroud of fog.

Darkhorse finally stirred. "Well! It matters not! We must find Cabe! That is all that matters!"

That, a legion of wolf raiders, and a Dragon King who does not act as one would expect, the Gryphon silently corrected as he held tight. *Other than those few things, we have nothing to worry about.*

—— XII ——

Cabe woke to the jarring sight of a Quel face looming over him. The long snout was mere inches from his own countenance. The warlock's nose wrinkled; the Quel's breath was putrid.

His head was suddenly filled to bursting with overlapping

images. Cabe gasped, put his hands on his head, and tried to shut the sensations out. He saw himself, the wolf raiders, the Quel, a vague image that must be the Crystal Dragon, a beach . . . there was just too much!

"Stop! I can't take it all in!"

Mercifully, the Quel presence in his head withdrew. As he regained control of his senses, the weary spellcaster sat up and surveyed his surroundings. They were in a small cavern with only one exit, an exit guarded by yet another of the underdwellers. Cabe counted three Quel in all, but then he realized that the third, off to the far side of the chamber, was slumped over. A single image touched his mind, confirmation from the one near him that their companion was dead and had been so for some time.

He wondered how long he had been unconscious. Cabe had faint memories of being pulled under, of watching the earth fill in above him. He recalled little else after that, for something had caused him to pass out.

The Quel inquisitor reached out and pointed by the warlock's right hand. Cabe looked down and saw a gem. He vaguely recalled it having been in his hand when the images had first struck him. He nodded understanding to the armored leviathan and picked it up.

Injury . . . urgent need . . . question?

The combination of images, sensations, and emotions was as close as the Quel could come to speaking in the human tongue. Cabe was aware of the communication crystal and found it a fascinating tool, but it took careful thinking to sometimes decipher what was meant. It was possible for the Quel to communicate to him without it, but then the images would have been less detailed and many of the projected sensations would have failed to even reach his mind.

They want to know if I'm injured in any way. He shook his head. Considering that any injury would have been the Quel's doing, Cabe was not entirely impressed by the subterraneans' concern. Still, it was unusual that they should place any importance in his well-being, unless they wanted something from him.

Something involving the wolf raiders?

The images projected by the one Quel, a female, if the warlock was correct, shifted almost the instant he formulated the question.

Although the question had merely been for his own contemplation, the Quel answered as best she could.

*Black shells . . . defenders . . . the hungry magic . . . defeat
. . . the city lost . . . statement.*

Statement. The manner by which the creatures communicated
made the reply sound almost matter-of-fact until one stared into
the dark, inhuman eyes of the Quel and saw the loss there. Her
city, the Quel city, was in the hands of the Aramites, who had
used some sort of magic spell to nullify the defenses. She and a
few like her had escaped capture, he imagined. There were only
a few Quel at any time and so they had not had the resources to
completely combat a foe as determined as the wolf raiders. If they
had, he suspected that the raiders would have found themselves in
the midst of one of the worst hand-to-hand struggles they had
ever come across. One Quel was worth more than a few human
soldiers any day, no matter how well trained the latter were.

Black shells . . . hunt . . . too few . . . statement.

He saw them hunting down a lone guard every now and then,
but such attacks were not enough. One by one, the secrets of
their cities fell into the hands of the invaders.

Cabe stiffened. "What about—"

The response was swift. *Sacrifice . . . hidden . . . suspicious
but unable to find . . . safe . . . for now . . . danger in thought
. . . statement.*

Their greatest secret was safe, but the Aramites were thorough.
They might at any time find it. The Quel did not even wish to
think about that, for fear that doing so might somehow bring the
discovery to pass. Cabe received a swift, curt look from the
female who told him there would be no more questions on that
matter.

He had no delusions that the underdwellers saw him as anything more than a means to an end. Their concern was for their
own kind; they saw in him only someone who shared an obvious
interest in seeing the black shells, as they called the raiders, gone
from the Dragonrealm.

"You don't make cooperation very enticing," he bluntly informed his captor. "What difference would it make for me to
help you?"

A single image of a tall, opaque sphere flashed into his mind.
For the first time, Cabe recalled Plool. The Quel still had the

Vraad hidden away and were attempting to use him as a bargaining chip. It almost made the warlock want to laugh. In one respect, there was a temptation to leave the Vraad where he was, for it would be the best way to ensure that he caused no further chaos with his Nimth-spawned magic.

Cabe knew he could do no such thing, though. Even Plool deserved a chance. Also, the Aramites *were* a deadlier threat to the continent, at least now. The Dragonrealm had survived centuries of Quel, confined as they were to only a few wandering above and below the surface of Legar. The raiders would never settle for that. They would seek to rebuild their power base. He was certain that other ships sailed the sea, other ships seeking a new port. The longer the wolf raiders had, the deeper they would be entrenched.

He would work with the Quel for as long as it was safe, but he knew better than to trust them. "What about the one who was with me? What about your prisoner?"

The answer was short, succinct, and proof that this was meant to be no partnership but rather a situation demanding his complete obedience to their cause. Cabe lost whatever little sympathy he might have ever had for his captors. Memories of his past experiences with the Quel returned to him. They were vivid and sometimes painful memories.

The warlock wished it were possible for him to just forget Plool, but he was not that sort of person . . . and the underdwellers certainly had to be aware of that.

His inquisitor rose and indicated he should follow suit. Rising stiffly, the wary mage followed the Quel to the tunnel mouth. The other creature, taller and definitely a male, waited until the two had passed before joining. The male moved with some stiffness, as if working with muscles long unused. The Quel were careful to keep him sandwiched in between, he noted. A brief touch with his mind also indicated that they were doing what they could to stifle his magical abilities, but their strength was not enough to completely disable him. His mind already shielded so that the gemstone he still had to carry would not betray him, Cabe pondered his possible options. Down here, his sorcery appeared to work, but what would happen if he tried to teleport to the surface? Could he do it safely? More to the point, did he have the concentration and strength to even perform the spell? He doubted it. Still, he was fairly certain he would be able to defend himself when it came time for the Quel to turn upon him.

The warlock wondered what he would do about Plool when that happened.

As they walked, Cabe, with growing curiosity, carefully studied the tunnel. It was a claustrophobic thing, not at all like the larger passages he recalled from his earlier encounters. There was barely room enough for one of the diggers to pass. More important, after the first few steps, the only sources of illumination became the occasional crystal embedded in the walls. They were of the same type as those in the vast tunnels, but so scattered and so few, it was as if they had been added only recently and with great haste.

This is a new tunnel. Very new. "Where are we going?"

He received no response from his companions. The more he thought about it, the more they seemed to be growing increasingly anxious. The warlock did not find that comforting. Anything that worried the Quel surely had to be fearsome.

There was only one thing he could think of that would put such uneasiness into the minds of his captors. One creature.

Only the Crystal Dragon.

They wouldn't! That would be suicidal!

Unfortunately, he could think of no other explanation. Cabe had intended on seeking out the lord of Legar, but now that he was possibly on his way to do just that, the idea had turned sour. Who was to say that the Crystal Dragon might not find his intrusion just as irritating as that of the wolf raiders? What had he been thinking? One could not just walk up and ask to see the Dragon King!

But that was what the Quel intended *him* to do. He knew that the moment they came to the end of the tunnel. Before him was a vast cavern that glittered so great that he had to shield his eyes for several seconds before they finally became accustomed to the brilliance. Gemlike stalactites and stalagmites, looking much like the jagged teeth of some great beast, dotted the cavern. The faceted walls reflected themselves again and again and again, an infinity of cold, gleaming beauty. Cabe began to sweat heavily, but not because of fear. The heat in the cavern was ghastly and when he stared at the floor, which was also of crystal, he knew why. Some subterranean source of heat buried deep beneath was what turned the chamber into an oven. It even gave the floor a reddish tinge. It was not enough to make travel across impossible, but the warlock did not intend to stand on any one spot too long.

What he saw beyond the chamber made him forget the heat. Carved into the far wall was a temple that, in many ways, resembled the Manor, a place that Cabe wished he had never left. Columns rose high, at least two stories. There were three doorways. Symbols that the warlock did not recognize formed an arc over each of them. Cabe knew that the work was very, very old, but it was still in immaculate condition. A sense of ancient power radiated from the temple.

He was on the threshold of the Dragon King's inner sanctum.

The Quel in front of him shifted to the side. *Journey . . . the crystal lord . . . (fear) . . . seeking an audience . . . statement!*

So this *was* to be his role. They wanted him to do what they could not, namely face the Dragon King and seek his aid. The warlock found himself amused. He was expected to go where they refused to tread and seek aid on their behalf. It almost made him laugh aloud. Their capture of him must have been a lucky but desperate venture. It said something for their ability to plot under dire circumstances but little for their bravery.

The male took hold of his shoulders and shook him. New images danced in Cabe Bedlam's head. *Audience . . . the crystal lord in his sanctum . . . dispersing the floating death . . . driving the black shells back into the sea . . . statement!/question?*

It took him time to decipher the last. The message was evidently a list of requests the Quel had for the Crystal Dragon, requests that they wanted Cabe to make. From the way the male gripped him, he knew that even the very thought of asking the drake lord for such aid unnerved the subterraneans. They *deeply* feared the might of the Crystal Dragon . . . and Cabe could hardly blame them for that.

He was prodded from behind. The Quel would not join him on this last part of the trek. They would trust that their captive would make the warlock do what they wanted. It had probably never occurred to them that Cabe might have gone even without a threat.

Slowly he entered the gleaming chamber. What wonders the

underground recesses of Legar held. It was amazing that the surface of the place did not collapse, considering how extensive the world beneath was. Of course, more than a little of it had been carved by intelligent hands, not the forces of nature. Those hands had made quite certain that their efforts would not end up buried in rubble.

Cabe still found it amazing, nonetheless.

The temperature was steady, which was fortunate. He still found he had to loosen the top of his robe. It was bad if not worse than being on the surface during noontime.

The walk across passed without incident, although at one point the Quel hooted something. He turned, but even holding the gem, he could not understand what they wanted. They did not appear to want him to return, so Cabe finally turned back to the glistening temple and continued on.

It was not until he stood before the carved structure that he discovered a problem. While there were indentations representing windows and doorways, none of them were real entrances. As far as he could see, the temple was nothing more than a vast relief.

There must be something! He stared at his reflection, distorted by the multifaceted surface, and thought. The Quel would not have sent him to this place if they had not believed it to be a way to the Crystal Dragon. Yet if they were too frightened to come this far, then perhaps none of their kind had ever journeyed close enough to see that this was no more than some sculptor's masterpiece. It hardly seemed possible, but . . .

"Who seeks passage?"

The voice, piercing, echoed all around him. Cabe stepped back from the temple and as he did an astonishing thing happened, for his distorted reflection, instead of copying his movements, stepped *forward*. Not only did it step forward, but it left the confines of the wall and continued toward him.

"Who seeks passage?" This time, it was definitely his macabre reflection that spoke.

"I do," Cabe responded, finally able to find his own voice.

Although the crystal golem—the warlock could find no better term for what faced him—looked his way, the eyes did not exactly fix on him. Rather, they appeared focused behind him, perhaps on the Quel. "You alone seek passage?"

"I alone seek passage, yes. I would speak with the Crystal Dragon."

The guardian was silent. It was eerie to stare at himself, especially a self who was twisted and jagged. Cabe reached up to rub his chin in thought, a habit he had long had, and watched bemused as the reflection followed the same course. Cabe wondered what the creature would do if he started to dance.

An eternity passed before the golem finally said, "You may pass through."

Cabe glanced beyond the golem. He saw no doorway. "Where do I go?"

The guardian looked at him with vacant eyes. "Follow."

He began walking backward.

After a moment's hesitation, the warlock obeyed. The crystal creature had no trouble walking backward, but the sight made Cabe stumble twice. He kept waiting for a passage to open in the temple wall, but nothing changed. As the guardian reached the wall, Cabe braced himself for the collision.

The golem melted into the crystal.

The warlock froze, uncertain as to what to do now. He stared at his reflection. Almost it seemed to be waiting for him.

Its mouth opened. "Follow."

"Follow?"

"Follow yourself if you would enter," was the only explanation he received.

He thought he understood, but that made it no easier. Nodding, Cabe focused on his reflection, tensed, and walked forward.

He closed his eyes just before he would have hit the wall and so he was never exactly sure what happened next. Instead of a harsh, very solid wall, the anxious mage walked into a substance that reminded him of syrup. Gritting his teeth, he continued through it. The voice of the guardian urged him on now and then. Despite being surrounded by the odd substance, the warlock had no difficulty breathing. That in no way meant that the crossing was easy on him. He was reminded of Gwen, who had been trapped in an amber prison by his father, Azran, and left there for nearly two hundred years. The thought of being so imprisoned sent a chill down his spine.

When his hand broke through to empty space, Cabe sighed in relief.

Only when he was free did he dare open his eyes. He did not look around but rather spun back and faced the wall through which he had passed. The warlock stared at it. To the eye, it was as it should have been, a crystal-encrusted barrier of rock. There was no passage and when he touched it, he felt only what one would expect to feel. Rock.

"If you are finished, huuuman . . ."

A drake warrior stood waiting for him in the new chamber, a drake warrior like none he had ever seen. Thin, glittering, his skin armor was an array of multifaceted jewels, not all of them the same color. There were deep greens, sunlit golds, ocean blues, and so much more. When the drake moved, it was a graceful movement, almost as if the creature were a dancer, not a fighter.

"Your Majesty?"

The flat, half-seen reptilian visage broke into a thin-lipped smile. "I will take you to him."

Cabe reddened slightly. He should not have assumed. It might be a mark against him now. The Dragon King might take umbrage at being mistaken for one of his mere subjects.

His new guide led him along a well-worn path that, like all else here, spoke of incredible age. Most everything down here had been built long before the Dragon Kings; Cabe was certain of that. He wondered if the Quel had built it. Possibly. Then again, they, too, might have come across it and decided to simply move in. Some additions looked more recent than others. Differences in style could be seen here and there. Everything gleamed, but fortunately not with too great an intensity.

They passed only two other drakes, both warriors like the first. He wondered how small the clan was. Some drake clans were larger than others. The Ice Dragon had sacrificed the last of his people for his master spell and several other clans had been more or less decimated over the past couple decades by their struggles with each other and the humans, but some, like Green and Blue, were actually increasing in number for the first time in generations. Cabe doubted that this particular clan was large. Legar could not support so many. Their principal source of food would have to come from the sea, for life was not abundant enough here. True, there were things that grew well under the surface, but these *were* dragons he was speaking of, which meant they needed meat of some sort.

Their journey ended before the mouth of another tunnel. Two warriors flanked each side of the mouth. Within, Cabe could make out only darkness.

His guide turned to him. "He awaits within, Cabe Bedlam."

"You know who I am."

"*He* knew. I simply obey." With that, the drake abruptly turned from him and walked away.

One of the guards used a lance to indicate that he should enter. Putting on a mask of resolve, the warlock stalked past the sentries and stepped into the darkness before hesitation got the better of him. It was not, he was grateful to see, like crossing through the wall. Instead, the moment he was through the entranceway, the darkness was burned away by a brilliant illumination. Cabe blinked, found himself blinded again.

"There isss an object in front of you, Cabe Bedlam. Pick it up. Itsss purposssse will become apparent to you."

The blinded warlock reached down, then recalled that he was still holding the Quel device. He started to pocket it, but a warning hiss made him halt.

"You have no more need of that. Drop it."

Cabe did . . . and a second later heard a crackling sound, as if something were melting. He did not dare try to look, but rather searched for the vague shape of the object the voice had mentioned. His hands came upon a curved item that upon very close inspection proved to be a visor of sorts. It was designed to be worn over the ears like a pair of the glasses that were now fairly common among humans. Gingerly he put it on, blinked a few times, and let his eyes complete the task of adjusting.

Even with the visor on, the chamber still gleamed. Now, at least, he could see it . . . and also its lone inhabitant.

"Welcome to my domain, Massster Bedlam."

He knew of the Crystal Dragon, knew what he looked like from the visions, but still Cabe was not completely prepared for the leviathan.

The lord of Legar was possibly the largest of the Dragon Kings he had ever seen. Like his counterpart Blue, however, the Crystal Dragon was sleeker than some of the others. Yet it was not size that so overwhelmed the warlock. Neither was it the image of a dragon who seemed carved from the very crystal he took his title from. The drake warriors had dazzled Cabe's eyes enough, but their monarch positively blinded. In fact, it was the Crystal Dragon who so made the room blinding.

What overwhelmed him was the age. There was no particular thing that indicated it, but staring at his host, Cabe knew that here was the oldest of the present Dragon Kings. Even older than Ice, who had claimed the mantle of age often. It was said that the drake lords tended to live a thousand years at best, mostly because of the violent world of their kind. The warlock doubted that any of the other Dragon Kings were more than seven hundred years old. They might have the potential for long lives, but the drakes always found conflicts to kill themselves in . . . much the way humans did. Unfortunately for the drakes, their kind did not multiply as quickly as Cabe's race did.

Sharp diamond wings spread. The huge head dipped down so as to better observe the tiny human. "You have ssssought me, Cabe Bedlam, and I have given you an audience. Do you now intend to ssssimply sssstare for that time?"

It did not help that no matter where he looked, all he saw was either the reflected image of the Dragon King's unique countenance or that of his own, uncertain visage. Each face was distorted. He felt as if they all watched him, awaiting his response.

"Your pardon, Your Majesty. This is, I hope you'll understand, much to take in."

"Isss it?" An unreadable look crossed the draconian features.

Try as he might, Cabe could not completely calm himself down. This chamber was by far the most daunting. It served some distinct purpose, a purpose that he could not help but think that the Dragon King was trying to hide from him. All this blazing brilliance, brought forth by the drake lord himself, was meant to distract. The warlock was not certain how he had come to that conclusion, just that it made some sense when he viewed the chamber and its lord as a whole.

"It is," he finally answered. Clearing his suddenly dry throat, Cabe continued. "You must know, my lord, that even though it was the Quel who led me here, I would have come to request an audience with you regardless."

"Then you are here about the black plague sssswarming over *my* realm." The Dragon King shifted. Although he pretended control, his movements looked forced to his human guest, as if the crystalline monarch was trying too hard to appear confident. The drake lord's entire body spoke of a creature at war within. Even his disinterested tone was too perfect.

What goes on here? This was not what Cabe had expected. "I am, yes. You should know. It is your summons that brought me here in the first place."

"My what?" The reptilian eyes widened. Almost it seemed that fear was the dominant emotion, but Cabe could not believe that was possible. What could frighten the Crystal Dragon?

"Your . . . summons. The vision and the dream."

"Visions . . . dreams?" Lifting his head high, the glittering leviathan turned his gaze toward the walls. The Dragon King had an apparent fascination for his reflections, but not because of any vanity. The mage watched him closely. Although he had only been in the Dragon King's presence for a minute or two, Cabe was already beginning to worry about the drake lord's sanity.

"You didn't send them?" Cabe asked after a long silence had passed.

Instead of answering his question, the Crystal Dragon quietly ordered, "Tell me of the visions."

Having few options, the worried spellcaster did that. He described his first experience and how he had shrugged it off. Then Cabe described the dream and how Aurim had also been affected. At that the reptilian monarch glanced his way, but the images soon snared him again. Cabe concluded with the vision he had suffered while recuperating in the hills of Esedi. When his tale was complete, the warlock waited for some comment.

Another long silence ensued, but at last the Crystal Dragon gazed down at him. The look in those great, inhuman orbs was enough to make Cabe Bedlam stiffen. There was sanity in them, but not much.

"I did not ssssummon you, warlock . . . or perhapssss I did."

"I don't understand." Why did it feel like he was always saying that? The frustrated sorcerer wondered if *anyone* understood what happened in the Dragonrealm. Sometimes it was as if life was but a game. A macabre game.

The great dragon unfurled and furled his wings over and over again. The talons of his forepaws gouged deep into the floor. Cabe looked around and realized that the chamber had grown darker.

"No . . . you wouldn't. No one would, warlock. That issss my bane, the sssssword that hangsssss over my head. *No one* understands what I live with." The cold tones only added to the image of a creature slowly going mad. "I thought of ssssummon- ing you, Master Bedlam, thought of it but did not." He looked away from the tiny human and studied the chamber from wall to ceiling. "To thissss place, though, ssssuch a thought wassss good enough." The Crystal Dragon hissed. "Away with you!"

Cabe's first inclination was that his audience had come to an abrupt end, but it was not he to whom the drake lord roared the command. Fascinated, the warlock watched as the images all around him faded away. The crystalline walls dulled. They no longer reflected. The illumination also faded, albeit not com- pletely.

"I ssssometimes think it hassss a mind of its own," the dragon murmured. He continued to stare at the now blank walls. "I ssssometimes think that the chamber controlsss me and not the other way." The Crystal Dragon laughed in self-mockery. "Ironic if true, would you not say?"

The warlock kept quiet. Noticing the lack of response, the behemoth tilted his head so that he could see his human guest out of the corner of his eye. "It takesss my thoughtsss, Cabe Bedlam, and makessss them reality. I can ssssee anything, any place, any perssssson in the Dragonrealm with the aid of thissss chamber. It showssss me the world ssso that I do not have to risssk myself and venture out.

"But there isss another sssside to it. Another side. It issss not ssssatisfied with my direct commandsss, no! It mussst have my deeper thoughtssss, my sssleeping thoughtsss!"

The massive drake stirred. Cabe wanted to step back, but something within told him it would behoove him to stay where he was. He had to maintain a strong front. "So you thought of summoning me but did not."

The Dragon King quieted at the sound of his voice. Cabe's calm provided him with an anchor for his sanity. "I thought of you more than once, recalling your part in the ssssstruggle with the dragon lord Ice."

Which might explain why there had been more than one vision. Perhaps each time the drake had thought of him, a vision had been sent. So he had journeyed here under a misconception. The dragon had not called him, but rather only *thought* about doing so. If he understood his host, then the chamber had taken his desire for Cabe's aid and acted upon it even after the Dragon King had chosen otherwise.

"I understood some of what I saw, but some of the images made no sense. The men in dragon-scale armor; what does it have to do with the wolf raiders?"

"Nothing!" snapped the Dragon King. Then, realizing how he had reacted, he withdrew into himself. "Nothing. A twisssting of random thoughtsssss and dreamsss. Nothing to concern *you.*"

Perhaps or perhaps not, Cabe thought. Whether or not it concerned him, it appeared he would receive no clarification from his host and the warlock had no intention of pressing the subject. He had no way of predicting what the Dragon King's reaction would be then.

"Then you don't require my aid?"

A pause. "I am the Crystal Dragon."

He knew what the drake lord's response was supposed to imply, but the hesitant manner in which it was spoken belied that implication. The Crystal Dragon was trying to hide something and failing miserably. Yet Cabe dared not make mention of that fact. It would be far too easy for his host to take out whatever frustrations and fears he had on the warlock.

"Your Majesty—"

"I have the ssssituation in hand, mage! That issss your ansssswer; be sssatisfied with it!"

"I only had a question, Your Majesty." When the Dragon King said nothing, Cabe dared push on. *"Was* it you who unleashed this deadly fog upon your own kingdom?"

His first thought was that he had indeed stepped over the line, for the Dragon King rose to his full height and hissed loudly. The chamber grew stifling. The leviathan spread his wings wide; his talons sliced at the air before him. He thrust his head toward the human, stopping only a yard from Cabe. The warlock struggled to maintain his composure even though every fiber screamed for him to run. Cabe did not consider himself a brave soul in the heroic sense of the word. He remained where he was basically because he knew that to run would be futile. Better to face a threat than turn one's back on it.

"I releasssed it, Cabe Bedlam! I releasssed the foulness upon my own domain and it isss my ressssponsssibility!"

"But to even call upon a shadow of Nimth's dec—"

"Nimth?" The Crystal Dragon recoiled as if Cabe had just informed him that he carried plague or some other dire disease.

Could he have not known? It was not a simple task to read those draconian features. There was fear there, but of what only the Crystal Dragon knew. "Yes, Nimth, Your Majesty. A world lost in time, ever dying. There was a race of sorcerers there, a race called the *Vraad*. They—"

"I *know* what they were! I know better than you!" The glittering behemoth shifted yet closer. "I know all there issss to know about their foul ways! Did you think I wanted to do this?" Again, the Dragon King looked away. His stentorian voice grew softer. "I knew what it wassss I would unleash. I have alwayssss lived with that. But it issss only a shadow, assss you mentioned. A shadow! No ssssubstance!" He quieted yet again. "But I fear it will not ssssstop them. They will be sssslowed, but not defeated. You are correct to be fearful of it. I dared let it go no further than I did, lessst ssssomething else come through. Things of Nimth wreak only deadly havoc in this world."

Cabe took a deep breath. He had to tell the Crystal Dragon. Only the lord of Legar could possibly send Plool back. It would not solve the problem of the wolf raiders, but it would prevent the Vraad from possibly causing further chaos. That, they did not need. If Plool could have been trusted, Cabe might have held his tongue, but Plool could *not* be and the warlock knew that.

"You . . . did let something through, Your Majesty. Someone, I should say."

The dragon's eyes narrowed. There was the slightest tremor in his voice, a tremor that shocked the mage despite all he had already noted about his terrible host. *"What . . . did . . . you . . . say?"*

"A creature . . . a man . . . of Nimth came through when you opened the way. A . . ." Would the Dragon King know enough about the history of Nimth? So far, it sounded as if he might know even more than the warlock did. "A Vraad sorcerer."

"You *lie!* The Vraad are dead and forgotten! I know! I—" The gleaming titan's denial ended in a roar that echoed again and again throughout the chamber. Cabe was forced to cover his ears. This time, he was certain that the Dragon King had lost permanent control. This time, there would be no escaping the obvious madness of the drake lord.

Yet . . . yet, the Crystal Dragon *did* calm. It was as if a different creature were abruptly there before Cabe, a creature more cold, fatalistic.

Like the Ice Dragon? He hoped it was not so. One of the few reasons that the Dragonrealm was not a dead, frozen waste was the leviathan before him. If the Crystal Dragon was now mad in the same manner as his counterpart to the far north had been, then the wolf raiders might become the least of the continent's worries.

"Wheeeerrre? Where issss it?" A scarlet, forked tongue flickered forth. "Where isss the Vraad?"

Cabe was regretting his idea now. He did not want to hand even someone like Plool over to the dragon; yet he had committed himself. "The Quel have him. If you could send him back . . ."

"Ssssend it back? Sssend the monstrosity back?" The Dragon King's maw snapped shut. He closed his eyes for a brief time. When he finally opened them, the Dragon King nodded and said, "You are correct, of courssssse, Cabe Bedlam. That would be for the best. Requiring little in effort, yesss."

"Can you take him from the Quel?" The warlock was startled to find himself asking such a question. He had grown up always believing that if any one of the present Dragon Kings was omnipotent, it was the Crystal Dragon. A few Quel should have required the least of his power.

Here the titan recovered his aplomb a bit. "I do not have to take him. They will *give* him to me."

The chamber gleamed. The crystalline walls were alive with not only the Dragon King's reflection but the mage's as well. The drake lord stared at one of the walls and suddenly the reflections melted away, becoming other images. They were images of another cavern, a place where a single Quel toyed with a device. The vision of the Quel was repeated from a thousand different angles and distances, but mixed in with those images was a more important one that Cabe focused on. The sphere that held Plool.

He frowned. It had a reddish tinge to it. It was the same sort of reddish tinge he associated with heat. Were they trying to *burn* the Vraad alive?

The shimmering leviathan leaned toward that particular vision. "He isss mine."

A host of identical Quel jumped as if bitten. A legion of startled, identical countenances looked around in panic. Cabe took some small satisfaction. He had no more sympathy for the Quel plight.

The Crystal Dragon spoke again. "You will give him to me."

The images faded away. Cabe blinked as he watched his own face multiply over and over across the chamber walls. No matter where he looked, he saw only his own uncomprehending visage.

"Hold out your handssss, mage."

Cabe obeyed.

"You hold the doorway to damnation."

In the warlock's hands was the very sphere that Plool had led him to atop the hill. It had not been taken by the Quel, the Crystal Dragon had summoned it back to him. He tensed, fearful that his grip might slip and send the fragile-looking artifact to the hard floor. If the door was broken, *all* of Nimth would flow into the Dragonrealm.

The dragon saw his dismay. "Ssssimple clumsiness will not bring about the end of our world, Cabe Bedlam. It would take tremendoussss power to even ssssscratch the surface of thissss toy. It would take more power than even that of a Vraad . . . or a hundred Vraad, if ssssuch cooperation wassss posssible."

It was unnerving to know what he held in his hands, unnerving to know that what he saw within was an entire other world. It was a world that his ancestors had twisted beyond repair and then abandoned . . . most of them. Yet Nimth had struggled and had survived, if what Plool had become could be called an example of survival. He wanted to throw the horrific sphere away, yet at the same time he wanted to hold it tight so that nothing, no matter how remote, would threaten it.

"It issss time."

With those words, the Vraad's deadly prison formed between them. The reddish tinge that Cabe had noticed before was still there, but it looked older, like a mark left over from something that had already happened. Were they too late? Had the Quel acted as the Crystal Dragon had been tempted to do?

Cabe was no longer certain he wanted to see the contents of the tall sphere.

"Hold the artifact before you. Be prepared."

For what? How? Why do those who say that never really explain?

The Dragon King eyed the spherical prison. He started to reach toward it, then hesitated. The reptilian nose wrinkled. Again, the Dragon King reached toward the sphere and again he paused. His expression went from wary expectation to puzzlement to growing fury.

"Thissss shell holdsss nothing! It issss *barren!*"

The warlock lowered the artifact in his arms. "Barren?"

"Empty." Long, narrow eyes burned into the warlock's own. "The Vraaaaad hasss essscaped!"

Cabe stared at the prison. He had misinterpreted the scorch traces. The marks were not the work of the Quel, but rather Plool himself working from within the trap. Both the warlock and his armored captors had underestimated the skills and tenacity of the eccentric Vraad.

"A Vraaaad loossse . . ." The Dragon King was talking to himself. "But I dare not . . . do I? I *musssst* . . . unlesssss . . ." He blinked and seemed to study Cabe anew. "Yessss . . ."

A taloned hand reached forth. The malevolent sphere tore free of the sorcerer's grip and flew to its master. It came to a halt only a foot or two from the dragon's snout and hovered there, waiting.

Cabe relaxed a little, realizing now that it was the device that had interested the Dragon King, not him. "What will you do?"

"What musssst be done. I musssst withdraw what I have unleashed. It will not sssstop . . . *stop* . . . the wolf raiders, but it will deal with that *thing* from Nimth!" Now that he had decided on a course of action, the Crystal Dragon sounded almost human in his speech patterns. There seemed no predicting how he would act from one moment to the next. Cabe hoped that this new attitude would remain for a time. "I must risk it. I will not allow that curse to reenter the world. When all that is Nimth is thrust back through the doorway, he will be weakened. He will be so weakened that the threat will become negligible!''

Weakened . . . with all traces of Nimth gone . . . What was it that bothered Cabe about that? Something about Plool and teleporting. Something . . . Of course! ''Your Majesty, if you could hear me out. Instead of what you do, let me try to find Plool first. He can be made to see reason. If you do what you plan—''

''It will be done.'' The finality in the drake lord's voice left no room for compromise. In his eyes, a single Vraad was more a threat than a legion of Aramites. It almost appeared to be a personal vendetta, as if the Dragon King had dealt with Plool's kind before. Could that be?

What was it that hid behind the mask that was the Crystal Dragon?

The glittering titan closed his eyes. Before him, the dark contents within the sphere shifted and turned. It was a trick of the eyes, of course. The artifact was only a doorway. Perhaps what the Crystal Dragon did disturbed some small area of Nimth, but he certainly could not control the entire world. That much was evident from his fear of anything Nimthian, especially a lone Vraad.

Cabe was torn. On the one hand, he wanted the madcap entity called Plool removed from his world because of what chaos the Vraad *might* be able to cause even restricted to this one region. On the other hand, the warlock despised what he considered murder. Plool was deadly, but Cabe would have preferred to try to turn the bizarre mage first. Plool was Plool only because of where he had been born.

He had to try again. If his words failed to convince the Dragon King, would he be tempted to action? Was everything else worth risking for a creature he barely knew? ''Your Majesty?''

The Crystal Dragon did not hear him.

''Your—'' Cabe Bedlam's mouth clamped shut. Suddenly the walls surrounding them had come alive with faces, but not all the same. There were copies of his own, some of them older, some of them younger. He saw the face of the Gryphon and wondered at that. There were others, though, and with a start, Cabe eyed the face of what could only be one of the raider leaders. A tall man with a short beard, much like the wolf raider D'Shay, who the Gryphon had killed years ago. His face was ghastly, a drawn, scarred thing. Yet, what bothered him most upon sighting that face was the expression, for in many ways it resembled a human variation of the present expression on the Dragon King's reptilian countenance.

Then, among all the other faces, he saw one that made him forget even that of the wolf raider leader. It was a face he had seen only in a vision, but one that had remained with him. A bear of a man, a leader, who wore armor of dragonscale. It was the face of a conquerer, one who brooked no defeat. There was something so compelling about the figure, something that reminded him of Shade. It was the man he had thought of as his father when the vision had controlled him. It was . . . *whose* father?

Cabe stared at the entranced drake lord. The thought was ludicrous. It was.

Dragon Kings do not live that long . . . and he is *a Dragon King at that.*

The Crystal Dragon hissed and his eyes flew open. His gaze shifted from the sphere to the wall . . . and to the image of the gaunt, scarred figure that Cabe had taken for the Aramite commander. Their eyes seemed to lock.

The sphere exploded.

XIII

A shiver ran through the sleepers. They did not wake, but something in the spell that had kept them under for so long had changed. What it was would have been hard to explain in any terms save perhaps to say that now they did not sleep so deep.

Not deep at all.

What are they doing down there with that blasted toy? Orril D'Marr stalked across the dark, fog-enshrouded camp trying to keep the men organized. Those who were supposed to be getting some precious sleep were still awake for the most part, the mist and rumors keeping many of them too wary to even lie down. The soldiers on night duty, meanwhile, were turning and slashing at shadows and ghosts in the fog. Sentries kept reporting sightings of creatures that did not, *could* not, exist.

All of this was taking him from his more important tasks. D'Marr had stolen a few precious hours of slumber for himself so that he would be alert for the project he had planned for this night. Tonight he had been planning to open the way to the hidden chamber and finally find out what it was that was so precious to the beasts that they were willing to suffer at his tender hands for it. The explosives were ready and he had chosen the blast points. There would be little damage to the areas nearby and none at all to his master's precious chamber.

That was if he ever had the opportunity to set the explosives. With both his lordship and the blue devil down below, still working after all these hours, Orril D'Marr was the senior officer available. That meant that he had to maintain control, which amounted to running around and beating the other officers until they began acting as their ranks demanded. The officers were his duty and the men beneath them were *their* responsibility. He did not have time to go running from soldier to soldier.

Something is happening. The fog swirled about, a violent storm of shadow and light. Sometimes, the area was lit for several minutes, as if the sun had risen and finally managed to slice through the mist. At least it had thinned a bit, he thought. Even when it was properly dark it was possible to make out shapes several yards away. Whether that change was due to some success on Lord D'Farany's part or was simply a natural occurrence, the young officer did not care. He was only glad it was happening.

D'Marr hated this place, but the damned heat and sunlight was preferable to this mess. So far this night, two men had simply disappeared and a third . . . well, there were some things that made even him queasy.

And that patrol scattered, more than a dozen men lost there, too. Oddly, that both irritated and excited him. The reports spoke of a huge dark stallion with a rider, the latter having a dozen different descriptions. The survivors all seemed to have been obsessed with the monstrous steed . . . no surprise, if it was what he thought it was. One of the spies from that kingdom,

Zou or some such nonsense it was called, had reported trouble involving a mage on a large black horse.

The Gryphon had an ally in this realm who matched such a description, a demon called Darkhorse. D'Rance, of course, had been able to supply that tidbit of information.

Two sentries stumbled across his path and swiftly backed away. They saluted, but the young officer just waved them aside. He had no time for men doing their duties. It was the ones who were not who would feel his wrath if they were so unfortunate as to cross him. D'Marr wanted to be done with this task. Once he had the officers under control and they in turn the men, he could return to the tunnels.

His mind drifted back to the patrol's encounter with the monster known as Darkhorse. The demon could not possibly have come across them by chance; he had to have specifically come here searching for the wolf raiders. Any notion that contradicted that was not acceptable to either Orril D'Marr or his lord. Even the blue man agreed with him on this matter.

The Gryphon had to be here. It fit. The black steed's appearance had come too quickly after their landing. He had a rider with him. If the rider had not been the damned birdman, then it had to be one of his friends. Either way, they could only have known of the raiders' presence through the Gryphon. It made sense to him.

Admittedly, there was some logic missing in the argument, but one other reason superseded all others in this matter. D'Marr recalled the attack on the port city. Lord D'Farany had hoped to accomplish two things there. One had been to steal a series of charts that would aid them in this venture and the other had been the hope that they would catch their greatest adversary off-guard.

They had been unable to kill the Gryphon that day, but his brat had paid for the deaths and defeats the empire had suffered. Not satisfactory, but it would do until the Gryphon's head decorated a lance tip.

And that time is coming soon. True to form, the bird had followed them across the seas. D'Marr had predicted he would and for once he had outdone the blue devil in that respect. *You're coming to me, Gryphon, coming to join your brat!*

His hand touched the pommel of the scepter. When he had finished the Gryphon, there would remain only the cat woman.

She would follow after her mate, being as predictable in her way as he was when it came to revenge. *Then I will have taken all three.*

No one would deny his greatness then.

His course took him around the camp until he returned to the mouth of the tunnel leading to the Quel city. The camp was at last in order. The officers were now in line and they, in turn, had the men under rein. D'Marr had done as best as was possible. Now it was time to—

A tall figure emerged from the tunnel. From his walk and his manner, D'Marr had no trouble identifying the northerner. The man looked bedraggled, exhausted. The young officer smiled briefly, then once more fixed his expression into one of detachment.

D'Rance saw him and did not bother to hide his own distaste. He tried to walk past his shorter counterpart, but D'Marr was having none of that. To know that the northerner had been put through the paces made his own tedious day more palatable. "Tired already?"

"You will play no games with me, Orril D'Marr. Our lord has struggled long and I was forced to help maintain him, yes?"

"And what could you do for him, blue? Wipe his brow when he sweated?"

D'Rance sneered. "The knowledge of a scholar is a greater weapon at times than the sword of a simple soldier, yes? You would have pounded on the crystal device with that toy on your belt, I think, as you did to the walls. Such effort, but so little result."

"You're a scholar of magic?"

The blue man suddenly lost interest in the battle of words. "I have given my all for our effort, little man, yes, and our Lord D'Farany knows this. I have been given leave to rest and rest I shall."

The exhausted northerner turned and stalked into the fog. D'Marr watched him disappear, then glanced at the tunnel mouth. All the blue devil's efforts would amount to little before this night had ended. Whatever favor he had curried with Lord D'Farany would fade when D'Marr revealed the secret cavern.

He started down the tunnel, finalizing his plans. He would need four or five men, just to be on the safe side. They could plant the explosives in the proper locations and light the fuses. There would be rubble to clear away, too, which meant that five or six men would work better. The most important task D'Marr would save for himself, however. It was he who would be the first to enter the unknown, he, the discoverer. *And whatever secret, whatever treasure lies behind there, I will be the first to know it*.

"Sir!"

Although his expression remained bland when he turned back toward the mouth of the tunnel, inside, Orril D'Marr was seething. *What do they want now?* "Yes?"

An understandably nervous officer even younger than he stood at attention at the edge of the entrance. No doubt he had been volunteered by his superiors for this mission. That way, if D'Marr chose to take out his wrath on someone, it would not be them. "Sir, I have been ordered to report that there is some confusion in the eastern flank. Several men have reported a roving light. Two went out to investigate and have not returned. Another man reports . . ."

He waited, but the other officer did not go on. "Reports what?"

"Someone laughing . . . from above him."

The corners of D'Marr's mouth edged downward. His work was *already* falling apart. If this was an example of the situation being under Lord D'Farany's control, then it was no improvement. Success was supposed to mean that the fog would either vanish or obey the commands of his master. It had, so far, done neither as far as D'Marr could see. If anything, this latest report indicated things had turned worse.

He returned to the surface and looked around. How he was supposed to keep this rabble organized was beyond him, but it was his function. That meant chasing down those incompetent officers and uncovering the truth about things that went bump in the fog. He was growing tired of this. There would have to be some changes made in the ranks.

"What's your name?"

"Squad Leader, Base Level, R'Jerek, sir."

The man's superiors had picked the lowest officer they could find. He still bore the R' caste designation. Anything above him would have the D' like D'Marr's name bore. His estimation of the value of R'Jerek's superiors dropped further. "Your immediate officer?"

"Captain D'Lee, sir."

"Lead me to him, D'Jerek."

"Yes, sir . . ." The younger officer paused. "It's R'Jerek, sir."

"Not after I'm through with your superior, *Captain*."

His guide said nothing more after that.

Orril D'Marr gave the tunnel one last glance. *Tomorrow*, he swore to himself. *It'll hold until tomorrow*.

So much power! Kanaan D'Rance stumbled toward his tent, which was, not by chance, away from the rest. As much as he would have been happier to sleep among the fascinating Quel artifacts, that was not allowed. Still, he had smuggled a few of the items into his tent, where he tried to understand and make use of them. His skills were growing; he had even managed to heal his hand without anyone ever discovering the truth. The streak in his hair was becoming a problem, however. He was certain that the Aramite leader suspected.

The secrets the trinkets held paled in comparison to the struggle that had gone on tonight, a struggle in which Lord D'Farany had all but triumphed. The mysterious adversary was vanquished; now, the Aramite commander only had to bind the magical fog to his control. Lord D'Farany was already talking of making use of the deadly mist, an idea contrary to his first inclination. Despite the wrongness of the sorcery tied into the fog, or perhaps because of it, the keeper now saw great potential in it as a weapon *for* the raiders.

Kanaan D'Rance agreed for the most part, but he differed with his master in one respect. He wanted control of the mist for himself. *There is a power there, yes? A different, alien magic!* It had repelled him at first, but now it attracted. The blue man felt he could accomplish great things with it once he learned how it had come to be. He needed time, though, time alone in that chamber. Time alone to study.

Thrusting aside the flap of his tent, the tall figure darted inside. It was not until the flap had closed behind him that he noticed something was amiss. Something that only his burgeoning magical senses could note.

With no effort at all, he created a small ball of light brilliant enough to illuminate most of the interior.

Lord D'Farany's work? Was he now toying with the blue man? He did not like the thought of ending up as one of the martinet's playthings. Orril D'Marr excelled at slow death, yes.

It was then he noticed that his carefully hidden collection of Quel artifacts had been taken out and scattered over his worktable.

Who would dare? This was not the way of Lord D'Farany. D'Marr, then? One of his spies? It made no sense; they could learn nothing from his collection save that he had palmed some pieces. The little martinet would know that such efforts would be a waste of everyone's time.

Somehow, he knew that this could not be the work of the Aramites . . . yet, who did that leave?

One of the figurines on the table, a small crystal bear, leapt up from the table and past his shoulder.

Stunned, he spun around, trying to keep track of it. The Quel talisman stood on the ground behind him, as motionless as it had been before its extraordinary leap into momentary life. With great caution, Kanaan D'Rance reached down for it.

The tiny bear sprang away from him, flying into the dark shadows in the corner of his tent. The blue man snarled and started for the spot. Although he could not see the artifact, he knew that it could go no farther. The tent would impede its progress. Now it was a simple matter of searching those shadows. The scholar in him took over. Once he found the peculiar little piece, he intended to study it thoroughly until he discovered the reason for its sudden animation.

A laugh from within the shadows made him pull back his questing hand.

A grotesque, round figure who could have not been hiding all this time squatted in the shadows. He could see nothing of the face except the long, narrow chin and the slash of mouth. The creature raised a spindly arm to the huge, broad-rimmed hat he wore and lifted it just enough to reveal the rest of the unholy visage. It was all D'Rance could do to keep from shouting. He stood there, petrified.

"A fascinating struggle; a struggle fascinating to me," said the intruder. "*Especially* to me."

"Who . . . ?"

The mouth shaped into a mischievous grin. A bony hand formed a fist, then opened again. In the palm of the hand was the elusive figurine. "Plool I am; I am Plool . . ." The grin grew wider. The eyes, the ungodly, crystalline eyes, glittered merrily. "A *friend*."

"Something has definitely changed, Lord Gryphon, and not necessarily for the better!"

The Gryphon noticed it, too. There was indeed a change in the air, or rather the fog. He shivered and was not exactly certain why. The change might have been for the better; they had no way of knowing otherwise.

Pessimism? More likely experience and common sense. The lionbird had been in too many dire situations not to expect the worst. Usually, through no effort of his own, he was proven correct in that assumption.

"What do you make of it, Darkhorse?"

The shadow steed snorted. "Nothing! I make absolutely nothing out of it. It is from Nimth and as far as I am concerned, that which is Nimthian is a threat to all!"

"Like Shade?" he could not help asking the eternal.

Darkhorse was prevented from answering by what sounded like a crack of thunder. He stumbled. The entire area was suddenly aglow even though it was still night. The Gryphon heard a rumbling, glanced down, and, with the aid of the mysterious light, saw the earth opening up before them. He started to point it out to his companion, but the stallion was already backing away. The chasm began to widen and from it poured forth a grayish substance much like clay.

"Can you leap over it?" He had seen Darkhorse clear gaps far wider than this one.

"I will do so once I am certain that it is *safe* to do so! Do not trust appearances in this place; there is usually more to come!"

That was when the molten clay turned toward them.

From the center of the bubbling mass burst forth a crude, thick tentacle. At the same time, the Gryphon felt his *own* body twist. He stared in horror as his arms began to lengthen and his torso started to turn sideways.

"Darkhorse!" The Gryphon struggled to maintain control of

his fingers, which were trying to bend backward of their own accord.

"Hold . . . hold on to . . . me!"

He did. As best as his distorted form would allow, he held on to the dark stallion. His fingers still struggled for independence, but his will was stronger.

The lionbird felt a surge of movement from the eternal, then the rush of air, foul air, as Darkhorse leapt.

It took forever to land, at least in the Gryphon's mind, and when they did, Darkhorse did not stop. He continued to run. Over hill and flat earth, the terrain did not matter. All the while, the light remained with them. They raced on for what had to be several miles before the Gryphon recovered enough to demand that his companion come to a halt. Darkhorse did not acknowledge his words, but he nonetheless came to a reluctant halt some few moments later.

The Gryphon looked himself over, wary of what he might find but determined to see what terrible changes might have been wrought on him. To his astonishment and relief, he saw that he was just as he had always been. Leaving the vicinity of the chasm had restored him to normal.

"Grrryppphhonnn?"

"Darkhorse?" In his relief at finding he had survived intact, the lionbird had nearly forgotten the one who had saved him. It had not occurred to him that the eternal might also have suffered some monstrous alteration. "Darkhorse! What is it?"

There was no response from the shadow steed, but he was shivering noticeably. The Gryphon glanced at the rocky ground beneath them, saw nothing out of the ordinary, and gingerly dismounted. Darkhorse continued to shiver. He did not even look back at his rider, simply stared ahead.

"Darkhorse?"

"I . . . cannot . . . fight it this time!" The shivering grew worse yet. The shadow steed stumbled back a step.

"Fight what?" How could he help the eternal?

"Fight . . . what almost took . . . control . . . when I was . . . with Cabe!"

The last word ended in a scream.

Darkhorse *melted*.

He was quicksilver, flowing in all directions. A black pool

with vague equine touches to him. The lionbird danced away from him, aghast. "Darkhorse! What do I do? What can I do?"

"Urra . . ." From the horrific mass rose a figure the color of ink. Cold, blue orbs stared out from a face that was and was not a copy of the Gryphon's own. Every detail of the Gryphon's own form was copied, yet it was a flawed reproduction. He raised one clawed hand toward what his companion had become.

The shape melted, but re-formed almost instantly. A thing of many arms and eyes, the latter all blue, sprouted before the Gryphon. He did not back away, although experience should have demanded otherwise.

As quickly as it had formed, this shape, too, melted. A new one, another humanoid figure, coalesced.

This one the Gryphon also recognized. "Shade!"

Shade, but with the definite outline of a face. Quick as the lionbird was in attempting to see those blackened features, he was not quick enough. Shade, the shape of Shade, rather, poured to the earth before the Gryphon could make out the details of his visage. The Gryphon watched the melting with some disappointment despite the circumstances. For all the years that he had known the warlock, he had never discerned the true features of the man. Not even Shade had been able to recall what he had once looked like.

Yet a new form grew, but this one, it turned out, was to be Darkhorse again. It was a slower shaping than the others, possibly because it looked as though the eternal was forcibly willing himself back into existence much the way the Gryphon had struggled with control of his fingers.

When at last he was fully formed, the ebony stallion shook his head and eyed his companion. "I had thought I had beaten the urge when last I was here, but the fog, Nimth, is stronger still."

"What happened to you?"

Darkhorse took an unsteady step. His form rippled. "Still not completely safe! You will have to give me a little time. What happened to me? I am even more susceptible to the wild powers of Nimth than you are! Ha! I am worse than wet clay in the hands of those powers! When I was here with Cabe, it almost happened. I fought back and succeeded then, but not this time! I failed! I was twisted into whatever shape it could derive from my memories. *Any* memory."

"Including Shade?"

The eternal steadied himself. "He will haunt me forever! I had forgotten that I had ever known his true visage. It was in the last days . . . or . . . was it long, long ago?"

That was all that his companion wanted to say on the subject, so the Gryphon turned to studying their surroundings. The odd light—*where is its source?*—enabled him to see maybe five yards away from them in any direction. He had no idea where they were save that they had gone farther west. Darkhorse had not thought about his course. If not for the Gryphon, they might still be racing through the fog. He was glad he had managed to speak out or else they might have kept on racing until they ended up in the middle of the Aramite camp itself. The lionbird did not want to confront his adversaries until he knew the advantage would be his.

He wondered how close they were. Close enough that his claws unsheathed in anticipation. The peninsula was very, very long, but Darkhorse moved swifter than the wind. What would take a true steed days to reach could take him only hours. The Gryphon was aware that his mount had paid no attention to his speed, so there was no satisfactory method of calculating where they were.

The mysterious illumination at last began to dim. Nothing remained constant here. From what the shadow steed had related to him about this foul mist, the lionbird was surprised the light had lasted this long. He was not sorry to see it go. Despite the temporary increase in visibility it had created, it made the Gryphon more anxious. Night was supposed to be dark. He was more comfortable with that. In the night, his reflexes and senses were an advantage over most foes. Hunting the wolf raiders was best done at night.

The Gryphon stared into the darkening fog. He could imagine the scene. Lone soldiers wandering in the night, unable to see much save with torches that marked them for him. If the warlock was their prisoner, they would lead the Gryphon to him. If Cabe was not at their mercy, then that would simplify matters for the lionbird. He would not have to hold back.

The images became so real that the Gryphon could almost see the shadowy forms and hear the clink of metal upon metal. His good hand clutched the grip of his sword.

He was jolted by a strange, whistling sound . . . then it became impossible to *breathe* as something thin and tight wrapped itself snugly around his throat.

"Gryphon! Beware!"

Ignoring the belated warning, the Gryphon reached down and drew his sword. He knew that it was a whip that encircled his throat and knew very well who was at the other end. What he counted on was the other underestimating his strength. The lion-bird was stronger than most humans, even despite his three-fingered grip. He took hold of the whip and pulled, at the same time bringing his sword into play. His attacker had no chance to react; the Gryphon's blade ran him through in the neck.

Pulling his sword free before the soldier could even fall, the Gryphon whirled about. No figment of his imagination were these men. He *had* seen shapes and heard sounds, but like a senile fool, he had paid them no mind. Perhaps it was time for *him* to die. When one grew old and careless, that was what was supposed to happen.

No, for your sake, Troia, and for the memory of our Demion, I will not!

They swarmed toward him. Darkhorse had described in detail his first encounter with the patrol and so the Gryphon knew that this second patrol was much larger and better prepared than its predecessor had been. Someone understood too well what they might be hunting and had supplied the soldiers with tools designed just for the likes of Darkhorse and him.

Even as he took down a swordsman, the Gryphon knew that he alone would not be able to escape the Aramites. *They must have heard us; they must have heard Darkhorse as he struggled.* There would be little aid from Darkhorse. The shadow steed was situated but a few yards to his left and already struggling against more than half a dozen attackers. Darkhorse and his opponents seemed at an impasse; they could not reach him, but he was still too weakened from his inner battle to do them any harm.

Already three swordsmen fought him from different angles. He was able to keep them more or less in front of him long enough to disable one in the leg, but others were already gathering. Four men with a net worked toward his back. A lancer and yet another swordsman joined his attackers. A pattern developed, a lance thrust followed by one or more sword attacks, generally together. The Gryphon fought them off, but he was forced to back up each time.

When the net came down on him, the lionbird knew that he had allowed himself to be played like a puppet. That there had been no other choice in no way assuaged his anger at himself.

His sword was yanked from his grip, but he had the satisfaction of severely clawing one of his captors before they wrapped the net tight around him. When they were done, he was trussed up like a piece of game . . . and to the wolf raiders he probably was. The Gryphon heard one of the Aramites call out to Darkhorse.

"Hold, demon, or we will fillet your friend here and now!"

He would have urged the shadow steed to ignore the threat, but someone rapped him on the side of the head, dazing him for several seconds. By the time his head cleared, Darkhorse had already surrendered.

"Watch him!" ordered the same voice, likely the patrol leader. "Commander D'Marr will want him in good shape for questioning!"

The Gryphon could not see his captors' eyes, but he noted that a couple of the men who were handling him stiffened at the mention of the name. *D'Farany's torturer*.

"Bind his mouth."

Someone shifted him around so that another guard could wrap thick cloth around his beak. In the darkness of reborn night, the lionbird could make out the outline of the demon steed. Darkhorse had lowered his head. Two Aramites were looping something around the eternal's neck. It could not be a rope noose. Something as simple as that would never hold Darkhorse. No, it had to be a magical bond of some sort, a bond whose power they trusted to work despite the tricks of the fog. The Gryphon was not certain he would trust any sorcery or sorcerous artifact while lost in this mist. He hoped their faith would come back to haunt the wolf raiders before this was all over. If not and their toys worked as they should . . . then it was all over already.

Unless Cabe was not a prisoner . . .

If not, where was he?

A pair of boots crossed his limited field of vision. They paused before him. "Make him docile for the trip. That'll keep the demon in line."

The Gryphon knew what was coming and braced himself for it. The blow to the back of his head was a good one, he was just barely able to note, for alone it was enough to send him spinning into unconsciousness. He would have only one fist-sized lump when he woke.

Provided the Gryphon woke at all.

Wake he did, but it was no relief to do so, for the Gryphon saw that they had reached the Aramite encampment. It was still night, he supposed, but there were many awake. He sensed a certain tension that permeated the area. The raiders were not at ease in this place. There was not much satisfaction in knowing that. His captors would be that much more anxious, that much more ready to kill him. Although he knew he faced potential agony at the hands of the Aramite inquisitor, the lionbird was determined to survive. He had given up part of his hand already and he was willing to give up much more if he was granted the deaths of Lord D'Farany and his men.

His eyes little more than slits, the captive continued to survey his surroundings. One item of vast importance was missing. He could neither see nor hear Darkhorse. What had happened to the eternal? Surely he was aware that the raiders would kill the Gryphon no matter what? They would be searching for methods of binding the ebony stallion to their will. The Gryphon was fairly certain that the wolf raiders would find some adequate device. This batch had probably stolen whatever they could before they abandoned their fellows back in the empire. *So much for the loyalty of the pack!*

He was dragged on and on, so long, in fact, that he almost believed they intended to drag him to death. It was not a very imaginative death, if that was the case. From D'Farany the Gryphon expected more. Something slow and agonizing.

This was *not* how he had planned it.

All at once, the Gryphon was dumped to the harsh earth. He suppressed a grunt and remained as still as possible.

"What is it now?" The voice was indifferent, almost bored.

"Sir, a prize most wonderful! It's—"

"Don't bother to tell me; show me."

"Y-yes, Commander D'Marr!"

Ungentle hands rolled him onto his back.

"Forget rolling him free. I have other things demanding my time, Captain. Cut him out of there."

Evidently in the darkness it was troublesome to make out anything more than his shape. A possible advantage? The Gryphon heard the sound of a dagger being drawn from its sheath. A blade flashed by his visage, but he did not flinch. With little care for his well-being, the soldier began to cut him loose. He tensed. If there was ever an opportunity for escape, it was when he was nearly free of the net. He was swift, far swifter than most of them would think. It was a slim hope, but if they bound him after this, his odds would shrivel to next to nothing.

A heavy boot landed atop his throat. The Gryphon gasped. He felt the tip of a mace against his forehead. Around him was nothing but silence.

"What are you gaping at, you fool? Finish releasing our friend here." Was there just a tinge of excitement in the officer's otherwise monotone voice? "He won't be trying any tricks *now*."

When the last of the netting had been cut away, the Gryphon was seized by both his arms and his legs. Only when he was certain that his prisoner would not be able to free himself from the guards' grips did D'Marr take his foot off of the lionbird's throat. "You might as well open your eyes all the way, bird-man."

The Gryphon did. Peering down at him was a round, clean-shaven countenance. At first glance, he almost wondered if the Aramites had been reduced to promoting children to the officers' ranks. Then, as they tugged him to his feet, he was better able to glimpse the eyes. Young, D'Marr might be, but he was by no means a child. There was more death in his eyes than most men the Gryphon had ever faced.

And is my son one of those deaths?

The Aramite commander stepped closer. The Gryphon cocked his head in sudden amusement as he saw that D'Marr came up only to his chin.

The head of the mace went deep into his stomach.

His guards would not let him fall forward or clutch his stomach in pain. As he gasped, he heard the young commander say,

"You've made an otherwise long and annoying night worthwhile, birdman. You have no idea how much I've waited for this confrontation."

"Shall I alert his lordship, sir?"

D'Marr looked at his prisoner, then at the guards, and then at last at the man who had spoken. He never seemed to look at any one thing for very long, the Gryphon noted, not even the face of an adversary whose image had become synonymous with Aramite defeats. "No. Now would not be the best time. Lord D'Farany has only just retired and his victory over the fog has cost him." The men looked confused over the last part of the statement, but D'Marr ignored them. He smiled ever so briefly at the lionbird. "I'm certain that we can find accommodations for our special guest until then. We need time to prepare the best welcome for him. We need time to properly plan his death. For that Lord D'Farany will want to be fully alert and able to *enjoy* his pain."

"I hope I will be a disappointment," the Gryphon managed to respond. He was still in pain, but it had subsided enough so that he could pretend it had vanished.

"You speak." D'Marr raised the tip of the mace to the underside of the Gryphon's beak. The lionbird could sense a spell of some sort, a strong, complicated spell, locked into the weapon. Judging from its owner, he was certain that the mace was a treacherous little device. "How entertaining. I'd begun to think you incapable. Don't worry yourself, Your Majesty . . . you are supposed to be a king or some such dribble, aren't you . . . my lord will hardly be disappointed. If you think that I'm eager for your company, you'll be amazed at his enthusiasm. You are the cause of all his suffering. Years of suffering."

"Good."

A shock coursed through his body. He would have fallen if not for the guards. D'Marr waited for him to recover, then held the head of the mace close enough so that the Gryphon could see how it had been designed. "That was one of the low levels. You'll be tasting the others—as many as you can take—when you're brought before our master."

"I am always eager to meet the men I want to kill. It has been a pleasure meeting you, in fact."

D'Marr started to smile again, but then he stared at the avian visage before him and the smile faded. "The only one you'll have the pleasure of meeting will be that brat of yours. The one who died much too quickly."

Demion . . . It was as if his heart had suddenly been wrenched from his chest. Blood madness took him. The Gryphon's world shrank. It was a world large enough to contain only two. One was himself and the other . . . the other was the *beast* who had killed his son.

No, two was still too many. He would not be satisfied until there was only one.

"Demion . . ." Nothing would keep him from the beast. He felt some sort of resistance holding him in place, but with a twist of his arms he freed himself. The monster backed away from him, eyes wary and prepared for struggle. Good, it would make his death that much better.

The Gryphon felt something pull at his arms again and this time he lashed out, striking flesh and bone. Not once did he look to see what the source of that interference was; his eyes could only see the black figure before him. The jackal.

He leapt, but the beast struck him with the scepter, sending him through a new crescendo of agony. Still the enraged Gryphon would not accept defeat. The pain gave way to his anger, his bitterness. He slashed at his adversary, but his claws caught only the hard metal of the beast's armor.

The net came down on him before he could strike again. Still fighting, the maddened lionbird was pulled to the ground. A blow to his head finally succeeded in lessening some of the blood lust.

"Don't kill him. Keep him bound." The beast stood where he knew the Gryphon could not help but look. His placid face broke into that brief smile again. "You are a feisty one, aren't you?"

"I will have you, D'Marr," the prisoner replied in much calmer tones. He was furious at himself for allowing his base instincts to take over like that. He had not served the memory of his son nor the love of his mate in any way by becoming the animal. There was a line between animal and humanity that the Gryphon had always walked. Now, he had allowed himself to fall prey to the unthinking side. It was never right to allow one side or the other complete control. Only with both sides in balance could he triumph. "I will have you and your master."

D'Marr squatted and pointed the tip of the mace at him. The top just barely flicked against the side of the Gryphon's face, who flinched before realizing that there was no pain this time. "No, that's for later, birdman. That and so much more." The Aramite officer rose. "Bind him properly this time and take him to the other beasts. They can stare at each other until he's needed for the festivities. Is the demon under control?"

"We've bound it as you've instructed," responded the patrol leader. "It doesn't seem to be able to free itself."

"Watch it. Make certain of that." The youthful raider yawned in the Gryphon's direction. "Now that we have things settled, you'll excuse me if I retire. I have so much to do tomorr— excuse me, later today." He pointed at the guards with his scepter. "These men will see to your discomfort. If you have need of anything, please ask."

"Just your head."

D'Marr tapped the side of the weapon against his palm. He stared thoughtfully at the captive, then politely asked, "And how long do you think before we might be graced with the presence of your cat? I'm looking forward to completing the set."

This time, the Gryphon did not respond. D'Marr was working hard to keep his mind in turmoil and he was achieving that goal all too well. As desperate as his situation was, the only hope that the Gryphon had was in retaining his calm.

"Well, I suspect she'll be here soon enough. I will be certain to greet her with open, loving arms." His countenance once more a bland mask, the young officer gave the tangled lionbird a mock salute and departed.

Watching him walk off, the Gryphon knew that he had to somehow free himself despite the odds. If he did not, then Troia *would* follow, as D'Marr had predicted. The thought of her in the hands of someone like the sadistic Aramite made him shiver.

I'm looking forward to completing the set, D'Marr had mocked. If the Gryphon did not find *some* way to escape his fate, without the aid of Darkhorse, apparently, it was all too possible that the deadly raider would do just *that.*

—— XIV ——

"Rise, Cabe Bedlam."

The voice sounded familiar, yet it also did not. Cabe, his body responding as if it had long ago given way to rigor mortis, managed to rise to a sitting position. He found himself staring at the blurred images of one countenance, a countenance that every facet of every reflective crystal repeated. It was the face of a man much like the one the warlock had seen in the visions, but despite the blurriness, he could see that this one was a younger, varied copy. A son, perhaps. Until the detail became much more focused, he could guess no more.

"You are resilient, warlock."

He turned to the source of the voice and only then discovered that it was not the images that were blurred, but rather his own vision. Not really a shock, considering what had happened.

Dragon Kings will be the death of me yet . . . even when they are not purposely trying to achieve that result.

"Your—Your Majesty?" He blinked several times, but to no discernible effect.

"Wait a moment. Your vision should clear. You were not, fortunately for you, struck in the eyes. I did what I could for you otherwise."

What did that mean? Cabe started to reach up with his left hand and was wracked by dagger strikes of pain. He quickly lowered the arm and clutched it with his other hand, which thankfully did not hurt. "What—what happened?"

"You deflected most of the fragments, but a few stronger ones broke through your shields. Only a few pierced you; it was the force of the explosion, which I fought to contain, that left you unconscious."

"The fragments. The sphere. One of the pieces struck me in the arm?"

He knew it was the Crystal Dragon who spoke to him, but still the voice sounded so different from *anything* he had heard before. What new change had the explosion wrought upon the

Dragon King's personality? "It did not strike your arm. It *pierced it*, warlock. The wound goes completely through your upper arm. I did what I could, but it will not heal for me. It may never heal, you understand, not completely."

Never heal. Much the way King Melicard's face and arm had never healed after the burst of magic that had maimed him. Cabe was aware that his own wound did not even approach the severity of Melicard's, but he could not help but be more upset by it.

"There are also small scars on your neck. You were very fortunate, warlock. Your skills are impressive."

Skills? More like pure luck! Cabe pulled his robe askew so that he could study the wound. A jagged, green scar surrounded by red, swollen skin marked the fragment's passage. With great trepidation, he touched it. The soft touch was still enough to make him grunt in intense pain. Bracing himself, the wounded mage touched the back of the same arm. Again, the pain struck him.

Never heal?

He was still staring at the wound when the Crystal Dragon spoke again. "We are both fortunate, Cabe Bedlam. When the sphere was shattered, the doorway to Nimth was closed, not opened. That was how the device was designed, but there was no true way of testing it except by an occurrence much like this explosion."

Cabe looked up. His vision had cleared enough so that he could now clearly see the Crystal Dragon. The drake lord looked unmarred, but that did not mean he had not been wounded. More important now was his state of mind. He seemed sane enough . . .

"What happened?"

"I underestimated the wolf raider leader. I underestimated so much. He has wrested control of the mist from me. Before long, he will understand something of how to utilize it. Things go from bad to worse." The glittering leviathan closed his eyes.

The warlock's gaze darted back and forth between the massive dragon and the face that stared at him from all directions, but his attention remained on the subject at hand. "What will you do now?"

"Nothing."

"Nothing?"

"I *must* do nothing!" The Dragon King's long, narrowed eyes opened again . . . and was this the first time that Cabe had noticed how crystalline they appeared? They were almost like the insane orbs of Plool. "I dare not! I will not lose myself!"

Cabe's gaze again drifted to the multiplied countenance covering the walls. This time, however, he studied them closer. *Not lose myself,* the leviathan had just said. Did that mean what Cabe thought it did?

"Who are you?"

The Crystal Dragon settled back. He seemed almost to welcome the strange question. The huge head turned and indicated the faces. "Once . . . I was *him.*"

Him. The faces in the visions. The eyes of Plool. The obsession with the foulness of Nimth. It all began to make sense to the warlock.

"You're a *Vraad.*" He found he was really not that astonished by the revelation. So much had pointed to it. Yet, if the knowledge that the Crystal Dragon had once worn a human form was not shocking, then the fact that he still lived was. How long had it been since the coming of the Dragon Kings?

"How did it happen? *When?*"

The dragon's laugh was harsh and humorless. "By the banner, I no longer even know, warlock! Centuries, yes. Millennia, yes. How many it has been I have forgotten! I have watched generations come and go, live and die! I have seen the rise of the Dragon Kings and I have watched their pitiful decline! The others passed on, but I lived! Ha! *Lived?* I am fortunate that I have not gone insane!"

The last word echoed throughout the chamber. Cabe stood, careful to avoid stress to his arm. He had to hear. "Tell me."

"Tell you?" The Crystal Dragon contemplated that. His expression was weary. "Tell you of Logan of the Tezerenee? The dutiful son, one of many sons, to Lord Barakas Tezerenee, he was. Not like Gerrod or Rendel or Lochivan, he was. Logan obeyed blindly as was proper. When the Vraad fled Nimth, he was there to aid his father. When Barakas claimed this land under the dragon banner, Logan was there to enforce that claim."

Cabe Bedlam listened transfixed as the history of the first

Dragon Kings began to unfold before him. The wound was all but forgotten as the time-worn leviathan spoke of the fatal error that had led to his present existence.

"It was the bodies, the bodies his father and Master Zeree and his brothers Gerrod and Rendel had created, created from the stuff of *dragons*! They were people-shaped, but they were dragons in heart. The spirits, the ka, of the Tezerenee crossed the path of worlds to this one and claimed those bodies. Claimed their own eventual destruction."

The sorcery-shaped bodies had worked well for the Tezerenee. Most of the other Vraad had crossed over physically, but that door had not been open at the time of the Tezerenees' crossing. So the folk of the dragon banner truly became dragon men, which served to increase their power and presence among the other refugees.

It was not until a few years later that people, not merely the Tezerenee, began to notice some changes. Their skill in sorcery faded, but even that was not so insurmountable a situation to the Tezerenee, who had always espoused the physical even while they made use of the magical. For a time, it served to make the Vraad more reliant upon the clan. Not enough to accept the rule of Lord Barakas, however. When he sought to take his rightful place, there was resistance. Strong resistance. It was that in the end that forced Lord Barakas to seek a new kingdom overseas.

"They claimed that land." The Dragon King did not seem to consider how the Tezerenee had made the long crossing from one continent to the other without ships and sorcery important enough to discuss. Recalling what little he had gleaned from Darkhorse over the years, the warlock wondered if this was where the eternal had fallen prey to the Vraad. It might explain the shadow steed's bitterness and, yes, fear where things relating to Nimth and the Vraad were concerned.

Lord Barakas had evidently expected to fight the Seekers, but the avians' civilization had collapsed in some war and only a few bands were strong enough to give them trouble. Flushed with success, they conquered the mountain stronghold of the bird folk and took its ancient secrets for their own.

Kivan Grath. Cabe recognized the place from the Dragon King's description. Kivan Grath, the mountain whose caverns would become the citadel of the Dragon Emperor. *Odd how he recalls so much but not how much time has passed. Then again, he may want to recall his humanity, but not how long it has been since he lost it.*

As he spoke, the Crystal Dragon seemed to shrink a little. More and more he became a man seeing a horror ahead than a great leviathan who ruled and was feared. With great unease, the warlock noted how the multitude of faces copied the drake lord's emotions. It was like being surrounded by a thousand thousand tormented ghosts.

"It may be that the land was fearful of them and although it could not destroy the Tezerenee, it made them into its own. Or perhaps the bodies themselves, formed from that which was dragon, at last sought to revert to what they had been meant to be. In the end, all that matters was the changing. First one, then another. No one understood then. No one saw it was happening to all, not merely a few."

He shuddered, blinked, then looked directly at his human guest with something approaching desperate envy. "I remember the pain that day. I remember screaming as my arms and legs stretched and bent at angles no human appendages had been meant to bend. Do you know what it feels like to sense burgeoning wings squirming beneath the flesh of your back and then having them burst fully formed through your *skin*? To feel and see your skull reshape itself and then realize that your eyes, too, are shifting, changing? To scream and scream again as the transformation tears through armor and sends you crashing to all *fours* . . .

". . . and then to know oblivion."

Cabe, thinking of his own fear of even the minutest shifting of form, swallowed.

The reptilian monarch looked down at the floor. "I recall vague images, the thoughts of a beast struggling to think. How long, I do not know. I only recall that one day I began to think as a man, but I was not *myself*. I was a *creature*. I was . . . a dragon. This land was supposed to be my kingdom. Years it would be before I remembered that it had been chosen for me by my father, that all of us had, despite becoming beasts, claimed our particular kingdoms." His laugh had more than a tinge of bitterness. "I have never known whether he gave me this peninsula because he knew what wonders were here or simply because I was one of the least important of his many sons."

It was child's play to seize these caverns. The Quel civilization had been in worse condition than that of the Seekers, disorganized and much too busy trying to devise a method to save their kind to note the danger until it was too late. The self-proclaimed Dragon King explored his new domain and in doing so found a place that the Quel had obviously shunned. There were no signs of recent activity. Nothing but a dark passage before him, a dark passage leading to the mouth of an even darker cavern. His arrogance and curiosity got the better of him. The passage was wide enough to allow him through and so with no reason to retreat, the dragon entered.

"There was no flash of memory, no flood of recollections. I entered the chamber and stalked to the center, fascinated by the glitter. I was not yet what you see before you, although my form had already adapted to my kingdom. Turning about, I studied this place from floor to ceiling and from wall to wall. When I was finished, it came to me that this would make a most proper citadel for such a magnificent leviathan as myself. This chamber, I decided, would be my sanctum.

"And *then* it was the truth overwhelmed me. Then I recalled who it was I had *been*."

Cabe waited, but the Crystal Dragon lowered his head to his breast, as if that distant moment was still too terrible to speak of even now. The warlock suspected he knew what had happened. The images surrounding a startled dragon, images of what he had been. Memories rising from the buried portion of his mind. It would be like awakening from a long, deep slumber, but a slumber whose peace had been shattered at last by a nightmare of untold horror. Only this was a horror that would turn out to be all too real.

"I can only say, warlock," the Dragon King began again, lifting his head just enough to eye his guest. "I can only say that it was as terrifying as the transformation, which was my last recollection. Now I saw what had become of me. I roared in anger and madness and it would not be exaggerating to say that on that day I put the fear of the Crystal Dragon into all that lived in Legar." He scratched at the floor with his talons. "Not that

I cared. My own fear was all that mattered. I tried to destroy this place, but you can see how well I did. Although it resembles other cavern chambers in this underground world, I think it lives, in a manner of speaking, lives and plots and does what it can to give it purpose. If the Dragonrealm is not a living thing, then it may be that this chamber is what guides the course of our land. Perhapssss it even viessss with the Dragonrealm for powerrrr.''

Cabe tensed, noting the change in the Crystal Dragon's voice. The human quality in it had given way to the more reptilian sibilance that he was accustomed to from the other Dragon Kings.

Looking more and more exhausted, the drake lord slumped back. The hissing became more pronounced with each breath. ''I wasss a man who wasss a beassst, but I knew who I wasss now and so I believed there wasss hope for my humanity. The others mussst have become like me. I decided to summon the other dragons, the onesss I was certain were of the Tezerenee, and bring them into the chamber one at a time. Surely, with all of usss once more knowing who we were, we could work to transform ourssssselves back to what we had been.''

It was not to be. He who had once been the Vraad called Logan summoned drake after drake into the chamber, only to find that none of them recalled even the vaguest of memories. One after another disappointment. When the last had been dismissed, he again attempted to tear the place asunder and was again defeated by the power that held the chamber together. He and he alone was evidently the recipient of the crystalline chamber's great sorcery. He had been *chosen*; that was the only answer that he could surmise. It would be useless to summon his brothers even assuming he could find them. They would be no different than the poor fools who were now his clan.

Humanity briefly crept back into the Dragon King's voice. It was as if there were a constant struggle going on between the two sides of his mind. ''And so through the millennia, I have remained alone, my mind a man's and my form a monster's. The chamber gives much: the ability to view the land all over, power that reaches beyond the borders of my domain, and, most devilish of all, *life eternal*.'' He allowed Cabe time to think of the ramifications of that gift, then resumed, ''But it does not give me the power to become the man I once was. Nothing has. If I try to transform, I risk losing control over my very thoughts. All that is left to me is my mind. After so long, *that* is little consolation, but I will not give it up. I have watched the others give way to generation after generation of heirs, each more of a monster than the lassst. I have watched the rise of humanity, who thinks that it, in turn, inherits from beasts and not from its own ancestors. I have watched . . . and watched . . . and watched.''

A lengthy silence followed. It was a silence that the warlock knew meant the tale was at an end, or at least as much of it as the drake was willing to tell him. There were many questions that Cabe wanted to ask, including whether Shade was one of the Tezerenee and how the Crystal Dragon had kept his immortality secret from his counterparts, even barring his hermitic existence. Perhaps someday he would be told the answers to his questions, but not this day. What he *had* learned was stunning enough. The Dragonrealm was ever a cornucopia of surprises.

The silence continued without foreseeable end. At last able to stand it no longer, Cabe dared speak. ''Your Majesty?''

There was no response from the massive form.

''Your Majesty?'' The warlock paused, then shouted, ''Logan Tezerenee!''

The Crystal Dragon's head shot skyward. Blazing, reptilian eyes fixed on the small, defiant figure standing before him. The monarch of Legar hissed. ''You have my attention. Make it worth the danger.''

Cabe Bedlam had had enough, however. He took a step closer and retorted, ''I don't fear the danger. If you were anything of a threat, you would be acting against the true problem, the wolf raiders. Instead, you remain here, dwelling on a past that is lost. If you care so little about your existence, then you should have ended it long ago.''

''Beware of how you ssspeak, human!''

''Listen to yourself! Is that a man speaking?''

The glittering behemoth rose to his full height. Even then, the warlock would not back down. He dared not.

''You are purposely trying to annoy me! Why?''

Pointing at the walls, Cabe responded. ''You've seen what's out there. *You* unleashed the fog. Now, instead of bringing down the Aramites, it may become a weapon they can use. You *have* to do something.''

''The fog will eventually dissipate! It must! It cannot hold itself together, not even if he commands it. The raiders will wipe themselves out trying to conquer this land and that will settle the situation." He hesitated. "Now leave me . . ." The Dragon King started to turn away. "I must rest."

Cabe could not recall ever becoming so infuriated with a Dragon King before. The very notion surprised him even now, but he knew that he was nonetheless fast approaching the point where he would lose his temper . . . and then probably his life. There were too many people relying on him, however, for the incensed sorcerer to give up.

"You've been hidden away here too long, content with observing through this device rather than seeing the world through your own eyes! You've become afraid of the outside, afraid of becoming part of the Dragonrealm!"

"*You* understand *nothing*!" roared the Crystal Dragon. "You understand nothing! I *cannot* leave this chamber! If I do so I lose *everything*! I will become as the others did, as I once was! I will be a creature, a monster, in form *and* in mind! I will lose myself! And this time it will be forever, I feel it!" The enraged dragon tried to calm himself down. "The sssame it isss if I exert my power too often, asss I nearly did when Ice sssought to end all things with his foul spell! I have rested much since then, but it is still not near enough!

"It almost happened once, when I decided to seek out some of the others and see if they, too, with the aid of this chamber could recall their past. As I started to leave, though, my head began to swim and my thoughts grew beastlike. I only barely made it back here. It was *three* days before my mind was calm enough to think my bitter experience through. I came to realize that only here was I myself. Only *here* could I survive intact."

Intact? Cabe found that debatable. His shoulders slumped in resignation. There would be no alliance with the lord of Legar. Now, Cabe was truly alone unless somehow he could find Darkhorse.

"Then there's no need for me to remain here," the warlock stated. He readied himself for the worst. "Am I free to depart or have you told me this fantastic story with the intention of keeping me here?"

The Crystal Dragon no longer seemed even interested in him. He curled up in what was obviously a prelude to slumber. It dismayed Cabe to see what the Dragon King had become. "You were free to go the moment you woke. You are free to go now."

What are you waiting for? the sorcerer demanded of himself. To his surprise, he tried once more to convince the Dragon King to see his way. "If you would only consider—"

Glittering, inhuman eyes that had been nearly closed widened. A hiss escaped. "I ssssaid *leave*!"

With those words, the warlock began to spin. Cabe gasped and tried to stop, but was helpless. He spun faster and faster, a frantic, living top. The cavern became first a bright blur and then a murky nothing. Cabe tried to concentrate, but the constant twirling threatened to make him black out. It was all he could do to keep conscious.

All at once, he simply stopped.

With a grunt, the stunned mage fell to the floor, but a floor that was hard and, strangely enough, very uneven. Cabe shook his head, then regretted the action as vertigo set in again. He settled with putting his head in his hands and waiting for the world to come to a halt on its own. Only when it finally did was he willing to look up.

Cabe first saw nothing. Wherever he had landed, it was pitch-black. Cabe summoned a dim sphere of blue light, then grimaced at what the illumination revealed. He was in another tunnel, but unlike the ones leading to the drake lord's lair, the malignant fog held sway here. That meant that Cabe must be closer to the surface. Closer to the surface and, he suspected, almost beneath the Aramite encampment.

With the Crystal Dragon's aid no longer a hope, the warlock was on his own. The surface was where he now needed to go, but which was better, he wondered, journeying in the direction he was already facing or turning around and seeing where the other end of the tunnel led? Did he *really* want to continue to the surface or would it benefit him to descend farther into the earth? At this point, it was impossible to tell which path led to the surface and which did not. One thing was certain: no matter which direction he chose, the mage would have to walk. As long as the tendrils of Nimth had hold of Legar above and below ground, the warlock dared not try teleporting save as a last desperate venture. There was too much chance of something going wrong with the spell.

Grumbling, Cabe at last chose the direction he was facing and started walking. What he hoped to accomplish without the aid of the Crystal Dragon, he could not say. Yet, even without the Dragon King's might behind him, the warlock knew he had to attempt *something*.

By the time he did reach the surface, Cabe hoped he would know exactly *what* that something was supposed to be.

One hour 'til dawn, yes? thought the blue man. It was hard to be certain in this godforsaken place, but that seemed a good estimate. Kanaan D'Rance estimated he had two hours at most to accomplish his task before Lord D'Farany rose. If all went as his grotesque visitor said, that would perhaps be an hour more than he needed.

D'Rance did not at all trust the macabre creature who had visited his tent, but Plool did indeed know things about sorcery that the northerner had never come across before. What especially interested him, however, was the stranger's knowledge of the magic that was the fog. With that to add to his own growing skills, the blue man would have need of no one. He could leave the mongrels to their own end.

The blue man entered the tunnel mouth and hurried down the deep, descending path. The guards in the passages would think nothing of him returning since his other work was down here, but those who kept watch in and around the chamber would be suspicious if he entered without Lord D'Farany. None of the Aramites trusted him that far. His skills were still not sufficient enough to deal with so many, otherwise he might have been able to do this without Plool's aid.

One thing he pondered about was why his bizarre ally could not work the Quel device himself. Plool refused to enter the chamber, not because he did not want to, no, but because he could *not* do so without endangering himself somehow. That, at least, was Kanaan D'Rance's humble opinion, yes. The creature needed D'Rance for that reason alone and that reason alone was why the blue man knew that the advantage was his. He was familiar enough with the magical device to know some of the things he could do with it, enough that he would be prepared when his ally turned on him.

Plool was still an enigma to him in most other ways and

D'Rance was willing to admit that he had perhaps been a bit too hasty in joining forces with the ghastly, deformed mage. Yet, when Plool had spoken of the power to be obtained by working together, it had been too enticing. More than enough power, horrid Plool had hinted, to make the dangers negligible.

He was a part of the mist, that much the blue man had gathered despite his ally's confusing manner of speech. Plool had come from *somewhere*, drawn to this place at the same time as the fog had been. Plool had originally wanted to go home, but he could not. To open that doorway would require more effort than both he and D'Rance combined could summon. Searching for such power had brought the sorcerer to the camp and the caverns, where he had observed enough to know that somewhere below the surface there was a thing of great potential. Yet, it was a creation of a foreign sorcery. Plool did not understand that sorcery and so had sought out someone who might. Someone who also would have an interest in aiding him. In return, he could show that someone how to manipulate the magic of *his* world. Then, his part of the bargain kept, he would return to that other place—*Nimth*, was it?—and leave the spoils to his temporary ally.

The skill and knowledge to control two very different types of magic. The blue man had taken the bait . . . but was careful only to hold the hook, not bite it. From studying the efforts of Lord D'Farany and devising a few secret theories of his own, he was certain that he knew more than enough to ensure that this partnership would end in his favor. D'Rance even suspected he knew almost all he needed to know about Plool's magic. In his own grand opinion, he certainly knew enough about the Quel's creation to guarantee that whatever else happened Plool would not be able to betray him.

Still none of the scattered sentries questioned his presence in the passages. Likewise, he crossed the abandoned city of the diggers without any trouble, save that the damnable mist, which somehow remained strong even down here, made walking a matter of stumbling every few yards. At least it was thin enough here that he could see the men just ahead of him. It would not do to walk into one of the guards. Some of them might be tempted to attack first and question afterward.

Each time, the sentries straightened as he passed, strictly because of his position as aide to their leader, D'Rance understood, and did nothing to slow him. He nodded to each man. With luck, this would be the last time he saw their ugly, pink faces.

Then, almost before he realized it, the blue man was at his destination. The entrance to the chamber stood before him. He saw two guards standing there, seemingly oblivious to him. That, D'Rance was certain, would change with a few more steps. He was puzzled, though, that nothing looked different. *Where are you, my misshapen friend? Something should have happened by now, yes?*

"Enter you may, whenever you like," a familiar voice whispered from his right. "You may enter whenever you like."

Although it took all his will, D'Rance neither jumped at the sudden sound nor did he turn in the direction it had originated from. The northerner already knew that there was no one to see. If Plool had been visible, the sentries would have been able to see him from this distance, if only as a strange shadow demanding investigation.

"The sentries are dealt with, yes?"

"Will be bothering you not; you will not be bothered."

The blue man grimaced. If the Aramites thought *his* manner of speech was strange, they should listen to this clownish figure.

Standing straighter, Kanaan D'Rance walked toward the two silent guards. Even with the mist, his identity should have become apparent to them, yet they did not move to bar his way. At the very least, they should have been calling out, asking what business he had here alone.

It was only when he stood face-to-face with one of them that he saw that the man looked somehow different. His eyes had a glassy, blank look and his skin was smooth and bright pink, almost as if it had been carved from wood and painted over.

The *mouth* . . . was it actually cut like—

The sentry suddenly bent over in a comic bow, one arm flopping loosely, and said in a familiar singsong voice, "Enter, O seeker of knowledge!"

D'Rance nearly choked. He stepped back from the horrific monstrosity. The guard straightened again. D'Rance could almost imagine strings holding the dead figure up and making it move.

The lower jaw of the macabre puppet slid down and Plool's chuckle filled the tunnel.

He cannot enter the chamber! Remember that, yes! A bit more shaken than he would have cared to admit, the would-be sorcerer walked toward the entrance. To the opposite side, the second guard slowly turned his head so that he was staring at the new-comer. D'Rance shivered as the man's head continued to turn beyond normal limitations. The sentry's countenance was a monstrous copy of the first man.

What of the guards inside? Had they heard nothing? Had Plool somehow dealt with them, too? How?

There was only one way to find out, of course. He stepped into the chamber.

Gods! What sort of creature had he aligned himself with? The blue man surveyed the carnage with growing horror. He had braced himself for the worst once he had seen what had become of the two guards outside, but it was Plool's playfulness that daunted him. The two sentries had been twisted into marionettes, puppets. Here, where the madcap monster could not physically go, Plool had chosen a different but still effective manner of mayhem.

As with the sentries outside, each soldier appeared to be standing ready. They would stand ready forever, or until someone had the nerve to remove them, for from head to toe they had been *pierced* by long, thin needlelike projectiles of metal. So great had been the velocity of the deadly needles that the guards must have barely had time to realize what was happening, for several still held their weapons. Glazed eyes stared ahead, eyes that might have barely acknowledged the flying death before it struck. Strangely enough, there was hardly any blood, which only served to make the scene that much more frightening for it gave the tableau an unreal quality. Recalling what little damage Orril D'Marr's scepter had done to this place, D'Rance swore under his breath. Plool's lances had penetrated armor and rock with little effort.

Plool himself might not be able to enter, but his power reached easily enough. D'Rance steadied his nerves. He would have to be on guard.

"Admiration later," whispered the peculiar voice from behind him. The blue man could feel those terrible, lopsided eyes on his backside.

"You should not have done this, yes? By damaging the walls, you may have ruined everything!"

"It will function; function it will. To your task."

Avoiding the accusing eyes around him, the blue man made his way to the Quel's great toy. Here was where he had the malformed spellcaster at a disadvantage, the blue man reminded himself again. Plool might be able to kill a dozen or so men with a single strike, but he dared not use his sorcery on the magical construct. Without the understanding of how it worked, Plool was more likely to destroy it. This was a thing requiring careful, physical manipulation of the patterns and crystals.

Thinking of crystals, D'Rance glanced quickly around the array. The Aramite talisman was still there, ready to be used as his key to unlocking the secrets of sorcery. He had been mildly worried that the Pack Leader might have decided to take it with him when he retired, but D'Farany had apparently assumed it was secure here. Kanaan D'Rance smiled at such egotistical naiveté.

As he bent over the platform, the blue man shifted so as to obscure one side of the array from his companion's sight. There were some adjustments to be made that he did not want Plool to know of. They would be of value when the time of betrayal came.

It took several minutes to organize the crystals to the pattern he wanted. So far, he had not had to summon much power to aid him in the binding of the new array, only enough to make the pattern stable. Still, even as little as he called made the chamber take on a reddish gleam. The blue man could feel the forces stirring above and around him, growing stronger with each passing second. Soon, he would have to move to the next stage . . . which meant including Plool in the spell.

How much of a fool had he been to go along with this insane scheme? A truly great fool, but it was often the fools, he knew, that became the masters.

D'Rance straightened. "I am ready, yes?"

"Do it, then," came the voice from the corridor. "All was explained to you."

The fog itself would be the key. Lord D'Farany had bound

the deadly fog to the Quel creation. He did not know the specifics
of how the Aramite commander had done that fantastic deed, but
that did not matter. All he needed was to seize control of the
magical cloud, spread its might to this chamber, which had
somehow been neglected by the fog, and use it to open the way.
He would have his power and the monster would have his path
home.

The would-be mage touched the shimmering keeper talisman.
In the process of combining the two sorceries, he would also
make certain that Plool would not steal all that power from him.
The blue man had seen D'Farany use the talisman enough to
know that redirecting all those forces away from where his misshapen companion expected them to go would be simplicity
itself. D'Rance smiled, his uncertainty giving way to confidence
as he saw how everything was under *his* direction.

His fingers gently played across the array of crystals. Every
movement that Lord D'Farany had performed was etched into his
mind. Now, all that careful observation was going to profit him.

I will be the greatest mage to ever live, yes! What other mage
had ever held in his figurative grasp two distinct and deadly
variations of sorcery? What other spellcaster could lay claim to
such power?

He traced the last pattern.

A bluish glow surrounded the Quel artifact, burning away the
reddish light and bathing the entire room in its own magnificent
color. *Yes, very appropriate!*

"Mind yourself!" Plool called. "You should mind!"

The blue man ignored the warning. He *knew* what he was
doing! As the glow strengthened, he glanced up at the macabre
legion surrounding him. The eyes of the dead guards watched
him, he thought. *The greatest moment and all there is to see my
victory are a score of blue-tinted ghosts and a monstrous jester
from beyond!*

Kanaan D'Rance reached down to again touch the Aramite
talisman. It would be the receptacle of all that combined might.
A receptacle that only he would wield.

A second later he snarled and pulled back *blackened* fingers.
There was blood where the skin had cracked the worst.

"This should not be hot," the northerner muttered, fighting
back the pain. Lord D'Farany had touched the talisman time and

time again during his experiments and never had there been any
visible sign of such terrible heat. The keeper was no god; his
fingers should burn as easily as D'Rance's had. What was wrong?

He spat on his injured fingertips and carefully wiped away the
blood. He would cure the wound when the power was bound to
him. The pain was not so much that he could not make use of
those fingers. A slight adjustment of the Aramite artifact was all
that was needed. A simple mistake was all it was.

Kanaan D'Rance reached for the talisman again.

This time, the blue man shrieked.

The hand he pulled free was burnt, torn, and twisted. Still
screaming, Kanaan D'Rance fell forward. His arm was a wave
that knocked aside crystal after crystal from the delicate arrangement. Blue light darted forth from the device to the walls and
back again. The northerner stumbled away from the wreckage,
only partially aware of what he had done.

"Plool!" he managed to croak. Through blurred eyes, the
blue man sought out the ungodly form of his ally in this venture.
Waves of agony coursed through his body. His lower arm was
not only burnt, it was also cut to ribbons. The blue man did not
wonder how the second had occurred; sorcery was just that way.
All he knew was that he needed help quickly and there was only
one who could provide that help.

No response. It was as if Plool had fled . . .

There was a sound like a crack of thunder, thunder that was
in this very chamber. Even maimed and in agony as he was,
D'Rance turned in curiosity.

A *hole* had formed above the battered array of crystals. Within
that hole he could see another world, a dark, violent, misty world
smelling of decay.

"I have d-done it, yes!" he hissed, the pain fading for a time.
"Yesss!"

It was beautiful in its own way. Beautiful and seductive.
Kanaan D'Rance stumbled back to the battered crystals, a trail
of blood forming behind him, and looked up. A smile spread
across his sweat-soaked face. "Y-yesss!"

The smile remained on his face even as he collapsed backward
to the floor.

——— XV ———

Bound and tossed among the captive Quel, the Gryphon felt the terrible change in the air. The fog began to move with more violence, at times becoming a veritable maelstrom. A chill ran down his spine. He stared at his fellow captives who, as one, looked up and then at each other.

The lionbird studied the other prisoners closely. They almost seemed to be anticipating something. The Quel were excited, almost . . . hopeful?

He renewed his efforts to free himself. The collar he wore around his throat prevented him from conceiving any spells, but that did not mean he did not try. Whatever was happening, the Gryphon did not want to be bound and gagged when it reached its climax. What could possibly make them so—

The Gryphon let loose a muffled squawk. There could be only one thing that so interested his fellow prisoners, but . . . could it be true? Was there a chance that the spell had been broken?

Had the wolf raiders, in their arrogant ignorance, woken the *sleepers*?

He struggled even harder. Dawn was fast approaching and the Gryphon had a suspicion that this was to be a day of reckoning. For everyone.

They woke.

There was no preamble, no slow stirring. Eyes simply opened and took in the dark. Stiffened forms slowly shifted, trying to make muscles work after thousands of years of ensorcelled sleep.

None of the sleepers were aware of how much time had passed. They only knew that they were all awake. They only knew that being awake meant it was time to reclaim what had once been theirs.

It was time to reclaim their world.

In the tunnels, a weary Cabe came to a halt as the first sensations of change washed over him. The warlock gasped at both the intensity and the source of those emanations. By now, he recognized the touch of Nimth too well. Something had caused a resurgence in the fog, a terrible growth. It was as if Nimth were trying to intrude farther upon the Dragonrealm.

The wolf raiders! It had to be them. They had control of the sorcerous mist. The Crystal Dragon would not have dared try opening a new doorway to foul Nimth. The Aramites, experimenting, must have done so themselves. Perhaps they had tried to discover the source or perhaps they had hoped to strengthen the fog's power.

What the reason was did not truly matter. What did was that everyone—every*thing*—might be in danger. This felt almost uncontrolled. The Aramites, even if they had a sorcerer of their own, might not understand what it was they played with.

Cabe could sense in what direction the magical ripples originated from, but he was still hesitant to try to teleport. It was because of that hesitation that he had spent so much valuable time wandering in what he hoped was the right direction. Teleportation had not worked the first time he had tried it in the fog and even if it succeeded now, he might find himself far from his intended destination! Yet there was no way of telling whether it would be possible to trace a path through the tunnels. For all he knew, they might lead him away from the danger.

The last was a tempting thought, but the dour mage knew he could not avoid the threat any more than he had avoided the rest of his mission. The magic was growing wilder by the moment. It could not possibly be under the guidance of anyone with the skill and knowledge needed. Cabe was not certain that even *he* had such knowledge, but there was no one else. The Crystal Dragon had made it emphatically clear that he wanted nothing more to do with the outside world.

"I've got to try," Cabe finally muttered. There seemed to be times between the ripples of newly released power when things almost became normal. If he attempted a spell, then . . .

He cringed as the next wave of sorcerous energy washed over him. So far, nothing had changed. No hands grew out of the walls. No creatures materialized from the ether. It appeared that Nimth did not immediately affect its surroundings, but that bit of good fortune could not last much longer.

The wave passed and an area of calm surrounded him.

Cabe teleported . . .

. . . and found himself staring into the dead eyes of a soldier who had been pinned to the wall like some gruesome decoration. Cabe bit back a yell and turned his gaze away, only to confront a similar grisly sight. He surveyed the walls in morbid fascination. There was no doubt in his mind who was responsible for this. Even the wolf raiders would not tolerate such insanity from their commanders. The Quel would not have killed in such a way; the damage to the chamber was extensive.

Plool had left his mark here. Only the Vraad would kill in such a manner.

Belatedly, the warlock saw the hole.

A black, oval space surrounded by a halo of wild light, the hole floated high in the center of the chamber. It was a small thing, but its simple presence here was danger enough. Cabe could sense the same malevolent power that permeated the fog, the power of ancient Nimth. As the hole pulsated, that power seeped into the Dragonrealm, adding to the foulness already admitted by the Crystal Dragon. There was a faint hint of mist in the chamber, but nothing approaching conditions on the surface.

He did not have to ask how it had come to be here. Cabe recognized the thing in the center as a creation of the Quel. It was a new creation, for he could not recall it being here during a previous encounter with the subterranean race. What its original purpose had been was impossible to say, although the warlock had some suspicions. The wolf raiders had usurped it for their own desires, obviously recognizing the potential power but not respecting the likely danger of trying to use the device.

By its side lay another body, but this one was different from the rest.

Cabe had never seen a blue man, although they had been mentioned briefly in one or two of the Gryphon's dispatches. Moving to the corpse's side, he inspected the body. The hood of the man's outfit had fallen away, revealing the silver mark of the warlock in his hair. His one hand was a burnt and ravaged horror that made Cabe greatly desire to look elsewhere. Shock and blood loss had likely killed him. Judging by the trail he saw, the foreign sorcerer had walked toward one of the tunnel mouths and then back again, as if he had not even noticed his life ebbing from him. Evidently, his dead counterpart had overestimated his

skill in manipulating the power and had paid with his life . . .
or perhaps Plool had overestimated it. Glancing up at the hole
again, he began to have some idea of what the Vraad might have
wanted and what the blue man might have been offered.

Where *was* the Vraad? Cabe could not sense him nearby, but
with Plool that did not mean much. Plool was like nothing he
had ever come across before; it might be that the Nimthian
sorcerer was invisible to his senses most of the time.

Rising, he studied the damage to the device. Crystal sorcery
was not Cabe Bedlam's forte, but he understood the basics. Much
to his regret, however, what he knew in no way aided him in
deciphering the scattered array before him. In his death throes
the blue sorcerer had pushed almost everything aside. Cabe had
no idea how to even begin re-creating the original design.

Yet, as he touched some of the crystals, certain images played
in his mind. He picked up one piece, wincing briefly in pain
when he raised his arm too high, and positioned it. Once that
was done, the warlock chose another piece and placed that in a
position on an angle from the first. Around him, blue lightning
crackled to life, but as it was high above him, he paid it little
mind. After assuring himself that the piece was in its proper
place, Cabe searched the pile again. It almost seemed logical
that the next two crystals that he chose went where they did. So
did the two after them.

Before his eyes, he watched the arrangement take place. Everything he picked up had its niche. There were some crystals
that interested him not at all, no matter how many times Cabe
tried to find a spot for them. He felt as if his hands were being
guided, but not by any source without. Rather, the sorcerer felt
he was being guided by some force within.

Had his grandfather, Nathan, known crystal sorcery? Was that
what guided the warlock's hands? The thought that he might be
drawing upon Nathan's past did not at all surprise Cabe. Nathan
Bedlam had known something about everything and had tried to
pass on as much of himself to his grandson as was magically
possible. There seemed no end to the skills the elder Bedlam had
possessed. If he lived to be three hundred, the warlock wondered
if he would ever feel he had lived up to his grandfather's legacy.

As Cabe re-created the pattern, he noticed that the hole's
pulsations decreased. The lightning, which had played about the

chamber throughout his work, now ceased. Encouraged, Cabe worked faster, trying to align everything. He soon depleted his supply of usable crystals, but still the array was not complete. Searching the floor, the warlock located several pieces around the body of the blue man. He reached down to gather them up, then paused. Just noticeable under the body and arm of the corpse was something that was not a crystal but still cried out to him to be used. Cabe gingerly moved the body to one side.

It was a carved object. A talisman. Whoever had carved it had fashioned it into the shape of a jagged tooth reminiscent of a hound's or a . . . a *wolf's*.

An Aramite talisman. To be more precise, a *keeper's* talisman. The thing radiated such power that he almost pulled his hand away. Yet, a feeling inside insisted that the warlock add it to his collection. The pattern would not be complete without it.

Cabe reached forward and started to wrap his fingers around the carving.

It flew backward from his grasp, heading in the direction of one of the cavern mouths behind him. Cabe turned, intending to give chase.

A hand caught the talisman. An elegant figure clad in the black armor of the wolf raider empire stepped forward. Despite his aristocratic features, there was a definite hint of insanity in his eyes. Sometimes the eyes focused, more times they did not. It almost seemed as if the newcomer were uncertain about which direction in life he preferred. Cold sanity or even colder madness. Cabe recognized the scarred visage from glimpses in the Crystal Dragon's sanctum during the battle of wills. Here was the victor of that battle.

"My precious . . . prize! My treasure! What . . . have . . . you done . . . to my . . . prize?"

He pointed the talisman at Cabe.

With but a thought, the warlock shielded himself. Tendrils sought to snare his arms and legs in a viselike grip, but his own spell held. The tendrils could find no grip on his person and slipped off. They tried again with the same result, then faded away.

The Aramite sorcerer did not even pause before striking with a quick, swordlike slash. Cabe parried a long, gleaming blade that formed from nothing with a magical blade of his own. The two traded blows for several seconds before the wolf raider withdrew. Cabe, his head and heart pounding and his arm in agony, did not try to seize the advantage. There was too knowing a look on the raider's marred face. He *wanted* Cabe to come to him.

The Aramite caressed the carving. "Who are you, warlock? I felt the tooth call to me, for we are bound together as two halves of a soul. Did you think that I would not notice? Kanaan should have known better, but I see that does not matter any longer. A pity for him."

He did not bother to answer the wolf raider. Cabe debated his chances of teleporting safely while continuing to fend off the attacks of the Aramite. From their brief exchange of spells, he could already see that his opponent was quick and a master of power. Cabe doubted his chances of simultaneously escaping and defending himself against the sorcerer. That meant it was to his benefit to take the offensive.

A shower of rock struck the Aramite sorcerer from behind. As he moved to defend himself, Cabe unleashed the second half of his assault. It materialized above his adversary's head, a leathery thing as large as a shield and resembling nothing more than a sheet. The wolf- raider, engaged in repelling the rock storm, did not notice the danger above him until his head was suddenly covered. He reached up to pull the sheet off, but the covering would not be removed. It wrapped itself tight around the face and helmet of the raider, cutting off his air supply.

Then it dissolved.

Cabe stepped back. The eerie eyes turned his way again. In the Aramite's grasp, the talisman fairly glowed. "I ask again, warlock. Who are you? I think you must know the Gryphon, our friend. I think that is why you are here. That would make you one mage in particular. What was the name? Yes . . . *Cabe Bedlam.*"

From behind the raider came the sound of many armored men running. The first of the soldiers reached the entrance, but when he sought to enter, the Aramite sorcerer waved him back. From the soldier's quick obedience, it was obvious who was in command of the invaders.

"Your chance to yield has forever passed, Cabe Bedlam."

The talisman flared.

Cabe tensed, but there was no attack against him. He glanced back and forth around the chamber, never letting his eyes completely shift from the raiders. Still he saw and sensed nothing.

Then, from all around him, there came horrible, wrenching noises. He could not place the sounds save that they reminded him of metal scraping against rock. The warlock took a step back and tilted his head enough so that he could see more of the right side of the room while still keeping an eye on his foe.

What he saw turned his stomach and almost made him forget the threat before him.

They struggled from the wall, freeing themselves slowly but surely with a strength far in excess of that of any living man. With eyes as blank as the sorcerer who controlled their strings, the dead sentries, the lances still piercing their torsos and limbs, shambled toward Cabe. Some had their weapons ready, but others merely reached for him. Caked blood splattered the floors and walls.

The warlock fought against the unreasoning panic rising within him. Necromancy was the darkest use of sorcery. Cabe's first introduction to it had been when Azran had sent the rotting apparitions of two of Nathan Bedlam's old companions, the sorcerers Tyr and Basil, to kidnap the young Bedlam and bring him to the mad mage's keep. That horrific meeting had forever left its mark on him, although he had never admitted such to Gwen. Cabe Bedlam disliked shapeshifting, but he *feared* necromancy.

Fear, however, did not equate panic. Not quite. He stepped around so that the Quel device stood between him and the Aramite. The wolf raider stirred, but, as Cabe had prayed, his adversary still held some hope of making use of the artifact and therefore hesitated to cast any spell that Cabe might deflect to it. That hesitation gave the warlock the extra breath he needed to combat the more immediate threat. Even if the barriers he had raised held, the unliving army was too great a distraction. If Cabe let them surround and harass him, he would eventually fall to his true opponent.

It was the metallic lances that skewered each of the undead that finally inspired him. Cabe lunged forward and reached among the crystals he had arranged earlier. Drawing upon the same knowledge that had let him create the pattern before him, he transposed three of the pieces.

A storm broke above his head. A lightning storm that raced so swift from one end of the room to the other that it created a web of ever-shifting design. The warlock ducked back as the bolts struck the array as well, creating a bluish glow about the artifact. From the other side of the Quel device, he heard the keeper shout in frustrated realization.

From his studies, Cabe was familiar with the attraction of lightning to metal rods. So, too, it was evident, was the wolf raider.

The chamber shook as the bolts struck. There was no escape for the undead, pincushioned as they were by so many lances. Some were struck several times in a single moment while others were touched but once. One or a hundred times, however, the effect was still the same. The raw power behind those bolts was more than enough to incinerate the stumbling corpses. Some few burst into flames while others simply dropped, their forms charred black. More than one literally burst, sending gobbets flying.

Cabe crouched on the floor, his cloak protecting him from the awful rain. From where he was, he could see that the other spellcaster had backed all the way into the tunnel. The raider's spells might protect him, but armored as he was, he evidently thought himself too tempting a target for the magic lightning.

The last of the unliving legion fell. Cabe felt some small pity for the unfortunate men, but reminded himself of what they had been. Whatever decency had once existed in them when they had lived, the Aramite war wolf had worried it to death. The Gryphon had spoken of many gallant folk among the raiders' race, but the soldiers of the empire were, with very few exceptions, not among them.

Risking the storm that still crackled above, the exhausted mage stood. Much to his dismay, the keeper chose that same moment to dare to reenter. Cabe would never be able to sufficiently describe the expression on that ravaged countenance, but he knew that the next duel between them would be the last.

The duel was never to be, though, for as the raider commander raised the talisman, the chamber shook anew with a frenzy that nearly sent both men to the floor. Someone cried out about earthquakes, but this was no natural tremor. The walls, floor, and ceiling were being buffeted from within, almost as if a ghostly fist was trying to battle its way out of the cavern. Only the shield that Cabe had raised against the Aramite mage was preventing him from being tossed and battered like a piece of soft fruit. As it was, each passing moment left him weaker and weaker, for the pounding was growing stronger with each wave.

Across from him, the wolf raider was also struggling against the tremor. In his one hand he clutched tight the talisman. Beyond the sorcerer, Cabe could make out the faces and forms of several of the soldiers. To his surprise, they moved as if barely hindered by the quake. The greatest force was confined to the chamber itself, at least for now. Once the crystalline walls began to crumble, who was to say how far it would spread.

The cause, of course, was the hole between Nimth and the Dragonrealm. Feeling much like a fool, Cabe realized that the struggle between the two sorcerers had upset the balance he had created. It not only had recommenced pulsating, but with greater intensity than previously. Worse, although the tremor made it impossible to focus long on the terrible hole, the thing's dimensions appeared to be *expanding*.

Damaged as they were from the deadly rain of spears, the walls were not long in commencing to crumble. Large chunks of rock crystal broke free and tumbled to the floor. Long, wicked cracks spread from one side of the chamber to the other. Damaged already and now with its support weakening, the ceiling, too, cracked and shook.

The entire place was about to collapse.

Having succeeded in righting himself, the Aramite sorcerer retreated once more to the cavern mouth. Although they did not exactly focus upon the warlock, not once did the raider's eyes leave the vicinity where Cabe stood. The talisman remained poised.

He means to trap me! Caught between the danger of the collapsing ceiling and the threat of the keeper's sorcery, Cabe initially did nothing but stand where he was. His adversary continued to back away until he was well out of the chamber. Then the Aramite stopped and waited. The warlock cursed his counterpart. The keeper was trying to make certain that Cabe's quandary became a fatal delay.

The warlock knew he could not hope to escape through one of the other exits, not with the keeper waiting to strike. Yet, that left only teleportation and while the spell had served Cabe well enough to bring him to this place, he knew that under present circumstances he now stood a greater chance of materializing a hundred feet above the surface than he did in actually arriving at his hoped-for destination. That was if the warlock did not teleport into solid rock instead of thin air.

It was the ceiling that made his decision for him. No longer able to withstand the battering, the entire thing collapsed.

Cabe never knew if the Aramite mage tried to prevent him from escaping. He was only aware of his own sudden desire to be elsewhere and that, combined with his skill and natural affinity for sorcery, was enough to make the spell happen. Even as the ceiling came down, the warlock vanished.

He did not reappear in solid rock nor did the harried mage materialize high above the surface of Legar. Rather, Cabe came to an undignified stop against a small rocky outcropping. He yelped in pain as his arm briefly rolled against the harsh surface, then grunted as he continued to roll downward.

The outcropping was a low one and so his descent was short, if bruising. Fighting back a moan, Cabe Bedlam looked up.

The warlock had *not* materialized a hundred feet in the air, but he *had* materialized three or four yards from the feet of one very eager soldier.

Mages popping into existence must have been a familiar sight to this veteran. Even as Cabe noted his presence, the raider was already charging him, likely aware that the only chance he had against a spellcaster was to catch him while his wits were still addled. Cabe caught a glimpse of a well-honed blade rising. He reacted instinctively, raising his own arm to block the blow. From anyone other than a sorcerer, this would have been but a feeble, fatal attempt. From Cabe Bedlam, however, the action was what saved his life. The soldier's blade came down . . . and stopped two feet from the warlock's forearm.

Cabe did not wait for the soldier to recover from his surprise. He made a cutting motion with his arm.

The wolf raider's head snapped back. The soldier grunted, then fell backward. He sprawled on the ground, his neck broken as easily as if the warlock had stepped on a dry twig.

I'll never get used to killing. That might be true, Cabe supposed, but it no longer prevented him from doing the deed. This journey was becoming too much for him. Where he had tried to avoid killing his adversaries unless pressed, he now considered it the only expedient route in this case. The wolf raiders were without pity; they would kill him outright or save him for a slow death. Worse, they were more than willing to let his friends and family share that slow death.

The sons of the wolf had to be pushed back into the sea. Even one was one too many.

I'm beginning to sound like the Gryphon, he thought. Why not? He had lived through the war through the lionbird's messages, hearing of the battles and deaths. While the war had from the start been in the rebellion's favor, the immense size of the empire had meant years and years of struggle to free the continent. Years and years of folk giving their lives to overthrow the night-clad soldiers and their masters.

The brief, contemplative respite allowed him to recover enough so that he could go on. That he was in Legar was obvious. That the mist seemed a bit lighter and the land a bit more visible made him suspect that dawn was coming fast. Cabe had wondered exactly how long he had been unconscious after the Crystal Dragon's sphere had exploded. Longer than he had imagined.

Where was he in relation to the Aramite encampment? That was the true question. Was the dead raider a lone soldier who had gotten separated from his patrol or was he a scout?

Cabe rose and took a step toward the direction the raider had come from. Despite the rocky soil, he could make out a partial track here or there, at least enough to give him a place to start. He continued on for several paces, then recalled one last thing. Turning, Cabe eyed his attacker. The corpse might not be noticed for quite some time, but he could not risk it.

The spell was simple, as had been the one that had so handily killed the soldier in the first place, and thus there was less chance of it going awry. The Nimthian fog was almost dormant for the moment, but that was not likely to last. The present calm was probably like the quiet before the storm. Cabe had not forgotten the destruction raging somewhere below him, destruction that would affect the surface before long. That was another problem that needed quick solving, but the warlock knew no way to close the portal without the now buried Quel device. Besides, he had enough on his hands at the moment as it was. All he could do was hope that some solution would present itself before all of Nimth poured through.

The spell began with a tiny whirlwind whose width was just enough to include the remains of the soldier. As the whirlwind spun, dust and dirt flew up and around the body. The compact tornado whirled faster and faster, dredging up more dirt and rock. Before long, it was impossible to see anything within. Cabe let the whirlwind spin for another two or three breaths, then made it stop.

When the dust had settled, there was no sign of the body. In its place was a small mound not much different from many other mounds formed by the uneven land. A close examination would reveal the truth, but Cabe was trusting the fog to work with him. Unless one of the other warriors tripped over it, no one was likely to find the remains for quite a while. By that time, the warlock would either be finished here or *dead*.

He grimaced. He *was* sounding too much like the Gryphon.

The trail twisted and turned, but Cabe somehow managed to keep sight of it. Before long, he came across more tracks, also from Aramite soldiers. The boot shapes were more or less identical and Cabe doubted that there could be too many other armies wandering around Legar. Most of the trails led from one general direction. At first, he was surprised at the ease with which he was able to follow the tracks, but as he came across more, it occurred to him that the wolf raiders were not being very careful about covering their trails. It seemed unlikely that they would be so careless unless he was—

In the distance, he heard the familiar clink of metal upon metal.

Cabe located a nearby rise and hid behind it. He peered over the top, ready to duck if someone looked his way.

The clink of metal was joined by the stomping of booted feet. In the mist, the warlock was just barely able to see the outlines of four figures wearing helms and carrying swords or lances. They were wolf raiders; they had to be. As Cabe had thought, the Aramites would not have been so careless about covering their tracks unless those tracks were in an area very, very close to the encampment.

A little more distance and I might have landed in the center of their army! He considered it fortunate that he had been forced to deal with only one soldier. This close, he might have found himself confronting yet another patrol . . . a better *prepared* patrol, this time.

Cabe allowed the foursome to pass. Once they had, the wary mage continued on. He was not exactly certain of what he hoped to accomplish, but the closer he journeyed the more something new began to drive him toward the camp. It was almost as if someone was calling to him. Not anyone malevolent; his senses were acute enough for him to know that. No, someone who needed his help. That was what it felt like to him. Even if he was wrong and the feeling of need was only a figment of his imagination, Cabe would have still been willing to invade the Aramites' camp. He had to know how many men there were and how well supplied the army was. Most important of all, he had to know what their plans were. Where might they strike other than Zuu? Without the Crystal Dragon's magical sanctum, which saw everything and everyone, skulking through the encampment was the only way by which he could hope to gather the information he needed.

So far, his last few spells had worked the way they were supposed to work. Cabe wondered if he dared one more. He was taking a risk with this one, for it required a much longer duration. There was a good chance that the spell would deteriorate unexpectedly in the sorcerous mist.

The sounds of camp life reached his ears. Even throughout the night there would be those who were on duty and those who simply did not sleep. Sleep had probably not been quick in coming for the Aramites, not in this magic-wracked fog.

He would have to risk the spell. If it worked, it would give him a free hand. If it did not, the Aramite keeper might yet have his life.

He cast the spell about him. Unfortunately, there was no way to tell whether he had succeeded until he confronted someone. Under normal circumstances, Cabe would have been certain of his success, but so long as Legar was blanketed, nothing was certain.

With great care, the warlock walked toward the camp. It was not far, he discovered. The first of the sentries came into sight only a few minutes later. A trio of wolf raiders conversed with one another. It was time for the changing of the guard. With the two sentries was an officer, marked so by the cloak he wore. What they were saying, Cabe could not hear, for their voices were too quiet. He braced himself and walked toward them.

One of the guards glanced his way. The warlock stiffened, ready to do what he had to do in order to protect his anonymity. His patience was rewarded, however, for after a brief moment, the raider turned his attention once more to his superior.

The spell worked. Unless Cabe drew added attention to himself, he would be able to walk unnoticed through the entire army. He was not actually invisible, but like Shade had done so many times in the past, he now blended into his surroundings. It was an easier spell and one that did not require as much will and power to maintain. It was also a bit more of a danger.

He was careful to give the trio a wide enough berth. Once past them, Cabe did not look back. There was too much ahead of him that needed his attention.

Cabe had seen armed camps before, but the organization and efficiency of this one dismayed him. He had assumed that the wolf raiders would be a more haphazard bunch after their flight from the war, but while the men and equipment did have that weary and battle-worn look to them, this was not an army of refugees. These soldiers were here to fight. They would grumble and their officers would beat some of them, but this was most definitely a force to fear.

Walking among an army that would have slain him in an instant if his spell failed, Cabe could not help but feel ill at ease. Nonetheless, he moved through the camp with little hesitation, noting the number of tents and men he saw and estimating how many more there might be. The warlock listened to fragments of conversations about the war in the empire and the decisions of the expedition's leaders. He heard the name "D'Farany" used more than once and always in fearful respect. From what he discerned, Cabe was certain that the Aramite sorcerer was the very same man. His worry increased a hundredfold. Under a leader like the keeper, the wolf raiders became an even greater threat. D'Farany was the sort of commander who would drive his men beyond normal limits, if only out of fear of him.

Several times soldiers on sentry duty crossed his path and during one such incident one paused before him, squinting. The guard tightened his grip on his sword, but after staring for several seconds, he blinked and continued on. Cabe's heart did not start beating again until the guard was far away.

The warlock was in what he guessed was the center of the encampment when, to his shock, he sensed an all too familiar presence. It could only have been because of the fog that he had not noticed it sooner. In fact, Cabe was certain that the sense of need he had felt earlier could only have come from this source.

"*Darkhorse . . .*" he muttered. *They have Darkhorse!*

Like a beacon, the shadow steed's presence drew him along. Cabe was forced to walk around several tents and avoid numerous sentries, but at last he saw a huge, looming shape in the distance. The ensorcelled mage glanced around. The light had not changed much for the past several minutes; this was evidently as bright as the day was to become. Cabe was relieved. It would be difficult enough to rescue Darkhorse, out in the open as he was, without more illumination further increasing visibility. For once, the fog worked to his benefit.

The distance that remained he covered in swift enough fashion, but the last few yards were still the hardest he had crossed yet. Not because of any encounter with sentries, but rather because he was at last able to see what had become of his old friend.

The ebony leviathan stood silent in an open patch away from the main encampment. Two sentries stood watch from a more than healthy distance, but they were there more for decoration and were not even looking at the captive. What truly held the shadow steed prisoner was a peculiar, metallic harness device that hung around his neck. From the harness stretched four thin lines whose other ends were looped around his legs just above the hooves. Cabe could detect the power ravaging Darkhorse even from far away. The baleful Aramite device was designed not only to hold its captive in place, but to slowly drain him of any will or strength to escape. Judging by the way the eternal's head dropped and how dim the once-blazing eyes were, the foul creation of the wolf raiders was doing its work and doing it well.

The guards did not notice him, but when the warlock was only a few yards from Darkhorse, the shadow steed raised his weary head. He did not look at the spellcaster, but Cabe felt a weak touch in his mind. Cabe shuddered at the feebleness of that touch. How had the eternal come to this?

He continued on past the guards, who looked too caught up in their misery at having had to stand night duty to ever notice a specter crossing their paths. The silent warlock walked until he was next to the prisoner, then turned around so that he could keep watch on the sentries while he and Darkhorse conversed.

"Can you speak?" Cabe whispered.

"That . . . power is still mine. I had . . . given up hope . . . for you, Cabe. My heart lightens."

The shadow steed's tone did anything but lighten his. This close, he could better feel the wicked work of the harness. Each moment further drained his companion of his might. Darkhorse, however, was almost all magic; if the harness was allowed to continue its work unheeded, it would eventually drain the eternal's very essence away.

"You can't shift?"

"No, the harness prevents that."

Cabe studied the diabolical creation while he talked. "How did you come to be here? Did the patrol capture you after we were separated?"

A little of Darkhorse's bluster returned. The harness might be sapping his strength, but the return of the warlock was a revitalizing force. "That rabble? They scattered in every direction and never came back."

One of the guards turned, a look of curiosity spread across his war-ravaged face. His comrade also turned, but seemed more curious about what the other sentry was doing. The first man took two steps toward the eternal and stared at him. With a casual turn of his head, the black stallion stared back. The guard swallowed and stumbled back, much to the amusement of his companion. Both men swapped glares at each other, then returned to their duties.

"Talk quieter!" hissed Cabe. "At the level I do."

"I have become . . . careless . . . but it is so good to see you, Cabe! I thought my obsession had cost you your life. In dwelling on the loss of one friend, one enemy, I did not pay heed when another friend needed me.''

"You were trying to protect me," the human protested, still attempting to find some way of removing the harness. He had to be wary; there were alarm spells woven into the arrangement. They were old, however, likely implemented when the harness had first been created. If he was careful, Cabe was certain that he would have no trouble bypassing them. Actually releasing Darkhorse from his magical chains was a more troublesome predicament. The sorcery involved in the evil work of the device was bound also to the captive. In trying to free his friend, Cabe might kill him instead.

"Do you have any notion as to how this may be removed?"

"I do not." Darkhorse sounded much stronger, if not any more confident. "Forget me, Cabe. There are other matters you would be better off attending to."

The warlock thought about the wild Nimthian sorcery loose below, but said nothing concerning it to Darkhorse. He could not leave the shadow steed here. Besides, with the stallion's aid, perhaps a solution to that situation could be discovered. "I'm not leaving you."

Both sentries turned. Cabe moved as close as he could to his companion. Darkhorse eyed the two raiders, and as had happened before, the soldiers quickly turned away. The dark leviathan's ice-blue orbs brightened in amusement.

He tilted his head toward Cabe. "Then hear this thought. You asked how I had come to these dire straits. When I discovered that we had become separated, I searched for you. Unable to find any sign, I returned to Esedi, hoping that you would also return there. Much to my dismay, I did not materialize where I had intended. Thinking that the same . . . the same had become of you, I searched the hills carefully. Upon my return to our original point of departure, I was greeted with a surprise."

As desperate as he was to hear the point of the story, Cabe did not try to hurry Darkhorse. The eternal would explain in his own manner and at his own pace.

Fortunately, this was not to be a long tale. "Awaiting me in the hills was none other than the Lord Gryphon."

"*The Gryphon!*" It was all the stunned mage could do to

keep from shouting the name. The one thing he had not expected was the lionbird's return from the war.

"The Gryphon, yes. He it was who joined me when I entered Legar this second time. He it was who was with me when a second and better-equipped patrol found us." The leviathan lowered his head, the gleam fading a little from his unsettling eyes. "He it is who is now, too, a prisoner of these jackals."

Which was why the shadow steed had surrendered, no doubt. Cabe forgot the harness. Turning to gaze out at the mist, he asked, "Where? Do you know?"

"There is a large, flat-looking tent to . . . to your present right. It is some distance from here. When I was being led here, I saw them put him in there."

"After I free you, we'll rescue him." His face was grim. The warlock had wished for aid in his mission and he had received it in the form of two prisoners, one weakened near to the point of collapse and the other . . . Cabe tried not to think about what the wolf raiders might do to their most hated enemy.

"You miss my . . . my point, Cabe. Rescue the Gryphon now for two reasons. The first is that he might have the knowledge to free me from this vile contraption. He knows the curs better than either of us. The second reason is of the most import; this morning he is to be presented to the leader by some despicable little monster calling himself D'Marr. I heard that much. If you do not rescue him very, very soon, I fear we will lose our only chance. This D'Marr sounds ready to treat the Gryphon to the tender mercies of the empire at this morning's confrontation. I do not think our friend is supposed to survive the event."

Cabe hesitated but a moment. As dire as the shadow steed's situation was, there was no argument that the Gryphon faced the most immediate threat. For years, Aramite spies and assassins had tried to put an end to what they considered the empire's chief foe. Now, that foe was in their clutches. It would be an inspiration to D'Farany's forces and no doubt a way of wreaking vengeance for his own personal losses if the keeper was able to present the Gryphon's battered and torn body to his followers.

"Show me again the direction," he finally whispered.

Darkhorse dipped his head toward the unseen tent. "The camp is starting to stir. They have not slept well this last night. Go swiftly but go very cautiously."

Cabe faced his old friend. "I *will* be back for you."

"I have faith. Your being here gives me new strength with which to battle this thing of torture. Now go!"

Slipping past the two sentries, the warlock again moved nigh invisible through the camp. He was pleased his spell still held true, but was aware that each moment made the chances of mishap greater. Cabe had to find the Gryphon, release him, and return to Darkhorse. With the Gryphon to aid him, they would surely be able to find some way to free the eternal. Darkhorse was also large enough to carry both of them, which would be a necessity once either escape was noticed.

He had just sighted the tent when a minor tremor shook the area. It was short and mild, but its appearance raised a muttering among the soldiers nearby, including those who had been sleeping before the quake had begun. Cabe gritted his teeth as he pondered what could be done. Had D'Farany tried to halt the destruction and failed or had he simply abandoned the underworld under the mistaken impression that the violence would not affect the surface?

Guessing was futile. Cabe set his mind on his present task. First the Gryphon, then Darkhorse, and finally escape. Once they were secure, then they could discuss their next move.

Although he was positive that he had found the correct tent, the warlock nonetheless decided to risk reaching out with his mind to discover who or what was inside. It might be that the lionbird had been moved to another location. It also might be that Cabe had chosen the wrong tent. Surely there had to be more than one tent so designed. Moving over to another, much nearer tent . . . just to be on the safe side . . . the warlock probed.

Gryphon? He sensed more than one being in the tent. There were several, in fact, and Cabe's impression was that they were all prisoners of the wolf raiders. Cabe investigated one of the other minds, then immediately withdrew in disgust. *Quel!* They had put the Gryphon in with a band of Quel.

At least I know that he's in there, too. His probe had been able to verify that fact even though Cabe had not actually linked with his former comrade. Still, it would be a wise move to alert the Gryphon to his coming so that the lionbird would be ready when the time for escape arrived.

Then, before he could act, a new presence invaded his senses.

Cabe flung himself against the tent and tried to shield his own existence from the other. He prayed it was not too late. If he was discovered now, it was the end for all of them.

Out of the mist came the tall, familiar figure of Lord D'Farany. The keeper strode across the camp accompanied by several men, including a much slighter but foreboding officer who carried on his belt a crystal-tipped scepter that radiated sorcery. The shorter raider was fitting his helm on his head and looked to have been only recently asleep. He was muttering something to Lord D'Farany, who nodded once but did not otherwise reply.

The keeper suddenly came to a halt. As all but the slight officer looked at one another in confusion, the Aramite commander shifted his gaze toward the tent where Cabe hid. The talisman in his hand glowed, but no discernible spell was cast. At his side, the sinister aide also studied the spot where the warlock stood.

Despite the years it seemed, only a handful of seconds passed before the raider commander turned away. The other Aramite continued to watch a moment longer, but when his master resumed his walk, the officer had to follow.

It was not until the danger to his own person was past that Cabe noticed where the party was heading. His fists clenched in frustration and he silently swore in the name of his Vraadish ancestors.

He was too late. The wolf raiders had come for the Gryphon.

XVI

As the day began, soldiers all around the encampment noticed changes from the previous days. The fog moved with renewed violence and this time with a virile wind behind it. There were tremors now and then, each a little stronger than the last. Some also left in their wake peculiar humps of earth almost resembling the upturned dirt left by the underground passage of a mole or gopher, only larger. That started muttering about the need for fresh meat, which was quickly quelled by officers, who secretly agreed.

No one paid too much attention to the changes. There was nothing that the army could do about them and rumor had it that the expedition was at last going to be moving on to better climes. That sort of rumor was more welcome and soon became the only topic of importance.

Meanwhile, the tremors increased and the mounds, sometimes appearing even when there *was* no quake, soon crisscrossed the entire camp.

The Gryphon ceased struggling with his bonds the moment he became aware of the sounds of armored men approaching the tent. Much to his dismay, the Gryphon had made very little headway in his attempt to free himself. D'Marr's men had performed a practiced effort upon him; try as he might the bonds had not loosened one bit. That he had less than a full complement of fingers on one hand did not help matters.

Both he and the Quel looked up as a soldier pulled the tent flap aside. A column of six men entered the tent, the last two being D'Marr and a tall, scarred figure who could only be Lord Ivon D'Farany.

One of the guards removed the gag around the Gryphon's beak. The lionbird opened and closed his mouth a few times to see if it still worked.

"You have not changed much after all these years, Gryphon," the Aramite commander commented in quite polite tones. He reminded the captive of D'Rak, the senior keeper at the time of his arrival on the other continent. The same tone was there, although in this case, it was tinged with borderline madness. The Gryphon did not have to look into D'Farany's unholy eyes to recognize the sickness.

"So, we have met before," he replied.

The keeper toyed with his talisman, one of the largest of the so-called Ravager's Teeth that the prisoner could ever recall seeing. "Under the streets of Canisargos, in the days when the true Pack Master still ruled, the Lord God Ravager smiled down upon his children, and I was chosen to be my Lord D'Rak's successor."

"Under the streets?" The Gryphon recalled battles and flight as he and the drake Morgis, the latter in humanoid form, were pursued by the minions of the empire. The keepers in particular had been avid hunters. That hunt had ended in chaos and destruction, however, when the spell that had prevented Morgis from transforming into a dragon had been broken. Bursting upward through the very streets of the massive city, the dragon, with the lionbird on his back, had flown off, leaving behind him ruin.

A lipless smile crossed the drawn countenance of the raider leader. "I led that patrol that fought you. When the dragon brought the city down upon the catacombs beneath, I was nearly crushed. I *did* survive though . . . only to suffer *much* greater later on, when our Lord Ravager's gift was withdrawn."

The Gryphon could still not recall D'Farany's features, but that had been almost twenty years ago and humans tended to change more with time. Sorcerers, even keepers, lived longer, but the Aramite commander had also suffered withdrawal from the addictive power of his dark master. That had probably done more to twist his features than the entire war.

Glancing about, D'Marr dared interrupt his commander. "Lord D'Farany, you said that we must have the camp ready to move as soon as possible. While the order has just gone out, we don't have much time."

"I am aware of what I said, Orril. I am. A pity, though." The eyes suddenly focused. "It is a pity, Gryphon, that we cannot make a grand ceremony of your death. I, for one, would have found it inspiring. I was thinking of first giving my verlok a few moments of your time and then allowing Orril to show us his prowess in the art of lingering pain."

"Death by vermin. My apologies for the disappointment." There was no great visible reaction from D'Marr, although his eyes might have flashed in anger for an instant. The lionbird tried to judge the distance between himself and Lord D'Farany. Even bound as he was, he was almost certain that a good push would send him rolling into D'Farany. It was a desperate venture, but if he was meant to die now he at least wanted one last chance at one of his foes. After what the Gryphon had learned from D'Marr about his son's death, he would have preferred the young officer's throat, but D'Marr was too far away to even consider.

"I will live with it . . ." Lord D'Farany gingerly shifted his grip on the glimmering talisman. "I made the brief acquaintance of a friend of yours, by the way. A dark-haired warlock . . . Cabe Bedlam was his name."

The Gryphon tensed.

"It would have been so cozy to bring such old friends back together, but he didn't want to come . . . so I left him buried beneath the rubble from a collapsed cavern."

Cocking his head to one side, the lionbird carefully studied his captor. The drawn face, the constantly moving hands, and the stiff body told him more than the keeper's words. Cabe might be dead, but that death had been costly for the Aramite commander. He began to ponder the sudden decision to break camp when it was obvious that the Quel city could hardly be stripped of all its prizes. Cabe or Cabe's death had instigated something that bothered Lord D'Farany enough to make him uproot his entire force without warning.

D'Farany took his silence the wrong way. "I thought you cared about your friends more. You are little more than an animal, birdman. It would be best if we just put you out of your misery."

By the side, Orril D'Marr removed the scepter from his belt.

A hand stayed the raider officer. "He does not die this morning. Have him readied for the journey. His death will entertain us on the morrow."

Looking somewhat disappointed, D'Marr nodded. He glanced at the Quel, who stared back with unreadable expressions. The Gryphon thought that they looked a bit too calm considering their situation. "What about these little beasts?"

Lord D'Farany did not even give them a glance. "Kill them before we leave, Orril." To his prisoner, the Aramite softly added, "I want to spend a little time with you before your death, birdman. I want you to know the pain and suffering you caused me all those years ago . . . and I know it was you. It had to be. I have never been whole since the day the gifts of the keepership were stripped from my soul." He stroked the talisman and again smiled that lipless smile. "But here I have come close."

With that, the keeper turned and departed the tent. His aides, with the exception of Orril D'Marr, hurried after. Only the young officer and the guards remained. The former studied the bound captives and scratched his chin in contemplation.

"I should do this all myself, but I've not the time. Too bad; it would've been fun." He swung the tip of the scepter around until it was pointed at the lionbird. "At least I'll have the pleasure of dealing with you later. Let's see if you can scream as long as your son did."

Holding back the rage that boiled up within him, the Gryphon calmly and quietly responded, "My son did not scream."

It was not merely his belief. He *knew* Demion had not screamed. Demion would never have screamed. The Gryphon was also aware that his son had died quickly and in the heat of battle. D'Marr had never had time to torture him.

That in no way released the wolf raider from the lionbird's vengeance. Somehow, he would take the little man down.

Seeing that his attempt to ruffle the feathers of his adversary had failed, Orril D'Marr replaced the mace on his belt and summoned the two guards. "Bind his mouth and kill those obnoxious beasts. Do you think the two of you are capable of executing those orders? I mean, they *are* bound hand and foot."

The soldiers nodded. D'Marr turned to go, then stopped to stare at the Quel again. He reached into a pouch and removed something too small for the Gryphon to make out. Crouching, the Aramite spoke to one of the Quel males. "I have decided to give you one final chance to save your miserable lives. What's in that cavern? What were you hiding? Speak to me!"

The Gryphon guessed that the unseen object in D'Marr's tightly clenched fist had to be a magical creation similar to the crystals that the subterranean race used to communicate with those not of their kind. Talk of a hidden cavern interested him, especially the cold silence it brought forth from the Quel that D'Marr had questioned.

"It's buried forever! There's no use keeping it a secret any longer! I want to know!"

It was interesting to see the bland mask of the young officer slip away. He had obviously become obsessed with this cavern.

"Bah!" The Aramite rose, then turned toward the lionbird. "Stupid beasts won't talk even to save their useless lives."

Likely because they know what your promise is worth. At least they can die knowing they've frustrated you in this. Aloud, he wryly remarked, "You seem a bit put out. What won't they tell you?"

D'Marr's face returned to its more common banality. "You.

You might know about it." He leaned over the prisoner. "Far beneath the surface, past the Quel city, there was a chamber with some sort of great magical device."

"Fascinating."

The Aramite looked ready to strike him, but held back. "It's what lies beyond, what I *alone* of the camp knows lies beyond, that interests me more. The beasties used sorcery—I witnessed the very end of that spell—to change the entrance to solid wall. There is something so valuable in there that they willingly die to preserve the secret. I was planning to set some explosives against one of the outer walls, but circumstances worked against me. Something *always* worked against me. Now Lord D'Farany says the passage is gone and we must leave here, but I still need to know what was in there." While he had been talking, Orril D'Marr had put away the tiny talisman and once more removed the scepter from his belt. He began poking the head into the lionbird's chest, but, fortunately for the Gryphon, did not make use of the weapon's more devilish aspect. "Do *you* know what secret they hide from me?"

Certain as he was of the cavern's contents, the Gryphon had no intention of passing that information on to the wolf raider. D'Marr could offer him nothing. The Gryphon had no love for the Quel and they certainly cared little for him, but here, for the moment, was a common foe. Let D'Marr's curiosity eat at him. It was a small, petty bit of revenge, but at least it was something.

"I have never been to the domain of the Quel."

It was an honest statement, as far as it went. The raider officer looked ready to strike him, but their discourse was shattered by another tremor, this one more violent than its predecessors. D'Marr almost fell on the Gryphon, who would have gladly snapped off the Aramite's throat with his powerful beak if given the opportunity. One of the Quel did seek to roll into a guard, but the soldier backed out of the way and, without ceremony, thrust a good length of his blade into the creature's unprotected throat. The armored beastman gave a muffled squeal and died. His companions rocked madly back and forth, but there was little they could do.

The tremor took long to settle. Now, the Gryphon had a better understanding of why the wolf raiders were beginning to break camp. This portion of Legar was no longer stable. That should not have been so, unless . . . *The fools must have played too much with things they did not understand!*

Collecting himself, D'Marr stepped back to the tent opening. He looked from his adversary to the sentries, his frustration revealed only in his eyes. "Finish the rest of those beasts and make him ready for travel. I want this tent struck immediately after. We march in one half hour. Anything or anyone not ready by then will be left behind."

With one last glance at the Gryphon, D'Marr vanished through the tent flaps. The two soldiers matched gazes, consulted among themselves for about half a minute as to how best to dispose of the bodies, then turned with grim purpose toward the captured Quel.

The Gryphon felt the ground beneath him rise and braced himself for another tremor. When that did not immediately happen, he looked down and saw that he now sat on one end of a spreading rise of dirt much like a mole's trail. The width of the rise spread as it neared the soldiers and their victims, in the end becoming twice as wide as either man.

Throwing himself to one side, the lionbird braced himself.

His sudden and peculiar action caught the attention of the two raiders just as they were about to dispatch a pair of the Quel. One of the guards sheathed his sword and started after the Gryphon.

The Aramite was thrown screaming into the ceiling of the tent as the ground before him burst skyward and several hundred pounds of armored destruction erupted from the depths of the earth.

The Quel was huge, even by the standards of the race. In one massive paw he carried a wicked, double-bladed ax that somehow he had managed to drag with him even while tunneling. The first soldier had still not recovered, but the second was already attacking. Much to the raider's misfortune, though, he thrust his blade too low and it shattered off of the rocklike shell of the newcomer. The Quel, completely silent throughout all, brought the ax around and proceeded to nearly cleave the armored soldier in two. Blood and much too much more decorated the interior of the tent, but only the Gryphon seemed to care.

Turning, the armed creature stalked toward the remaining

raider and buried one edge of his deadly weapon in the chest of the still dazed man, who managed another short scream before he died.

The Quel threw down his weapon and began freeing the other prisoners. Dragging himself along like a snake, the Gryphon tried to move as far from the sight of the Quel as was possible. So far, they were all ignoring him, but one of them might decide to leave no witness to the escape.

A soldier stepped through the flap. "What goes—?"

Reaching for his ax, the rescuer rose to face the stunned newcomer. Two Quel whose hands had been freed hurried to undo the bonds around their legs. The Aramite was not so caught off-guard that he was not able to defend himself. His blade was out and biting before his hulking adversary was able to bring his own weapon into play. This time, the Quel was not as lucky. The wolf raider caught him in a fairly unprotected area near the neck and managed to slice off a good piece of flesh. The Quel fought back a hoot of pain and swung. His ax passed through where the human's chest should have been, but the wary raider had fallen to a crouch. The soldier started to shout at the top of his lungs.

Meanwhile, the lionbird, who had continued to move away from the battle, found himself against the side of the tent. He rolled over so his face was toward the material. Seizing the heavy cloth in his beak, the Gryphon tried to either tear a hole in it or pull it free from the ground. There was no other way out.

A true tremor struck. He lost hold of the material but quickly regained control. Unfortunately, the tremor continued to grow in intensity. It was all he could do just to hang on.

Then, someone tugged on the tent from outside. The Gryphon was so surprised that he lost his grip again. A figure in a robe peered inside.

"Gryphon?" asked a not-so-silent voice. The quake rumbled on, making it hard to hear anything below a shout.

He looked up into the worn but ready countenance of the warlock Cabe Bedlam.

"It would be nice to occasionally meet under more pleasant circumstances," the imprisoned lionbird managed.

That brought the shadow of a smile to the visage of his old

friend. Cabe started to crawl in, but the Gryphon shook his head. "Pull me out! There's Quel in there!"

Cabe glanced past him and nodded, likely having known already. The Gryphon was glad the tremor and the anxious work of the wolf raiders was keeping most others from noticing the battle yet, but was certain that that would change in the next few seconds. The warlock seized him and dragged the lionbird out. Then he pointed at the ropes around the Gryphon's arms and legs. The bonds loosened and fell to the ground. Rubbing his wrists, the former mercenary tried to remove the collar from around his throat. A sharp, immediate pain on each side of his neck made him cease his efforts.

"Let me." The warlock reached forward and touched the sides of the collar with his index fingers. There was a brief, reddish glow. Cabe took hold of the Aramite creation and pulled it apart.

"My gratitude." The Gryphon rubbed his sore neck. He noticed Cabe glancing at his maimed hand. "A gift of the war. A gift I blame on men such as Ivon D'Farany and Orril D'Marr."

"I've met the first. Is the second a shorter, younger officer?"

"The same. There's a blue man from the north of the empire that completes the set."

Cabe shook his head. "That one's dead. Would-be sorcerer. Killed himself with overconfidence, I think. These tremors are the result of that."

The Gryphon straightened, the news bringing him some little pleasure. Still, there was no time to savor the death. "Tremors aside, we cannot remain here. The battle will draw others."

"I have a spell. One that makes others ignore me unless I confront them. Let me include you under its shield."

Tired as he was, he only nodded in reply to the warlock's suggestion. Cabe blinked and, a moment later, smiled in satisfaction. Then, his face clouded again. "Now we have to return to Darkhorse and rescue him."

"Darkhorse?" The Gryphon was too ashamed to admit that he had been thinking of searching out D'Marr and his master. It seemed that the eternal was not the only one with an obsession.

"He's not far. Over there," the warlock continued, pointing. "I came across him first, but the trouble is I can't release him as easily as I did you. The harness device they have on him is linked to his very being. I've not seen its like before.''

"I have. They call it a dragon harness in the empire. It saps the power and will of the minor drakes and makes them docile. The wolf raiders also use it on other, more intelligent creatures. I was fortunate that they thought the collar was sufficient. Evidently they wanted me hale and hearty for my prolonged execution.''

"Can you release him?"

"I think so. I think I know how.'' As he started in the direction that the mage had indicated, Cabe grabbed his arm. "Wait! There's something you should know about these tremors . . .''

"Tell me. Quick.''

Condensing the story to only the most basic details, the tired spellcaster told of his meeting with the Crystal Dragon, the battle of wills between the Dragon King and the keeper, Cabe's ouster from the drake lord's realm, and, lastly, his discovery and duel in the cavern.

"And as the hole grows more unstable, this region of Legar grows more unstable as well," the Gryphon commented. The quake had begun to subside, but both knew that the next would not be long in coming . . . and it would probably be the next one that they would have to fear the most. There was a point of no return that had to be fast approaching. "Is that everything you know?"

"All that's necessary." Cabe Bedlam was hiding something, something that concerned the Crystal Dragon, but the lionbird assumed that whatever it was, the warlock felt it was not important to their immediate danger. He knew Cabe well enough to trust that decision. Later, they would talk.

"We'll worry about—Dragon of the Depths!"

The ground exploded, tossing the two in opposite directions. Even as the Gryphon landed hard on his back, he knew what was happening. This was no tremor, but a much more localized threat.

Another Quel had burst through the rocky soil. The Gryphon continued to back away . . . only to find the earth behind him sprouting into a new mound. He rolled aside just as a second Quel tore his way through to the surface.

All around the Aramite encampment, the same thing was

happening. Mounds formed, became craters. Bursting forth from each of those craters was a Quel. Wherever there was a trail of dirt coursing through the wolf raiders' camp, there sprouted the armored, hooting figure of one of the subterraneans. One by one and then a dozen by a dozen, they burrowed from the deep to the day. Many carried large war axes, but others were satisfied to use their claws. It mattered not where they rose, be it open ground or beneath a stack of weapons, the Quel came on and on and on. The Gryphon knew that there would be hundreds of them, hundreds of tawny, hulking behemoths whose sole intention was to rid themselves of the surface dwellers. Like an army of the unliving released by the Lords of the Undead, they kept coming.

The *sleepers* were not only awake; they were angry.

Few folk alive knew the full story, although the legend had spread across the Dragonrealm. Once, before the Dragon Kings and before the Seekers, the land had been ruled by the Quel. Their race had prospered for a time, but like so many others preceding them, the armadillolike creatures had watched their empire decay. The avian Seekers became dominant.

The Seekers and their immediate predecessors shared one common trait. They could not accept a rival for power. The bird folk sought to eliminate the last bastion of Quel domination, the peninsula. What the Seekers did instead, however, was unleash a spell so terrible that not only did it nearly succeed in driving the Quel to extinction but also the avians. The bird folk retired to what few rookeries remained to them and tried to rebuild their depleted population. They would never succeed in raising their numbers, for many of their females would die.

As for the Quel, they sought a different solution to the disaster. Their already inhospitable land ravaged and the neighboring regions little better, the survivors devised a plan by which the race, through high sorcery, would slumber until the day would come when they could reclaim their realm. The notion had been suggested even before all the destruction, but the Seekers' monstrous spell made its casting a necessity.

So the Quel race, excluding the sorcerers who had devised the spell, gathered into one of the largest of the underground chambers. The sorcerers and their apprentices would remain awake long enough to complete the grand spell and train successors, for there had to always be a handful to monitor events, keep the sleepers safe, and know how to awaken them when the glorious day came.

Something went terribly wrong, however, and those who knew how the spell worked perished in the process of casting it. It did put the race to sleep, but the secret of awakening them was lost. One other part did succeed; for each Quel who died, a successor was brought back to waking. There would be guardians, watchers, but none who understood what had happened. Over the centuries, the Gryphon knew, the Quel tried an endless variety of methods to bring their race back to life. They had never found success.

Until today.

Trust Nimth and the wolf raiders to wake something as unsavory as the Quel race! he thought. What would happen to the Dragonrealm with the Quel awake, the lionbird could not say. In his opinion, it could only be ill. He doubted that their long slumber had taught the overgrown armadillos the concept of sharing their world.

Around the Gryphon's vicinity alone more than a dozen Quel had already risen. He looked for Cabe but did not see the warlock. That was not too surprising. The Gryphon had been thrown back several yards. It was a credit to the lionbird's astonishing constitution that he was able to rise relatively unharmed, albeit more than a little dazed, by his flight and landing. Much to his dismay, though, the same Quel who had knocked him aside desired to change his good fortune. Heavy, taloned paws reached out for him.

He ducked and called out Cabe's name, fearful that his companion was unconscious or worse. There was no response. The rising din made it impossible to hear any one voice unless the speaker was within a few feet. He gave up just as the monster attacked again, this time slashing down with his fearsome claws. Again, the Gryphon evaded him, but barely.

There were more sounds of battle. The wolf raiders had recovered in swift fashion. Years of war had no doubt made the wolf raiders well practiced in everything. *They should thank me.*

He dodged yet another swipe from the leviathan's paws, all the while searching for something with which to combat the Quel. His reach was nothing near that of his adversary, so hand-to-hand was an option that the Gryphon wanted to reserve for last.

The lionbird found his weapon in the form of a pole tangled in the remains of a tent someone had been dismantling. He gazed at the deadly top of the staff with grim satisfaction. *Only the Aramites would make tent poles with pointed tips at the end.* Better still, the makeshift lance was made of good hardwood. Metal would have been best, but the Gryphon was not about to argue. He freed the pole, swung it around, and immediately jabbed at the Quel. This time, it was the beastman who backed away.

Taking advantage, he pressed the attack. The Quel hooted and took a defensive swipe at the wooden shaft.

It snapped in half.

Seizing the initiative, the massive creature stalked toward the Gryphon, all confidence now. Glancing around, the lionbird saw that there was no other object that he might use in place of the shattered pole. It was the lance or nothing.

In his long, bloody history, he had killed with much less.

The lionbird lunged. Surprised by the short figure's temerity, the Quel left himself open. The Gryphon, well aware of the weaknesses of the race, aimed for the not-so-armored neck.

Backed by his momentum, the jagged end of the pole went into the tender throat and up into the back of the head. The Quel squealed mournfully and struggled with the staff, but the wound was mortal. Wheezing and with blood flowing down over his torso, the digger finally slumped forward. The Gryphon barely had time to leap out of the way before several hundred pounds of dead behemoth crashed to the ground.

The behemoth's fall put an end to any other use of the pole, for the weight of the monster was enough to crush the staff into several small, meaningless pieces.

Only when his own battle was over did the Gryphon truly notice the growing intensity of the war around him. Men screamed or shouted or did both. The pain-wracked hoot of a Quel now and then pierced through the other noise. There was the constant clash of arms and orders cried out by the wolf raiders' officers. Above, he heard the roll of thunder, which would have made him believe it was going to rain, save that the rumbling never ended, just went on and on and on. Now and then, there was green lightning.

The earth began to shake again. From the severity of the new tremor, the lionbird knew that the end was very near. *The Quel's world must already be a maelstrom of destruction!*

Which is why they have come to the surface fighting, replied a chilling, vaguely familiar voice in his head.

I know you! The Gryphon's eyes widened. His mouth went dry. He still recalled the details of the battle against the Ice Dragon.

Then you know that I may be an ally.

Cabe said—

The voice became defensive. *I have changed my mind. I will aid your efforts.*

"Because the Crystal Dragon's own domain is *also* at risk?" the Gryphon could not help asking out loud.

The lord of Legar did not reply to the question. Instead, he acted as if all were settled. *You may rest easy where Cabe Bedlam is concerned. The warlock will know his part to play in this. If all goes well, all will be ssssettled before long!*

The Gryphon did not miss the sibilance toward the end. He recalled Cabe mentioning the Dragon King's struggle with sanity, but was careful to shield the thought from the drake lord. At the moment he was willing to accept almost any help, even that from a mad creature like the Dragon King.

What do you want of me?

You must free the demon steed. I will show you how the dogs' toy can be removed.

That's all? What about all this?

The Dragon King's voice began to fade away. *We will ssspeak again when you have reached the ssstallion . . .*

"Come back here!" the lionbird squawked. It was no use; the link the Crystal Dragon had created was no more.

The drake lord had spoken of Cabe playing a part. He feared for the human, knowing from the past how Dragon Kings toyed with their "lessers." Still, the Crystal Dragon *had* helped save the land from his bone-numbing counterpart.

Whatever the case, the Gryphon had lost Cabe and pandemonium now reigned supreme over the wolf raider encampment.

Freeing Darkhorse was the only path left to him. Cabe might even be there, despite the Crystal Dragon's hints.

He knew that he would have chosen to rescue the eternal, regardless of what else happened. Not only did he owe the shadow steed much, but, astonishing as it was to sometimes believe, Darkhorse was a friend. A loyal friend. The Gryphon could not have left him behind any more than he would have left behind Cabe or his own wife.

The Gryphon began wending his way toward the area where Darkhorse was supposedly being held. In each hand he carried a blade retrieved from the corpses of mangled Aramites. The path was not an easy one. Not only was the spell cast by the warlock no longer protecting him, but a pitched battle had spread across the entire camp. The Aramites were fighting back against the Quel with lances and arrows. There were even explosions on occasion. Oddest of all the things that he heard was a series of high-pitched notes being blown on battle horns. He did not understand what purpose that served until he spotted soldiers with battle horns working in conjunction with a row of lancers. The lancers would try to pen in two or three Quel. All the while, the hornmen would take turns playing as sharp and long a note as they could. To the Gryphon's shock, Quel within a certain range nearly fell to their knees as they tried to block the noise out. Weaponless and in aural agony, the subterraneans were easy prey for the lancers.

You see all possible things in war. The Aramites were holding their own, but it was a bloody fight. The lionbird felt no sympathy for either side as he wended his way through torn tents and twisted corpses of both human and Quel persuasion. He wondered if Lord D'Farany or the treacherous little D'Marr was among the dead. Likely not. *Evil like those two seems to live on until the very last.* If they escaped, he would have to hunt them down even if it meant scouring the Dragonrealm for them. Such men had a way of attracting new followers to replace those they lost. Even without an army, the keeper and his aide were dangerous to everyone.

The fighting, it soon turned out, worked in his favor. The wolf raiders and the Quel were too occupied with each other and the growing quake to pay him much mind. He *was* forced to do battle more than once, but none of his adversaries was equal to his skill, not even the second Quel he confronted. The latter he caught while the underdweller was still rising from the earth. It cost him one of his swords, the tip of the blade having become lodged between the natural plates in the creature's armor, but he left the dead Quel on his back, · half of the immense body still below the surface.

Then at last he came upon Darkhorse.

The black stallion struggled weakly against the harness that kept him in check, but his efforts were next to nothing. The Gryphon studied the area and saw no guards, which was as he had hoped it would be. Why, after all, guard something that was helpless while monsters from the depths of the earth were invading the camp? Nonetheless, he kept a wary eye on his surroundings as he completed the last bit of the trek. One could not be too careful.

Darkhorse looked up. "Lord . . . Gryphon. Good . . . to see you about. Where is Cabe?"

"He is safe." What could he tell the shadow steed? That the warlock was supposedly a pawn of the Crystal Dragon? *Speaking of the same, where are you, Dragon King?* The lionbird would definitely need assistance with the harness. He could sense that its spell was far more complex than the ones he had seen before.

There was still no response from the Crystal Dragon. The Gryphon tried again, but still without success. All the while he tried also to follow the pattern of the spell that worked the harness.

"Can you not free me?"

"I should be able to, but it is going to take longer than I had hoped. I was *supposed* to have help."

Darkhorse did not pretend to comprehend the last statement, but he dipped his head in understanding to the first part. "I will do what I can, Lord Gryphon, from within. Perhaps with the two of us striking at it . . . at it, we shall have an easier time."

"I hope so." The Gryphon stumbled. It was becoming more and more troublesome to maintain his footing.

The shadow steed's eyes closed and his head slumped. Had not Darkhorse given him some warning, the lionbird would have been dismayed. Darkhorse had entered what was the equivalent of a light trance in the hope that he might be able to assist in his own release. Working with renewed confidence, the inhuman mage began retracing the lines of the spell. Somewhere he had missed the beginning thread. Somewhere . . .

He had it! The Gryphon used his magical senses to follow the thread. He saw how it wound around the collar of the harness and split off, but the new threads did not go to the bonds around Darkhorse's legs. Rather, they returned to the beginning. He probed a bit further and found where they reconnected. The secret of the spell started to unravel before his eyes.

Then, a thousand needles turned his nerves to jelly.

The pain was almost enough to make him black out, but the Gryphon had fought against pain in the past. He fell to his knees, then would allow himself to fall no farther.

From behind him, the lionbird finally heard the sound of boots on rock. This time, he was able to roll away before the weapon could strike him in the back. The roll became a crouch, albeit an unsteady one. Only then did the Gryphon realize that his sword was not with him. It now lay at the feet of his attacker, who he had not heard because of his intense study of the harness.

I am getting old, he thought. *But it looks as if I may not be getting much older!*

"I *knew* I'd find you around here. Even in the midst of all this chaos and danger, you'd come to aid a *friend*. How sweet."

Orril D'Marr drew circles in the air with his magical scepter, circles or perhaps bull's-eyes, for the design centered around the Gryphon's chest.

"You *can't* leave now. Time to finish things, birdman. Time to die. After all, your son is *waiting* for you."

—— XVII ——

Cabe recalled being thrown aside when the Quel had burst from the ground. What he could not recall were the several seconds after that. Cabe only knew that he opened his eyes to the sight of a squalid whiteness. It took him several seconds more to discover that he had become entangled in a tent. The befuddled mage fought his way out of the canvas, then hurriedly looked all around him to see if he was in immediate danger.

He was not. The battle had been carried away from where he was. The Quel who had surprised the duo was nowhere in sight.

Neither was the Gryphon.

Cabe began to suspect that he had been unconscious for more than a minute. He reached back behind his head, which proved to be a painful mistake, for the warlock made use of his injured arm. That led to another few seconds while he struggled to fight the new agony.

I can do nothing about the arm, but I have dealt with your head injury.

"Wha—?" Cabe started, then clamped his mouth shut. *Why did you do it?*

There were actually two questions in that one. The voice, the Crystal Dragon, answered both. *You struck your head on a piece of wood in the tent. The wound was severe enough that it demanded immediate treatment. I need you as whole as possible for what we musssst do.*

The Dragon King had chosen to aid him after all. It was not too surprising to the spellcaster, not when the Crystal Dragon's own kingdom must certainly be threatened. Cabe was careful to avoid any comment or thought about the Crystal Dragon's earlier reluctance. The warlock needed a solution and it appeared that only the lord of Legar had one.

At least, he *hoped* that the Crystal Dragon had a solution.

"But the Gryphon—"

Isss on his way to free the demon steed. He knowsss what your tassssk is to be.

My task? the warlock asked in silence.

There issss only one force capable of driving the evil of Nimth back to where it belongsss! That isss the evil itssself! With the sphere and the Quel platform no more, there isss only one object with ties ssstrong enough to the cursssed sorcery of Nimth to be of ussse! We must have it!

Only one object. Cabe could think of only one, but surely not *that.* "You don't mean Lord D'Farany's talisman?"

The silence that greeted his question told him that the keeper talisman was exactly what the Crystal Dragon meant. The warlock shook his head. There had to be something else.

There is nothing else! It mussst be the tooth!

Cabe stood his ground. *Even if I can find him in all of this, he'll never willingly give me that thing!*

I shall do what I can to aid you. I promissse you, Cabe Bedlam, that if there were another way, I would take it! Thisss will either sssave all . . . or it will put an end to usss asss well!

Not a statement evoking confidence, the spellcaster thought wryly. However, his link with the Dragon King was strong enough that he knew the other was not lying. The talisman was the only chance they had.

First, though, Cabe had to find the tooth and take it from a sorcerer more than capable of killing him with it.

He isss to your right at the far end of the camp. I will guide you, but you mussst hurry!

Hurry he did, but not before he first recast the spell making him unnoticeable to those around him. It might or might not work in the midst of all this anarchy, but Cabe felt safer. An invisible shield would have protected him better, but he wanted to save himself for the confrontation with the Aramite commander. The peculiarities of sorcery demanded that while the power was drawn from without, the will and strength of the mage was often paramount to maintaining many of the spells. He did not pretend to understand it; Cabe only knew that those were the rules.

Did a keeper have to abide by the same rules?

His path was surprisingly clear of violence, despite all he heard and saw around him. There was still no way of knowing whether either force had gained the upper hand. A Quel died with three bolts in her neck; the Aramites were quick to learn the weaknesses of their much larger foes. However, the Quel were learning, too. Those that did not have weapons tore from the earth massive hunks of rock, which they threw with uncanny accuracy at their smaller, quicker opponents. Cabe came across one body whose face and upper torso were crushed beneath a rock probably as heavy as the warlock was. He had always been aware of the astonishing strength of the diggers, but this new reminder struck home.

In some places, the threat was not from either side, but from the land itself. Crevices had opened up throughout the area and more were opening every minute. Cabe saw one man plummet to his death as the surface under him abruptly caved in. The warlock himself had to leap across growing ravines more than once. Only the Dragon King's guidance kept him on his course.

Then, amid the fighting armies and the trembling earth, Cabe saw Lord D'Farany. The keeper and three other raiders, all officers, were attempting to seize control of a number of horses penned up nearby, but were having limited success. Two animals were nearly saddled, but the other horses were too overwrought and fought the wolf raiders.

D'Farany was mounting one of the two animals readied for flight.

Cabe started to run. He wanted to be as close as possible before he attempted a spell in this chaos, but his time was limited. The Aramite commander looked more than ready to leave his men behind if they did not hurry. Evidently Lord D'Farany had decided that the Quel attack was too long of a delay to risk. Even if his men defeated the underdwellers, which was not a certainty, the time lost would be too great. This entire region was heading for total collapse.

In his anxiousness to cut the distance between the keeper and himself, the warlock did not watch his path closely enough.

He tripped over something large and moving, falling face first into the inhospitable soil with a jarring crash.

Groaning, Cabe looked up, fearful that the Aramite commander had already fled. What he saw was not the wolf raider, but rather a mouthful of jagged, yellowed teeth. The teeth were in the wide-open jaws of a monstrosity the size of a small dog, but more rodentlike in appearance. It had positively the ugliest countenance that the bruised mage had ever seen, and that included such creatures as the Quel or ogres. It looked hungry. Very, very hungry.

He tried to roll aside as it leapt, but the horror twisted in the air, and as Cabe turned onto his back, it fell upon his chest. Cabe gasped as all the air went out of him. The warlock was barely able to get his hands up in time to keep the beast from his throat. It snapped at him and the foul breath was almost enough to kill him, teeth or no.

His arm was in agony and a second snap by the thing added

to the pain in the form of a shallow wound. He was able to push it back just enough so that the strong jaws could not keep hold. The viciousness of the beast was so astonishing that Cabe hardly had time to concentrate. Twice he failed and both times the monstrosity's horrid maw moved a little closer to his throat.

With a last desperate push, Cabe finally managed to put the ratlike beast at arm's length. Ignoring the throbbing pain, the warlock glared at his catch.

It squealed. Squealed in fear. He allowed himself a slight smile. It was nice to have something afraid of *him* for once. Despite its mournful squeal, however, he did not stay his course. The punishment had been chosen. The beast twisted and turned in his grip and as it did, it shrank. It shrank to the size of a rabbit, then a robin redbreast, and then the rat it so resembled. Even that was not good enough. Cabe did not stop until his attacker was no larger than an acorn. At that point, he closed a fist around it and, stretching back his good arm, *threw* the vermin as far away as he could manage. The tiny beast vanished into the fog.

Cabe turned back, fearful that he was too late, but he found that Lord D'Farany had *not* yet departed. In fact, the keeper was looking in his direction and not smiling in the least.

The warlock searched his mind for the presence of the Crystal Dragon but could not reestablish the link. The Dragon King had seemingly abandoned him at the worst possible instant.

D'Farany spurred his steed and guided the animal slowly toward his enemy. He made no attempt at a spell but the warlock sensed the power flowing about the wolf raider, power whose source lay in a pouch at the hip of the Aramite. Behind him came the three officers, one astride and two on foot. *They*, unlike their master, were armed and ready to kill.

"You should be dead. Like I once was. But I came back to life and so have you. I think you must be, in your own way, as tenacious a foe as the Gryphon," D'Farany remarked, the lipless smile just barely coming into play.

"In some ways, more so. Is this raider loyalty I see before me? You weren't long in abandoning your men, were you?"

The officers took his slight as the final insult and moved to cut him down. Lord D'Farany raised a hand, halting them in midstride. "I do not abandon my men. I abandon wars that are lost and I have, in the past, abandoned sanity, but I do not

abandon my men. I have the power to save them right here."
He patted the pouch. "And as long as I have it near, I can do *anything*."

The earth tried to swallow Cabe up. Literally. The ravine that opened had boulders for teeth and a sinuous, seeking column of clay that acted as a hunting tongue. Cabe had wondered if the keeper could control his power even when the talisman was not in his hands. Now he knew, although the coming of that new knowledge had almost been a second too late.

Yet, the warlock had been expecting the worst and so he was ready. Cabe rose above the gaping mouth and beyond the searching tongue. He felt D'Farany work his power. The tongue, like an earthen snake, followed after him, growing to match whatever height the dark-haired mage dared.

A violent wind turned Cabe's flight into a spinning terror. He first thought it was the Aramite's work until a chance glimpse showed that D'Farany, too, was having trouble controlling his sorcery. While the warlock was finding it nigh impossible to direct his flight, the wolf raiders were now having to do combat with the animated creation of their master. The column of clay darted in and out, first matching blows with the two officers on foot, then trying to seize either rider.

Nimth was overwhelming all of them.

Dragon King, where are you?

I . . . sssspell . . . it will . . . The message in his mind was meaningless garbage. Cabe struggled to force his will upon the spell he had started. In a sense, he finally succeeded, for suddenly the startled mage was plummeting earthward.

Cabe was unable to keep himself aloft, but in the last second, his will was strong enough to create a cushion of air, making his landing only a bit harsh. Lord D'Farany's creation did not seize him when he touched ground, which he assumed meant that it still fought with the Aramites. That proved true enough. In fact, the serpentlike appendage had wrapped itself around one of the horses, throwing the officer riding the steed to the ground, and was even now dragging the poor creature kicking into its maw.

Two soldiers pursued the trapped animal, but Lord D'Farany barked an order, causing them to backstep. Shrieking, the steed was pulled into the magical jaws. As the hapless mount disappeared from view, the mouth simply vanished. There was no sign of the ravine and no sign of the unfortunate beast.

Seemingly satisfied, D'Farany then pointed at the third man, the one who had been thrown off the horse, and said something unintelligible that the warlock assumed was an order to see to the condition of the injured officer. The two remaining officers obeyed without hesitation.

The keeper glanced in his direction. One hand went into the pouch where the talisman was kept. Lord D'Farany wanted a more direct control over his spells. The talisman was useful as a focus, but Cabe knew it was also a crutch of sorts to a sorcerer's imagination. Those who relied on talismans concentrated too much sometimes on what was in front of them, for that was where their toys were focused. That meant that on occasion they left their other defenses weak.

So he hoped.

The warlock did not wait for his counterpart to retrieve the tooth. Quite suddenly, there were ten Cabes all about the area. Each one moved with purpose, but not the same purpose as his twins. Some stood where they were while others moved toward the keeper and his men.

Among the latter was the true Cabe Bedlam, who now stood far to the right of his previous position. It was a risky spell, as all were in this place, but it had worked like perfection. The false Cabes moved their hands about in mystical passes that actually had no meaning. Creation and control of the illusions were actually not a great strain for him. They required much less power than true conjuration. Now he only had to hope that his adversary fell prey to it.

D'Farany did pause, losing a precious second or two while he studied his multiplied opponent. Then he pulled free the talisman and pointed it at one of the farther images. Out of the corner of his eyes, Cabe watched the duplicate ripple, then fade away. He hurried his pace. Just a little closer . . .

Swinging his arm around, the keeper brought the talisman to play on one image after another. His steed, made jittery by the madness around him, struggled with the Aramite, slowing D'Farany's work another critical few seconds. The warlock edged closer, glancing now and then at the other raiders. The two officers were still bent over the third, who would not be rising soon, if at all, from the looks of him. Cabe did not fear the two remaining. Only their master was a danger.

Then it was that Lord D'Farany's deadly talisman was pointed directly at him . . . only to continue on until the keeper had fixed it on the illusionary Cabe to the warlock's right.

The Aramite had assumed that one of the ten must be his adversary. He was wrong. Cabe walked among his duplicates, but to all eyes but his own, he was not there. Not unless they looked close. Cabe had relied on the tremors and his duplicates to draw attention from himself. Meanwhile, the same spell that had allowed him to enter the wolf raider encampment now allowed him to move toward the keeper. As long as D'Farany had other things to occupy his sight, he would not see the warlock. Of course, there were limitations. The nearer Cabe moved, the more chance there was that the Aramite sorcerer's will would overcome the spell. Had he tried to actually reach Lord D'Farany and pull him from the saddle, it was likely that Cabe would have been attacked long before he was close enough to do anything. Fortunately, he had no intention of getting *that* close.

At least, not at first.

He reached his destination just before D'Farany, still battling his anxious steed, focused the talisman on the last of Cabe's duplicates. The keeper was having trouble maintaining aim, which was what the warlock had hoped for. It gave him just enough time to prepare and then to unleash his own assault.

The ground before the nervous stallion exploded in one bright, raucous burst after another. The bursts of light appeared all about the steed, growing noisier with each consecutive explosion. Already flighty, the stallion could take no more of the happenings around it. It bucked and reared, trying to escape the explosions.

Lord D'Farany fought in vain to remain in the saddle. He first slid back, then fell forward as he tried to grab hold of the saddle with the hand not clutching the carved tooth. In the process of grasping, the keeper lost his hold on the reins.

Not daring to pause, the warlock turned on the remaining pair of wolf raiders, who even now rose to aid their master. Cabe dealt with them in the simplest of manners, using a tiny portion of his skill to raise two heavy stones and fling them toward the duo. Neither man had a chance to deflect the oncoming projectiles. Helms or not, the stones struck with enough force to knock both officers senseless.

Unable to collect his thoughts enough to control his beast, Lord D'Farany was finally thrown off his horse. The fall was not as harsh a one as Cabe had originally hoped, but the bucking stallion did manage to toss the keeper almost exactly where Cabe had wanted.

Now he leapt.

The determined spellcaster fell on top of his counterpart. D'Farany, still dazed by the fall, was unable to prevent Cabe from getting a grip on his wrists. Only when he realized that his precious talisman was no longer in his hand did the keeper truly begin to struggle. He did not even attempt a spell, although perhaps his kind needed their tokens on their person. The only magic that the warlock could recall D'Farany using on his own was when he had summoned the talisman to him and that might very well be only possible because of his link to the thing in the first place. There was too much that Cabe did not know about Aramite sorcerers.

Cabe, searching while he fought, saw the object of both their quests only a yard or so away. To his dismay, it was inching its way toward the two. Recalling how the tooth had flown to the hands of the Aramite sorcerer, he realized that as long as the keeper could think, D'Farany could summon the talisman to him. Only the fact that he battled with Cabe kept him from already retrieving his cursed trinket. A minute or two and he *would* control it again.

That time the warlock would not allow him. This close to each other, he, at least, knew how risky it was to cast any sort of potent spell. However, there *was* one more illusion he planned on trying. He only hoped that his imagination and the Gryphon's descriptions in a long-ago letter would be enough.

Cabe's visage melted, becoming the dark, murky outline of a great and terrible lupine creature with burning eyes and a toothy maw capable of taking in whole a man's head.

Lord D'Farany's face grew blank, then twisted into a horrific mask of reverence for the beast he saw above him.

Releasing one of the keeper's wrists, Cabe formed a fist and punched D'Farany in the jaw with as much force as he could muster. His hand ached for a time after, but the results were well worth the pain.

"Sometimes the direct way is the best way," he muttered to the unconscious keeper. Only against a man such as D'Farany would an illusion like the one Cabe had cast succeed. The Gryphon had described his meeting with the Aramites' rabid deity, the lupine Ravager, spending some length on the ghostly image of the monster and the devotion the keepership displayed for their darksome god. D'Farany had reacted exactly as the warlock had calculated. A good thing, too; he would have been at a loss as to what to do next if his trick had failed.

The talisman! said a sudden, familiar voice in his head. *There is little time left to undo the damage!*

"If I'd had a little more help with this," the warlock snarled, climbing over D'Farany, "I would've been done earlier."

I mussst consssserve my sssstrength!

"What about mine?"

The talisman! the inner voice roared.

I have it! he sent back, more than a little bitter. Out loud, Cabe asked, "What now?"

Now, came the oddly hesitant but unusually controlled voice of the Dragon King. *Now you must hold it together at all costs. You must not allow it to shatter, lest all we manage to do is unleash further decay and chaos from the realm of my past!*

That sounded like nothing Cabe desired to be a part of, but he nonetheless held the talisman tight. "What are you going to do?"

The keeper's toy is the only thing still with a link to Nimth and the dark power of that wretched world. It is not one I would trust long to survive the effort, but it is all we have. I will take the power of Nimth and use it as only one born of the Vraad could. I will take that power and bring peace to my realm . . . peace or death.

"But—" Cabe's protest died on his lips as he felt the first surge of power flow into and then out of the talisman. Almost immediately he understood what the Dragon King had meant about holding the talisman together. There was so much energy, so much of the *wrong* magic being forced through it that the tooth was being stretched beyond its abilities. The Crystal Dragon was using it as more than just a receptacle or a focus or even both together and the strain was tearing it apart.

The Crystal Dragon's voice grew indifferent, distant. *Let the power of Nimth at last do something worthy. Let Legar hear its power . . . and then let Nimth be silent forever!*

From all around, there came a sound, a piercing sound that suddenly simply *was*. It was powered from the great forces pouring through the hole between worlds, but it was transmitted from all around. The storms, the wind, and the wild, drifting magic gave way to a trembling. It was not a quake. Cabe could only think of it as the entire land *vibrating* and the faster the frequency of that vibration, the greater the intensity of the sound.

Keep your mind on the talisman! Let the ssssound drift away! I shall—

The deafening noise sent the warlock to his knees, but he did not lose his control. It was not because of the knowledge that the spell would fade unfinished, but because he knew that to do so would mean his death. He only hoped the spell's success would not mean the same.

Then, coherent thought was no longer possible. There was only the sound. The damning sound.

As Cabe fought against the verlok, the Gryphon's own battle commenced. It began with circling, as the two wary opponents sized up each other. The lionbird did so in silence; Orril D'Marr was the opposite.

"When I found the tent in ruins and the bodies of the beasts and guards lying there—but not yours—I was furious. To have caught you at last and then have you slip away . . . it was just too much. I've waited too long!"

The Gryphon glanced over D'Marr's back at Darkhorse, who remained motionless. There would be no help there, not that he wanted any. D'Marr was his and his alone. As much as the young officer wanted him, the Gryphon wanted the wolf raider more. Even though practicality was screaming that escape was the only option for either of them, neither would have stepped back now.

D'Marr's scepter glistened as Legar once had. The Aramite made two jabs with it, always withdrawing before the Gryphon had a chance to grab the deadly little tool by its handle. He was aware of how useless his power was against the wolf raider while D'Marr carried the mace. That was not a great disappointment to the Gryphon. Demion's death demanded a more personal struggle. Orril D'Marr had to be made to know what it meant to kill one of the Gryphon's own. Besides, he did not want to trust to sorcery too much in this place. A thing like the scepter might work here, but spells cast might kill the caster instead.

Around them, the earth shook and crevices opened. Green lightning still played with the plain. Neither fighter cared in the least. They had come almost to the point where interference by anyone, be it Quel, wolf raider, or one of the Gryphon's allies, would result in a bizarre alliance between the duelists against those interlopers. Only the rampages of the realm itself stood any chance at all of coming between them.

"Would you like your sword, birdman? Perhaps asking for it politely will gain you something." The Aramite's visage was still damningly indifferent. His eyes were not.

The Gryphon displayed his talons. "I have these. They are all I need for you."

"We'll have the sword, anyway," D'Marr remarked, kicking it toward his foe.

Puzzled and wary, but knowing the sword *would* cancel out the advantage of length the wolf raider presently had, the former mercenary retrieved the blade. There was no lunge from D'Marr, merely that shadow of a smile. The lionbird had met few men who could unbalance him the way that this one did. Nothing about the Aramite could be trusted, not even the way he breathed. Still, now the Gryphon had a weapon he could make use of without coming dangerously close to the scepter.

"Whenever you are ready, D'Marr."

The wolf raider laughed . . . and brought his mace into play while the Gryphon was still marveling over the peculiar reaction from the normally diffident officer. He only discovered the reason for that laugh when his blade came up to parry the attack. As the two weapons struck each other, Orril D'Marr pulled his back, bringing the head of the scepter into contact with the metal blade.

The Gryphon was unable to stifle his scream.

He dropped the sword and stumbled away as quickly as he could, all the while keeping blurred eyes on the position of the

Aramite. D'Marr was not pursuing him, however. He was simply smiling at the Gryphon's misfortune and at the success of his trick.

Compared to this present attack, the blow he had taken while engrossed in the effort of freeing Darkhorse had been only a bee sting. The lionbird could not stop shaking. His head pounded and his legs threatened to fold.

"That's a setting somewhere in the middle, birdman," smirked the raider officer. The true Orril D'Marr was coming to the surface at last. "Didn't you know that all I have to do is touch something you're touching? Could be metal. Could be cloth. If you wear it or carry it, you'll feel the mace's bite. My predecessor was wonderful with detail like that."

"What—what happened to him?"

"He was slow to realize my potential, but then the accident took care of that oversight." Even if the raider's words had not been clear enough in their meaning, the Gryphon would have understood what D'Marr was saying. The path to promotion in the Aramite empire was littered with the bodies of those not quick enough to know which of their brethren wanted their throats. It was encouraged; after all, it was the law of the Pack. The better officers would weed out the lessers.

Before him stood a prime example of the former. The tradition of blind obedience was for the lower ranks, the line soldiers, and those you feared enough to serve.

D'Marr gave his scepter a lazy swing. "Shall we have another go at it?"

The Aramite thrust with the mace, a maneuver that would have been foolish if not for the horrific ability of the head. Dodging aside, the Gryphon utilized his exceptional reflexes and slashed out at his adversary's weapon arm. Talons tore at ebony armor to no avail. The officer's armor was of a grade much higher than that of a common guard. Nonetheless, D'Marr backed away, aware that he was growing just a bit too careless.

Still, under the oncoming pressure of the scepter, the Gryphon was pushed farther and farther back. Each step was a precarious venture in itself, for not only was the ground increasingly uneven, but the intensity of the tremor had become so great that even on the flattest surface it would have been a challenge to maintain his footing. Even Orril D'Marr, working with a vast advantage over the lionbird, was finding it difficult to keep steady.

"Why don't you come to me, bird? Are you part chicken? Is that what all those feathers mean?" The Aramite officer pretended to lunge. "Are you going to prove as much a coward as that stripling of yours?"

If he hoped to goad the Gryphon into a frenzy as he had nearly succeeded in doing the last time he had mentioned Demion, the wolf raider was mistaken. For the memory of his son, the lionbird was trying his best to keep his instincts in check. They would have their uses when the moment came, but they could not be allowed control.

At that moment, his foot came down upon a small crack in the earth, a crack just wide enough to catch the heel. The Gryphon weaved back and forth, trying to regain his balance. Orril D'Marr charged at him, the scepter ablaze in hideous glory.

It was not the Gryphon who ended up falling. By dropping to a crouch, he managed to just barely stabilize himself. The eager raider, on the other hand, stepped on a portion of ground that that tremor had loosened but not broken up. D'Marr's heavy boot was more than enough impetus; a good piece of earth gave way, scattering about, and the Aramite went sliding down on his back.

It was all the feathered fury needed. He turned his crouch into a leap at the throat of the murderer of his son. Gasping, D'Marr twisted away, but not quite enough to escape untouched. The Gryphon went crashing into the harsh soil, but the claws of his maimed hand caught the side of the raider's neck. D'Marr shouted out in agony. The smell of blood reached the Gryphon and he felt the wetness spread down his fingers.

There was no time to savor the strike, for the Aramite was far from dead. Orril D'Marr continued to roll until he was facing his adversary again. Despite the fall, he had kept hold of the scepter, which he immediately swung at the sprawled figure beside him. The Gryphon blocked it with his arm, careful to meet the scepter at the handle. He tried to twist his hand around and grab hold, but D'Marr was having none of that. The wolf raider scrambled back, then rose to his feet. Blood was seeping from twin scars running along the side of his throat. The smile had been replaced by growing fury and perhaps a hint of fear.

Standing, the lionbird showed the raider officer his blood-soaked fingers. "The first taste, D'Marr. The first taste of my revenge. I will not stop until the skin on your face has been peeled away the same way one would peel away the hide off of a dead wolf. I doubt if there will be as much call for your hide, but I know two, counting myself, who will prize the experience."

"I'll see your head mounted on a wall first, birdman!" The wolf raider came at him again.

The Gryphon ducked the initial swing, then slashed at D'Marr as the raider's arm went by. Again, his talons caught on the armor, but he pulled away before the Aramite could swing the scepter back. D'Marr managed to kick him in the leg. The Aramite underestimated the lionbird's strength, however, and instead of sending his foe to the ground, he almost lost his own balance.

The Gryphon leapt once more. Orril D'Marr was not able to bring the mace down in time. The two collided and fell, locked in mortal combat. D'Marr would not release the scepter and the Gryphon had to put all his effort into maintaining a three-fingered grip on that arm. They rolled on for several yards with first the lionbird on top, then D'Marr, and so on.

It was the sound that almost put an end to the battle for both of them. A high, agonizing sound that cut through the ear and the mind. The duo separated, each seeking only to cover their ears and save their sanity. The Gryphon barely noticed that the earth no longer shook, but rather vibrated, a somewhat different and puzzling movement.

Orril D'Marr had thrown off his helmet and was rummaging in his belt pouches for something. He had dropped the mace, but the Gryphon was at first unable to act. It was all he could do to stand. A part of his mind pushed him on, though, reminding him that if he died Troia would come next. She would face Orril D'Marr on her own. For her and the sake of the child yet unborn, he could not allow that.

He took a step forward . . . and almost lost his life. Cracked and broken by the tremors, the cavern-riddled earth of Legar could little stand up to the constant vibration now occurring. Whole areas of the surface began to collapse into the underground system the Quel had established over the centuries. The ground before him gave way just as his foot came down. Only his reflexes saved him. As it was, the Gryphon lost his balance and slipped. His legs dangled over the new ravine for a time, but with effort he was able to pull himself back up.

A hard boot struck him in the side.

Orril D'Marr stood above him, a peculiar set of coverings over his ears. The Gryphon recalled the wolf raider speaking of working with explosive powders; D'Marr must have designed the coverings for his projects. It was clear that they did not completely filter out the sound, but they worked well enough for the Aramite to move about without having to hold his ears.

Unable to concentrate enough to shapeshift, the lionbird could do nothing about his own predicament. It was a wonder he was not deaf by now. Part of his magical makeup, no doubt. Still, deafness was the least of his worries. The greatest was that D'Marr once more had his foul toy in hand and this time he looked ready to try its strongest touch.

Knowing he could not be heard over the horrible sound, the wolf raider leaned over his shaking adversary and mouthed out an arrogant farewell. That proved to be his fatal mistake. Despite his knowledge of the Gryphon, Orril D'Marr was evidently unaware of the stamina and resilience of the lionbird. He thought the Gryphon too overwhelmed to have any fight left in him.

That was just the way the Gryphon wanted it.

His spinning roll caught the wolf raider's legs. The Aramite officer went down under him, but did not lose the magical mace. The Gryphon easily caught the awkward strike that D'Marr tried, then began to bend the raider's arm back, bringing the scepter toward its master's face. Although he felt he must soon black out, the former mercenary pushed with all his might. It was time for Orril D'Marr to understand what his victims had gone through.

The ground shifted, sinking lower on one side of the duelists.

Cursing, the weakening lionbird tried one last effort. Throwing his full weight into it, he forced the scepter into the wolf raider's snarling visage. D'Marr, however, twisted aside and the jeweled head went past his face. The snarl became a smile.

The tip of the scepter grazed the raider's shoulder.

Lying as he was half on his adversary, a prick of pain coursed through the lionbird, but it was little compared to what D'Marr must have felt. So very close, the Gryphon could not help but hear the scream. The Aramite had said that armor would be of no help and he had been all too correct.

Fueled by his agony, the wolf raider managed to throw the Gryphon off of him. He also succeeded in dropping the scepter as well. The ground tipped even more, but Orril D'Marr hardly noticed. He was still hunched together, trying to recover.

The lionbird had given his all, but now he realized it was time to get away. The area was collapsing and it would do no good to die here if he could ensure otherwise. Half stumbling and half crawling, he abandoned the Aramite to his fate. If they both survived, the Gryphon would be more than happy to renew the struggle. Staying here was simple foolishness.

Behind him, D'Marr recovered enough to realize his danger. He searched for the mace, found it, and hobbled after his enemy. When he had seen that the tip was coming toward him, he had tried to lower the weapon's intensity. It was all that had saved him. Now, though, D'Marr let the full power of the scepter rise again. One way or another, he would kill the birdman. He would.

About to pass out, the Gryphon rolled over and saw the wolf raider stumbling toward him. He also saw the ground just beyond his own feet begin to crack. The lionbird dragged himself back a bit more and watched in fascination at the tableau that unfolded before him.

Orril D'Marr obviously felt the earth collapsing, for he started to run toward his foe. Still suffering from the effects of his own toy, the Aramite stumbled and fell to his knees. He dropped the mace again and as he fumbled with the handle, trying to get a grip, the ground he knelt upon finally broke completely loose.

The last glimpse the Gryphon had of Orril D'Marr was the image of the wolf raider, his face composed one final time into that bland mask, raising the scepter to throw at his cursed enemy.

Then . . . there was only a cloud of thick dust as tons of rocky earth crumbled into the vast crater.

Demion . . . he managed to think. *Demion* . . . *he is no more, my son. The monster is dead*.

He settled back, willing to let oblivion take him, when a

darkness covered him from head to foot. There was blissful silence and none of the oppressive heat of Legar. Too weak to wonder, the Gryphon merely accepted everything.

A stentorian voice broke the silence. "I . . . will protect you as . . . well as I can, Lord Gryphon! I cannot . . . promise you . . . but we may survive this yet!"

At the moment he did not care. All he wanted to do was sleep. Sleep for the first time in almost two days . . . and sleep *well* for the first time since his son's death.

XVIII

No part of Legar was left untouched by the sound, yet just beyond the interior edge of the peninsula, the region of Esedi and the kingdom of Zuu in particular heard nothing. Those who might have been curious enough about the fog to attempt an excursion into Legar would find themselves turning away in great unease. Even the agents of Lord D'Farany who attempted to return to the camp could not find their courage. Instead, they scattered northward, suddenly certain that it would be wise *never* to return to the inhospitable land of Legar.

Within Legar, the spell of the Crystal Dragon did its work. The Quel, whose hearing was far more sensitive than that of most other creatures, including humans, fell to the ground hooting in dire agony. The wolf raiders were unable to take advantage of their misery, for they, too, suffered from the terrible, piercing noise. Several Aramites simply stumbled off of the edge of newly formed cliffs and plummeted into ravines and craters. A few of the Quel did the same, but the pain was so great most of the tawny behemoths simply crouched on the ground and tried to block out the sound. Tunneling into the earth was no escape, for the vibrations collapsed passages with the ease that a foot could crush an ant. The shells of the Quel were strong, but not *that* strong, and even if they survived, they could only hold their breath for so long. In truth, there *was* no escape.

Cabe, almost oblivious to the world, still struggled to hold the

Aramite talisman together. *Ssssoon . . .* the Crystal Dragon had promised. *Ssssoooon it will be at an end.*

There was something strange and frightening happening to the mind linked to his, but Cabe had little opportunity to pursue the matter. All that was important was to keep the tooth from being destroyed . . . and keep *himself* from being destroyed while he was at it.

Around the camp, the Quel began to die. The sound shook their very being, destroying them through their ears. Enhanced by sorcery, it was an inescapable hunter, for there was nothing on the surface of Legar sufficient to dampen its intensity.

On and on and on it went. The fates of the Gryphon and Darkhorse concerned Cabe, but by this point he knew that nothing could be done if it had not been done already. The Crystal Dragon had not warned him of the enormity of what he was doing and for that Cabe was angry. Recriminations would have to come later, however.

That was providing that *later* actually came.

The first . . . ssstep isss complete! Now, the time hasss . . . come to . . . clossse forever the . . . portal!

"Ungh!" Cabe Bedlam's entire body shook as the flow of power suddenly reversed itself. He had thought that the strain had been great before, but so awesome was it now that he almost lost control. For a single second, the talisman was beyond his ability to suppress. Then, just before it would have shattered, the warlock succeeded in regaining control. Sweat soaked his body. The pain in his arm was laughable in comparison to what wracked his system now. He was certain that he was going to die, yet somehow the weary mage held on.

Slowly, ever so slowly, the vibrations lessened. The sense of wrongness in the air, the sense of Nimth's intrusion, weakened.

Almost . . . Cabe thought, trying to encourage himself. *Almost!*

A long, spindly hand *tore* the tooth from his grasp.

Jerked back into full consciousness, Cabe's first reaction was to scream as pure sound invaded his mind. He clamped his hands over his ears, which did little to lessen the agony, and turned to see what had happened.

Plool, looking not at all affected by the spell, scampered

merrily beyond Cabe's reach. The macabre figure held the tooth high. His broad-rimmed hat was pushed back, revealing a V-shaped smile and bright, crystalline eyes that flashed in triumph. Whether he had simply stolen the talisman for the sake of his own survival or had thought that he could use it to turn the Dragonrealm into another Nimth, only the Vraad knew. Plool finally stopped, folded his legs underneath him, and, floating, tossed the tooth from one hand to the other.

Cabe knew he shouted, but not even he could hear his warning.

The Vraad lowered the talisman and his unsettling orbs narrowed in intense concentration. Tendrils of fog stretched toward him like children seeking their father. An aura formed around Plool. The thing in his hand glowed so bright it blinded.

The tooth exploded.

No longer held in check by either Cabe or the Dragon King, the power filling the talisman had at last stretched the boundaries of D'Farany's toy beyond its limits. Possibly the Vraad had not completely understood the dangers of the spell when he had stolen the talisman from Cabe. The sorcery of Nimth did not always follow the same rules as the sorcery of the Dragonrealm; the warlock's sparse knowledge of the other world included that bit of information at least. Unfortunately, such knowledge was too late to save the eager Plool.

Raw energy flowed over the Vraad and for a short instant, Plool resembled a deflating sack. So horrified was the warlock that he almost forgot the pain shaking him apart. Plool did not scream; he did not even appear to have time to notice his destruction. The madcap figure simply collapsed into an ungodly heap that, thankfully, dissipated immediately after. The spell that the Crystal Dragon had begun had been designed to absorb and make use of Nimthian magic. Perhaps Plool had literally been too much a creature of that foul sorcery.

With the Vraad gone, the realization of what Plool had done occurred to the pain-stricken mage. The talisman was gone and there was no way of completing the spell. There might not even be a way of dousing the horrendous noise.

WARLOCK! the voice burst through the noise. *YOURRRR POWERRR I MUSSSST HAVVVE! WE ARRRE ALMOSSST THERE!*

He did not argue. To tell the truth, Cabe did not have the

strength to argue. At that moment, the Crystal Dragon could have had anything he wanted from him. Cabe only wanted the screaming to stop.

It did. Just like that. The fog burned away before his very eyes, returning the rule of day to the blazing sun. The ground ceased vibrating. It just *stopped*. All was as it had been before the coming of the wolf raiders . . . save that now there were new ravines and valleys all over the peninsula and bodies decorated the new landscape wherever one looked.

Cabe Bedlam crumpled to the ground, suddenly very much drained. He recalled the shouted plea for his power, his strength. The Dragon King had borrowed power through him to finish what they had begun, but he had almost used Cabe too much. To draw so much sorcerous energy into the warlock and through him use it had nearly burned Cabe out in the process. He was thrilled that they had finished the grand spell, but he truly wished that there had been another way.

Still, whatever the human spellcaster had suffered, the Crystal Dragon must have suffered more. He had guided the spell throughout. It was his will more than Cabe's that had been pressed. Knowing how fine a line the drake lord's mind had treaded before this, the warlock wondered if there was anything much left.

Your Majesty?

Silence. It might be that the Dragon King had simply broken the link, but Cabe knew somehow that his hermitic ally had truly suffered. How serious the damage was, there was no way of knowing unless Cabe returned to the sanctum. For all he knew, that chamber, too, was now a memory crushed under tons of rocky earth.

All but a few residue traces of Nimth's evil had vanished. Even without being there, Cabe knew that the hole had been sealed and that the power to seal it had been the magic inherent in the fog. Nimth's own might had been used to force it from the Dragonrealm. The Dragon King had used Cabe's added strength to force the alien magic to do his bidding, something only he, who alone understood both powers, could have done. All of this the warlock understood even though no explanation had been given to him. He simply knew because he had been a part of it.

Gryphon! Darkhorse! The images of his two friends formed
in his mind. How could he have forgotten them? Thanks in part
to him, they might even be dead, for the Crystal Dragon had
never revealed to the warlock whether he had actually protected
the two from the killing sound as he had Cabe. Cabe did not
trust the Dragon King enough to have faith in their well-being.
He turned, intending to head back to where the shadow steed
had been held.

Lord D'Farany stood before him. Yet another thing that Cabe
had forgotten. He silently swore and prepared to do battle even
though he doubted that he had enough will to raise a feather an
inch from the ground much less fight to the death with the keeper.

D'Farany, however, merely stood there, his blank eyes staring
in the direction of Cabe but not at him. The spellcaster took a
tentative step toward the raider and noticed that his mouth was
moving. Lord D'Farany was muttering, but only when Cabe
stepped even closer did he understand anything of what the
Aramite commander was saying.

"Gone . . . tooth . . . empty . . . so . . . empty . . . cannot
. . . cannot . . ."

The keeper had survived one loss of power, but only after
madness had claimed him for a time. Cabe, staring at the shell
that had once been a man to be feared, was fairly certain that
this time madness had staked a permanent claim. The warlock
looked around. The other raiders were gone; a sinkhole larger
than the Manor and its grounds combined revealed the fate of
both the officers and the horses their spies had bought or stolen
for the never-to-be-released invasion of Zuu or whatever it was
the Aramites had planned. Of the two groups, Cabe felt much
more sorrow for the horses than for the raiders.

He turned back to the keeper and reached out a hand. As much
as he despised the man, Cabe could not leave him out here, not
in this condition. "Come with—"

Slapping his hand away, D'Farany, the pale, marred visage
twisted into a look of suffering and loss, cried, "*Empty!* It can
never be filled! I can never be *whole!* I can never be . . .
be . . ."

The raider commander slumped into Cabe's arms. Under his
weight, the warlock fell to one knee. After a short struggle, he
managed to lay the still form on the ground. Cabe looked into

D'Farany's ravaged countenance, then felt his neck. He uncovered the Aramite's wrist and checked there, too.

Ivon D'Farany, whose name had meant terror for almost a decade to those fighting against the wounded empire, was dead. He just could not stand the loss a second time, Cabe concluded. No man so in thrall to his power could have. *The Gryphon will be pleased, at least.*

That returned him once more to the fate of his companions. Leaving the corpse where it was, the warlock worked his way back to the camp. Compared to now, his first crossing had been the simplest of tasks. Legar was now a ruin and parts of it were still in the process of collapse. He came across no life in the areas he first wandered; most of this part had sunken into the underground kingdom of the Quel, taking all with it. A few bodies, both human and otherwise, still littered the place. A little beyond, though, Cabe could see hundreds of silent, unmoving forms. On a rare occasion, he spotted a few human figures, wolf raiders, but there was no fight left in them. They either ran if they saw him or simply walked on, ignoring him as they ignored all else. He doubted whether the latter had much left in the way of sanity. Not everyone had died because of the piercing noise, but looking at the survivors, he was not so certain that the ones who walked were the more fortunate.

Of living Quel, Cabe saw only signs. Burrow holes dotted the ravaged encampment; at least several score, probably more, of the diggers had made it back to the safety of the underworld. Several hundred more, both above and below, would never threaten Legar or the Dragonrealm. The survivors would certainly not, either, at least in his lifetime. He crossed his fingers on that score, but judging by what he had felt earlier and seen now, it would take the Quel several generations just to repair the damage. It would take them several more to rebuild their population, if that was at all possible. True, as long as one existed, they *would* be dangerous, but not nearly as much as they would have been if nothing had stopped their return.

So no one will ever truly understand the threats that so briefly rose here. It was ironic. The Quel sleepers had been a legend to many and a true danger to a few who knew. The Aramites, in as great a force as they had brought, could have brought the western part of the Dragonrealm to ruin even if they were finally defeated. The hole that had been opened, the hole that had allowed so much of poor, decaying Nimth in, spreading its sickness . . .

He did not want to even think about what would have happened if that had been left unchecked.

To his great relief, Cabe suddenly detected a familiar presence not too far off.

Darkhorse? he sent out.

For a moment there was no response. Then there came a slow, hesitant touch, followed by an equally hesitant response. *Cabe? Do you really live?*

I do! Where are you?

Follow . . . follow the link. Cabe, Lord Gryphon is injured.

The eternal sounded none too good himself. Summoning what will he had left, the warlock immediately teleported.

The devastation that greeted him was even worse than what he had already seen. The carnage brought on by the battle alone was sickening. For all their ferocity, the Quel had met a foe equally matched. Their size and armored bodies had not given the subterraneans the great advantage it should have. At the same time, the swiftness and well-honed battle skills of the wolf raiders had not saved them, either. It was a wonder that there had been any left to perish in the collapse of the surface.

Yet, it was Darkhorse who stunned Cabe even more than the horrible sight around them. Instead of the valiant black stallion the dark-haired mage was familiar with, a grotesque thing with primitive appendages and a vague, animallike shape flowed before him. Only the ice-blue eyes were still there, but they were so pale they now seemed almost white.

"Darkhorse?"

"What is left of . . . of me, friend Cabe." Even the voice was subdued. "With . . . aid from . . . Lord Gryphon, I was just . . . just able to free myself . . . but it was almost too much . . ."

Cabe could not think of anything to do for the eternal, but he was willing to try. "What can I do? Is there anything?"

"I am beyond your help, Cabe. It will be up to . . . to me to recover . . . that will take . . . time. Best that you see . . . see what you can . . . do for the Lord Gryphon . . ."

"The Gryphon? Where is he?"

"Within me . . ." The murky, shifting form flowed to one side and as it did, the outline of the lionbird's form appeared. Cabe swallowed hard when he saw how still his companion was. "Is it too late?"

"He lives . . . but like me . . . he has been drained . . . drained of nearly every . . . thing. I protected him from the . . . the sound, which did not . . . harm me as it . . . did him." The eternal grew silent.

The warlock knelt beside the Gryphon and felt for a pulse. It was there, slow but steady. Then it jumped a bit. The Gryphon suddenly opened his eyes.

"Cabe?"

"It would be nice to meet under better circumstances once in a while," returned the warlock, smiling.

The Gryphon tried to rise. "The Aramites!"

Cabe eased him back down. "Dead or scattered. The same holds true for the Quel. Most are dead, I think."

"My son . . . his murderer . . ."

"*Demion?*" Neither Darkhorse nor the Gryphon had made mention of this terrible news before. "When? Who did it?" Fury rose within the spellcaster. If the lionbird was beyond avenging his only son, Cabe would try to find the strength to do it.

However, the lionbird shook his head. "No, Cabe. Demion's murderer . . . Orril . . . D'Marr . . ." The look of disgust on that avian visage spoke volumes concerning the wolf raider. "He lies in that crater there . . . buried under several tons . . . of earth." The Gryphon pointed at the gaping hole with his maimed hand. "D'Marr never did find out . . . the great Quel secret . . . was the Quel themselves. I would have liked . . . to see if *that* would have cracked that . . . mask of his." He laughed very briefly, then sobered. "My son can rest. *I* can rest . . . but only for a time. Lord D'Farany—"

"Your son, you, and Troia can *all* rest, Gryphon. The keeper is dead. I know. He died right before my eyes." In response to his companion's questioning stare, the warlock explained the Crystal Dragon's spell and the use of D'Farany's talisman. He also spoke of Plool and the Vraad's swift and foolish death. The very end of his tale he reserved for Ivon D'Farany's inability to suffer so great a loss twice in one lifetime. Addicted to his power, he could not survive a second withdrawal. "He collapsed in my arms and when I studied him close, I saw that he was dead."

"A—a fitting way for him. I thank you, Cabe."

The warlock shook his head. "I was only a part of it. The one who guided me through much of this, albeit not always with my approval, wa—"

"Cabe!" Darkhorse suddenly called, sounding more like his old self. He was still a shifting, near-formless thing, but the eyes seemed a bit brighter . . . and now very concerned, too. "I think I see . . . see soldiers approaching!"

With the Gryphon too weak to be of use, Cabe tried his best to make out the shapes in the distance. It was not noon in Legar, a fortunate thing, but the sun was bright enough already to force him to squint. He would have to create copies of the Dragon King's eye protectors when he had the opportunity. That is, *if* he had the opportunity. The figures did resemble soldiers and their high helms, at least from this distance, were shaped akin to the wolf's head helms of the Aramites.

"Some surviving officer must have . . . have reorganized survivors," the lionbird added, becoming exhausted by the continual task of trying to talk coherently. "We'll have to fight . . . them."

Glancing at his friends, Cabe was not particularly hopeful. He might be able to get off a spell, but he was not certain as to its potency. If the wolf raiders had any sort of magical protection, then the three of them had little chance. Their greatest hope, Darkhorse, did not even have the strength to reshape himself.

The figures were still too distant. "Could they be soldiers from Zuu?"

"Are they leading horses?" asked the Gryphon in return.

"No, they're on foot."

"Then, they are . . . not from Zuu. A soldier of . . . Zuu always has . . . his mount with him. Besides, they . . . do not . . . wear armor at all resembling . . . resembling . . . that of the raiders."

That was true, but Cabe had hoped. He continued to watch, thinking that maybe the soldiers would not see them, when he noticed a newcomer. It was a rider on some beast not a horse. Cabe's brow wrinkled. Then, the rider turned a little in the saddle and abruptly became a blinding, glittering beacon. The other soldiers, turning, also seemed to suddenly blaze with the glory of the sun.

"They're not wolf raiders," he informed the others. "They're allies." *I hope,* he added to himself.

The gleaming warrior astride the riding drake might have been the same one that Cabe had mistaken for the Crystal Dragon, but the warlock could not be certain until the warrior spoke.

"Master Bedlam. I am Gemmon, my lord's first duke. Pleased I am to have found you and yours alive in all this ruin."

"You were looking for us?" The perfection with which the drake spoke did not really startle Cabe any more than the interesting fact that the dragon men were not using the forms they had been born with, which would have made searching Legar swifter and easier. The Dragon King's human tastes had no doubt spread to his subjects.

"For you and survivors of both abominations. My lord leaves nothing to chance, although the humans will have scattered eastward and the curssssed Quel will burrow very deep. We lack the strength to hunt them down, but there are those lying among the dead who must still be dispatched and others wandering about that must be rounded up and dealt with in some manner."

Cabe was not certain whether the drakes were putting the badly wounded to death out of pity or their need for further satisfaction. The warlock knew that he did not have the strength to fight for those lives and, in truth, he was hard-pressed to find a reason to spare either the Aramites or the Quel. Still, it did bother him . . .

"I have been instructed," the drake continued, "to assist you and yours across the border into Esedi. Servants of the Green One will be there to help you return to your loved ones." He eyed Darkhorse with some confusion. "Although as to what—"

"I will make do," retorted the eternal. He sounded even stronger, but Cabe was not certain whether that might just be a front before the minions of the Dragon King.

"You have our gratitude," the warlock interjected, not desiring a confrontation. "But there is one thing I must ask."

"What is that?"

"I'd like to speak to your master. I insist upon it."

The warrior looked uncomfortable. "He . . . hasss secluded himself from all for the time being. The sssspell was taxing, even for him."

Cabe noted the nervousness, but would not be put off by the drake's fear. "Tell him I will make my visit short."

"I can tell him nothing. He will not even sssspeak to me, human."

Glancing at the Gryphon and Darkhorse, Cabe said, "Then see to my friends. Help them on their way to the border. I'll join you all when I can."

The Gryphon stirred. "Cabe, surely you do not . . . intend to simply . . . simply materialize before a Dragon King . . . especially *this* Dragon King."

The warlock was already rising. "I do. Call it concern."

"Concern? For the Crystal Dragon?" Even the drake warrior found this a bit incredulous.

Shrugging, Cabe replied, "If not for him, then maybe a little concern for a man who once called himself Logan."

He vanished while the others were still puzzling over that last statement.

XIX

"Whaaat do yooou want, ssssorcerer?"

Cabe, who had just materialized, was taken aback by the horrific change in the Crystal Dragon's voice. His voice was now more reminiscent of a true Dragon King.

Undaunted, the warlock replied, "I came to see how you were. I think I know something of what you went through, wouldn't you say?"

The Crystal Dragon was a hill of gemstones pressed tight against the far end of the chamber. There was little light and the walls were dull, opaque things. Cabe could not even see the drake lord's countenance.

"I . . . ssssurvived. You need know nothing morrre."

It would do no good to press the point, Cabe decided. He was disappointed, but knew that there was nothing he could do. Instead, he asked, "What will you do about your kingdom? Legar is in ruins. If my help would be of any value to—"

From the darkness rose the head of the lord of Legar. An inhuman rage controlled his draconian visage. Narrowed eyes with only a hint of crystal in them glared at the presumptuous little figure. "Caaan you not underssssstand? I want nothing from you, huuuman! I want only ressst! Privacy and ressst! Why did you perssssissst in coming here?"

"Because of Logan Tezerenee."

His words doused, for a time, the flames of anger. The Crystal Dragon recoiled into himself, looking much, much smaller. "I know the name . . . myyyy name . . . it isss me . . ."

"Logan," the warlock dared use the name. "Your kingdom is in chaos and you risked yourself in the end. By no means will I forget that it was all in your own self-interest, but what you did affected the rest of the Dragonrealm, too. Your subjects will need help in rebuilding Legar. There are prisoners and wounded from the wolf raiders who might be best turned over to other humans. Perhaps my friends and allies will be willing to aid you. Instead of the wreckage you now rule, there might even be a chance of turning the peninsula into a land of life. They could meet with you and perhaps—"

"No!" It was not anger this time, but rather fear that drove the Dragon King. His eyes widened and he hissed madly. "No. If I allow them so close, they will discover the truth and then I would be in danger! They will be furious that I have tricked them all! I might be forced to leave this place and I cannot! I cannot! I have exhausssted myssself more than I ever dared! The outside world in any form isss now a danger to me! Only here and alone am I ssssafe!"

Cabe could not believe what he was hearing. "You're wrong! Listen to yourself—"

With but a terrible glance, the glittering leviathan silenced him. "Your aid wassss mosssst appreciated, Massster Bedlam, but you will leave now! My ssssubjectssss will ssssee to your needsss all the way to Esssedi! Now go! I mussst ssssleep!"

"Logan—"

"I am the Crystal Dragon!" the behemoth roared. Draconian jaws opened wide . . .

Cabe teleported away before the Dragon King did something either of them would regret.

He found the Gryphon and Darkhorse waiting for him, the latter, to the warlock's surprise, once more in his favorite form. A short distance from them, their reptilian escort waited in growing anxiety.

"What happened?" asked the Gryphon, lying atop the shadow steed. Darkhorse, the warlock would discover later, had not trusted the drakes. His obsession with Shade was at an end; now his greatest concern was for his living friends, including the Gryphon. Drawing upon his incredible will, he had not only succeeded in re-forming, but then had shaped himself so that the lionbird could rest comfortably on his backside. It was a peculiar sight, but one so welcome because of that peculiarity. Almost the mage was able to forget his meeting with the Crystal Dragon.

"We should leave. I may have just outstayed our welcome."

"What happened?"

Cabe shook his head. "I can't be sure . . . not yet."

The others did not understand, but that was probably for the best because even Cabe was not certain that he understood. He only understood that more than ever the line between Logan Tezerenee and the Crystal Dragon had become blurred. Which way, if either, the lord of Legar would eventually turn was anyone's guess. The only thing of certainty was the fact that be he drake or man, the lone inhabitant of that darkened sanctum would not leave that place no matter what happened. It went beyond the precious safeguarding of one man's mind; the Crystal Dragon had been in seclusion for so long that he could not bear either the thought of leaving his chamber or allowing the world inside.

One of the warriors offered him a beast. Cabe took the proffered riding drake and mounted, hardly paying any attention to what he did. The warlock continued to stare at ruined Legar, picturing in his mind the Dragon King dreaming of the face he had once worn in a world that was forever barred to him . . . by himself.

The drake duke signaled for the party to commence eastward. Cabe allowed everyone to precede him, even Darkhorse and the Gryphon. Only with reluctance did he finally urge the dragon beneath him forward. Legar still haunted him. If not for the Crystal Dragon, even what little remained intact would no longer have existed. Alone, the warlock doubted that he could have succeeded.

So much power and so long a life, he thought, finally having to turn his eyes to the path before him. *Yet, despite that, he's forever a prisoner of himself, fearful of losing a humanity that he might have already lost long, long ago.*

The notion was enough to make him ride in brooding silence for the rest of the journey to Esedi . . . and for some time after.